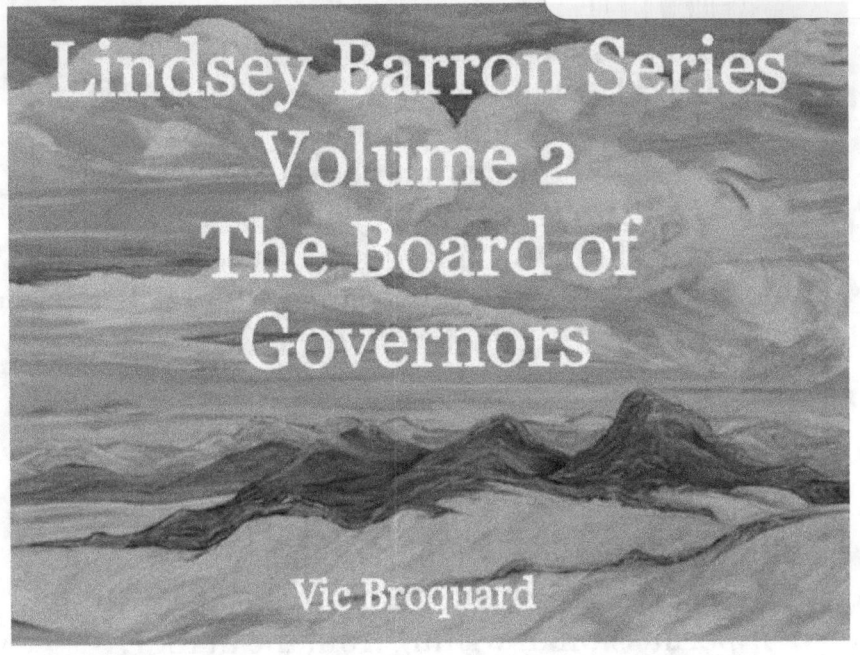

Lindsey Barron Series
Volume 2
The Board of
Governors

Vic Broquard

©2007, 2011, 2012, 2013, 2014 by Vic Broquard
Fourth Printing; ISBN: 978-1-941415-47-4
Published by:
Broquard eBooks
http://Broquard-eBooks.com
author@Broquard-eBooks.com
103 Timberlane
East Peoria, IL 61611

Artwork by Crooked Willow Studios.

For Morgan and L. Ron Hubbard

Table of Contents

Chapter 1—Summer Vacation

Lena Barron, now Compton, having been married a few weeks, looked out of their new ranch home's window at her daughter, Lindsey Barron. She was saddling her horse called Betsy, while chatting with the neighbor children who came to escort her over to their house to play. The loving arm of Lloyd around her waist, she observed, "My precious little girl is growing up so fast, Lloyd! When she went off to Bradbury's School of Magic last year, she had never had so much as a single friend in the world, except me. Now look at her. She has hands now and so many dear friends! It makes me want to cry." She did in fact have wet eyes. Lloyd gently dried them for her.

"Some days, Lena, I marvel myself at how fast life changes. Sometimes, it's the same old, same old for years on end. It was like that with me, Lena, ten of them in fact. Then, I take this assignment to come protect you and my whole world changed! I met you, fell in love with you, and now find myself a rancher as well as working for the Department Defense, Magic Bureau. So much in my life has changed for the better in the last year that I don't have words for it. Your late husband said it best; I can't top him. I just agree one hundred percent with him. How did he put it? Oh, yes. 'Your mother and you have taught me that love is the most important aspect of life.'"

Her previous husband, Samuel Rabnor, was killed when Lindsey was five. She was now thirteen. His quote came from the letter Lindsey had recently found in the bank vault that she had inherited from her father.

For a dozen years, all of this was hidden from everyone's knowledge, and Lindsey had born the brunt of the results of that secrecy. During her first year at magic school, the pieces slowly fell into place, revealing the truth behind her life. It began with her father, who had also attended Arthur Bradbury's School of Magic, located somewhere near Telluride, Colorado, one of the most exclusive magic schools in the country. After he graduated, he had become a Dispeller, that is, a wizard who is exceedingly adept and skilled at canceling evil wizard's spells, so they could be apprehended by the authorities.

His skills became legendary, perhaps the best Dispeller the world had ever seen. During that time span, one wizard went bad, extremely so. His name was Dominus Malefic. His most trusted henchmen were called Death Stalkers, because that's what they did—stalked others and killed them for their master. After an incredible reign of murders, robberies, and worse, the Department of Defense hired the Rat Pack to apprehend these criminals. Sam led the foursome called the Rat Pack, though no one knows why they chose that name. Able Monument was their Tracker, one who could follow the trails left by wizards and witches by detecting the nearly invisible traces of the magical energies left behind. Bill West had been their Eliminator, the one who was skilled at bringing about the actual capture of the wrongdoers. Bill could not do his job while the criminals were casting death spells at him. It was Sam's task to nullify those so Bill could get off his entrapment spells. Mabel Pruit was their Diviner, the one would could foresee just where they criminals would strike next, allowing the other three to home in on their prey.

The Department of Defense hired the Rat Pack to apprehend Dominus and his gang. This they did, some two years before Lindsey was born. Instead of putting these men to death, as befitting a man who had thirty-six known murders to his credit, the Department of Law imprisoned him. Capital Punishment had been banned for a century now. Dominus swore to take revenge on the Rat Pack. However, they had not captured all the Death Stalkers or his many other supporters, who remained in positions of power and unknown. Barely two months after the capture of Dominus, Mabel and all her immediate family were murdered.

The remaining members of the Rat Pack then went undercover. Sam Rabnor changed his name to Sam Barron, leased a secure vault for a hundred years, stored all of his possessions and funds there, and disappeared from society. He pretended to be a down on his luck norm. Norm is the word used to describe normal people in the world who do not possess any magical abilities. Ninety percent of the population of the world is norms, however. He moved to Plano, Colorado, a tiny, remote town, not even on many maps, in the high plains of eastern Colorado, over a hundred miles east of Colorado Springs. There, he took on a job as a ranch hand working for Lena.

Lena owned a tiny, nearly worthless gully ranch one mile south of Plano and entirely surrounded by giant farming corporations. Though extremely poor by monetary standards of the day, Lena was kind, compassionate, a good rancher, and had great self-pride in her own independence. She was a survivor, eking out a living on her ranch. Sam fell madly in love with this rugged western woman and married her. A year later, they had a daughter, Lindsey.

Unknown to them, a large chemical company had buried a lot of toxic waste nearby, and over time, the barrels had rusted, leaking Thalidomide into their water well, from which Lena drank. Lindsey was born in perfect health, just without any hands. For five years, until his death, Sam cried over this horrible situation. He had millions of dollars in his secret vault, and only a tiny fraction of that would be required to pay the Department of Magical Healing to re-grow hands for Lindsey. However, he couldn't do it, because as part of that process, they would take DNA samples from her and compare them to the Universal DNA database. That, he couldn't afford to have happen, for then the entire world would know that Sam Barron was actually Sam Rabnor, and the Death Stalkers would surely kill Lena and Lindsey! For five agonizing years before he was killed, he continued to pretend he knew nothing about magic and had little money.

When she was five, she discovered his crushed body beneath their tractor, a victim of some horrible farming accident. Only a few months ago, did the world discover that he had been murdered by magical means; the accident was faked. Lindsey and her mother continued ranching, and she spent six horrible years going to the one room school in Plano, enduring a life without hands and daily taunting and teasing from the other children, who saw her as some freakish thing.

Then, last June, out of nowhere from their point of view, the Bradbury School Seeker came to visit them, offering

Lindsey a full academic scholarship to the school of magic, all expenses paid! Already, Lindsey had been doing all manner of magical actions, though she did not know that was the source. She only called it her "invisible hands."

During the first few months there, Lindsey, as their Special Needs student, had all manner of difficulties, as one might expect. However, in Plano, her daily escape from school was running the entire mile home as fast as she could run. Yes, Lindsey had developed into a fast long distance runner. At magic school, she was encouraged to join the track team and soccer team. During their first track meet, she had just helped her team to a big lead when a disgruntled fan of their opposition used a magic spell to trip her. She fell and broke each of her arms in three places. The school doctor, acting on his own volition, took this golden opportunity to not only heal her broken bones, but to re-grow her missing hands!

Just as Sam Rabnor had feared, the instant that he entered her DNA into the database, as required by law, it flagged him as her true father! Before long, everyone knew that her father had been the famous Dispeller who had captured Dominus Malefic. Worst still, this man had just escaped from prison and was now wreaking havoc around the country once more, having killed at least another dozen men and women.

This prompted the head of the school, Governor Alister Broadwell, to request someone from the Department of Defense to guard her mother, Lena, at their ranch south of Plano. Enter then Lloyd Compton, a single wizard who accepted the posting. In the following May, the two decided to get married when Lindsey returned home for summer vacation. Likewise, the giant farming corporation offered Lena fifty thousand dollars for her ranch, many times more than the gully land was worth just to get them out of their way. She accepted primarily because another ranch, many times better than hers, some forty miles further east and a bit north, came up for sale.

On June 3, they wed in a private ceremony and then moved to their new ranch. Lloyd had been discrete in all these actions. They left no traces of Lena Barron's whereabouts; it

4

seemed that she had vanished. Hopefully, this would give her some added protection from any possible revenge by Dominus. Indeed, Lloyd found he really enjoyed ranching Lena's style. No, she had no half million dollar farming equipment, but used good old horsepower, incredibly ancient technology. Yet as she repeatedly demonstrated, the cost of operation was nearly negligible, unlike the thousands of dollars in fuel the other rancher's heavy equipment consumed. Repeatedly, she proved that the ways of the ancients were extremely cost justified when farming a very small ranch, such as theirs.

From their various crops and horses, Lena expected to triple her yearly profit this year, perhaps bringing in fifteen thousand dollars. Still, by modern standards, she was classified as being in dire poverty. Yet, Lena did not see it that way; she had all that she desired, including her self-respect, a fabulous daughter, and now a loving husband.

At school, Lindsey made a number of dear friends, the first true friends that she had ever had. They accepted her when she had no hands, helping her with her needs, standing up for her, and defending her, something no other children had ever done for her. One of these was Amanda Whitewater, a full-blooded Apache who lived on a small ranch on a tiny Indian reservation around Arapahoe, Colorado, just over the line from Kansas. Lindsey had long brown hair and green eyes like her father had. Amanda had long black hair and bushy eyebrows with thick lips. Amanda was also a long distance runner. Together, last year these two joined the track and soccer teams.

Amanda had two older brothers, who were also on their team and long distance runners. The four ran the twenty-mile relay race together. Now Lindsey and Amanda were second year students. Her younger brother, Jim, was now a fourth year student, while her older brother, Tom, was a fifth year student. Tom also had a girlfriend, Sandy, a full-blooded Arapaho, who lived in town and worked at the gambling casino. Yes, the major claim to fame was the Indian Casino, which brought in huge revenues to the five hundred who lived on the reservation.

Amanda also had a younger sister, Fern, who would be attending Bradbury's this fall as a first year student. Both Tom and Sandy were Yellow Hall's Floor Monitors, the students who assisted and helped out the other students of Yellow Hall. Sandy, the girls; Tom, the boys. At school, the students lived in one of five connected dorms or halls. Each had a color and students of like personalities lived in the one best suited to their temperaments.

Her Seeker had explained them this way. "The Yellow Hall is for those wizards and witches who are brave and fearless, who prefer thought as a means of solving a problem, who are cheerful, and who like light and air. In contrast, the Blue Hall is for those who love water, who are compassionate and caring, and who believe that emotions should be used to solve problems. Many in the Blue Hall are healers, succoring those in need. Now the Red Hall is fiery for those who believe passions rule, who believe love is all, and that hot emotions should be used to solve problems. Brown Hall represents the earth. Here are those who love to grow things, both plants and animals, stalwart and dependable to a fault. They believe honest efforts solve life's problems. Those in the Black Hall stand for pure logic. Seeing themselves as all important, some are foolhardy and take risks to solve problems. Might and strength, effort in other words, are their hallmark."

At the end of the school term, a Formal Dance is held. Last May, Jim had asked Lindsey to go to the dance with him. Lindsey had never been on a date before and found the experience extremely rewarding, though she could not explain her feelings about it as yet. Amanda had told her that Jim had a crush on her, but she couldn't really relate to that.

During their encounters with Dominus Malefic last term, Amanda had begun displaying the rare Tracker abilities—the ability to see and follow the magical traces left after the casting of spells. She had used her skills to lead a rescue party to find Lindsey. Lindsey, on the other hand, had developed into a fledgling Dispeller herself, casting all their Grade 0 and 1 spells both non-verbally and without the use of her wand. In their sixth year, students would finally make an attempt at non-verbal casting, but one in a hundred might be able to cast a few this way. Without the use of a wand in casting was an extreme rarity, making the number of true Dispellers few indeed, as few as the true Trackers.

Lindsey's other dear friend was Pam Betts, from Sterling, far to the north of Arapahoe. Homely, with two large front teeth with a big gap in them, she was a computer genius, having won the Microsoft's Top Computer Student award her last three years before entering Bradbury's last year. Pam turned out to be a natural born Sleuth, another rare skill. It was she that had first figured out that Dominus had kidnaped Lindsey, the spell he was using to infiltrate the heavily protected school, and sounded the alarm when she deduced that he was trying to steal the ancient relic.

Her other girlfriend, Kathy Townsend lived far to the west in Limon. South of there in Pueblo lived her fourth friend, a boy of Mexican descent, Emilio Lopez. Because the four of them had managed to thwart Dominus Malefic's plans to steal the ancient relic, Lindsey, Amanda, Pam, and Emilio had received the Bradbury Distinguished Service Medallion.

Finally, when the other students returned home for summer vacation, Governor Alister had taken Lindsey into Denver to find out what was in the secure vault that her father had left her. That's when she found her father's letter to her, written when she was four years old. He left her over five hundred thousand dollars, a smaller fortune in gold, silver, platinum ingots, along with gemstones. Further, the vault contained numerous magical items that Sam had had. Alister insisted, as had her father in his letter, that she wear three of these for her own protection.

The Chameleon Robe would blend her into whatever terrain was around her, making her extremely hard to see, and it would totally nullify any spell from Grade 0 through Grade 4. The Runner Pin would prevent anyone from being able to summon her against her will or charm her. The Runner Ring prevented anyone from scrying on her, to learn her thoughts and plans.

He left her his Staff of Power, Margarete. This she also brought back with her. Only powerful wizards and witches have such staves, and no student other than Lindsey had one.

With it, she gained more potential to avoid being killed by Dominus and his thugs. What Lindsey found most exciting about Margarete was the staff's ability to come to her on command from wherever the staff was located! "Margarete: Come." Presto, the staff would move to her hand from wherever it was at when she called for her.

This sunny, late June day, Jim and Amanda rode over to escort Lindsey safely to their place. The three chatted as Lindsey saddled up Betsy. Lena and Lloyd watched them discretely from the ranch house window. Lena had never seen her daughter as happy as she had been this summer, which was in part why her eyes watered so. Her daughter was growing up rapidly.

"I'm sure glad that you volunteered to help us clean up the ranch," Jim said cheerily, as the three rode down the arroyo behind Lindsey's ranch. "Dad doesn't often throw a party. He's the absentminded inventor type."

"Well, my room and Fern's room are always neat and perfect," Amanda teased her brother. "If you put things back when you are finished with them, you would not have much to do."

"Yes, but I take after dad, so does Tom. If dad can leave stuff around, so can we," Jim suggested a way that he could somehow be right.

"I'm just so happy that Pam found a way to come and visit us," Lindsey exclaimed, ignoring the brother-sister barbs. She liked both of them and did not want to take sides.

"Me too. Her email said that her Aunt Wilma wanted to bring her boys to the casino and that she might as well bring Pam along. She didn't say how old her cousins were, but Sandy says that they have to be eighteen to get into the casino on their own, sixteen if an adult is with them."

"Rats, that leaves me out again," Jim complained. "I'm only fifteen, but I guess Tom might be able to go with them, that is, if her Aunt is taking them." They turned up the first gully on their right, heading up and out of the arroyo. At the top where the Whitewater ranch began, all three paused and looked back out over the view. The heat waves made the distant aspens wiggle and move, yet the view was inspiring.

They could see for miles. Neck reigning, the trio headed on up to the sod ranch house.

R. B. (Running Bear Whitewater) had built their home as an energy efficient dwelling. Its walls were three feet thick, and the rooms were mostly below ground level. Lindsey still liked the curious look that the sloping roof had, merging seamlessly with the ground at the rear of the home. However, as always, tons of odd, rusty items littered the grounds. Some were actual magical inventions of R. B. The group rode past the mess to the corral and unsaddled their horses, allowing them to seek the shade of the many trees that lined the split rail enclosure. The attached barn was built of adobe and was even dirtier inside than their house.

Fern and Tom came out to greet them. Tom complained, "Just in time, mom says the whole house *and* the outside must be cleaned! We're never going to get both done!" Fern giggled and waved to Lindsey.

Luci, their mother, stuck her head outside the door and called out, "Hi Lindsey. Boys, why don't you start with this outside area first. I want it spotless for our company." Lindsey waved back.

"Half of this stuff is dad's magical things and the rest is trash," Tom said, looking at the mess. "Okay, Jim and I will identify what's what. You three collect up what we decide is trash. Fern, go fetch a whole lot of trash bags, please." Resigned to the task, Tom's leadership skills rose to meet the challenge, as he issued orders.

Picking up an abandoned soda can, Amanda said, "Mom's right. It's only ten and it is ninety out here already! Going to be a scorcher by afternoon. Chill!"

"Chill! Sure is. I'm sweating already," Lindsey replied, tossing another can in the sack held by Fern.

"Me too, please," Fern begged.

"Chill!" Amanda waved her wand over his sister, and her body felt a forty degree drop in its surface temperature. Of course, it began to rise immediately, but she appreciated the brief coolness.

By lunchtime, they had the grounds looking better than it had in a decade. Luci called them in for something to eat.

Lindsey enjoyed eating with the Whitewaters. Luci was a good cook and had accepted her as if she were a third daughter. As always, the table conversation was anything but boring. Tom had gotten his father to discuss what he thought Dominus Malefic's next actions might be. Lindsey was all ears.

R. B. explained, "Well, the one thing that I know is this lunatic is methodical to a fault. Twenty to one, he'll break out his other nine Death Stalkers from prison."

"Yes, but dad, according to MagNews, they moved them into nine different prisons, just after Dominus broke out. How's he going to find them?" Tom protested. He had other ideas about what the murder might do next.

"Son, little in this world is a secret for long. Had he had all of his henchmen with him when he went after the rod, Lindsey would likely not be with us today. He knows that. His own failure to be methodical cost him that ancient relic. No, son, he's going to get the rest of his men back next."

"Enough of this talk, R. B, Tom. You are scaring Fern. Besides, I need them to clean the whole house this afternoon. Honestly. R. B., you should be cleaning up your workshop as well," Luci suggested, grinning at him. He grinned back. Both knew he did not intend to do so. That he offered to have a party was his big contribution.

"Let's see. Party is tomorrow afternoon. We're six, you're three, Lindsey, and Pam has four, so we need dinner for thirteen. On no, what an unlucky number. R. B., we can't have thirteen people here!"

"Mom! Don't panic. Sandy's coming; that makes fourteen," Tom teased her.

Brushing her hair back in relief, she replied, "Oh yes, I forgot about her. Yes, fourteen, that's so much better. Morning Dove once had a party for thirteen, and four got sick during it, so we ought to be just fine, that is, if everyone comes. Oh no, I forgot your Aunt Monane Tumble; she's coming too, along with her husband and three children. That makes nineteen, so now we're quite safe from any jinx. Whew. Now then, children, keep your hands off and out of the pies and cakes. They are for the party. Time's a wasting, so get to cleaning, please."

Year old magazines, newspapers from five months ago

stained with ketchup, empty soda cans, as well as some unidentifiable objects, littered the front room. The kids got started filling up more garbage sacks. Luci stuck her head in from time to time, adding encouragement. "Just you wait until you have four teenagers, then see how clean your house will be!" she said to Lindsey and Amanda.

"But I'm only twelve," Fern protested, "and my room is spotless. I don't see why I need to clean up in here."

"Isn't that your hot dog wrapper from two nights ago?" her mom pointed out. Fern blushed. Lindsey presumed that it was. By late afternoon, the Whitewater home was spotless, even the stains on the rug and sofa had been magically removed. After thanking Lindsey profusely for her help, Jim and Amanda helped her saddle up, and the three rode back to the Compton's ranch, providing her an escort, in case of trouble. Everyone was still just a bit on edge over Dominus Malefic's threat to kill those who had imprisoned him fifteen years ago, along with their families, as he had done to Mabel Pruit's.

Just after lunch the next day, Lloyd hitched up Lena's old-fashioned buggy, and the three enjoyed the ride over to the Whitewater ranch. Indeed, over the last three weeks, these two families had become close. Lena really enjoyed the company of Luci, and they held much in common. Even though Luci was a witch, she preferred many of the "old ways." Lloyd marveled over the miraculous inventions of R. B., who thoroughly enjoyed showing off his many useful magically enchanted inventions.

Soon, the three joined the six and the constant chatting among friends began once more. Lena and Luci headed into the kitchen, their private world, interrupted only magically by someone lifting another cold soda from the refrigerator. No one actually walked into the kitchen and got one manually, not in this household.

Around one p.m., a car drove up near their corral. At that instant, one of R. B.'s inventions activated. A stuffed owl spoke up, "You have visitors arriving by the corral." Lindsey gave a start, and said, "Now that *is* cool, Amanda!"

She grinned, "Come on; it must be Pam!" They rushed

outside to greet their company. It was indeed Pam. A very fancy Cadillac 4000 Series M had parked beside the corral, near the Compton's buggy. This super luxury car had everything a wizard or witch could want in transportation, including an autopilot, which, once you punched in the coordinates of your location, drove you to that location flawlessly. Pam was climbing out along with two older boys, and her Aunt Wilma.

Just at that same instant, four others suddenly appeared beside the group. Inside the home, the owl spoke, "Four have just teleported to the corral. Monane is here." However, Lindsey didn't hear the owl. It was Monane and her family, R. B.'s sister.

"Wilma, I see that we are just in time," Monane greeted the new arrivals.

As the others came out of the house, it was introductions all around. Wilma was about the same age as R. B and Monane, in their late thirties. Wilma, Lindsey noted, was very fit, strong boned, a no nonsense type of woman. Her brown hair was short—the easy to care for style. She had piercing eyes, however, and Lindsey felt that she was keenly observing her, when she was introduced. "So very pleased to meet you at long last, Miss Lindsey Barron." Her handshake was firm and solid.

Her husband, Tom, was in real estate and traveled the high plains daily. He was tall and thin, but well dressed. Their two sons were twins and were eighteen, gangly youths, Bill and Ted. After the introductions, Tom took the boys to the casino in Arapahoe, promising to be back long before supper. "They'll be broke quite soon, I expect, Wilma," he said.

Monane was likewise an Apache, with long, black hair and darker skin, very similar to Amanda's appearance. She too was quite fit, Lindsey noticed, with eyes that did not miss a thing. "It is a pleasure meeting you, Lindsey. Amanda has told me a lot about you." Lindsey smiled and shook hands with her, again a solid shake. Her husband, Rufus Tumble, was a rancher, and Lena and Lloyd hit it off with him at once. He was keen on just how they managed to run the ranch using horsepower.

They had two children as well, Louisa was a witch, who was working in a dress maker's shop in Sterling, designing custom made dresses. Louis was a wizard, who loved to work with automobiles, adding extras to Cadillacs that came from the norm factory in Detroit.

Just as the Cadillac left with the gamblers, Sandy arrived on her horse and more introductions were needed. Once everyone entered the house, various people congregated with those of similar interests. Lindsey soon found Pam, Amanda, and herself sitting alone with Monane and Wilma. Monane said, "Lindsey, may I call you that? It seems better than Miss Barron."

"Of course, otherwise, you sound like one of my school teachers," she replied, and the three girls giggled.

"Good, I wouldn't want to sound like Professor Janice Smith. Is she still teaching first year's their first spells?" Monane asked.

Again, from the giggles, she assumed so, but Lindsey replied, "Yes, I had an awful time with her, when I first got there. Pam came to my rescue, and after that, she was definitely fair to me."

The older women smiled, and Monane asked, "Amanda has told me about your adventures with Dominus. I believe Pam has told you about it, Wilma." Her friend nodded. "Yet, I always prefer to hear such stories from those who lived it. If it doesn't bother you to talk about it, Lindsey, would you mind entertaining two older women with all that happened at Bradbury's, all that involves Dominus Malefic? We both would dearly love to hear your side of just what happened."

Once more, Lindsey found herself going back over all that had happened to her and her friends during their first year. Both Pam and Lindsey noticed that these two women seemed keenly interested in her story and their eyes never left her throughout. When she finally finished, Monane gave her a bit more to think about.

She explained, "Yes, Governor Alister knew what he was doing. He managed to get Dominus to use his most powerful spell, a limited form of a wish, on him. If he had not, Dominus would have been able to regain control of the rod, Lindsey, taking it away from you as you handed it to the First Rider. However, Amanda, you shouldn't worry what would have happened to Lindsey had you not been able to track Dominus to that cabin. Alister also knew where they were and was magically observing everything from Lindsey's head. He takes the protection of his students very seriously. While you were most definitely tortured something hideously, Lindsey, he would never had permitted any permanent harm to befall you. His record in this account is spotless."

Wilma added, "Indeed, stories are accurate. Nice job, Pam. It seems that we, Monane, are looking at three very gifted young ladies, a Sleuth, a Tracker, and a Dispeller."

"Well, they still need five more years of schooling, my dear," Monane countered Wilma's rather brash statement.

"Dinner's ready," called out Luci. Everyone headed to the dining room. R. B. had magically enlarged this room to hold the large gathering comfortably. Tom and his sons had returned. Both twins looked dejected; they'd lost, of course. Lindsey later learned from Pam that they thought that they had a foolproof system worked out to win big at the roulette table. Now they believed their father and mother, who had told them that the house always is the big winner.

The mountain of dirty dishes was handled in less than a minute, to Lena's complete wonder. With so many experienced witches present, the Clean spells went faster than the others could put them away.

Once that chore was done, R. B. explained, "Now then, time for the dancing. Of course, we realize that the music we prefer is most definitely not what you children prefer, and vice versa, I might add. Hence, I have taken this opportunity to adapt my latest invention. Behold, our living room becomes two dance halls. The moonlighted one is for us adults, while the one with the silly disco lighting is for you children. While you are inside your half of the room, you'll only hear your music, not ours. If you don't like the music, blame Tom. He picked the music for you. Lucinda Morning Dove, may I have the pleasure of this dance?" He gallantly offered his wife his arm. Lloyd followed his lead and took Lena's arm; the others followed suit, entering their half of the dance hall room.

Not to be outdone, Jim said, "Miss Lindsey Barron, may I have the pleasure of this dance, whatever Tom has picked out?" The girls giggled, but Lindsey offered him her arm. Quickly, the others piled into their half, eager to hear the latest rock tunes that Tom had picked out.

Occasionally, Lindsey looked over at the other half of the room, where the adults were dancing slowly and formally, in stark contrast to the wild gyrations of the younger set. Time flew by rapidly. Soon the hour drew late, and the dance finally ended. Once more, they gathered around the dining room table for pie, cake, and drinks. Then, it was time for goodbyes.

However, Pam stayed on for a week with Amanda, sleeping in her room with her so that she could visit her dear friends. While the three had little time to talk among themselves today, tomorrow would be all theirs, once the chores were finished. Lindsey gave Pam and Amanda a hug and joined her folks in their buggy.

Early the next morning, Lindsey rose and got her chores finished before breakfast. Shortly after that, Pam and Amanda came riding over to visit her. After a tour of Lindsey's new ranch, the three went into Lindsey's room for serious conversations.

"Have you checked your email today?" Pam suggested. "I got our fall schedule today. I wonder why they were so late in coming this year. Perhaps it has something to do with Dominus and his bunch." Hastily, the other two booted up their laptops, and the three compared their schedules. No surprise, they were identical.

```
 8:00 Biology
 9:00 Algebra I
10:00 Physical Education
11:00 Government/Music
12:00 lunch hour
 1:00 English/World History
 2:00 Divination/Necromancy Theory I
 3:00 Alteration Theory I
 4:00 Spell Casting—Grade 2 and 3
 5:00 Dinner
```

"Ugh, we have one less magic class this year," Pam

complained.

"Yes, but I dread the necromancy part," Lindsey added. "I think it is terribly wrong to animate dead bones and dead people."

"Zombies," Amanda explained, "Tom says they are called zombies. I think that is just plain gross! They ought to make that an elective or something."

A pair of incoming emails appeared simultaneously on all three computers. Emilio and Kathy had just gotten their schedules and wanted to compare schedules. Indeed, the five were going to be in the same classes again this year. Back in Pueblo, Emilio breathed a sigh of relief. He greatly depended upon the others for help in many of these subjects, especially math, which now looked impossibly hard.

Emilio also asked them if they had seen MagNews today. Lindsey realized that she had forgotten to listen to the news all summer. Her life had become full of wonderful things, and she just had not had time to spend listening. For the last three weeks, the news had been the furthest thing from her mind. Quickly the trio logged into the web simulcast of MagNews, the magical news station.

The news announcer, Hugo Whitefield, who many thought was a handsome devil, blonde hair, blue eyes, charming smile, whiter than white teeth, faced the camera, as if speaking directly to the viewers. Lindsey had the uncanny feeling that he was right here in front of her.

"Yes, wizards and witches, it *has* happened. While the Department of Law kept insisting that this would be impossible, the impossible has happened. During the night and early this morning, Dominus Malefic freed all nine of his remaining Death Stalkers! Yes, the ploy of putting each prisoner in a separate, undisclosed prison has failed utterly. Supposedly, only one person knew the locations of these men. The death toll stands at fifteen guards at the nine prisons! The US Senate has called for an immediate investigation of how this could have happened. Even the Board of Regents is demanding an explanation from the Department of Law."

Hugo leaned even closer to the camera, his face becoming a picture perfect image of deep worry and concern.

He seemed to be speaking directly to each of his viewers, "I urge each of you to immediately implement all means available to you to protect yourselves and your loved ones from these vile, heartless, criminals." He leaned back changing his countenance to that of a learned, trusted professor.

"KMAG and I have prepared a list of Always Followed Rules for Safety. These will scroll across the bottom of your screen as I speak. One. When traveling, always travel in a group of at least four, and never, ever go anywhere by yourself. Always have someone at your departure and destination locations know your plans and your expected time of arrival. Two. If you see any suspicious activities, men lurking about, call either 911 or MAG911 immediately to report it. Three. When you are in your own homes, triple lock all entrances, including windows. Hurricane shutters are recommended for all windows. If possible, get all these Wizard Locked. Four. Prepare a plan of escape, should your home be attacked. Drill your family on the escape routes at least once a week. Five. In the event of an attack, prepare a safe house to which you and your loved ones can flee. Later, we will present an entire hour devoted to the best ways and means you can use to protect your loved ones from these wicked men."

Hugo leaned back and presented a perfect, relaxing grin to his audience. "I am pleased to announce that KMAG has suddenly found all the missing video tapes from fifteen years ago, when the Rat Pack apprehended these vile criminals. At the bottom of this hour, we will be playing a thirty minute summary of the best of this footage! Stay tuned for some incredible footage, long thought lost from KMAG archives! I promise you folks, you will find this video summary highly informatory!"

"I look forward to seeing you at the bottom of the hour. Until then, this is Hugo Whitefield, saying so long for now, and keep yourself safe!"

"Wow! Footage of the Rat Pack!" exclaimed Lindsey. "Maybe they will show some of my dad. Pam, is there any way that I can make a copy of the video if dad is in it?"

"Darn, I didn't think I'd need anything but my laptop on this trip, Lindsey. I left the rest of my stuff at home. Hey, I know a way. I can setup a video capture using my dad's computer, then download it, and remove it from his server when I get home, turn it into a mp4 file for you, and email it to you. How's that?" Pam, the computer geek, replied, grinning, her large front teeth prominently displayed.

"Super, Pam!" Lindsey replied. "Thank you. Gee, do you really think that everyone ought to be going around everywhere in groups of four?"

"Honestly, I think Hugo is overreacting," Amanda interrupted. "Look, they are only just under a dozen men. How can they begin killing people they don't know, you know, families and such? It doesn't make any sense at all. Why would they be killing random people anyway? I think it is just sensationalism at work."

Intense. That's the only way to describe the three as they watched the video of the Rat Pack, an interview done some fifteen years ago. Lindsey stared at her father, who was then in his late teens, displaying a boyish cockiness and playfulness she'd never seen. Mabel, their Diviner, looked rather plain, with short blonde hair and slightly crooked nose.

Bill and Able, the Eliminator and Tracker respectively, in contrast to the playful Sam, appeared quiet and reserved, allowing Sam to do most of the talking for the group. The two's appearance was quite unremarkable, faces one might see in any crowd. Yet, Lindsey was drawn to their eyes, something about the eyes of Bill and Able transfixed her attention, almost as if she had seen them before, somehow.

"Your father must have been their leader, Lindsey," Pam concluded as the interview ended. "He certainly did most of the talking and explaining. Bill and Able said very little, quiet types, I guess. Your dad sure was cool, though." Lindsey grinned, very pleased for the compliment, though she was coming to grips with the fact that he was something of a teaser himself. Lindsey had enough teasing to last a lifetime already.

A little later, both Jim and Tom arrived to escort the girls home. Jim commented, "Mom's gone off the deep end with Hugo's advice. We are now under orders to always travel in a group of at least four." Everyone groaned at this new twist. It would crimp their plans. Now they would have to get Jim and Tom to accompany them the short distance to Lindsey's place.

Tom added, "Well, I did get her to compromise a little. Only Jim has to go with me to get Sandy each late afternoon. Don't make any traveling plans weekdays between four and five, that's when Sandy gets off work and drops by our place."

"Who's going to bother us way out here in the isolated high plains?" asked Pam. In Sterling, she could see some merit in traveling in groups, but here?

Vic Broquard

Chapter 2—Bus Troubles

August 23, the school bus came to the Whitewater home to pick up Fern, the new first year student, for her orientation week. Both Tom and Sandy, the Yellow Hall Floor Monitors, also had to return to school with her, since part of their duties was to help the new students get their supplies and learn their way around Bradbury's.

Because of the threat of Dominus Malefic and his band, the remainder of the students was told to be ready to return on August 29, two days early, and to expect long delays while each student was examined to make sure he or she was not one of the Death Stalkers masquerading as a student. Lindsey heard this delay had happened last year, but now she got to experience it herself. At nine in the morning, she stood on her new porch, five duffle bags of possessions ready to go. She had said goodbye to her mom and stepfather already, though both were watching from the front window. "She looks so grown up, Lloyd," Lena commented, as the two looked at the teenager.

Pop! The Bradbury school bus suddenly appeared. Across the front banner scrolled "To Bradbury's School of Magic." The school logo was also plastered across both sides of the yellow school bus as well as above the rear emergency door. Yet this was not your ordinary school bus, rather it looked more like a double decker Greyhound bus, a mixture of a London two-decker and a Greyhound coach. A large cargo bay below held the students' gear. Two stories of seats meant that this bus could carry at least a hundred passengers. Jimmy, a young man in his twenties stepped off to greet her. A solemn faced second man also got off, his badge indicating that he was from the Department of Defense.

Jimmy had long blonde hair, tied back in a ponytail, and blue eyes with a small blonde moustache. As he smiled, Lindsey saw that he was still missing his two front teeth. "Bradbury School of Magic. I's a pleasure seeing you again, Lindsey Barron. 'om, here, will check you ou' 'o make sure you is you and no one's hiding in your bags. Then, I'll pu' your bags

20

below, ma'am." He still had immense trouble with his t's.

Tom came forward and waved his wand over Lindsey. A bit annoyed, Lindsey replied, "Honestly, how is that going to detect if I'm not who I am? When Dominus was being me, that spell wouldn't have detected him as me." Tom ignored her and waved her onto the bus, while he began inspecting each bag and her staff. He shot her a long glance over his shoulder, though she did not see him doing so, as she climbed on the bus. She would be the first student to have her own Staff of Power!

Lindsey moved quickly to the rear of the bus, where Jim and Amanda were sitting in their favorite spot, the very last seat. "Hi, sure is kind of dumb of them," Lindsey remarked.

"We know," her two friends chorused. "Took him five minutes to check us out. This will be a long morning until the bus gets loaded up."

"Well, soon we ought to pick up Kathy and Emilio," Amanda offered a more hopeful note. Indeed, it took all morning before they had finally picked up all the students; close to a hundred were jammed into the bus, when it finally began the lengthier portion of their journey, across southern Colorado to somewhere near Telluride.

Kathy, Emilio, Lindsey, and Amanda chatted together, while Jim moved up front to talk to some of his older friends. "I always like this part of our trip, because we get so see the mountains and forests," Amanda commented as the bus flew along US 160 through the San Juan Mountains and Forest. Zipping through the streets of Durango at a hundred miles an hour, the bus traveled in twisted space. Still, it was creepy as they apparently "moved" through other cars and trucks as if they were not really there. Not long after that, the bus turned north on State 145 and entered the long, picturesque drive up to near Telluride.

This area was quite remote; only three tiny towns lined this magnificent road, which traversed the valley to the east of the towering range of mountains. Last year, they had studied astronomy in their science class, and the four now knew that Mount Wilson Observatory lay just north and west of them. While they were chatting about this, suddenly the bus made a loud bang. It lurched violently and suddenly stopped, heaving students forward in their seats. Thankfully, everyone had obeyed Jimmy and had their seat belts fastened.

"What happened?" Lindsey asked over the terrified shrieks coming from some Red Hall girls up front.

"Dunno, we must have broken down," Emilio suggested.

"I didn't think these buses could break down," Amanda replied. "I thought that they were magically enchanted and all that."

"Quiet!" the loud voice of Tom, greatly amplified by a spell, thundered throughout the bus. Instantly, silence came. "That's better. We are having some kind of problem with the bus. I would like everyone to exit the bus slowly and safely and in an orderly manner. Stay close together over there on the hillside by those trees, while Jimmy and I see if we can figure this out. Don't go straying around! Thank you."

One by one, the students climbed off, talking hastily, voices full of concern. The four joined Jim and his older friend. Jim was saying, "This shouldn't be happening. These are magically enchanted buses."

"You're right about that, Jim," Francesco, Emilio's older brother and fifth year Brown Hall student, replied.

"Maybe it's sabotage!" Henry Freeze, the Black Hall fifth year student ominously suggested.

Deiter Cross, the Black Hall boy who had teased Lindsey relentlessly all last year, spoke up, "Well then, we had all better look out. It's probably Dominus coming for Lindsey again. Lindsey, here comes Dominus." Several other Black Hall students snickered at his jest.

Lindsey realized that here was a big difference between her dad and herself. She now knew that her father, non-verbally and without a wand, would have cast some spells onto Deiter in retaliation. Lindsey wouldn't do such a thing.

"Just ignore the creeps," Jim came to her defense. They watched as Jimmy and Tom crawled underneath the bus.

"'his is no' supposed 'o happen!" Jimmy called out. "Wha' do we do now?"

Tom slid out from under the front of the bus. Even from

this distance, Lindsey saw that his face had gone white. He brushed off his suit and came over to the milling students, standing at the side of the road. Behind them, the mountain slopes rose, but on the western side the slopes rose to jagged mountainsides.

"Sabotage, students. Someone has used a remote controlled bomb to blow up the bottom of our engine. Sixth, fifth years, I want you to form up a perimeter around the younger students. Expect more trouble. Miss Barron, I suggest that you summon your staff. This is not a drill, students. Be alert for trouble, while we try to summon some aid," Tom explained. Several Red Hall girls shrieked in alarm, but before they could begin to complain, he added, "Don't panic! Fear is our worst enemy. Focus, wizards and witches. This is not a time to be out of control of your senses." His serious mien only added to the overall fear and tensions.

"Margarete: Come," Lindsey commanded. Many watched in surprise as her Staff of Power came flying from the cargo hold to her hand. This gave many something else to discuss, while the older students began to organize the younger ones.

"Circle, form into a circle," Jim ordered. Francisco and Henry Freeze began stationing the older students around the clump of younger ones. Lindsey and her staff stood close to Amanda, Emilio, and Kathy. "Please, keep talking to a minimum. Each of you is to stand guard over the area you are facing. Like the ancient TV westerns, you know, a circle of covered wagons fighting off us Indians." Many chuckles momentarily lightened the chilling mood. He was an Apache after all. Amanda and Lindsey faced eastward, looking up the beautiful, but relatively steep meadow that climbed skyward from the valley floor and road.

Reduced to whispering, words flew unrestrained. "Do you see anything?" "No, how about you?" "This isn't supposed to happen." "Are we under attack?" "It must be Dominus." "I don't see anything yet." "What are we supposed to see?" "Will we be all right?" "I think we ought to have had more protection." For several minutes, whispered comments flew in all directions.

Something began moving around in Lindsey's skirt pocket. She reached down to feel it. "Oh, it's the lucky foot," she whispered to Amanda, who glanced down at her pocket too. "Golly, it's getting a bit frantic, Amanda."

"Dad said it warned of danger," Amanda recalled her father's words. "Look out, but from where? I don't see anything yet!"

Lindsey looked all over the flowered meadows and the ever-rising hillside, but saw nothing, yet her lucky rabbit's foot only jumped around more wildly within her pocket, rather annoying her. "I only see a chipmunk with a stick in its mouth," she said grimly to her friend.

Amanda looked at the small rodent too, but then her smile changed to fear. "It's displaying magical energy traces, Lindsey! It might not be a chipmunk!"

While they stared at the small furry creature, it suddenly began growing, morphing into a tall and bearded man wearing black robes! The transformation took less than a second. Jim, Francisco, and Henry now saw the man, as well as many others who were looking in that direction. The stick in its mouth became a wizard's staff in his hand. All who were facing his direction heard his magical spell command words. "Ball of Fire!"

Two seconds from being a chipmunk, a giant ball of flames began forming just beyond the edge of the circle of nearly a hundred students! "Suck It!" Lindsey screamed, forgetting that they were supposed to be silent. Just as the leading edge of the flames reached Jim, the entire spell evaporated. Its magical energies arced into Lindsey's staff. Three seconds after the transformation of the rodent, wild screams of terror and panic erupted from the center of the circle of students. The younger ones panicked! At that same instant, three magical missiles from Jim hit the attacking wizard, but had no effect. Amanda saw some kind of energy shield surrounding the man nullify her brother's missiles.

One second later, Henry's lightning bolt arced across the hundred feet and struck their ambusher in his chest. Again, Amanda watched that same shield absorb that one as well. A peal of thunder drowned out the screams of the

24

younger students, who were helpless against such an opponent.

One second after that, Francesco's spell activated, Lindsey heard his command words, "Dispel his magic!" Amanda saw the energy shield surrounding his body disappear!

"Poison Cloud: Kill!" their attacker screamed. Everyone saw a sickly, yellow cloud of vapors appear just before the tightly packed group of children.

"Suck It!" screamed Lindsey, once more. Again, just as the cloud reached Jim, who began to cough, the spell disintegrated, and its energy arced into her staff.

Amanda screamed louder over Lindsey, "His magical shield is gone! Attack him!" She waved her wand and a magical missile flew to where her fingers pointed, striking their attacker.

Now, many wands began waving and making a downward movement. The second year students' most powerful spell in a situation like with was to fire a single Magical Missile. While one alone would not do much harm, close to one hundred would be fatal, even to the strongest of opponents. Just as the first of the missiles struck the man, he commanded his staff, "Teleport: . . ." As usual, the words of his destination were not heard. Instantly, he was gone, and piles of magical missiles struck the ground where he had been standing.

Covered in dirt and oil, Tom, wand at the ready, came rushing up to the group, but their attacker was gone. The entire group was deadly silent. All wands were poised for another spell. All eyes looked at the spot in the sloping meadow where the man had been. "Well done, students! Well done indeed!" Tom spoke encouragingly to the group. "He'll think twice before attacking you again, I'm sure." Tom tried to convince the students that the worst was over, though Lindsey detected a faint trace of uncertainty in his voice.

Everyone watched for a minute or so, but only the winds blowing through the tops of the more distant white pines could be heard. "Okay, I think he is gone. Continue your vigilance, while I see if I can repair our bus," Tom ordered and ran back to the bus.

"Good moves, Lindsey," Jim said. "Saved our butts twice, mine in particular." He smiled at her. Lindsey stared at the ground momentarily. Of course, now everyone began whispering about how Lindsey's staff had absorbed both destructive spells.

"But you were the one who spotted him first," Lindsey whispered to Amanda. "You deserve big credit too."

"I'd rather not be in the lime light. I can't handle it as well as you can, Lindsey," her dear friend whispered. "Will he be back?"

"I'd expect so. After all, he hasn't hurt any of us yet. That must be his purpose, I think," Lindsey whispered back. The two scanned the meadow and hillside repeatedly looking for more signs, but saw none as yet.

"Sh! Stay alert, everyone!" Henry called out. "This isn't over yet!" The noise subsided a little.

Everyone heard a rumbling noise, coming from far up the valley slopes to the east. "What's that?" many voices asked nearly simultaneously. Shortly, everyone knew. A giant boulder came smashing through the trees, bouncing over several boulders as if it was a huge rubber ball! "I got it," called out Francesco. "Disintegrate: Rock!" he commanded, making a circling motion with his wand. The boulder shattered into ten pieces.

While much of the huge boulder was gone, ten smaller pieces clattered on down toward the tightly bunched students. "Push!" yelled Jim. The older students followed his order. With a sideways motion of their wand, a dozen voices called out, "Push Rock." Lindsey watched amazed, as the smaller fragments went flying off in many other directions, eventually landing in the road around the bus, but hitting nothing.

"That was a close one!" Jim exclaimed. "Stay alert, everyone!"

Henry, now coming to grips with their opponent's strategy, ordered, "Gang, let's put up a series of Force Walls between us and the hillside there, just in case he pushes more down upon us. I'll put up the first one and the rest of you anchor yours to mine. Form a barrier between us and fan it out to protect the bus as well. That's still our ride to school!" Lindsey, Amanda, Kathy, and Emilio watched, fascinated to see this new spell in operation. A shimmering wall appeared around the eastern edge of the group, fanning out at a forty-five degree angles to either side of them. Now a boulder would be deflected harmlessly around the bus and the students.

Nervously, the group waited. Tom cursed and said "Clean!" about ten times. He slid out from under the bus, entirely covered in transmission fluid. "What a darn mess! I can't fix it," he said to Jimmy, who stood there wringing his hands.

The lucky rabbit's foot in her pocket began vibrating once more. "He's trying something else," Lindsey called out. All eyes scanned the slopes and meadows to the east. A dark grey wall of fog began slowly creeping down the slopes towards them, growing larger with each passing second.

"He's trying to obscure us so he can do something bad to us," Jim called out. At once, several older students cast, "Dispel Magical Fog." Several of the attempts failed to dispel the fog that now reached their force wall, which momentarily held it at bay, though it slowly began rising up the sides of the wall. Just as the creepy fog reached the top of the wall, Francesco's dispel activated. The fog vanished only to reveal another one was coming their way!

Hastily, the ten older students cast their dispel spells. At last, that one too vanished. Suddenly, the earth began shaking under their feet. Many called out "Earthquake?" Yet this did not really seem quite like an earthquake. A few seconds later, everyone saw a huge landslide coming down at them, splintering the pines in its path as if they were but matchsticks!

"More force walls!" screamed Henry in a panic. At that exact instant, four people dressed in their robes appeared beside the bus. Governor Alister waved his wand and commanded, "Freeze!" Instantly, the landslide halted in its path, as if frozen in time. "Get the children into the bus, Cho Lin, I will hold the landslide a while."

Everyone turned around and saw an angry looking Governor Alister, his arms outstretched as if holding back the landslide. Professors Cho Lin, Huan Su, and Delius Dogs moved toward the frightened students.

Delius spoke, "Kids, onto the bus immediately!" Hastily, the hundred students rushed towards the bus. Looking like a ghost, Jimmy stood by the door motioning them inside.

As Amanda and Lindsey walked past Cho Lin, their Yellow Hall Counselor, both grinned at their professor, who had given them both special lessons last year. Cho Lin returned their smiles and gave them a wink. Lindsey and Amanda relaxed, knowing that they were now completely safe.

In just a couple of minutes, all were aboard. Jimmy took the driver's seat. Sitting in their usual spot at the very rear, her group watched as the three professors stood behind the bus and simultaneously cast the same spell, "Push." Slowly the bus moved forward, while Jimmy steered it onto the roadway. Several times the professors had to cast their spell, stopping only when the bus was safely beyond the landslide. Only then did the small group see a door appear beside Governor Alister. They watched as he stepped through the door and appeared behind the bus at Cho Lin's side. The landslide now continued its thunderous roll, stopping at the roadway, though blocking the entire road with debris.

Quickly, the four cast other spells. Lindsey and her friends watched numerous magical shovels quickly un-burying the roadway. Finally, the three professors climbed onto the bus. Governor Alister was the last to board. "Now then, is everyone safe and unharmed by this little adventure?"

Satisfied that no one was injured, he waved his wand once more, "I hope that you find the remainder of the trip most interesting. I thought it would be nice to ride into Bradbury's being pulled by a team of twenty white horses. What do you all think?"

Indeed, a team of horses appeared in front of the bus, which began rolling on down the road. Spontaneously, clapping and cheering broke out among the students. Cho Lin walked to the back of the bus where the small group made room for her to sit with them. "Welcome back, Lindsey, Amanda, Kathy, Emilio, and Jim. I see you had some practical spell use today," she said calmly, though Lindsey detected a faint trace of concern in her voice, as though she were trying to make light of just how serious this accident had been.

Jim outlined what had happened to the bus. When he got to the attack portion, Lindsey interrupted him, "It was Amanda who first spotted the magical enchantment on the chipmunk, and we watched him morph into his real form. If Amanda had not spotted that when she did, I wouldn't have had time to activate my staff, and the ball of fire would have hit us all."

"That's true, professor," Jim concurred. "Our counter spells, came a few seconds after Lindsey removed the immediate threat.

"Professor Cho Lin, how soon will we learn how to dispel magic?" asked Lindsey. "That spell saved the day several times. I don't know how many times that Jim, Francesco, and Henry cast that one, but it was a lot to help us out."

"Dear, I will speak to Alister about it, but I would think that he may have that one be the very first one taught to you second year students. However, Lindsey, your staff should be able to cast that one for you. Please bring your staff and visit me as soon as you are settled in at school. We need to see just what all it can do for you and see that you know how to activate them." Lindsey grinned; this was incredibly perfect for her.

By the time that they finished outlining all that had happened, the horse drawn bus arrived at the parking lot of Bradbury's School of Magic. Alister rose and spoke, "Today, students you have learned a valuable lesson. If you all stick together and work together, you are stronger than these Death Stalkers. Alone, you would have been killed, but working together, you defeated him. Well done, all of you and a particularly well done to you older students. I thank you. Now, let's get inside, I'm sure that you want to get unpacked and get something to eat. I for one would like a cup of tea. Professors, will you join me for tea in my office, once you see the students safely inside?"

Sandy and Tom were waiting for their Yellow Hall classmates as they disembarked. Indeed the Floor Monitors for the other four halls were also present, rounding up the students on their lists as well. Sandy said, "Okay, Lindsey, Amanda, Kathy, you are in room six this year. Pam is already here waiting you." Hastily, she told the others which room was theirs.

"Is it true, your bus was sabotaged and you were attacked?" Sandy asked. "We've heard all sorts of wild rumors. Professor Cho Lin was interrupted right in the middle of her orientation meeting with the first years and dashed off like there was no tomorrow!" Seeing the girls with their many duffle bags standing beside her, she added, "Oops, sorry, I forgot." She waved her wand and commanded, "Move: room six." Lindsey's many bags disappeared from the parking lot, appearing beside her bed in her new room, startling Pam, who now knew that her friends had finally arrived. She ran down to greet them as they walked up to the pentagram dorm building.

One by one, Sandy moved each girl's possessions up to her room. As a group, they began the walk through the main gates, passed the Admin Hall, heading to the dorms, located in the center of the pentagram shaped campus. "Yes, a bomb of some kind blew out our bus engine or something like that. It just stopped dead alongside of the road," Lindsey began. By the time they reached the outer doors to the dorms, Pam was there anxiously awaiting her friends.

"You are all right? Oh, that is good news. We heard awful rumors," Pam said as she hugged each of her roommates in turn. A few minutes later, inside their new dorm room, the three once more explained to Pam what had happened. She listened eagerly but asked way too many questions that the three could not answer. Who was the Death Stalker? Did they recognize him? What got blown up?

"Yes, my staff actually worked and sucked up two nasty spells," Lindsey finally had a question she could answer.

"You should have seen it! A ball of fire was just about to fry Jim, the older boys, and the rest of us. They were in the process of trying to cast a dispel spell, when it was sucked straight into Lindsey's staff. Impressive," Amanda vouched, while Kathy nodded enthusiastically.

An hour passed rapidly, as the three girls filled Pam in on the details. At last, the foursome headed down to the

Bookstore to get all their needed books and supplies for this year. The store was crowded with nearly five hundred other students all scrambling to get their supplies. As they stood in the different long lines, the only consistent topic of conversation among all the students was the sabotage of the bus and the attack on the students by a Death Stalker. Occasionally, Lindsey, Kathy, or Amanda was interrupted from their tasks by others asking them about the frightful event.

Suppertime arrived just as the quartet finally made their last purchases. After dumping the piles of books and supplies in their room, they raced down to the dining room, where the first years had already begun gathering for the formal dinner. They joined Emilio, Jim, and Fern, who were already there. "Glad you three are here. Now you can answer everyone's pleas for details of our attack," Jim teased them. "Besieged, that's what it's been like."

Tom and Sandy arrived, out of breath. They had been run ragged today, not only with their duties to all the first year students during orientation week, but also with the early arrival of everyone else. "Thank goodness no other buses were attacked," Tom said as they sat down near Fern.

Becky Salinos, their sixth year captain of Yellow Hall's track and soccer team, dropped by to ask, "Lindsey, do you really have a Staff of Power? I mean, it's all over the school—that you used it to save the whole bus load."

"Yes, my dad left it to me. Tom, the Department of Defense man, told me to have it at the ready when we got off the broken down bus. I'm glad he did or we might not be here now," Lindsey replied.

"Super cool! Can I see it after supper? I've never seen a real one, you know, up close and all that. Can anyone but you touch it? I mean without getting cursed or something?" Becky added, "That's if it is cool with you, if I do so, I mean."

Lindsey grinned. The whole school now knew that she had a Staff of Power, while not even all the professors had one. She knew that many of her friends really wanted to see one close up. "Sure, after supper, Becky."

"Attention please," Governor Alister signaled the

assemblage of students to their first formal dinner as a group. At once, a hush fell over the large room. All the professors sat along their long table perpendicular to the many rows of student tables. Lindsey noticed that, unlike last year, many of the teachers had very grim faces.

"Welcome back, one and all. I am most happy to see you again. Before we begin tonight's feast, I would like to express my sincere thanks to all of those on the bus that was attacked today. Yes, to quell rampant rumors, for the first time in recent history, one of our school buses bringing students here from the central high plains was attacked. An explosive device was placed beneath the engine and triggered while en route here. Once the students were evacuated, a Death Stalker appeared and attacked some hundred of you students. All halls were represented. He was not singling out any particular hall as some might suggest."

"Yes, Miss Lindsey Barron does have a Staff of Power. I helped her attune it to herself a few months ago. Between the brave efforts of the fifth and sixth year students and Miss Barron, a total disaster was averted in a timely manner. She used her staff to absorb two of the Death Stalker's spells, either one of which would have very likely killed most all the students, while the older students fended off many other spells, including a landslide and a falling boulder headed into their midst. In fact, once the older students had removed the Death Stalker's magical protective spells, as I understand it, every one of the nearly one hundred students let lose a volley of magical missiles, forcing the Death Stalker to make a hasty exit."

"Students, there is a very valuable lesson to be learned from this harrowing experience. By acting together, by working together, you found yourselves more powerful than a single, highly skilled Death Stalker. Yes, we indulge in Hall rivalry and competitions, but in the end, we are all students of magic. In trying times such as these, by working together, respecting your fellow students, we can triumph over evil men. Respect the positive aspects of those in other Halls, though their beliefs might not be yours."

"Okay, I've lectured quite enough for one day, let the

feast begin." He waved his hands and the tables filled with piles of steaming, hot food—six different courses from which to choose. For a time, everyone forgot the excitement of the day, diving into the delicious meal. Emilio sampled from all six main courses, naturally.

Around six that evening, nearly all the Yellow Hall students gathered in their large commons to watch the giant TV screen and the MagNews, which all expected would discuss the attack on the school bus. Hugo, his broad smile and whiter than normal teeth, appeared precisely on time. His report, however, was not quite what many had expected.

"The top story today is the unprovoked attack by Death Stalkers upon an Arthur Bradbury's School of Magic bus, which was bringing a hundred of our children back to school. Yes, nothing is safe any longer, not even our children's school bus. A remote controlled explosive device was detonated, forcing the bus to stop at a precise location where a Death Stalker lay in waiting. Sources close to the near tragedy reported that a Ball of Fire was cast, but just as it began to burst upon the helpless children, the spell was absorbed into a Staff of Power. Who do you suppose held that staff? Why, none other than Miss Lindsey Barron herself!"

"This whole sordid affair raises many questions that KMAG wants answered. Has Governor Alister Broadwell been taking the safety of our children for granted? Why would Governor Broadwell put a Staff of Power into the hands of a second year witch, entrusting her with such power? Would not it have been far better to put it into the hands of the Department of Defense guard, who would know how to use such? Why had not Governor Broadwell foreseen such an attempt and taken stronger preventative measures? Why did he leave the students to fend for themselves, their very lives at stake, for so long a time before intervening on their behalf? Is he getting too old for the job? Many have been asking that question."

"In our latest KMAG survey, eighty percent have grave doubts about the job that Governor Broadwell is doing. Some are going so far as to call for his replacement. KMAG tried to interview Governor Broadwell to put these questions to him,

Vic Broquard

but he refused to be interviewed. Of course, this only adds to people's ever growing suspicions! After all, it was his failure to protect the Rod of the Apocalypse this spring that led to the total destruction of that ancient relic."

Infuriated, Pam yelled out, "What did you do, Hugo? Interview five worried parents and get four to say they were worried? Eighty percent, bah. You are missing the whole point!" She turned to her friends and added, "I've had enough of his drivel. I'm going for a walk." Pam was quite angry, and her four friends left with her.

Walking northward, Pam continued, "You should have seen just how fast Professor Cho Lin reacted and responded! Five seconds and she was on her way. Honestly, they acted as fast as humanly possible."

"I know, Pam," Emilio soothed her. "They were there in the nick of time. What's with Hugo and KMAG anyway? What's the point of riding Governor Broadwell like that?"

Since the school term had not yet started, no one had any homework to do. The group found many others also out for a walk as well. Shortly, two Red Hall girls came up to Lindsey. Peggy West, a second year student like themselves, had been on the bus with them earlier today. Her friend, Monique Blackburn, a fourth year student and fellow computer whiz, was with her. Lindsey noticed that their cherry red lips seemed even redder than normal, but perhaps it was merely her not having seen them for several months.

"Lindsey, can I have a word with you?" Peggy asked, timidly.

"Sure, we're just calming Pam down. Hugo's newscast was rather awful," Lindsey replied.

"I, I want to thank you for saving my life today. If it hadn't been for you, I'd have been burned to death. I owe you one. If you ever need anything, let me know, and I'll try to help you."

"Thanks, but you helped too, casting your Magical Missile helped drive him off of us," Lindsey added, hoping to allow Peggy to gain some self-respect.

"Yes, and since Peggy is my friend," Monique broke in, winking at Pam, "you can count on me too. You need

34

something, let us know. You have friends in Red Hall. Besides, Pam would shoot me, if I allowed any harm to come to you," she teased her friend Pam, who blushed. Monique had taken Pam to the formal end of term ball last year. "One just has to protect the ones you love, at least that is how we all feel in Red Hall. I mean, I've no love at all for Deiter Cross and his sidekicks, so I won't feel any obligation to help those boys. We in Red Hall will do anything for those we love; that's what's important to us, you know. You need some help, Lindsey, you say the word, Red Hall will be there to help you."

"Thanks, both of you. I will, but I think that we are safe while we are here at school. After all, the attack came out there on the road, not here on campus," Lindsey replied. What a difference a year made, she thought. At the start of last year, she was looked upon as a helpless cripple, a Special Needs student, probably just a figurehead.

Just then, a group of Black Hall students passed them, going the opposite direction. Henry Freeze, a fifth year student, called out, "Hey Lindsey. Thanks for your help today. Impressive. You should think of joining Black Hall. We can use more important people in our hall."

Deiter Cross, who had been relentless in his teasing and taunting of her all last year, said antagonistically, "Yeh, thanks Lindsey, though with that staff of yours, I don't know why you didn't do more to save us."

His always-angry sidekick, Loyd Armstrong, added, "Yeh, thanks Lindsey. It's all Alister's fault, you know. He ought to have protected us better. One lousy Department of Defense man, ha! I told my father about that, and he is going to raise heck with the Board of Governors about Alister."

Lindsey nodded to the passing boys. Once they were out of earshot, Pam observed, "Well, that's a change, Lindsey. At least they are thanking you for what you did. That's a step in the right direction. Maybe everyone is realizing the wisdom in what Governor Alister said at dinner."

"I don't think so," Monique responded, "Black Hall always acknowledges someone who has demonstrated superior fighting skills, such as you did today, Lindsey. You just got their attention today, that's all. Take it from me. I've been around here longer than you have. By Monday when classes start, they will have forgotten all about it. But we won't!" She gave Lindsey a warm hug, and the two went their way.

Pam said, "She's really a cool person, you know. I like her a whole lot, and she likes me, even though I am rather ugly. My dad says I'm now old enough to wear a bit of makeup. Monique says that it might help me look better, and she is going to give me some lessons on how to do it later on. You are all welcome to come too. I'm sure she wouldn't mind sharing her skills with you three."

"Well, I'm game," Kathy said. Lindsey and Amanda remained quiet; neither had any real interest in such matters as yet.

Lindsey suddenly remembered that Professor Cho Lin wanted her to drop by after supper. "I nearly forgot! I'm supposed to go see Cho Lin. I'd better rush over there. See you all in a little while." As she walked rapidly to her professor's office, she summoned her staff to her.

"Sorry that I'm so late, professor. Honestly, with all the excitement, I forgot."

Cho Lin smiled. She'd let her long, black hair down and changed into a silk dress for the evening. "Accepted. Honestly, I was also rather busy myself, so the timing is perfect. Thanks for bringing your staff. Governor Alister insists that I help you learn and master all the powers of your staff."

"Here, I brought along dad's list of what Margarete can do, though I don't know most of the spells yet." Lindsey handed her the paper her father had left her on her staff's capabilities.

Cho Lin looked them over for a time. "Ah, yes, a staff tailored to a Dispeller. Your father has had this one specially made for his use."

"How can you tell?" Lindsey asked, curious about this aspect. That her father had this one made for him seemed important to her. Margarete was even more special to her now.

"For one thing, the spells she innately possesses are very different than normal Staves of Power. Many of these spells you will be learning this year. It can cast a Continuous

36

Light. Normally, we place the light source itself on the top of the staff, rather like a torch. Your simpler Light spell only lasts a few minutes, but this one lasts indefinitely. It will cast four Magical Missiles at one time. She will cast a Ball of Fire or a Lightning Bolt; these are your primary attack spells. It will also cast a Paralysis spell and a Levitation spell, plus a Fly spell. However, her true powers lie elsewhere. She can cast Dispel Magic spells, and she can provide you with personal protection, it's called Lesser Invulnerability. That's what the Death Stalker had on himself today. Most spells through Grade 4 will have no effect on you while this spell is in effect. That gives a Dispeller a distinct advantage. It can cast Skin of Stone, which Amanda made good use of during your soccer game with Black Hall last term."

"Whenever you suspect trouble is coming, have her cast the Invulnerability spell on yourself followed by a Skin of Stone. That way, you cannot easily be harmed by either weapons or lower level spells, giving you a decided advantage. Now the final spell she can cast is the Teleport spell. This one, I strongly advise against using until you have learned to cast that spell yourself. Witches can get into a whole lot of trouble with this one. If you are off in your casting, you may arrive with half of your body buried in the ground or five hundred feet in the air. I once knew a wizard who made a mistake with his Teleport spell. His feet materialized in solid stone beneath his feet. The only way to free him was to amputate his feet, and then he spent a month in the hospital re-growing new feet. He was lucky."

"I promise I won't touch that spell!" Lindsey replied, horrified at potential consequences of this spell.

"Good girl. Now then, let's walk over to the Hall of Evocation and practice casting these spells from your staff. She's absorbed quite a bit of spell energy today. Good practice dictates that she be left half charged so that you have the capability of absorbing a goodly number of spells."

On their way, she added, "Oh yes, you can also use her as a staff to bash someone. If you get in a good physical strike, she can cause almost as much harm as a good sword strike. Of course, once we start practicing the spells, we will likely draw a crowd of curious students, who will want to watch us. Will that be okay with you?" Almost as if reading her mind, she added, "I will make sure you don't embarrass yourself." Lindsey grinned and nodded.

Sure enough, just after the first Ball of Fire detonated in the outdoor casting area between the tall columns, curious students began congregating, sticking around to watch the demonstration. Among these were her four friends, of course. Even Monique and Peggy showed up to watch the display of spells.

After an hour of practice, Lindsey had everything down pat, excepting for the Teleport spell, which they ignored for the time being. She found using the staff incredibly easy, as well as recharging it, when its stored magical energies ran low. By eight o'clock, she and her friends walked back to the dorm. Lindsey felt more confident than she ever had felt before.

Chapter 3—First Days of School

Monday finally came and the quintet walked into their first classroom, joining over two dozen other students. Since Deiter Cross and his fellow Black Halls sat at the rear, they sat near the front. Lindsey was pleasantly surprised when Professor Jasper Jones arrived at his desk, lecture notes in hand. Deiter had not taunted her or picked on her—a drastic change from last year, when he was merciless to her. "Put away your wands," Jasper said grouchily, "no magic needed in this class, except your brains, if you haven't forgotten them during the summer. This year we are studying biology, the life science. First, we will learn about the plant kingdom and then the animal kingdom. Near the end of the year, we will study that topic that you are all anxiously awaiting, the human reproductive system and sex education. Clearly, some of you may well need this information." Many of the girls blushed, while Emilio squirmed in his seat, somewhat uncomfortable.

As they got out their new textbook, the girl next to Lindsey, giggled and whispered, "This is my favorite subject, you know, plants. I'm Audrey Lemon, Brown Hall." She was an average looking brunette, short and curly, but with sad looking blue eyes. Her clothes looked, well, definitely second hand. Certainly, her textbook had been used before. "Plants are *so* interesting, you know, not like people." Lindsey smiled and started to reply, when Jasper began lecturing and frantic note taking ended all other thoughts.

When the bell rang and everyone began gathering up their things, Deiter Cross commented rather loudly, "Oh look. Lindsey has found another lemon! Miss Lemon is a lemon." His companions from Black Hall chuckled at his taunt.

"Just ignore him," Lindsey said firmly. "Come with us Audrey. I'm Lindsey Barron."

"I know. Everyone knows you, especially after last year. He killed your dad, didn't he?" Audrey said sympathetically.

"Who? Dominus?" she replied, taken aback by the surprise question.

"Yes, well, he killed both of my parents, you know," she answered rather morosely.

"I'm sorry, Audrey. I, we didn't know. Did it just happen recently?" Lindsey asked, but couldn't help but feel for her. She was also rather short, the top of her head only reached Lindsey's nose.

"Oh no. It was fifteen years ago, right before he was captured. He killed dad and put a horrible curse on mom. She died right after I was born. I've lived in orphanages all my life." She sighed. Lindsey thought that this definitely explained the young girl's appearance.

"Oh how awful!" exclaimed Amanda.

"Gosh, compared to you, I'm very lucky," Lindsey replied, "I still have mom, and I knew my dad for five years before he was killed. It must be terrible living with strangers all your life. My dad left me an inheritance, though I only found out about it in June. Did your parents leave you anything?"

"A very small trust fund, which barely pays for Bradbury's, is all. That's why I like plants so much." Lindsey didn't see the connection, but had no time to inquire since they had just entered their next classroom for Algebra I.

"Come on; up front where we can see better," exclaimed Pam. "This is going to be a super cool class!" Emilio groaned in protest. Any class that Pam thought was going to be cool was likely to be a nightmare for him, as he hated math. Only with Pam's help had he managed to pass geometry last year.

Herbert Mac Elroy, his white hair thinner than last year and even more disheveled than before, welcomed his new students with a compassionate smile. "Hello all of you once again. So glad to see you are still studying math. This year we are going to be studying the basics of algebra, a most useful bit of mathematics indeed. Let me put this another way. Suppose that you want to go to a rock concert and take some of your friends, but you also have to take along some of your younger siblings. Ticket prices are five dollars for a teenager but only two dollars for younger children. You have thirty-five dollars to spend on tickets, and you must also bring along five younger children. How many of your friends can you afford to bring along?"

Pam shot her hand up at once. "Miss Betts?"

"Four plus yourself, professor," she answered immediately.

"Excellent. Algebra will aid you in solving this little problem rapidly. Unfortunately, it will not solve the problem of how to get out of having to take your younger siblings." Everyone laughed at his keen insight. These new teenagers, who had younger brothers and sisters, were at that age when they rather wished their siblings would disappear, at least occasionally.

An hour later with several pages of notes completed, the class made a beeline to the Stadium for PE class. "Kind of strange having PE this early in the morning," yawned Audrey, who was following on the heels of Lindsey's group. "I hear we get to play volleyball this year."

"What's that?" asked Lindsey, who had never heard of this sport. No one played it at her grade school in Plano.

"You don't know volleyball?" asked Pam incredulously. "Everyone knows about volleyball, don't they?" Emilio, Kathy, and Amanda agreed with her.

"It was my favorite sport in grade school," Kathy added. "Don't worry, Lindsey; we all will help you. It is pretty easy to pick up."

"Pretty easy to get trounced, if you are as short as I am," Audrey countered.

Betsy Walls waved her wand, and all sixteen girls found themselves wearing their gym clothes. "Now then, volleyball time! Everyone knows the rules, I assume." Lindsey shook her head no, but Betsy merely added, "Well, if you don't, you soon will. Now this half are on team red, and the other half are on team blue. Red's on this side of the net; blue's over there." She blew her whistle, and the girls hustled to take their positions. Audrey positioned Lindsey and began telling her what to do.

On the blue team, Peaches Colt from Black Hall, who also reveled in teasing Lindsey, appointed herself their captain. On the red team, Kathy took charge. However, within a few minutes, everyone discovered that only Lindsey had no idea how to play. Peaches continued to urge her team members to hit it to Lindsey, who constantly fumbled the ball.

However, Lindsey enjoyed watching Kathy, who liked to play close to the net, where her tall size allowed her to hit smashing drives over the net. By the end of the period, Lindsey was at least bouncing the ball up in the air so that others could have a chance at returning it over the net. Audrey patiently kept showing her how to set up the ball when it came to her, and to Lindsey's relief, it began to work. "When you are as short as I am, you have to be good at setting it up. I'm never going to be able to drive it down their throats like Kathy, not unless I suddenly grow a foot."

The hour passed rapidly. Close to the end of the period, Betsy again waved her wand. All the girls felt completely cooled off, cleaned up, and back in their school dresses once more. "I rather miss not ending sooner so I can take a nice long, hot shower," Kathy commented.

"This is *so* much more efficient of our time though," Pam pointed out. The girls chuckled and picked up their bags, joined the guys, and headed off to Hall of Humanities for their next class.

While they were waiting for their teacher, Deiter called out, "Oh look, Lemon has no fruit yet. Neither does Lindsey for that matter." Several girls around him giggled, Audrey's face reddened, but Lindsey didn't understand this taunt at all.

"What's he mean?" she whispered to Audrey, who was again sitting on her right.

"Breasts," she whispered back, slumping down in her chair, trying to be invisible, just as Lindsey had done so many times last year.

"Well, we are only thirteen!" whispered Lindsey back. Until this moment, she had not given hers any thought at all. She looked at Audrey and her friends. Indeed she and Audrey were a little less developed than Pam and Amanda. Lindsey decided this taunt was idiotic and forgot about it for now.

Professor Jerry Thalmus, in his fifties and their history of magic teacher last year, entered. "Good morning. You will be seeing a lot of me this year. I teach government and also will be co-teaching your Grade Spells later this afternoon." He was normally the Abjuration Magic instructor.

"Now then, the way that the class goes this year is as follows. On Mondays, Wednesdays, and Fridays, I will be teaching you the principles of government of the norms and the government of us magic users. On Tuesdays and Thursdays, Professor Cho Lin will be teaching you music. Now there are two types of governments, and you must pass both of them to get your degrees. However, we will begin with our own first, and in the spring, we will cover the system that the norms use."

"There are five magical departments: the Department of Law, the Department of Defense, the Department of Healing, the Department of Magical Misuse, and the Department of Records. Each of these departments has a main branch in every country. In larger countries, such as the US, there are numerous sub-branches. For example, Pam Betts' father is head of the High Plains of Colorado Branch Office of the Department of Magical Misuse." Everyone turned to stare at Pam, who buried her head in her book, as if something there was of vital importance.

"Each of the heads of the sub-branches reports to the higher department, until the heads of these five world Departments report directly to the topmost order, the Board of Regents. This most powerful group, the Board of Regents, is ultimately responsible for all things magical. It is composed of twelve elected members representing the entire world. Of course, the larger countries have a member, for example, there is a US regent, a Chinese regent, a Russian regent. Others represent areas, such as the African regent and the European regent. Each area or country elects their regent, who serves a six year term. If you pass this class, then you will become eligible to vote in the next election for the US regent, coming up in three years."

"Finally, and perhaps more of a concern for us, is the remaining group, which also reports to the Board of Regents, that is the Board of Governors. This group is composed of twelve members who are called Governor Generals, one for each of the corresponding twelve regent countries or areas. The Governor General of the US controls the numerous schools of magic in our country. Specifically, he or she appoints the school's governor. In our case here at Bradbury's, the Governor General has appointed Governor Alister Broadwell as our school leader. He runs all things administrative for our school."

Pam, evidently very curious about something Professor Jerry had just said, raised her hand. "Yes, Miss Betts?"

"Did I understand you properly in that Governor Alister is appointed to his position by the Governor General?" she asked. Lindsey had no idea why she asked this question. Neither did any in her group, save Audrey, who listened eagerly to his reply.

"Yes, that is correct. Governor Alister has been appointed to run Bradbury's School of Magic. I believe that he has been in this position for over two dozen years now." He then continued his formal lecture, while Pam wrote in notes using large capital letters the word "appointed."

Last year, Professor Jerry managed to lecture in a monotone voice that quickly put his History of Magic students to sleep. Government turned out to be no exception. Nearly the entire class was startled awake by the bell sounding, though their hands had been writing bits and pieces of notes on their pads. Their first homework assignment was in large letters on the board. Research the names of all the twelve Governor Generals on the Board of Governors, when they were elected to this post, and when their term would expire. It was a library project or a MagGoogle project. The entire class rushed out of the room, heading for the dining hall for lunch.

After lunch came World History class with Professor Elaine Mac Elroy. Right away, Lindsey discovered that this class, while interesting indeed, would require lots of homework papers. Yet, everyone counted the minutes until the next class, their first magic class of the year.

As they gathered in the Hall of Divination classroom, Deiter began to pretend he was Professor Mary Ann Thornby, eyes darting all over as if someone was about to attack him. He even ruffled up his hair to look as scattered as she did. Mary Ann walked in, but evidently didn't see his antics. Lindsey now knew why. She had been horribly attacked by Dominus Malefic and had never fully recovered. Yes, she was in constant fear—

terror in fact. Yet, she was an excellent divination teacher. Her hair flew in all directions; her socks did not match, and her eyes darted all over the room at a hundred miles an hour, before she finally settled down.

"Class, I already know all of you, so let's dispense with roll call. For the first half of this year, you will be learning advanced divination theory from me. In the second half, you will report over to the Hall of Necromancy for your beginning necromancy theory with Professor Delius Dogs." Deiter and his group let out a series of "Yes'!" From what Lindsey had seen of the building and the attitudes of those in Black Hall, coupled with the fact that Delius was their Hall Councilor, she dreaded this course.

"Many of the spells that you will be learning this year involve the art of divination. With many of these spells, you must be convinced that you are going to see what you have asked to see. With others, you must be able to read the tiny imprints of magical feedback that your spells give you. It is my task to get you prepared to sense these faint clues, for faint they will be at their best. A good diviner must be a good observer or he or she will fail miserably. Your Identify spell from last year is a prime example of what I am speaking." Everyone remembered that it had taken them a week of study to determine the properties of her magical rings, for example. It was tedious work at best.

"Yet, this year, we are going even farther into the art of divination, to the point where you can read the thoughts of another, see through another's eyes, and even hear what another is hearing. Yet, once more, I must caution each one of you. When you are doing this spying upon another's thoughts, you must keep the four inviolate rules in mind.

1. Thou shalt not use magic to injure or harm another unjustly.

2. Thou shalt not use magic to kill another unjustly.

3. Thou shalt not use magic to steal from another that which is not yours.

4. Thou shalt not use magic to force another to do something against their will unjustly."

"Scrying on another and then using that information

unjustly will land you in prison! I'm warning you right now that reading another student's thoughts and using that to embarrass them or to cheat on a test will land you in the Department of Magical Misuse immediately!"

She seemed to calm down somewhat and said, "Please get out your textbook and let's begin at chapter one, please." When the bell rang ending the class, Lindsey was certainly not ready for it, she was quite interested in these new principles. However, everyone had to make a dash over to the Hall of Alteration on nearly the opposite side of the campus from the Hall of Divination.

Professor Arthur Thornby, forty-three and husband of Mary Ann, taught alteration magic. Lindsey had not yet had him as a teacher. He was definitely mild mannered. After calling roll, he began, "Welcome to Alteration Theory. Why do we need this theory? Well, it's simple. Very soon, you will be learning the Alter Yourself spell. Has anyone wished to be somewhat taller, more muscular, thinner, or prettier? Well, with this spell you can. However, be advised that at first these changes will last only a few minutes, but with time, practice, and experience, why, they can last much longer. It is a very useful spell at times. For example, by altering yourself into that of a merman or mermaid, you will be able to breathe underwater."

"Hence, when you are casting any of the alteration based spells, students, it is imperative that you know what you are doing! If you attempt to make yourself prettier and goof the alteration, you can look quite ugly. I know. I've seen many a student botch such spells. Now then, let's begin at the beginning. I find that is always the best place to begin. Chapter one, please." Again, the hour passed swiftly for the thirty students, fascinated by what was possible in the arena of alteration magic.

When the bell rang, Arthur said, "Well, so much for theory. Now then, I'm also your main teacher for your Grade 2 and 3 spells, so for once, you don't have to change classrooms. However, you may take a ten minute break."

No one took a break; rather everyone began chatting at once. "Have you all taken a peek at the spells we're going to learn how to do this year?" asked an excited Pam. "Ball of Fire, Lightning Bolt, way cool!"

"I can't wait to get to being able to cast the Flaming Arrow spell," Amanda added her thoughts.

Emilio chuckled, "I'd expect that. You're an Apache, after all." Everyone chuckled.

Shortly, Professor Jerry Thalmus entered and joined with Professor Arthur. "Shall we begin?" Arthur suggested ahead of the bell. Everyone eagerly took their seats at once. "In light of recent events with the school bus, Governor Alister has asked us to jump ahead and teach you a Grade 3 spell first, before beginning with the usual Grade 2 spells. Open your book to page forty-two, there you will find Dispel Magic, which is where we will begin. Jerry has graciously volunteered to teach you this one, since it is, after all, abjuration magic. Jerry," he motioned for him to take over the class.

Professor Jerry began, "Students, this is a most critical spell for any wizard or witch to learn and learn well, for it is nearly the only way to undo or to counter magical spells and their effects. Let's begin with what this spell can never do or accomplish. First, it can't undo the magical enchantments of magical items, such as rings of invisibility or Staves of Power or even your wands. The only thing it can possibly do to such items is make them inoperable for a brief minute or two at most. Second, it cannot be used to destroy such items. For example, with the Rod of the Apocalypse that Lindsey ran into last year, a Dispel Magic cast upon it would have done nothing at all."

"Third, when you cast this spell, there is always some slight chance of success as well as some slight chance of failure, always. Let me explain more fully. Today, you will be using the spell to counter your classmate's spells. Both you and your classmate are of the same level of experience, novices in this case. Hence, when you are successful in its casting, the odds are fifty-fifty that your spell will work as intended, cancelling the other's spell. On the other hand, if I were to cast a spell for you to attempt to dispel, because my skill level is much greater than yours is, the chances for you to be successful are drastically reduced to about one in ten, perhaps.

Yet, there is always a chance you will be successful, even against me."

"I want to put this into proper perspective. Suppose that it is not me who is casting the spell but Dominus Malefic himself. Ah, now I can tell you that your chances of being successful drop to the lowest possible, about one in twenty! How about me trying to dispel one of Dominus' spells? Ah, my chances are also reduced to around two in five!"

"What about the reverse? Suppose you decide to cast a spell at Dominus, and he uses his Dispel Magic against it. His chances increase to about nineteen in twenty that he will succeed in ruining your spell! If he were to attempt to dispel one of my spells, his chances of success are around three in five or better."

"So if Dominus is so powerful, why does Governor Alister wish you to learn this spell immediately? Because there is *always* some chance of success! Now for the sake of Miss Barron, who possesses a Staff of Power, your staff will appear to be about as powerful as I am, with respect to its Dispel Magic spell."

"Class, there is another aspect of this spell that makes it powerful. Remember the old norm saying, 'If at first you don't succeed, try, try again?' Well, that applies very strongly with this spell. Say that Dominus has charmed one of your friends into working for him, and you wish to undo that charm. If you repeatedly cast your Dispel Magic spell, eventually, you will be successful in undoing his charm spell. So it takes you ten minutes to undo it instead of a few seconds? Do you follow me?" Everyone nodded.

"Now with this spell, you, the caster, can specify how the dispel is to operate. If you do not specify anything, then the spell will affect a cubic space about thirty or so feet on a side. Sometimes, this is useful because it may well undo several magical spells that are in effect on more than one person or object in that space. The norm's have a saying here too, 'Killing several birds with one stone' or something like that."

"Other times, you may wish to be more directive in its action. In the case of a charmed friend, you could add that as its keyword when you cast it, as in Dispel Magic: Charm. Or

Dispel Magic: Ball of Fire, which may stop an incoming ball of fire."

"Now find your partner and let's begin. One of you will cast a simple Light spell, positioning it on the end of your wand, please. Your partner then will attempt to dispel the light, before the light spell ends of its own accord. The wand motion is a simple outside flick, as if you were flicking a fly off of a piece of cake."

"Finally, remember that the word abjure means that you are formally, solemnly renouncing a belief or claim. When you cast the spell, be convinced that the light will be gone. Once again, always remember that it is your *conviction* that makes this spell work."

"Oh, I nearly forgot, will Miss Barron and Miss Lemon please pair up together and come up here with me? Governor Alister's orders for this spell only." Lindsey looked at Amanda, her all time partner in spell casting last year. What was this all about, she wondered. Amanda moved over and partnered up with Audrey's partner, Jen, while the two girls walked hesitantly up to the teacher's desk. Jerry waved his wand and produced two chairs for them, positioning them behind the large desk. Lindsey relaxed a little. At least the desk would hide them from their classmates.

After the two seated themselves, both looking a bit nervously at Jerry, he squatted down. "Alister's orders. I'm to train you two personally. Okay, wands at the ready. Audrey, you produce light and Lindsey will attempt to remove it."

"Light!" Audrey commanded and a light appeared, shining brightly from the end of her wand.

"Dispel Light! Oops. Dispel Magic: Light!" Lindsey commanded. Nothing happened.

"Did you really believe that there would be no more light, Lindsey?" Jerry asked.

"Er, not really," she admitted. "Dispel Magic: Light!" Audrey's light spell was canceled, as Lindsey's wand activated. Both girls smiled at each other. Perhaps this was not going to be so difficult after all.

"Again," Jerry requested. This time, her wand activated, but the light was not cancelled. Hence, she did it again, and the light went out. "Excellent, if at first you don't succeed, try again. Perfect attitude, Lindsey. Now switch it around and you make the light."

Lindsey commanded, but did not activate her wand, "Light!" The light appeared. Now Audrey began her counter spell, rather timidly. After some coaching, she, too, had her wand activate and Lindsey's light extinguished.

Jerry asked, "Lindsey, you don't need to vocalize your light if you don't want to do so." She grinned. What a huge difference this year was becoming. All last year, Professor Janice had continually hounded her about having her wand activating, when she could cast them all non-verbally and without a wand. Her light reappeared. For the next ten minutes, the two girls continued to practice until both were routinely accomplishing the task, either on the first or second try, since the odds were fifty-fifty for them.

"Excellent, both of you. Now, Lindsey, try the spell either non-verbally or without your wand, which ever you find easier." Lindsey nearly jumped out of her chair! She was that happy about someone finally allowing her to do just this! Within ten minutes, Lindsey had the spell working perfectly without using her wand. After another ten minutes, she did not have to vocalize the spell either.

"Wow! You did it! Incredible, Lindsey!" Audrey exclaimed, greatly excited that she was part of helping Lindsey get this one done almost innately.

"Very, very well done, Lindsey. I now understand why Alister asked this of me. Incredible. However, let's turn it around. Audrey, see if you can also do it without your wand and non-verbally."

"Is this possible for me? I mean she's Lindsey and can do them, but I've never cast that way last year," Audrey wondered.

"We have time to try, Audrey. Remember, it's conviction that matters. Give it a go," Jerry suggested. Lindsey produced her light once more. Audrey went to work. Jerry continually coached her, spotting every little nuance that she flubbed. Finally, near the end of the class period, Audrey thought "Dispel Magic: Light" and it worked!

"I did it! I actually did it!" Audrey nearly jumped out of her chair with excitement.

"Superb, Audrey, very few students at Bradbury's could ever do what you have just done. Now, let's work on it some more and get it perfected," Jerry praised her and nudged her back into practice. By the time the bell rang, Audrey was also quite comfortable in casting this single spell both non-verbally and without her wand.

Jerry waved his wand and presented both girls with a large chocolate bar. "Don't eat this before your supper, mind you. Incredible display of magic, girls, very, very well done! I have to hand it to old Alister, Arthur, he knew what he was doing here with these two."

Arthur's eyebrows raised, "Both?"

"Both!" Jerry stated flatly.

The two ran to their friends to tell them what they had done and to find out how their friends had fared. Lindsey relaxed when she learned that all her friends had been successful with the spell. "Emilio's going to need lots more practice, I'm afraid," Pam said; she'd been his partner today. Jen was just as excited as her friend Audrey was, when she learned what Audrey had done. All seven chatted together as they headed to the dining room.

Pam bragged a bit, "Well, after all, Lindsey is on her way to becoming a Dispeller, so she ought to be able to cast this one as a Dispeller would."

"But I'm not a Dispeller," Audrey replied. "How come I can too?"

"That I don't know. Perhaps we can ask Professor Cho Lin about that, Audrey. There must be a reason why you can cast that one silently."

A reason? Suddenly, Audrey knew the reason; her face flushed slightly as she realized why. She vocalized only a portion of her realization, "Oh, now I can protect myself from other's spells." However, Lindsey suddenly realized the rest of it. Audrey and she were not that different. Both were subjected to taunts, teases, and worse from others. Now both girls could easily undo any magic sent their way without saying a thing or using a wand. Both now had a big increase in their own self-respect.

As they approached the tables in the dining room and just as Jen veered toward the Brown Hall tables, Audrey asked, "Lindsey, would you mind if I came over to Yellow Hall tonight to study with you and your friends?"

"Sure, one more is always welcome. We are usually there around six," Lindsey replied, and the two groups went to their own Hall's tables.

"How'd your day go, Lindsey?" asked Jim, as Lindsey and her friends sat down. He had arrived moments before them, sitting two heavy bags of books down on the floor.

She felt her stomach tingle slightly, though she knew not why. "Great actually. We learned Dispel Magic today. Everyone's got it down."

Amanda had to brag to her brother a bit, "Yes, she and Audrey of Brown Hall both were doing it non-verbally and without their wands. Can you believe that?"

"No kidding? Really? Audrey too?" Jim asked, sincerely interested.

Lindsey's face felt uncomfortably warm, "Well, yes, we both did. Governor Alister wanted us to twin on that one spell. I think he somehow knew that we both would be able to do it. It was great really. Professor Jerry spent the entire class period working only with us two, no one else."

"Incredible! Super cool, hot shot!" Jim complimented her and her face warmed even more. It hadn't when Amanda had praised her. Why should it when Jim did so? The food arrived, and everyone began grabbing for their favorite dishes.

"No Emilio, an ameba is an animal," Audrey explained in her sad sounding voice, "I think you are thinking of a lichen. Those are what grow on rocks." The six were in the Yellow Hall study working on today's homework. Audrey had joined them. Actually, the five appreciated her even more, because they had discovered that she already knew quite lot about the plant world, making their biology assignment easier to do. Each had Audrey check over their lists of small plants.

"Thanks, I knew that. Don'na know why I wrote that one down," Emilio replied, rather bored with the whole biology subject, and this was just the first day.

"You just need to put out some real effort, that's all, Emilio, like we do in Brown Hall—good honest efforts will solve any problem," Audrey suggested, though Lindsey thought that her new friend was about to cry at any moment, but over what, she had no idea.

"That sounds too much like work to me," Emilio teased, but was actually being quite honest about himself. Audrey managed a fleeting smile, however.

"You really do know an awful lot about plants," Pam complimented her, as she finished her plant list for tomorrow's class. "How come you know so much about them?"

She sighed before replying, "Well, when you've lived thirteen years in twelve different houses with a dozen different families, none who really wants you—only the stipend the government gives them for taking care of me—you might too. I mean, plants are the only things that have been kind to me and given me their love, you see. I have Greeny—he's a Norfolk Island pine from New Zealand. I got him when I was five when one mother actually gave me a small allowance, which I used to buy him. He's now almost four feet tall and goes everywhere I go. He's in my room."

Emilio came out of his boredom, "Rats! Senorita Audrey. That's just awful! Twelve different families! That's horrible! Criminal! Despicable!"

Pam explained, "Well, that *is* the way the norm's Department of Family Services operates, you know. They dole out funds to families to take in and raise children who have lost their parents and have nowhere else to go. The orphanages are even worse, according to my dad. He's the director of the Department of Magical Misuse in Sterling."

"You must have gone to a bunch of different grade schools," Kathy added. "Geesh, you probably haven't had any long lasting friendships, moving around so much."

"Seven. No, I stopped trying years ago. I had one, Molly, but I cried for weeks after I had to move again. Never seen her after that. No, only plants. They are my friends. Good ones too. They don't make fun of you or tease you either. You can talk to them. Did you know that plants actually listen to you? If you are nice to them, they grow even better. If you are nasty to them, they wilt or get diseases or sometimes even die," Audrey explained in her sad sounding voice.

"I don't know how I could have survived all that, if it was me," Kathy said sympathetically.

"Effort. Just continuous effort to survive. When it's only you, you either put forth the effort or perish. There's no one to comfort you or to push you, only yourself. In the end, isn't that all that any one of us has—their own self?" Audrey replied philosophically.

"I think friends have a lot to do with it," Lindsey tried to explain her newfound viewpoint. "I mean before I came here last year, I had zero friends—didn't even know what one was. Then, I met these guys. If it wasn't for Pam and Amanda and Emilio, Dominus would have killed me last year. I think with friends, you have someone you can rely upon when trouble comes."

"You said it!" Amanda replied vehemently. "You can count on us. That's what friends are for, as I see it anyway."

"Yes, it's just like Governor Alister says; we are stronger as a group of friends than we are alone as individuals," Pam learnedly pointed out.

"Say, what's this Cradle of Civilization thing? I'm looking at our history assignment. Was there some kind of baby cradle relic, kind of like that Rod of the Apocalypse?" Kathy asked, somewhat confused. "Are we supposed to find this wooden cradle somewhere? Does it have magical properties or something?"

Pam gave an exasperated look, "No, it's not a cradle cradle. That's a metaphor meaning where the first human civilization sprang up, at least where documenting evidence is available to prove it. I think it is referring to the Tigris and Euphrates rivers area in Iraq. I guess we had better hit our history books."

"Why should we hit them?" asked Kathy. "Does something magical happen when we do that?" Emilio and Audrey couldn't keep from chuckling. Kathy always took things literally; her conservative mind would not allow otherwise.

The next day, instead of government, the class had their

first introduction to the world of music. While Lindsey, Pam, and Amanda had some private lessons with Professor Cho Lin last year, this was their first class with her as their teacher. "Welcome to music class. We are going to explore the long musical history of our world and you will be expected to choose an instrument to learn how to play. At the end of the year, each one of you will be playing a short piece for the whole class. I know, it can be a bit embarrassing, so I'm telling you right at the start about it. Practice, practice, practice." Many students groaned noticeably.

"Ah, groaning before you even know what instrument and genre you will play, I see." She teased the complainers. "You groaners, I take it that you don't like the music of the Sick Dogs?" Cho Lin was referring to the most popular rock and roll music group of the world."

"You mean we could choose to play the guitar and play Downer's Love?" asked Deiter. That was the number one song on KMAG's Hit Parade these days.

"Yes, you may. It is music isn't it?" she smiled at him. This got everyone's full attention, naturally. "First, today we are going to take a whirlwind tour of nine centuries of music, spanning the world. As you listen, see if there is one sound, one instrument, out of all you are hearing that you would like to be able to play. Yes, the human voice or singing also counts. First, we will sample what is known as Western Classical Music. It began with troubadours back in the twelfth century. Usually a single instrument played the tune, accompanied by percussion or sometimes a drone instrument. No, you cannot choose to play a drone all by itself."

For the next few minutes, the class listened to the mournful sounds of King Richard's Lament, a peppy saltarello played on a nasal sounding shawm, then two early Renaissance polyphonic motets, and on into the Baroque era with its concerti grossi. A bit of Mozart highlighted the Classical Period, yielding to Beethoven and the Romantic era. When she arrived at the Modern Period, she explained, "You see, a hundred years ago, they thought that all the good music had been written, and thus the composers went off the deep end, so to speak, producing pieces that simply put are not musical. That spelled the ultimate death of western classical musical developments." Indeed, the squeaks and squawks that she played next sounded nothing like music to Lindsey's ears.

"Traditionally, the music of other countries, that is, non-US, non-European, is called Non-western Music. Silly of them, I grew up with traditional Chinese music, and when I first heard Western Classical Music, I thought it was totally weird and strange. It is a matter of viewpoint." She rapidly played historical samples of the classical music of other lands.

"Then, there is another whole side to music, that of popular music, music designed to tell a story, to dance to, to have fun with, or as you prefer, to rock and roll to." She played bits of the popular music through time for a wide number of countries, including African Pigmy music, with its complex rhythmic patterns. Yes, she ended the whirlwind tour with a brief bit from Downer's Love, which everyone loved.

"Now then, during the rest of the year, we will be studying all these musical groups in detail. However, the rest of today will be spent figuring out what instrument you wish to learn this year. Bear in mind, some instruments are much more difficult to master than others are. When you give your final recital before the class, the difficulty of instrument will be taken into account. By that, Mr. Cross, if you choose to play the drums, which are relatively easy to do, I will expect a great performance from you. On the other hand, if you chose the violin, which is much harder to learn, then your recital can be a simple piece. The whole point is to get you introduced to making music."

"Bradbury's will provide you with the instrument of your choice. This is because it is far easier to learn to play on a high quality instrument than one cheaply made. We wish to make this as easy for you as possible. However, if some of you wish to purchase your own instruments, either here at the start or possibly at the end of the year, I will help you obtain the proper one for you."

"Okay, I will now come around to each of you and help you get your choice made. Once you have made it and I have retrieved your instrument, please go down the hall to the room marked 'studio.' Inside, find the room with the number that corresponds to that which is carved into your seats. Each booth is soundproof so you will not be overheard nor distract other students. Automatically, your instructions for playing your instrument and lessons will appear there when you enter your booth. Now then, who has their choice ready?"

"Mr. Cross?"

"Electric guitar! I want to sound like the Dogs!" She waved her wand and a fine looking rock and roll style guitar appeared, along with a heavy amplifier. Beaming, Deiter picked them up and headed off to try them.

Emilio chose to play the drums, but he wanted to play American Indian rhythms along with Mexican ones as well. Amanda had a hard choice. In the end, she desired to learn to sing traditional Apache songs. Cho Lin teased her a bit, "Very cheap costing instrument." Everyone giggled. "But then I rather expected that you might desire to sing your traditional songs. Have fun."

Kathy chose the flute, while Pam chose to play the acoustic guitar, hoping to sound something like the old Jethro Tull sound from the 1970's. Audrey chose to play the medieval pipe and drum, so that all by herself, she could make a full, rich sound with percussion and melody.

Poor Lindsey was the last person in the class to choose an instrument. "Well, you've certainly had a lot of time to ponder the decision, Lindsey. What will it be?" Professor Cho Lin smiled at her star pupil.

"I can't decide between two. Can I hear a bit more of that harpsichord music and the Corelli concerto? It's a tie between the violin and the harpsichord," Lindsey replied.

Cho Lin raised her eyebrows. She had not expected either of these choices from Lindsey. In fact, she had predicted that Lindsey would be a flute player. With a wave of her wand, the two selections replayed in the room, one after the other. "Can I hear some other selections of each, please? I'm in love with both sounds," Lindsey pleaded. The sounds of a Renaissance galliard filled the room, followed by a bit of Rameau. Next, she played a bit of the Four Seasons by Vivaldi.

At last, Lindsey made her choice, the harpsichord. As she headed off to find room six, she realized that, until her hands had been re-grown last year, she would only have been able to sing. Now, a completely new world of possibilities had opened up for her. Inside her booth, she found a small keyboard instrument, made of wood with an elaborately done wooden cover that was opened to allow the sound to come out better. She placed the instructions as shown on the top and followed them. The instant she made her first sound, she knew that she had made the right choice. She was in love with the quill-plucked sounds!

The last page of the instructions told her that she ought to come to this studio for at least an hour every day to learn and to practice. Indeed, all the students had this same message on their last pages as well. Homework. Lindsey smiled as she read it, more homework, only this one would be fun, not work.

At supper, Becky Salinos cornered everyone. Of Mexican ancestry, the sixth year Yellow Hall student tossed her long, black, curly hair over her shoulder. "Tryout's will be after supper. Sorry for the short notice, I kind of forgot, what with all my new classes and all." Becky was the new team captain of Yellow Hall's track and soccer team. "Fern is probably a shoe in, but to be fair, we have to allow anyone who wants to try out for the team to have an opportunity to show us what they can do. Stadium at seven?" she asked imploringly.

"Sure, Becky," Lindsey replied. "I forgot about it too, sorry."

"Fine here, how about Jim and Tom?" Amanda asked. "Say, what did you do to your hair? It looks good on you this way."

Becky smiled and tossed her curls once more. "I took a tip from you two and let it grow longer over the summer. Looks more mature, don't you think? Oh, yes, they will be there too. I'd better check with Sally. Excuse me." She spied Sally just sitting down at the back of the room where the older students preferred to sit and hustled over to her.

"She does look more attractive, don't you think?" Amanda asked her friends. On that, they all agreed. At seven, Lindsey, Amanda, and her sister Fern, walked over to the Stadium, just north of the dorms. Fern was more than a little nervous, so much was now happening so quickly.

"Just relax, sis. You can do a six-minute mile easy. Just keep pace with us and you'll do fine," Amanda coached her. When they arrived, the rest were already there waiting for these three. "Hi all. How many are trying out?"

"Just Fern," Becky answered. "If you can run, you're on the team. Honestly, I think that the Apaches have spread fear into the hearts of all the other Yellow Hall students. Either that or they don't like to run or get clobbered in soccer." Everyone chuckled, if Fern was on the track team, then the four Apache siblings comprised nearly half the team.

"Fern, Tom and Jim say that you are a miler not a sprinter or long distance runner, right?" Becky looked for confirmation. Fern nodded. "Good. Sally's our sprinter, which means that you will be taking Bill Ferny's place in the mile relay race. That means you are teamed up with Emilio, Jake, and me. In the mile relay race, you only need to run a quarter of a mile before you hand off the baton to one of us. However, there is some strategy in choosing which order we run, who goes first, and who goes last, that sort of thing."

"Cool! I think I see. You need someone who can sprint down to the finish line the best," Fern replied.

"Right, so what I want to do tonight is have the eight of us run a mile—that is twice around our track here. Sally will give us the signal that we are coming down the finish line when we have a quarter mile left to go. I want all of us to pour it on so that we all can judge who is going to be best in which order in the relay," Becky explained.

After limbering up, the eight took their positions at the starting line. Sally gave them a count down, and all eight took off with the Apaches setting a solid six-minute mile pace. Both Lindsey and Amanda, having practiced long distance running over the summer with Jim, easily found the proper pace. Lindsey recalled how she had struggled a good deal last year in finding the proper pace, but now it was second nature to her. For Lindsey and these Apaches, running was somehow a vital part of their nature, their being.

The mile went all together far too quickly for these four. Sally gave them her yell, simulating the last quarter mile of a race. This once, all eight gave it everything they had, racing against each other to the finish line. As Becky expected, Amanda edged all the others out, crossing well ahead of her brothers and Lindsey. However, she was more concerned about how Emilio, Fern, Jake, and she finished, as they would be the racing team for the mile relay. Fern crossed it first, followed by Jake, then Becky, while Emilio finished last. All their times, Sally pointed out were under a six minute mile!

Once they cooled down, Becky announced, "Okay, Emilio, you will lead off for us. You pass to me as second. I will pass on to Jake as third, and Jake, you hand off to Fern, who comes down the finish line. What's with you two, Fern, Amanda? You keep beating your brothers. I would have thought it would be the other way around."

Amanda grinned, "We know how they run and hold back until the last moment before accelerating. It's always close, though." Tom patted his sister on her back, while Jim did the same to Fern.

"I say it's because we kept threatening to tickle them if we catch them," Jim teased Fern. They all laughed for a bit.

"Okay then, that's all settled. If we all run like we did tonight, we ought to get another chance at the Nationals this year. That would be something. Now about soccer. Fern, have you ever played it before?"

"Yes, in our grade school, a little, but norm's soccer is so very different from Wizard Soccer," Fern replied hesitantly.

"Well, Bill used to play left middle field, so I am inclined to start you there so that the rest of us don't have to get used to playing new positions. How's that sound to the rest of you? Emilio is our right middle fielder, opposite you. Sally's our goal keeper, and she's the best short distance sprinter we have, perfect for the job." The others agreed, and the nine headed back to the dorms and their homework.

While they walked, Becky said, "I'll let you know as soon as I know what the schedule of games will be. I'll know probably this Saturday. Sally and I are absolutely swamped with homework this year, and it's only the second day! I'm inclined to suggest that we limit our practices to one time a week. How's that sound to you all?"

"Good for me," Lindsey replied. "We've got to learn to play musical instruments this year on top of everything else, so once a week sounds fine with me."

"Yes, we forgot to tell you about the music thing," Jim apologized. "Big waste of time for me. I never did play the flute worth a darn."

"Don't sweat it too much, Lindsey, Amanda, Emilio. If you do well on all the other music theory and recognition tests, even playing miserably won't lower your grade significantly," Becky explained. "I think that they just want you to have the experience of learning to play and performing once. Most students are absolutely awful when they give their recitals. I know I was."

"Me too," Sally added. "I was all thumbs trying to play the recorder, which was supposed to be the easiest to play. After you hear your classmates making awful sounds, you can relax and do the best you can. Don't worry too much about it."

Chapter 4—The Virus

Friday came. Lindsey was not alone in yawning at the start of biology class. Indeed, nearly every student wiped the sleep from their eyes. Summer vacation's idle time had vanished this week, replaced by long study periods. Professor Jasper Jones had just collected their papers listing many single celled plants, when a very worried looking Professor Herbert Mac Elroy stuck his head in their classroom. "Excuse me, Jasper. I need to borrow Miss Pam Betts immediately. Students, algebra class is cancelled today. Use the time wisely to make sure you are caught up."

Everyone turned to look at Pam, who hastily packed up her books, trying not to notice that all eyes were on her. Lindsey and Amanda shot her a glance that asked, "What's up?" She silently shrugged, indicating she had no idea. Lindsey could not think of a single rule or action that Pam could have done to get into trouble. Yet, something was going on here. Professor Herbert looked grim indeed.

Lindsey remembered that Professor Herbert had taken Pam out of class once last year, when he needed her help with the school's computer network. Someone was trying to hack into it. Perhaps it was happening again. She whispered her theory to Amanda, while Audrey strained to hear too.

Pam had to walk very fast to keep up with Herbert. "Someone is trashing our computer network, Pam. Ah, thank you for coming, Monique," he said to the fourth year Red Hall student, who came rushing out of her classroom in the Hall of Humanities. Monique flashed Pam a smile, showing her white teeth in sharp contrast to her bright red lips. She too had nearly to run to keep up with Herbert, her long blonde hair fluffing out behind her. "Someone's trashing our entire computer network," he repeated for Monique's sake. As they approached the Admin Hall, three boys raced to join them. Pam recognized them at once, Harry a sixth year from Black Hall, Tom a fifth year from Brown Hall, and Silas a fifth year from Brown Hall. Again, Herbert repeated what was happening, as the small group raced into the Admin building and descended the stairs into the first basement floor, which housed the huge computer network system.

An operator who Pam had never seen before looked positively frantic. "Sir, half of C: drive is gone already! I can't stop it!"

"I've brought help, Sam. These are the sharpest computer minds on campus." This time, he didn't even bother giving them a visitor's card as they entered the otherwise secure computer facilities. All five gazed at the operator's console.

"Wow! Files are being deleted at an alarming rate," Silas pointed out.

Harry added, "Quick, everyone. Laptops up and running. Professor, we need instant cabling to the network and administrator access!" Hastily, Sam and Herbert plugged in five network cables and gave an end to each student, who hastily plugged it into their laptops.

"Login as Administrator and frazzled101," Herbert gave out the key password.

"Tom, Silas, let's work on stopping it. Monique, see if you can find a way to slow it down and identify it. Pam, see if you can identify it and see where it is coming from," Harry took command.

Shortly, Pam began to poke around the system. Indeed, all the logs had been deleted. From all indications, she noted, they went first. Carefully, she undeleted them over on to her laptop and opened them up in several windows. "Got the logs recovered," she called out.

"It's called CEROL.EXE," Monique added. "It's sucking up over half the cycles of the network. Task Mon's terminate has been replaced; can't manually abort it now. Clever hack indeed. Only a reboot will kill it now."

"Yes, I see it now, Monique," Tom called out.

"I've got its priority lowered to the bottom," Silas replied. "Good going Monique. Herbert, we need to see what all it has done to the basic system before you try a reboot. It may have altered things so that when you reboot, it will regain control again."

"I see, so if I reboot and run a restore, it will still be there, deleting the files even as I put them back," Herbert replied. "Ingenious plan, but perhaps the person wasn't that clever."

"Okay, Tom, Silas, and I are going to see what alterations, if any, this cerol had made to the system files. Monique, help out Pam; let's see if we can find out where it came from and who is behind it," Harry ordered.

Monique slid her laptop beside Pam's and looked over her friend's shoulder. Pam quickly sent copies of the logs from her computer over to Monique's laptop. "Professor Herbert?" asked Pam inquisitively. "What are all these ports from 4000 to 4700 used for? There has been a lot of activity through them."

"It is our clever way of tracking each of your laptops. You see, when we give out the free laptop to each student, we assign a direct port link to each one. From the logs, we can see any access from any specific student's computer into our secure system. If you, Pam, used your laptop to hack into our grades file to change student grades, we would be able to track back that hack to your computer, via that port's access. Each laptop comes in on its own assigned port. I thought up that scheme myself. It's worked perfectly all these years," Herbert replied.

"Clever. Monique, let's see where cerol came in from, shall we?" Pam suggested. The two friends began working over the recovered logs furiously.

Tom called out, "Can anyone send me a file from your system?" He called out the name of one of the system files used by the Windows operating system. Harry sent him the needed file.

Harry added, "I've dumped the memory of the task monitor. Indeed, it has been altered. How can that happen anyway? I thought Microsoft fixed that hole. You're not supposed to be able to write to that read-only memory now, once it's loaded."

"Device driver can," Silas replied. "They are the only ones left with enough privileges to do that. Look for something that was running as a driver, Harry."

Presently, Tom exclaimed worriedly, "Herbert, for god's sake don't try rebooting just yet! He's hacked the system in such a way that if you reboot, it will re-infect the system and do even more damage. It's got the names of your most recent backup files in there, scheduled for immediate deletion!"

Herbert wiped the sweat pouring from his forehead. This was the worst hack his system had ever had to date. "I've a ghost copy of the boot drive locked away in a safe. Will that do?" he asked.

"Yeh, that's about the only way to get rid of this nasty cerol," Tom concluded.

"Port 4327," Pam announced. "It came in from 4327."

"On it Pam," Monique replied, her red lips pressed tightly together as she typed away, searching. "This can't be!"

"What?" asked Herbert.

"It belongs to Bill Ferny. He's graduated, right? And no longer a student? It came in from the port assigned to his laptop," the Red Hall student explained, looking worriedly at Pam. Bill had been the captain of Yellow Hall's track team last year.

Herbert logged into his own laptop and began typing away. Meanwhile, an idea formed in Pam's mind. She hacked into her father's server located in the Department of Magical Misuse in Sterling. Quickly, she brought up the GeoSat Locator program and tuned it to her own computer, which she discovered was using port 4044. She pressed the Locate button, and shortly a map of the US appeared. Using mouse clicks, she zoomed in on the indicated location. She saw Telluride appear and then Bradbury's school appearing. Clever, she thought. This program bypassed normal magical enchantments that kept the schools from being physically located on norm's maps of Colorado. She clicked the Follow Signal button and then sent a low-level ping message to port 4327.

"What *are* you doing? What *is* that program?" whispered Monique, keenly interested in the images on Pam's computer. She had never seen this program before.

"Sh. You aren't seeing this. I could get into big trouble with this one," Pam whispered back. She began to zoom in on the target of her ping. "Oh my!" she whispered, and then quickly terminated the program and closed all the windows. "Professor Herbert, Monique and I have an important errand to run. We'll be back shortly. It's about the computer used to infect ours."

Herbert was highly distracted with what he was seeing on his screen and just muttered, "Okay." The boys cast both a curious glance, but Pam didn't reveal anything. After all this could be a wild goose chase.

Once outside the Admin Hall, Monique exclaimed, "Was that what I think it was?"

Pam whispered, "If I am right, that is the location where the laptop of Bill's is located. Got your wand ready? We could be running into big trouble, if whoever did this is still on the computer."

Monique drew her wand, "Okay, I'll be ready with my dispels. Have you learned that one yet? If not, I will protect you, my love." Pam blushed as the words registered in her mind.

"Yes, Governor Alister ordered us to learn Dispel Magic as the very first spell. I am a bit slow with it yet. It's only been a couple of days since we learned it." The campus was strangely deserted at this early hour in the morning. Some six hundred students were in their classrooms along with all the professors. It seemed a bit eerie and spooky to be walking on the empty grounds. At the Library building, they ducked down the stairs and headed to the tunnel that connected the Library to the dorms.

"Silent Steps," commanded Monique. Pam smiled; their footsteps made no noise at all as they walked along the stone tunnel's floor to their dorm. Specifically, Pam was heading to the southern section, directly below Black Hall. As they approached the long corridor, both girls paused to listen, straining their senses to hear if anyone was just up ahead of them. At last, hearing nothing but their own breathing, they crept up to the garbage dumpster directly below Black Hall. No one was around.

All the garbage from Black Hall ended up down here, coming from above down long chutes. "Open!" commanded

Monique for Pam. The lid of the large dumpster opened up.

"Rats. How am I going to get in there?" asked Pam.

"Levitate: Pam," commanded Monique, with an uprising of her wand.

"Cool!" Pam exclaimed as she gently rose in the air. She latched onto the sides of the dumpster and looked inside. "I see it."

"Levitate: Me!" Monique said firmly and quickly joined Pam. Below them on top of the large mound of garbage lay the laptop.

"We need to get it out of there without touching it. Fingerprints might still be on it," Pam advised.

"Levitate: Laptop," Monique commanded once more, and the laptop rose up towards them.

The two girls slowly descended to the floor, while the laptop floated up and out and down beside them. Monique cancelled her spells. "Dirty!" Pam commanded, waving her wand. Fine bits of dirt appeared over the laptop. She looked at it closely.

"Fingerprints! You are right, Pam, there are a bunch of them. Now what?" Monique asked.

"We photograph them, that's what. As soon as I give this to Professor Herbert, he's likely to send it to the authorities, who will want to lift these prints to find out who used it, but I want to know too. Here, make it even dirtier, while I get my cell phone out to take pictures of them."

A few minutes later, having taken a dozen close-up shots of the smudges, Monique gently blew the dirt away, leaving the prints intact. Using the bottom of her robes so that her exposed hands did not leave more prints on the laptop, Monique picked it up. Pam sent the photos to her computer back in the Admin Hall. Then, the two walked back to the others in the basement of that hall. With great pride, Monique announced, "Gang, here is Bill's computer, the one used to send the virus hack into the school's network. Pam located it, and it is covered with fingerprints!"

Wild exclamations came from the three boys, while Herbert said, "Incredible detective work, ladies! I'll get this sent to the Department of Law immediately. Perhaps we will be able to find the culprit after all. I've some terrible news. There is no easy way to say this, but Bill Ferny has died. Car crash in the mountains. Department of Law is investigating, circumstances are a bit unusual, so they say. It's beginning to look more like murder to me, though, what with this laptop appearing. Wherever did you find it, Pam?"

"In the trash dumpster below Black Hall," she replied.

"But how did you know it was there?" Harry asked. "That's my hall. You aren't thinking that I had anything to do with this, are you?" he suddenly became very defensive and hostile toward Pam and Monique.

"Not unless those are your fingerprints on the laptop, Harry," Monique defended Pam, before Pam could even formulate a reply.

"No one is accusing anyone, Harry," Professor Herbert attempted to defuse the growing hostilities.

"What about her? She knew just where to find it. I call that more than suspicious," Harry continued to counter.

Monique again saved Pam, "She used a locator program, pinging its port number. I saw the location appear on her laptop. I had to use three levitates to get it retrieved. So are your prints on the laptop, Harry?" she threw it back at him. He glared at the two girls.

"No," he finally admitted.

Breaking the tense atmosphere, Pam asked, "So what have you all found out while we were gone?"

"We stopped the program," Harry began. "We've analyzed the machine instructions that the cerol put into several existing system files. Yes, it was designed to wipe out all backup copies as soon as they were being loaded upon system recovery. Nasty piece of work."

"What I don't understand is why?" Pam thought out loud. "Altering someone's grades, retrieving secret information, these would make sense. Why delete all the normal Bradbury website? What good does that do anyway?"

"Gives me a nasty headache," Herbert replied. "I see what you mean, though, Pam. Even if the whole site were trashed, eventually, I would get it back up, if I had to wipe the drives clean and restore everything. I agree, I don't see the reason behind this attack, unless it is to frazzle my nerves. Okay, while I get this laptop to the authorities, will you five lend Sam a hand to get our system back up and running? It's been down for hours now. I'd like to have it back to normal as soon as possible."

This, the five enjoyed immensely, aiding Sam to purge the corrupted files and then begin the lengthy ghost restore, followed by reloading the many drives. Shortly before ten a.m., the group had the entire system back up and running. At last, the five left the Admin Hall, heading off to their next class. As Pam walked towards the Stadium and her PE class, Silas tagged along for a ways. "I'd sure like to know about that locator program of yours. Mind sharing it with me sometime?"

Pam flushed. "Er, sorry, I, er, can't." She left it at that, not daring to say that she'd used her father's program, having hacked into the Department of Magical Misuse's computer system. Silas grinned as he headed off to his next class, resolving to keep a sharp eye on this secretive young girl.

"What was that all about?" whispered Lindsey the second Pam joined them, standing in line, waiting on Betsy to change them all into their PE clothes. Quickly, in a hushed voice, Pam told them what had happened. Abruptly, their discussion halted as Betsy rushed them onto the volleyball courts.

Later as the group got together to walk to their government class, Pam added, "It was sent to us via Bill Ferny's laptop computer, but Bill's been killed today. Professor Herbert said something about a car crash, but now he thinks it may have been a murder!"

"Oh no, not Bill!" Lindsey and Amanda said in unison. Both were visibly upset all throughout government class. He had been their coach last year and a star runner. Besides, he was only eighteen! To Lindsey and her friends, this seemed a senseless murder. The computer attack was mostly harmless, just a nuisance attack.

At lunch, Amanda told her brothers about Bill, and they relayed it to Sally and Becky. By evening, word of Bill's murder was all over the campus, along with the botched attempt to wipe out the school's computer network. As the students gathered for supper, Governor Alister looked somber.

Before the food appeared, he spoke, "Students, it is with a sad heart that I have to relay this news to you. One of our own recent graduates, Bill Ferny of Yellow Hall, has died today, under suspicious circumstances. The Department of Law is conducting a thorough investigation. Bill led Yellow Hall to third place in the Nationals last year. His untimely loss affects us all. Before we eat, let us take a minute of silence to honor him." The entire dining hall was silent.

During the meal, Lindsey noticed that both Sally and Becky were very upset over this news. Both tried unsuccessfully to restrain tears, but failed. Before they finished, both hurriedly left the room. Tom, Sandy, and Jim went after them.

A subdued group gathered in the commons after dinner to watch the KMAG news. Surely, Bill's murder would be on the air. However, not a word of it was mentioned! Instead, Hugo's lead story was about the website.

"Well, if you attempted to access the Bradbury School of Magic today, you would have found their computer system trashed! Yes, someone unleashed a virus, which erased all the school's files, knocking them off the web for half a day. Inside sources have told KMAG reporters that no significant damage was done. None of you has to worry about your grades having been altered. To this reporter, this does seem to be yet another incident outlining the shortcomings of Governor Broadwell. Ignoring that incident last year, already this year, his school bus security was found wanting, and now his own computer system has been breached. Yes, confidence in Governor Alister Broadwell's ability to run the school is definitely being called into question."

Lindsey and her group didn't stay to listen to the rest of the newscast. Adjourning to the study hall, Lindsey whispered, "The nerve of Hugo! What does Alister have to do with some creep trying to bring down our school's website? He should have been reporting on poor Bill."

"I bet they don't do anything about finding who killed Bill," Amanda stated flatly.

Just then, Audrey and Monique entered the Yellow Hall

study commons, looking for the group. "I just wanted to say how sorry I am about Bill's murder," Monique said. "From what I knew of him, he was a fine fellow. If you need a shoulder to lean on, let me know."

"Thanks, Monique," Lindsey replied for the others. "He will be missed. I hear you were instrumental in helping Pam find his computer."

Monique's white teeth flashed, outlined by her bright red lips, a twinkle in her eyes, "Yes, you have not yet learned the levitation spell, but you will soon enough. I was very glad to be able to help. Do you suppose that Dominus is behind all this?" She'd asked the question that she most wanted answered.

Something that Alister had told her came to mind. "Dominus is methodical to a fault." Lindsey suggested, "You know, he may well be at that. He definitely has it in for Governor Alister. I think he blames him somehow for his capture or something."

Relieved, Monique replied, "Well, that makes the whole mess make some sort of sense. After all, why would anyone just want to trash our website? Obviously, we have backups and can put it all to rights in short order. Well, I have to go study my new spells. Let me know if I can do anything for you. Bye Pam." She winked at Pam, who flushed slightly, and then left.

"That's so horrible about Bill," Audrey added. "I feel sorry for him; after all, he only just graduated. Imagine working so hard for six years here at school only to be killed three months after graduating. Sick, if you ask me. I do hope they catch the ones who did this and kill them. Well, Pam, I took many notes for you in biology class. We ought to go over them soon, so you don't get too far behind." Once more, Friday night was spent hitting the books. Pam wanted to do other things, but she knew that she had to keep up. She was behind one whole lecture in biology now.

Becky entered the room and spied them. "Ah, here you are. I have the schedules a bit early. A week from tomorrow we race against Brown Hall. Then the following Saturday, we play soccer against Blue Hall. Nothing after that until springtime.

Nice schedule this year, don't you think?"

"Yes, great, only two Saturdays. I'm glad that we don't have to race or play in the mud and snow," Amanda replied.

"Darn, I was hoping we would get more time off from studies," Emilio groaned. Amanda punched him playfully.

"Well, I'm off to find the others. I think that they are in the library. Don't forget practice tomorrow at one," Becky added and left.

Saturday morning, Lindsey, Kathy, and Amanda slept in, having struggled all week to get back into the rigorous groove of magic school and its demands. Pam, however, rose early, long before the others. Quietly, she booted up her computer and examined the dozen sets of fingerprint images she'd taken via her cell phone. If she was back home in Sterling, she could just sweet talk her father into running them against the Unified Database. Half a century ago, all the law enforcement groups pooled their databases into one, making identifying fingerprints an easier task for everyone.

Pam was at school, not home. While she knew that she could hack into her dad's system and run the prints herself, she also realized that ultimately her father would learn of it, likely getting into trouble over it. She sighed and resigned herself to composing an email to her father.

Dear Dad,

I have a special school project that I need some help with. I am enclosing a dozen fingerprints that I took. Can you possibly run them through the UD for me and send me the results? If I am right in my proposal, some of them ought to belong to Bill Ferny.

You remember Bill; he was Yellow Hall captain last year, who led our team to third place in the Nationals. I just heard that he was killed in a car crash today, so I can no longer ask him for a sample to check against these. Such a terrible tragedy. Everyone here is upset or sad over the news.

Anyway, I am working on a special project for Professor Herbert Mac Elroy. My thesis is that some of these belong to Bill, but the others I am not sure. Can you please help me out with my project? Thanks, dad.

Things are great here. I love it. I've met this new girl from

Brown Hall, Audrey, and she knows an awful lot about plants. She's been helping all of us with our plant biology studies. You never told me biology is so hard! With Audrey's help and a lot of hard work, I aim to get an A in biology anyway. Oh yes, Governor Alister has had us all learn a Grade 3 spell the first day. I am proud to say that I can now cast a Dispel Magic spell!

Love,

Pam

She sat back and reviewed her email letter. *Well, it is a special project that I'm doing for Professor Herbert. After all, I found the laptop, and it is really the only clue that we have left to follow at this time.* Pam justified her request to her father and pressed Send.

Just then, Agent retrieved a new email to her. Her heart skipped a beat, as she saw the sender was Monique. She opened it and read.

Dearest Pam,

Meet me in the dining room. Breakfast. I've some news about the hack. Bring computer.

Love, M

Pam sent a hasty acknowledgment and got dressed, being careful not to wake her roommates. Carrying her laptop, she headed downstairs and over to the dining room. A few of the older students were already there, widely scattered about the room, drinking coffee, tea, or milk along with their breakfast. Monique was not here yet, so she went through the cafeteria line, helping herself to bacon, eggs, waffles, and a large milk.

No sooner had she sat down than Monique entered, nodding to her. Her friend also went through the self-serve line and brought her tray over to join Pam. She wondered how she had time to put on her makeup this early in the morning. Monique's lips were perfectly red as usual. "Hi, glad you were up. I wasn't sure you wouldn't still be sleeping." Monique looked around to make sure they were not being overheard.

Nibbling on her waffles, Monique explained in a hushed voice, "Axelrod did some research." Both Monique and Pam were well known members of the Voodoo Underground

Website, a site where the best computer hackers of the world met online. Pam was known only as Madam Fingers, while Monique was a boy called Axelrod. Monique had figured out Pam's secret identity last year, when they had helped Professor Herbert solve the attempted break-in to the school's computer network.

"I searched for cerol virus. No hits, but then I asked around about it, and Sly One pointed me in the right direction. Here, look at the description for Lorec Worm." Monique opened up her laptop, and brought it out of hibernation mode. It was opened to the site and Pam read over the lengthy description of the worm.

"It matches everything but the code overwrite of the Task Manager and the capability to restore itself on a reboot," Pam whispered back.

Monique leaned close to her, so close that Pam could smell her scent. "I asked about who had the skills to rewrite it, and again Sly One pointed me to the logs. Look at this." She rapidly entered a few mouse clicks, bringing up another window. Pam read the log. Tommy Bomber was asking around for someone who might know how to rewrite the Task Manager code. Bait and Switch replied that he did. Immediately, Tommy Bomber asked for a private chat. The log ended there.

"I bet anything that Bait and Switch did the coding for Tommy Bomber!" Monique flashed her smile, white teeth surrounded by a sea of red.

Pam thought for a moment. "Say, I've seen some of BS's coding. He always inserts his signature code somewhere in what he writes. Do we still have the machine dump of what was in that rewritten Task Manager code?"

"Yes, I've got a copy from Harry here somewhere," Monique replied, growing more excited by the minute. She sent the file over to Pam's computer. Pam opened up the file using her Hex Editor, rather like a word processing document, only this one showed the hexadecimal display of numbers, with potential machine or assembly instructions that corresponded to it on the right. Pam entered a Find command. A second later, the screen highlighted a section of four bytes, which contained the machine encoding for the letters BSSB, Bait and Switch's signature. Immediately preceding these bytes, Pam noticed a jump instruction that caused the computer to step over these four bytes to find its next instruction, proof positive that this was his signature.

"You are good!" Monique whispered lovingly to Pam.

"So are you," Pam whispered back. "Now we have to find out who this Tommy Bomber fellow is. I bet anything he was the one who planted the cerol virus using Bill's laptop."

"Yes, but Pam, do you know what this means?" Monique looked a bit pale, Pam thought. "Whoever did this must be a student here! After all, only the staff and students can get through the gates! Look how Dominus got in here last year by morphing himself into a duplicate of Lindsey. Either one of Dominus's men is masquerading around here as a student or the culprit is one of our students!"

Pam paled. She had not yet reached this obvious conclusion. Either there was an outsider pretending via that horrid spell to be one of their fellow students—that student being in the same grave, deadly peril as was Lindsey last year—or one of their own students was a traitor to the school! "I, I cannot imagine that Alister has not taken stronger measures against another Morph Oneself into Another spell," Pam said hesitatingly.

"Same thought here. Alister is a wise old bird, for all his pretense of being an old fuddy duddy," Monique whispered up close to Pam's ear. "More likely we are dealing with a traitor student. Black Hall, I'll bet money on it! After all, it was in their dumpster that we found Bill's computer."

Pam suddenly realized that Professor Herbert had probably had this very thought when they returned with the laptop yesterday. That was why he looked so pale and upset when the girls showed him what they had found. "Traitor! Here inside Bradbury's! God!" Pam exclaimed, almost forgetting to keep her voice down.

"Well, if there is a traitor in our midst, Pam, we had best keep a sharp look out," Monique advised.

"He'll try again," Pam thought aloud. "Look, he was successful once. Surely, he'll try something else. We have to find out who this Tommy Bomber fellow actually is."

"Okay, I'll work on that aspect. You see if you can find out if someone is using the Morph Oneself into Another spell. Can't your friend Amanda tell?" Monique asked. Amanda was a fledgling Tracker, one who can both see and follow the faint traces of residual magical energies left after the casting of a spell. In the case of the Morph Oneself into Another spell, the magical energies would be continuously emitting, since the person would be constantly appearing to be someone else. Just then, Lindsey, Amanda, and Kathy came walking into the dining room, sleep still in their eyes. The trio spotted Pam and Monique, heads close together, and headed their way.

"Morning, you two are up awfully early," Amanda yawned.

"You are the hardest worker I know," Kathy pronounced. "I need food!"

"Hi, you are at it early today," Lindsey said.

"Amanda, go get some food and come here. We've got something vitally important to tell you," Pam whispered. A short while later, the three sat down beside the two. Quickly, Pam pointed out the obvious. Since they found the laptop that had been used to infect the school's computer in the dumpster underneath the Black Hall dorm, some student had unleashed the virus. There was a traitor in their midst!

Amanda readily agreed to spy on all the Black Hall students that she could. Indeed, for the next couple of weeks, with every Black Hall student she met, she looked for magical energy traces, similar to the not-Lindsey body, which had been Dominus impersonating Lindsey last year. At first, Lindsey just could not believe that one of their fellow students had been a part of this sabotage of the school's computer network. It seemed so unlike any student would do this. Yet, what other conclusion could be drawn from the evidence?

On Monday, Amanda began covertly staring at the Black Hall half dozen students in her class. Pam worked out the logistics on a paper for her. Bradbury's had six hundred students equally placed within six year groupings and within five halls. That meant that there were some one hundred second year students all total. Their classes had only around two dozen in them, mostly the same group as they had been all last year. Thus, reasoned Pam, there must also be three other similar groups, whose classes were at different times during the day. Only at meal times, did Amanda get to see all the hundred second year Yellow Hall students at one time and place. Actually, all six hundred were present at suppertime.

Last year, Amanda gave this no thought at all, content to make new friends, and try to keep up with all the homework. Now that she'd accepted this assignment, she struggled with the logistics, instead of listening to Professor Jasper discussing the pollination of plants. *Look Amanda,* she thought to herself writing out the numbers on her note pad, *one hundred second years, twenty-five to thirty of them are in my various classes. That means there are three more groups of us, so our professors are occupied four hours each with all of us. Now if I add in the other five years, assuming there are twenty-five of them in a class, then that means twenty more classroom hours, twenty-four all told. This doesn't add up! Only Professor Herbert teaches math, Professor Jasper, science, Professor Elaine, English, and Professors Hank and Betsy, PE. How can they teach twenty-four hours of classes per day?*

At lunch, she caught up with her brothers, Jim and Tom. "Guys, Herbert is the only one teaching math, right?"

"Yes, sis, only ancient Herbert," Jim teased her, "I've got him at three in the afternoon. Why?"

"But there are at least a hundred of you fourth years," Amanda argued.

"Sure, but we're not all in the same classes together, just like you second years. A hundred of you, but your class isn't that large is it?"

"Precisely my point, hot shot. Six year groups and each is broken into four classes each, that's twenty-four class hours for math. Please tell me how Professor Herbert manages that one?" Amanda declared flatly, convinced she had come up with something that her brothers had not figured out.

The dumbfounded look on Jim's face told her that he'd never realized this tiny detail before. His face grew slightly red. and he could think of no reply. Tom did, "Simulcast, Amanda, the math, science, and English classes are simulcasted. I'm not sure how it works exactly, but Sandy and I had it explained to us when we became the Floor Monitors. After all, we have to help the first year's get orientated to Bradbury's. They just use four different rooms at the same time, that's all. Simple."

Far from simple, Amanda looked more confused than before, and she rather wished she had not even discovered this anomaly. She bit her lip and twisted her long, black hair. What about four identical PE classes, she wondered. There was only one stadium, how could four classes of students be there running or playing volleyball at the same time, when she could only see her own class? Her mind reeling, she moved to join her friends.

"What was that all about?" asked Emilio, when Amanda finally sat her tray down beside him.

"Anything yet?" Pam asked, interrupting Emilio's query. Pam was eager to see if there was indeed morph magic going on within Black Hall.

Munching on her chicken nuggets, Amanda explained what she'd discovered and heard from Tom. She ended by asking, "What is this simulcast thing?"

Chewing on her salad, Pam mumbled, "What an idiot I am! I should have figured this whole thing out last year. Golly, do I ever feel like the class bumpkin!"

"I wondered where all our other classmates were," Lindsey said, feeling just as foolish as Pam. "How could we have all missed this obvious detail?"

With her mouth stuffed with greens, Pam got her laptop out of hibernate mode, her fingers rapidly typing a search. "Simu-cas," she tried to say, spewing a bit of salad out of her mouth. Flushing and holding her hand over her mouth, she pivoted her screen so the others could see the large ad on her monitor.

> Simulcast5000: This latest magical classroom device allows your teacher to teach up to six classes at the same time. Comes with complete instructions. So simple that it can be used by a child. Specify the number of simulcasts desired. Price: negotiable.

Mystery explained, Amanda finally answered Pam's

original question. "Our class is fine, no magic. About the only time that I'm going to see the others is here at meals and occasionally around campus. This is going to take time." Pam sighed; she'd preferred to know the answer by tonight so that she could move forward on the detective work.

Chapter 5—Minor Calamities, Major Calamities

Saturday dawned bright and sunny, though the fall chill was in the air. Aspens on the mountainside behind Bradbury's had turned to gold. Several elk herds had passed around the walled campus heading for lower pastures. Becky fluttered over her team members all morning, discussing strategies for their first track meet. "She's just nervous," Amanda whispered to Lindsey, as they got into their track outfits. "I would be too, if I had to be the captain." Lindsey chuckled. A streak of sympathy coursed through her as she watched Becky braiding her long hair for the sixth time.

At last, Becky ordered everyone to lineup, and the team walked up to the Stadium, along with hundreds of other students, who took the afternoon off from their studies to watch the track meet. While a soccer match drew nearly everyone at school, only about a fifth showed up to watch a track meet. Last year, Lindsey, the new Special Needs student who had at that time no hands, brought nearly everyone out to see the meet, well, really to see her in person. As they walked to the Stadium, memories of her first track meet flooded Lindsey's mind. Born without hands, she had always run the mile home from school to escape the humiliation cast upon her by her classmates in Plano. She had become a natural runner and last year, had helped her team set a new track record in the twenty mile relay race. Yet, as she passed the baton to Jim, a disgruntled Black Hall student had cast a Trip spell on her, causing her to fall hard to the ground, breaking her arms in three places. The doctor had taken this opportunity to re-grow her hands for her, changing her life around entirely. Lindsey hoped that nothing would go wrong today. "Please, let nothing bad happen," she whispered to herself.

As she entered the Stadium grounds this time, Lindsey noted only about a hundred students were in the stands, mostly friends of the runners. Professor Blake Smith, again, was the announcer. "Today, we have Yellow Hall, fresh from their third place finish in the Nationals last year, taking on Brown Hall. On the inner track, we have Red Hall challenging Black Hall. Now remember, during the track race, no magic is allowed. Save your magic spells for the soccer games. After last year's attack upon Miss Barron, Governor Alister has asked me to warn the spectators that any interference with the runners, whether magical or otherwise, will mean instant expulsion from Bradbury's."

"Now then, for the benefit of the first years, here's how it goes. First, there is the one hundred meter dash, and the winner gains five points for their team. Second, comes the mile relay race, and the winner gains ten points for their team. Finally, the twenty-mile relay race, the really big one where the runners each must run five miles before handing off the baton, yields twenty points for the victor." He then began to announce the contestants for the two pairs of simultaneous games.

"Go get him, Sally," Becky tried to infuse her short distance runner. A minute later, Sally returned to the cheers of her teammates and the few Yellow Hall students in the stands. She'd beaten Bill of Brown Hall by mere inches. Now it was time for Fern to make her debut.

Lindsey and Amanda both recalled their own nervousness last year, when they ran for the first time. "Relax, find your pace," Amanda whispered to her sister, who definitely had a case of nerves. Worse, Fern would be the last runner and thus had to watch her three teammates race before her turn came, which only added to her agitated state.

Amanda stood beside her sister, coaching her. Fern's nervousness only escalated when she saw that the Brown Hall runners had opened up a sizeable lead on Emilio. As Sally came racing towards Fern, pushing as hard as she could to catch Alan of Brown Hall ahead of her, Amanda coached, "You can do it, find your pace and then do what we always do to Jim and Tom. You can do it, Fern."

As Sally approached, Fern began to run, getting up to speed. At the three-quarter's mark, Sally handed off the baton to Fern, who sprinted on down toward the finish line. Sally jogged to a slowdown, eyes staring ahead, watching Fern. The Apache girl, who had long legs, took great strides, nearly that of her older brothers. Amanda noted that Fern found the pace and now began her final push. The Brown Hall runner made the common mistake of giving it his all right from the baton handoff. Fern did not, finding her normal pace instead. As the finish line drew closer, only then did she then began to increase her speed gradiently. In contrast, the Brown Hall runner found himself tiring as Fern closed the gap.

The Brown Hall runner's hundred yard lead rapidly dwindled to less than a foot as he crossed the finish line. Professor Blake called out, "Incredible finish! Did you see that finish! The Apache very nearly did it! I've never seen such a catch up. However, Brown Hall won, so it's Brown Hall, ten; Yellow Hall, five."

Fern looked dejected as she jogged back to the others. "I blew it," she wailed.

"No you didn't, I blew it," Emilio admitted. "I ate too much lunch and ran too slow, cost us a hundred yards. I'm sorry, Fern." The others quickly agreed with him, which made Fern feel better about her performance. However, now the four had to take their places for the long race. Within a few minutes, Black Hall triumphed over Red Hall, taking a fifteen to zero lead in their competition.

Lindsey, warmed up and ready, took her starting position, determined to help set a new track speed record. After all, the conditions were perfect for doing just that, no snow, no rain, no mud, no heat, and no cold. "Go!" Professor Blake called out and Lindsey shot off like a rocket, finding her usual pace almost at once. Having practiced all summer, she ignored her competitor and set her own pace, doing exactly six-minute miles. Amanda, Tom, and Jim all gave her thumbs up signs as she flew past them, re-enforcing her certainty that she had her pace.

Her Brown Hall competitor, having failed to make her speed up to his faster pace, slowed down, trying to match hers. As the minutes passed, he slowly began to fall behind her, though Lindsey paid him no attention. Indeed, Lindsey didn't see this as a race, as much as a challenge to see how fast she could make the five miles. This was the one thing all four had agreed upon over the summer: ignore the other racers and run their own way, against the clock. When Lindsey poured on the speed coming down her last quarter mile, she found she still had enough to make this last mile in under six minutes. After a perfect handoff to Jim, she slowed down and jogged for some time to cool down, though she now put her attention onto Jim.

After he had finished his first mile, she realized that this year nothing bad had happened to her. She smiled in relief and said "Thank you!" Shortly, Emilio came over to tell her how she had done. "Becky's stop watch put you at 26:25! Fabulous time, Lindsey. I feel like such a heel, having let you all down." His attention was still on his pitiful performance.

"Don't pig out so much next time," Lindsey replied, not able to think of anything more appropriate to say to him.

When Jim handed off to Tom, he had increased Lindsey's lead to nearly a quarter mile. A bit later, Emilio reported Jim's time to him, 26:20. A half hour later, Tom passed the baton to Amanda, his time ended up to be 26:15. When Amanda finally flew across the finish line, the Brown Hall runner was a half mile behind her. Her time was 26:10.

"Incredible! A new Bradbury track record! Yellow Hall has just shattered their own record set last year, 105:10!" The small crowd cheered loudly, while Amanda continued to cool down, Lindsey, Tom, and Jim, jogging beside her, cheering her incredible final push.

Boom! A tremendously loud explosion shattered the cheering. In slow motion, all eyes turned to the easternmost section of the stands, where a giant ball of smoke was rising. The bleachers began collapsing—students falling off in all directions. Many wands activated, Gentle Fall spells cushioned the fall the older students. However, screams pierced the chill air. First year students had not learned this Grade 1 spell yet. They were only doing their first useful spells of Grade 0.

Pandemonium broke out at once, Lindsey and her fellow team members raced to the stands, where arms, legs, heads, bodies, sprouted in all directions from the pile of rubble, which a moment before had been the stands. Only the stands beneath the Yellow Hall supporters had been destroyed. Lindsey and the other members of her team began helping their hall mates out of the rubble. Pam and Kathy had been seated on the top row. Lindsey and Amanda raced around the rubble to the rear to help the two stunned girls.

"Are you okay?" Lindsey yelled to Pam and Kathy who were trying to get up. Covered in a fine dust, the backs of their robes were singed.

Both girls screamed "What?" as if they had not heard Lindsey.

"Are you okay?" she repeated, but at once, Pam and Kathy realized that they could not hear much of anything.

A look of utter panic came over Pam's face as she screamed, "I can't hear anything!"

"God, I'm deaf! I can't hear myself!" screamed Kathy.

"Clean! Clean!" spells began firing all around. Now Lindsey could see that both did not appear to be wounded, save for their hearing.

"Take them to the Infirmary!" a loud, commanding voice bellowed over the din and confusion. It was Governor Alister, who took charge.

Lindsey put her arms around Pam and led her toward the Infirmary. Amanda followed suit with Kathy. Glancing behind her, Lindsey saw the other members of her track team helping others as well. Now all the students from the other halls joined in. Still looking back frequently, Lindsey saw that the professors were carrying those who were badly injured themselves. Their bodies were levitated and floating along following Lindsey's lead.

"She cannot hear!" Lindsey nearly screamed at Doctor Caterwall. She'd brought Pam into the Infirmary. "Kathy too. Lots more are coming, doctor."

"What was that explosion?" he asked.

"Stands blew up," Lindsey replied.

She helped Pam onto an emergency table. Amanda did the same with Kathy. The three nurses began scrambling to handle the long lines of other wounded students making their way to the Infirmary. Doctor Caterwall quickly examined both of Pam's ears, then Kathy's.

He made a drinking motion and handed each girl a

small cup of liquid. Pam gulped it down and yelled, "I can't hear anything!" Lindsey put a finger to her lips, trying to tell Pam to use a lower volume.

Doctor Caterwall waved his wand and a message appeared before all four girls. It read:

Temporary hearing loss. You will be fine in a little
while. Go back to your dorm and rest. If your hearing
is not back to normal by supper, come back to see
me. C.

Pam nodded, Kathy too. All four saw the large crowd coming in the doors and quickly made an exit out of the back door, the two leading the other two along.

The shock had worn off Pam. The healing drought made her feel calm and thoughtful. As the four headed towards their dorm, Pam waved her wand and sent Lindsey a message.

Take me back to the stands. I want to see what happened. P.

But you are supposed to rest! L.

Lindsey's counter message appeared before Pam. Kathy asked to go to her dorm before she collapsed altogether. Amanda took her up to their room, while Lindsey had no choice but to take Pam back to the disaster scene.

Ten unknown men wearing bib overalls were hard at work uncovering the debris. "Who are they?" Pam asked rather loudly.

"Her hearing is gone—the blast," Lindsey hastily explained to several workers who had looked up at the two girls. A rather annoyed look on their faces suggested that they shouldn't be here.

"We're the janitorial staff. Please stay back; it's a bit dangerous right now. Best if you take your friend to the Infirmary," one man with a clean cut beard suggested politely. The other nine ignored the two and continued to move the twisted pieces of metal and wooden boards out of the pile.

Lindsey messaged Pam, who was still not about to leave. Her curiosity was about to burst. Someone tried to kill her, and she wanted to know all the details. However, Lindsey managed to push Pam back a hundred feet, partially mollifying the workers. Lindsey was even more curious about the workers, however. Until now, she'd only seen the teachers and hall parents. She realized that someone had to be cleaning out the classrooms, dorm rooms, cooking their food, cleaning the hundreds of dirty dishes. Where did the food come from? Lindsey began to realize that there must be a whole lot more going on around Bradbury's than what the students actually saw on a daily basis. Now she, too, was curious, but about different things than Pam.

"Hey, I can hear a bit now," Pam said very excitedly. "It's coming back! I was terrified I would be deaf forever! Scared, really."

"I know, me too. That was horrible. Who would want to harm students anyway?" Lindsey asked, mostly rhetorically.

A deep voice behind the two girls answered her, startling both. "Now that is a very good question." Whirling, the saw a grim faced Governor Alister standing behind them, drying blood covered his suit, probably ruining it, Lindsey thought. "Your hearing coming back Miss Betts?"

"Yes, sir, little by little. I wanted to come here and look for clues," the somewhat shaky, but determined voice of the thirteen year old girl replied.

Alister smiled, "I thought that you might. You may stay; just remain back here until it is safe. Ben, any signs of more explosive devices?" He called out to the man with the neat black beard.

"No sir. Only this section. We've recovered a few wands and purses—couple stadium horns. We've made a pile of the student's possessions over there. No additional bodies in the debris. Looks like you got them all out of the ruins. Casualties?"

"Good. Good. It could have been far worse. Six have some broken bones, but no one is critical. No deaths, though quite a few have a temporary hearing loss from the concussion. We were very, very fortunate, Ben. Are we ready for the reconstruction?"

"Aye, sir. Allow me to get my men out of the way, in case it collapses," he replied, signaling the other workers, who moved back out of the way.

"Now let's see what we have here," Alister said calmly, as if this sort of thing happened daily. "Reconstruct bleachers," his wand made an up sweeping motion. Accompanied by wrenching, screeching noises, the metal frame began to reassemble itself as best it could, while not actually repairing any damage. Boards flew up into their original locations. Many were splinters, but the pieces went back to their original locations, hanging often in space, as if some invisible threads were holding them up.

"Ah, that's better. Now let's take a close look, shall we, Miss Betts?" Pam grinned broadly for the first time since the explosion. Just then, Amanda came running up to them.

"Kathy's resting. You guys didn't come back, so I came to see what's going on. Wow. It sure got mangled!" she exclaimed. The stands looked like something out of a war photo in her history book.

"Ah, Miss Whitewater. It seems I cannot keep you three from appearing on the scene," Alister teased the three. "Now that you are here, Miss Whitewater, put your skills to work. Any traces of residual magic? Are we dealing with a magically caused explosion or a normal explosive device? That is the first question that must be answered." Amanda grinned, another chance to practice her budding skill.

She concentrated and began sweeping her attention over the twisted, skeletal remains. Bright and shiny were the existing magical tendrils of Alister's, which held the ruins in approximately its original position. After a few minutes, she ventured her opinion. "Governor Alister, I see your magical energies, a large number of Gentle Fall energies, but nothing else."

"Very good, Miss Whitewater. We both concur on this detail. Normal explosive device it must have been. Now, Miss Betts, shall we move in for a closer inspection? With any such device, there ought to be bits and pieces of it still somewhere around." Lindsey and Amanda stood back watching the pair, as did the number of workers.

They made a pair, Lindsey noted, the tall governor and the significantly shorter teenager. Both were bending over, examining the small debris on the ground and what remained of the metal base of the stands. "Clean!" both repeatedly commanded as they carefully moved about the origin of the blast. Ben moved over to Lindsey and Amanda.

"Never had an explosion on campus before. Your friend, she is a detective?" Ben made conversation, though Lindsey saw at once that he was quite curious that Alister was allowing a student to search the rubble with him.

"Yes, she's planning to be a Sleuth when she graduates. I'm glad that Governor Alister is allowing her to practice some," Lindsey replied. She guessed that Pam had just found something, because she had her cell phone out. It looked like Pam was taking some pictures. While they watched, a plastic bag appeared beside Alister and several small bits floated up from the ground and deposited themselves into the baggy.

After ten minutes, Alister and Pam walked back to Ben and the two girls. Pam had a satisfied look on her face, but Alister did the speaking. "Well, no doubt about it, a normal explosive device, probably military grade C-4. We've recovered what's left of the detonator, and I'll get it to the Department of Law immediately for analysis. Ben, you have my permission to repair the damage. Oh, I almost forgot." He turned and used his wand to undo the reconstruction, collapsing the stadium deck once more into a pile of rubble.

Alister walked over to the pile of student possessions. "Return to owners!" he commanded, and the pile vanished. The three girls looked at each other and exclaimed, "Cool!" All three wished that they knew this spell, a most useful one indeed.

While they were walking back to their dorm, Pam explained, "I took photos of the detonator pieces. There was so much dust on them that I believe we have good fingerprints again. I'm going to compare them to the ones from the laptop computer. I bet anything that they are the same. We have at least one school traitor on campus!"

An hour later, Pam was convinced that the two sets of prints did indeed match. She had the two best prints up side by side on her monitor for her three friends to see for themselves. Lindsey had no idea what she was seeing, content to believe in Pam, likewise with Amanda and Kathy. It looked more like two darkish smudges with lines in them to the girls. Pam was very satisfied, however, and sent a message of her findings to Governor Alister.

At suppertime, half of Yellow Hall and a dozen from Red Hall appeared in the Infirmary, all wanting to help feed the dozen, who had to remain there overnight while their bones healed. Pam and Monique took turns feeding a first year Yellow Hall girl named Alisha, whose arms were both broken. By the time that everyone retired to the commons, the MAG news was on again. Books in hand, the study group paused to hear if anything would be said about the attack on their classmates.

Huge, flashing his brilliantly white teeth with his fake smile, began, "Disaster has struck Bradbury's School of Magic once again! An explosive device went off bringing down an entire section of bleachers. Many students were horribly injured in the explosion. Some may never hear again! What everyone wants to know is how could Governor Alister Broadwell allow such a catastrophe to occur to his students? Rumors are circulating that the old man has finally lost his touch. Many are calling for his resignation. That our children are no longer safe at Bradbury's is the commonly held view that KMAG reporters are hearing from terribly worried parents."

"Come on; who wants to listen to such drivel?" Pam said disgustedly. Audrey, who had just entered the commons, joined them in the study hall. Plants now became the topic of discussion, as the six worked on their biology homework.

During the week, spell casting became quite fun. Professor Arthur Thornby, Alteration Magic, began putting them through their paces on the many alteration-based spells of Grade 2. "First up is Alter One's Appearance. Again, it is a conviction based spell, you must harbor not the slightest doubt that the alteration will fail. Girls love this spell, I've found, so you guys out there be wary of your girlfriend's appearance from now on." Everyone chuckled.

Indeed, this class period was one of the most enjoyable Lindsey ever had. Classmates were suddenly growing three feet taller or shorter. Some gained a little weight, while many others chose to lose some. Facial features changed. Indeed, half of the Black Hall girls, led by Peaches, suddenly appeared to look an awful lot like Lindsey. The class roared over this tease, even Lindsey could not help laugh at the imitations of herself, some overly fat, some thin, some with pimply faces, even one with a large wart on her nose. Of course, the spell duration was only around ten minutes. Still, it was fun.

With that spell finished, Professor Arthur launched into many more new spells. Now Lindsey could create a light that did not go out every ten minutes or so, a Continual Light spell. Even more interesting for Amanda, they learned how to create total Darkness in a sphere around themselves. Lindsey enjoyed the Large Pocket spell, which allowed her to enlarge her dress pockets magically so that they could hold nearly five cubic feet of stuff, particularly books. Now she would not have to carry around her heavy backpack. More importantly, the items stuffed in these pockets weighed virtually nothing at all. The only drawback was that the spell only lasted for half a day.

On Wednesday, the group met outside the Hall of Alteration, where they began to create a better fog based spell. Already Lindsey had made good use of creating small fogs to obscure vision, but now the fog was very dense and appeared just like a bank of fog coming in off the ocean. However, Lindsey took this at face value; she'd never been anywhere near any ocean.

On Thursday, they again met outside, only this time they were widely spaced in pairs. Before each were a locked door and a locked chest. "Today, you are going to learn a highly useful spell! Have you ever found yourself accidentally locked out of your house, forgotten your key to your trunk, lost your keys? Well after today, that barrier will be forever a thing of the past. The Open Lock spell will open any mechanical lock, even some magically locked ones as well. The Lock spell locks any mechanical lock, including bars and deadbolts." He continued with a lengthy explanation.

Finally, on Friday, the class took up the Levitation spell. Amanda's comment spoke volumes, "Cool! These are really great and useful spells that we are learning this year!" Since everyone had learned to Gentle Fall from a height last year, no one was particularly troubled by their partner lifting them high above the Hall of Alteration.

What was different this year compared to last year was spell difficulty. Last year, two and three spells were taught each class period. This year, only one spell was attempted each class period. Further, as far as Lindsey and her classmates were concerned, the spells were extremely useful ones indeed.

Friday night, the gang gathered for supper, moaning the mountain of homework the professors had assigned. "Don't they know it's soccer weekend?" Emilio complained bitterly.

"Hey, Emilio isn't bored anymore," Amanda teased him. He glared back at her. "You'd better eat full tonight and don't overeat at lunch tomorrow before our big game." She remembered to remind him.

Multi-colored ribbons, a blend of the different hall colors, draped from the ceiling, nearly a hundred of them forming arc upon arc overhead. Soccer season had arrived, at least in the dining hall. The six hundred students along with the faculty ate their dinners, choosing from five major entrees this evening. Amanda sat on the far side, her back to the wall, so that she could observe the Black Hall students way over on the opposite side. Looking through the rows of Red Hall, Blue Hall, and Brown Hall students to get to the two rows of Black Hall students was most challenging, unless she stood up. However, occasionally a brief hole would appear and she could get a good look at another student. Still, this method was getting her nowhere on Pam's request to see if any of them left a magical energy trail.

Behind her was the buffet isle, which was not in use this evening. On the opposite wall behind Black Hall tables was the long conveyor belt on which students placed their trays when they had finished eating. Just as Amanda got another view of a third year Black Hall student, boom, another explosion occurred. The floor shook, but the loud concussion was totally muffled, sounding more like a deep underground blast. Amanda had a clear view of the conveyor system. Trays upon trays filled with plates, silverware, cups, bits of food, and fluids began rising in a graceful arc, expanding up and outwards over the Black Hall student tables.

Screams followed briefly the cavernous boom, as if the flying objects were being somehow choreographed. Over the dim, the thunderous command of Governor Alister bellowed, "Freeze!" For the first time, Lindsey actually saw Governor Alister using his wand, though she had not seen him reach for it. All the flying debris hung in space, as if their time was frozen.

"Floor Monitors, please escort all your students safely to their dorms. Faculty, stay here with me. Miss Betts, Miss Whitewater, will you remain seated. Calmly, calmly, return to the safety of your dorm rooms now, please."

Sandy and Tom jumped up, knocking over their glasses; milk and water flowed over the table, but no one noticed. "Yellow Hall students, orderly, now. Follow Sandy," Tom called out. To her he added, "I'll bring up the rear and make sure we don't lose anyone." He was referring to last year when the wolves broke into the dining hall and Lindsey and Amanda were knocked down the stairs by the stampeding students trying to get up the stairs to their rooms.

Lindsey desperately wanted to stay with her friends, but was forced to follow. Jim took her hand along with Fern's, making sure that they did not run into any further trouble. As she looked over to the other side of the room, many of the Black Hall students were ducking underneath the falling trays and frozen, falling liquids. Surreal. She also heard numerous comments about why Pam and Amanda had to remain behind.

Fern, near tears, said to her brother, "He doesn't think that Pam and Amanda had anything to do with that, does he? Why is he making them stay?"

Lindsey answered for him, "Pam's becoming a good Sleuth and Amanda, a Tracker. I suspect that he wants them to have a look-see, rather like on the job training we've read about. Don't you think so, Jim?"

"Yes, yes, that must be it," he replied, grateful for Lindsey's quick answer.

"But who would want to blow up the dirty dishes?" Fern continued; more questions kept appearing in her mind.

"Probably the same person who wanted to blow up the stadium stands," Jim answered her this time.

Eerie silence finally fell in the dining room. "Alister, is it wise to keep the two second years in here?" asked Professor

Janice, who had given them a very hard time of it last year. Pam had finally gotten her to stop picking on Lindsey by blackmailing her. Professor Janice now detested Pam, but there was little she could do about it; not then, not now.

Smiling, Alister replied, "I'm all for giving our Sleuth and Tracker real live experience. It so beats simulations. Now then, Miss Whitewater, see if you can detect any magical energy traces, other than mine which is holding everything still for the moment."

Amanda concentrated, but saw nothing. "Your magical energy is overpowering, but I don't see anything else," she replied conservatively.

"Neither do I," he gave her a confirmation.

"Allow me to make a catching net, Alister, before you release the trays," Professor Blake Smith suggested. He waved his wand and a huge plastic like sheet began appearing, wrapping totally around the objects that were hanging in space. Once he had it secure, Alister released his spell and the mountain of objects, bits of food, and drink continued in their original trajectories, but were caught in his enormous sheet. Once they had been caught, he lowered it to the floor and released his hold on it.

"Professor Janice, will you stand guard here, please? The rest of you, please accompany me to the basement, you too," he nodded to Pam and Amanda, who fell in line after the professors. They went to the stairs and headed down to the main tunnel nexus, located directly below the dining hall. Here the many shortcut tunnels that ran to all the other campus buildings connected at this nexus. Acrid smoke stung their nostrils as they reached the stone floor.

"Clean!" many voices called out; the smoke disappeared. Amanda was grateful that she was here at the rear. The smell was awful.

"Oh my god!" Pam could not help but say as she finally reached the nexus. Part of the northeastern wall had been blown apart, revealing a giant room, which no one had known was there, the dishwashing area. Well, Lindsey and her group had suspected it was there, because last year they had stumbled upon a map on which someone had marked many secret rooms. Pam remembered that there had been a room indicated about where the hole in the wall was located. The secret kitchen room, if their map was to be believed, lay inside the northwestern wall down here.

"I believe there will be some casualties inside," Alister spoke sternly. "First task is to find and rescue the staff. Second task falls to Miss Whitewater and Miss Betts, but you two may help us with the wounded if you are able. Come, I have a bad feeling about this one." Again, the two teens allowed all the professors to go inside first. While they were carefully picking their way over the rubble, a concealed door opened to Pam's right. Several cooks peered out.

"Is it safe to come out?" one asked Pam.

"I think so; we are going inside to look for those who are injured. Are you and the other cooks all right?" she replied.

"Yes, shaken up, but otherwise fine. The tunnel connecting the dishwashing room to the kitchen has collapsed," the middle aged woman replied.

"That probably saved you from all the smoke and blast," Pam advised. Her mind was racing to reconstruct what had happened. They didn't get to enter just yet. Professor Herbert came back out towards them, carrying a badly burned young lad over his shoulder. Unconscious, the boy was only moaning. Professor Cho Lin called out, "Door: Infirmary." A magical door appeared before him, and he stepped through it, while Pam held the door open for him. The door did not disappear.

"Perhaps it is best if we stay here and open the door," Amanda suggested. Pam agreed, not wanting to have to help someone so near death.

"This is just awful," Pam whispered. "This time, surely someone has been killed."

Professor Jasper stumbled his way back out, carrying another badly burned lad. Pam opened the magical door, and he stepped through, nodding grimly to her. Not long after, both Blake and Jerry brought another two out. The young women were levitated and being gently pushed long so as not to further touch their badly burned bodies. Amanda saw that part of their clothing had been burned into their skin. It was awful even to look at their bodies. Huan and Arthur also brought another pair out and through the door, using the same levitate and push method. No one was saying any words, however. It was grim work and done quietly. Herbert and Jasper stepped back from the Infirmary after Huan and Arthur entered the door. Without a word, the two headed back inside the fire blackened room for more.

Some ten minutes later, Governor Alister stepped out and spoke to the girls. "It is a sad day for Bradbury's. We lost two of our staff. Ten more are in very serious condition. If you wish, it is safe for you to enter and observe. If you prefer not to do so, I will understand."

Both followed him inside, carefully picking their way over the debris blocking what used to be the secret door to this room. Cho Lin had placed a dozen bright light spells around the ceiling so that everyone could see very well. Black soot covered everything. A gaping hole that led up to the conveyor belt allowed the dining room's light to enter the room as well.

"Wizards and witches and professors, it is now time for us to make our observations. I believe that we have about ten minutes before the Department of Law people will begin arriving," Governor Alister said quietly. "I remind you that this in now a case of murder, not a mere prank gone bad. We have ten minutes to find some answers for ourselves."

Amanda began moving around looking for magical energy traces. At last, she gave up, "Governor Alister, I'm afraid that there are so many magical things down here that I can't sort them all out. It's just a huge jumble. I'm sorry to let you down." She sighed, knowing that when the situation really demanded her keen skill, she had only let them all down.

"Oh, I fully agree with you, Amanda. With so many enchantments within this room before the blast and with so many that we ourselves cast to rescue the staff, it is truly impossible to tell. Let this be a lesson for you. Trackers can be thrown off the scent by just such a confusion of magical energies. Well done." Her watering eyes dried up, as she realized fully what he meant.

Professor Jasper and Pam finished conferring. He spoke up, "Alister, Pam and I believe we have located the detonation point. Here, right below the conveyor belt system.

See the radial markings on the walls and how the downward concussion caved in the connecting tunnel?"

Everyone gathered around to see what the two had observed. "Are you sure?" asked Professor Blake.

"Nothing is a certainty, but science indicates that this is the likely spot. Ask Herbert to give you a statistical certainty approximation if you so desire. Now if only we can find any pieces of the detonator."

"If it was the same kind that was used on the stadium," Pam volunteered, "look for small, black colored bits of plastic with some metal encased within. The detonator was at the center of the blast and will not be so covered with soot, which came afterwards."

Many eyes began poking around the area. "Is this something?" Professor Cho Lin levitated a one inch piece of black plastic up from the debris on the floor. Pam and Jasper looked at it closely.

"Bingo. Well done, Cho Lin. Yes, that is a piece of it. Can you dirty it a bit so we can see if there are any fingerprints on it, please?" Jasper replied. She smiled and lightly dusted it. Both Jasper and Pam looked very closely at the fragment, Pam casting Light directly onto it. Hastily, she took out her cell phone and took a quick picture. "One finger print for the Law boys to work with," Jasper replied with a smile.

"Oh dear lord above!" a deep, bass voice sounded from the entranceway. A tall man in a black suit, white shirt, and tie stood staring at the rubble of the dishwashing room. Four more peered in over his shoulder.

Governor Alister said, "You have a murder to solve tonight. Two of our staff have died already. Ten badly burned are in the Infirmary; some may not make it. We've recovered the detonator. It has a fingerprint on it. We will get out of your way and let you conduct your investigation, Samson."

"Alister, you stick around and fill us in; the rest, give your names to my assistants and return to your quarters or whatever duties you need to perform," Samson said with authority and sternly. One by one, the professors and the two girls filed out, stating their names, which were dutifully written by one middle aged woman, dressed more like a man than a woman. Her eyes rose when she saw that the last two were students, not faculty.

"What happened? What did you find out?" Lindsey blurted out the very instant that Pam walked in their dorm room. "How bad is it?"

"Really, really bad. Murder, Alister says. Two workers died! We saw horribly burned people being taken to the Infirmary. The Law people booted us out. They don't seem very friendly to us," Pam replied hastily. "Amanda, you tell them. I want to check the fingerprint we found." Near tears, Amanda did her best to describe what they had seen. She had never seen such carnage, such destruction.

"The same person did this one too," Pam defiantly announced, her hands on her hips. "Message: Alister," she commanded and sent him the confirmation of the prints. "Darn, now dad is worried!" A bit of Dirk's Dog, the latest pop tune, announced an incoming email of the highest urgency. "Dad's already heard about it, gang. Perhaps you should phone your parents and let them know we're okay." Hastily, she typed a short message to her father, but soon found that she was relaying all that she had discovered these past few weeks. She ended by asking him what kind of explosives required the type of detonators she'd found.

"Mom and dad were relieved to hear the news," Amanda hung up and explained to Pam. Lindsey and Kathy had similar comments, though neither of these girl's parents had heard of the latest bombing. "I wish there was something that we could do."

"Let's go down to the commons and see if anyone has any more news," Kathy suggested. Shortly, they walked into Yellow Hall's commons, which was packed. Nearly every student was here. Pam saw Audrey and Monique's hands waving over the crowd, and she steered the foursome over to them. Both girls were eager to hear what had happened with Pam and Amanda. This time, Amanda allowed Pam to fill them in. She found it too awful to continue to repeat. Jim, Tom, and Fern came over to her, and she latched on to her brothers. Crying at last, she did tell them what she had seen.

Pam, Audrey, and Monique joined the growing group.

"Monique says that with so many badly burned victims, the Infirmary staff will need some help, like with feeding them and such. We should go offer our services, don't you think?"

Lindsey remembered how all her friends had come to feed her when she was helpless in the Infirmary. "Let's do it. You all helped me, so it's the least that we can do for them."

"Right, we should organize relief helpers," Sandy interrupted. "Tom, I'll take a bunch down there and see what arrangements we can make. You see who else might be willing to volunteer. I'll message you as soon as I find out anything."

"Thanks, Sandy," Lindsey replied, as the Floor Monitor led Pam, Kathy, Amanda, Audrey, Monique, and Lindsey down to the Infirmary. Dozens of men and women from the Department of Law were arriving via the main gates. None looked friendly at all. One stopped them, but since Sally was the Floor Monitor, the group was allowed to continue on their way.

The stench of burned clothing and flesh assaulted their nostrils. Just inside the building, a very upset nurse came bustling out to meet them. "We are volunteering to help in any way we can, from feeding them to whatever you might need," Sally explained. "How can we help?"

"Here, put these on," she handed them sterile dresses and gloves. "Put the masks over your mouths, and I'll get you on my next trip. Lost another one; it's absolutely horrid."

The girls quickly changed, looking now like seven nurses. Nurse Matilda returned and led them into the emergency ward. "Put these to work," she said to Doctor Caterwall. "Kathy, follow me." She took Kathy into the next room, where a young man was entirely wrapped in bandages from head to foot. Only an opening for his nose and mouth were visible. "He's sedated at the moment. If he regains consciousness, tell him he is on the mend, but he needs to drink as much of this potion as he can. I will leave it to you to administer it to him. He won't be able to do it for himself, not for several days. Burn patients are in enormous pain." Kathy agreed and sat down on the chair beside the man. Tears trickled down her cheeks as she stared at the unconscious lad.

Meanwhile, the others began cleaning up the floor of

the emergency room. Doctor Caterwall explained that before he could administer the healing potions, the burned clothing had to be surgically removed from the patient's skin. Otherwise, the blackened, sometimes melted, material would become fused with the new skin growth. The older girls soon caught on to his technique. Because of their help, the other two nurses were soon free to begin removing the debris from other patients.

Nurse Matilda continually moved from patient to patient checking on their vital signs. "Cardiac arrest!" she yelled. Everyone stopped and raced to the young woman. Feverously, Doctor Caterwall worked his miracles, and her heart began beating once more. Meantime, Sandy took over removing the bits of clothing on the man that he had been working on, and, when he returned, he complimented her and allowed her to continue. He began doing the same on the critical woman.

Occasionally, he had to stop to assist the other two nurses. Lindsey felt a little relieved when those two patients were being heavily wrapped and bandaged. She used her Levitate spell to move them into the next room, where she and Audrey now sat beside them. Kathy explained what they needed to do when their patients awoke. Already, she had helped the lad take two sips. "He keeps going in and out of consciousness."

Two hours later, Doctor Caterwall finished the last patent and brought her into the recovery room. He pulled off the facemask and told the others it was now safe to do so. "Three dead, nine in terrible pain and condition, but if they survive the night, they will likely make a full recovery. I want to thank you all for lending a hand."

"Doctor, everyone wants to lend a hand," Sandy explained. "Tom has lots of volunteers lined up. Just tell me where and when."

He looked exhausted, as did the three nurses. "Incredibly kind of you Red and Yellow Hall ladies. As bad as this one is, I accept. These nine will require around the clock care for several days. Have Tom send nine to relieve you, but make sure that those he sends can stomach it. This is the worst

I've seen in my life, though I've heard of worse."

Sandy sent Tom a detailed message and fifteen minutes later, Tom, accompanied by eight other Red and Yellow Hall students arrived. "Thanks Tom and all of you. This is a grim sight to have to confront. Let's keep it to two-hour shifts. I will speak to Alister about the volunteers missing some classes. We will need the assistance for a couple of days at least."

"You got them!" Tom replied. "I've let the other Floor Monitors know and volunteers are lining up to help out. Sandy, when you get back, meet with the other monitors and get a schedule worked out, will you?"

Outside the Infirmary, all the girls took deep breaths, flushing the acrid smells from their lungs. Audrey was crying though. "I could sense the pain that they were in, overwhelming pain."

"I thought I was in bad shape last year when my hands were cut off and my mouth sewn shut," Lindsey said softly, "but that was nothing compared to these poor people. I wish there was more that we could do for them." Everyone echoed her sentiments.

Later that night, a message arrived for Becky, who relayed it to her team. "All soccer and track meets are cancelled until further notice. Alister's orders, I think it has something to do with the Department of Law," she explained. Upset, yes, she, like many others, had been looking forward to the games and to winning the school soccer trophy this year.

While everyone was moaning and groaning about the cancellations, Pam was becoming infuriated for an altogether different reason. The Law people were not answering her questions nor releasing any definitive information on the recent bombing. Infuriated with the lack of communications, she hooked up several of her Spy Cams around the facilities. One pointed to the main entrance gates; another, she positioned to have a good view of the destroyed entrance to the dishwashing room; the third, she placed on the roof of the Yellow Hall penthouse positioned to show a broad field of view all the way back to the entrance of the school. Pam was determined to get some answers one way or another.

At midnight, a sleepy Sandy woke Lindsey. "Your turn's

time to watch over the patients. Sure you want to do it?"

With a yawn, Lindsey whispered carefully. She did not want to wake her friends. "Coming." A minute later, she quietly closed her dorm room door and followed Sally. "I wish you didn't have to keep taking us down there. How are you going to get any sleep?"

"Becky is taking the next watch and then Sally has the dawn group. Audrey and Peggy of Red Hall are going to join us, that way Leann can get some sleep. Honestly, I am amazed how many students have volunteered to help. You won't get another turn until tomorrow night, Lindsey. Ah, here they come."

"Hi Audrey, Peggy. Looks like we pulled the midnight shift," Lindsey whispered, though outside the dorm there was no real need. The moon shone brightly; the air was quite crisp; golden leaves rustled across the green lawn. For once, she noted that the Red Hall girl did not have her lips cherry red. Both were still wiping sleep out of their eyes.

"Hi Lindsey, we probably won't have much to do," Audrey answered.

"Why are we whispering?" asked Peggy. All chuckled. As they entered the Infirmary, Sandy waited to escort the others back to the dorm; then she could sleep for a long time. The night nurse greeted them with a whisper and led them into the recovery room, where the nine heavily bandaged men and women were lying. The nine others being relieved were all from Brown Hall, but Lindsey waved anyway.

"If they awake, get them to sip the potion. If they need anything else, come get me. Thanks for helping out," the nurse said. Quickly, the three joined the others who were already here, taking seats close to the sleeping victims. In the dim light, Lindsey at last saw who was sitting across from her at the side of a young lad.

She whispered, "Hi Deiter. Glad you wanted to help out." Deiter had made her life nearly unbearable her first year here at school, constantly belittling her, teasing her, taunting her relentlessly. However, he was here helping, so for the moment she put that in the past.

"Hi Lindsey. I, I never realized that someone was

cleaning up all our dirty dishes after we put them on the conveyor. I feel sorry for these people. Three have died, did you hear?"

"Yes, terrible. I do hope they catch the murderer. Alister is calling it a murder scene, at least that's what I've heard."

"Yes, it was all over the KMAG news. Stupid Hugo is calling for Alister's resignation, saying this is all his fault. I'd like to know just how this is the Governor's fault. Ticked me off. He had no sympathy for these wounded staff, so I, well, I had to volunteer. Many of us in Black Hall have volunteered, you know," Deiter said civilly to her. Lindsey smiled; this was the first time that Deiter Cross had ever just talked to her like a normal person. She wondered if it took a disaster to make him human.

Just then, the lad he was watching stirred and moaned something horribly. "Help him to sip, Deiter," she suggested. Deiter inserted the straw into the man's mouth, since all else except two nose holes was covered in bandages. After taking a few sips, the powerful potion put the lad at ease, and he drifted back into a deep sleep. Deiter sighed, relieved.

"Burns like this are supposed to be almost unbearable," he whispered.

"Sure are," Peggy whispered back. "Pain can be so great that they just want to die. Gosh, I hope they survive." Red Hall students allowed their emotions to rule. Lindsey certainly felt what she was saying. It was as though Peggy had placed a wall of emotion behind her few words.

After a time, Deiter whispered, "Lindsey, did it hurt really badly? I mean when Dominus cut off your hands last spring?"

"Excruciatingly, but I was stunned and paralyzed. I couldn't move a muscle or even cry out in agony. It was short lived and turned into a dull pain rather quickly, though." Deiter didn't say anything after that, but he did take a number of glances at her when he thought she was watching her patient.

During the two-hour watch, the nine often drifted off to sleep themselves, only to be stirred awake by the sudden moaning from a patient. The potions quickly helped the misery of the patients. Tom came with the next relievers around two in the morning. As the small group walked back across the heavy dew upon the grass, Deiter whispered, "This has been rather a humbling experience."

Tom replied, "Yes, Deiter, just awful. I can't believe that three innocent people are dead, their lives snuffed out by the Mad Bomber. That's what Hugo is calling the maniac, the Mad Bomber."

"Come look at this, gang!" Pam woke everyone up around eight the next morning. Complaining girls staggered out of bed and tried to focus their eyes on Pam's laptop. "Bomb-sniffing dogs! They've brought bomb-sniffing dogs on campus! Cool!"

"You think there are more bombs about to go off?" Kathy said, a rising note of panic in her voice.

"Two so far, why not more," Pam answered grimly.

"Come on; let's get something to eat," Lindsey said. "Oops! I wonder if the dining room is even open? How are we going to eat?"

"Only one way to find out; come on," Amanda replied, heading out the door.

A large barricade blocked the destroyed side of the dining room. A very large sign read: Place dirty trays in a pile here. Volunteer dishwashers requested. See Professor Cho Lin at breakfast to lend a hand. Governor Alister Broadwell

"Well, I'm volunteering," Amanda said, stuffing a sweet roll in her mouth, while looking for Professor Cho Lin, who was not yet here.

"Morning Pam, Amanda, Lindsey, Kathy," Emilio greeted his friends. "What's this? Dishwashers? Hey, did you see the signs on the exit doors?" None had gotten that far yet. "All students are confined to the dorms, except those volunteering to assist in the Infirmary. That's what they say." He groaned, "First, no soccer. Now we can't even go outside. Boring."

"Guess you now have no excuses to keep you from doing your homework," Pam teased him. He made a mock groan and stuffed his mouth with an entire waffle.

"Clean!" Lindsey commanded. She had placed her

breakfast dirty dishes by the growing pile. However, she decided at least to clean them up. Her friends did likewise, and Pam added an addendum to Alister's note. Clean spell your dirty dishes before stacking them, please. Lindsey chuckled as others began following their lead.

A while later, having checked the signs on the exit doors of the dorm, they went into the commons. Several times, from Pam's Spy Cam on the roof, she could see the men leading the bomb-sniffing dogs around the campus. "This will take all day," she complained.

"Well, they do need to check every room of every building," conservative Kathy replied. "Then, we can feel safe again."

"Yes, but what if the Mad Bomber plants his bombs shortly before they go off, eh?" Pam replied. Kathy's optimism was short lived.

"I suppose that you are right," Kathy admitted. "That would make more sense. So what are we to do? Like wait for the next bomb to go off and hope we are not burned to death?"

"No, figure this out; catch the maniac, and put him behind bars where he belongs," Pam said flatly.

Monique and Audrey entered the Yellow Hall commons. "Ah there you are, Pam," Monique exclaimed. "Do you know that the school is officially on lock down? Some are predicting more bombs will go off."

"What's a lock down?" asked Lindsey, who had never heard the term before.

"That's when all the students are locked in their rooms to keep the attackers from getting to them," Monique replied. "We are like in prison here. I don't like it."

"Who's predicting more bombs?" Pam noticed the salient thread of her friend's comment.

"I overheard two Law men talking. I snuck down the stairs to the tunnels, but they are all blocked off. Okay, so I used my invisibility spell. I wanted to see for myself," Monique admitted.

"Look, all of you. These Law men aren't going to find another bomb ready to go off!" declared Pam sternly. "I'll bet you anything that the dogs will come up empty."

"Why?" asked Lindsey.

"The Mad Bomber isn't stupid, that's why. Look, if you were going to blow up things, would you set a whole bunch of bombs and then explode only one of them? Not likely, because for sure you know they are going to make a sweep of the school looking for additional unexploded bombs. Either set them all off at once or set them days apart. I tell you that they will not find anything."

"What if it is one of the Black Hall students?" Amanda speculated. After all Pam had been insistent on her trying to see if one of them was somehow magically altered, such as the not-Lindsey had been last spring. "Wouldn't he have the bomb making stuff in his room?"

Pam paused to think this one through. "No, while that would be easy, it is awfully risky. If I was the bomber, how could I hide all that stuff from my three roommates, eh? Not likely at all."

"Whew, that does make sense when you say it like that, Pam," Kathy replied. "We are not likely to be bombed here in our rooms."

Pam suddenly became very silent. "Pam?" Lindsey questioned.

"Eureka! We are missing a critical detail! One that we have all been overlooking, and it is as plain as the nose on my face, as plain as my ugly front teeth!"

"Senorita Pam, you have not got ugly teeth," Emilio broke in, unwilling to let her belittle herself. She smiled at him, but continued.

"Where was that last bomb set?"

"In the dishwashing room," Lindsey replied mechanically. "Oh my god! I see what you are thinking!"

"What? Tell us!" Amanda insisted, not yet grasping what was so important about the deadly bombing.

Pam straightened up; she noticed a number of others had stopped watching the big screen TV and were listening in on their conversation. "How many of you knew the precise location of the dishwashing room before the bomb went off yesterday?" Since a number of others were paying close attention to her, she yelled it out, "This is a test: How many of you knew where the dishwashing room was at before the bomb yesterday? Show of hands please, especially you older students. Please?" Not one hand went up.

"I didn't even know that we had dishwashers," Sandy sheepishly admitted.

"Me either," Tom fessed up as well.

"There you see, now what does that tell you eh?" Pam said triumphantly.

Someone called out, "An inside job!" Now the crowd began buzzing over this tidbit of information. Pam pulled her group into the study hall, which was deserted. It was Saturday morning. No soccer, school in lock down. No one was remotely interested in studying right now.

"I don't think that students are supposed to know where these hidden working rooms are located," Pam explained. "If we knew where the pantry was located, what's to stop us from raiding it for a midnight snack? Or filch a bit of extra provisions or whatever. No, the school is purposely keeping all the supporting staff and spaces hidden from us students. Honestly, there is no real reason that we should have known about the dishwashing room or staff who worked there. Actually, has anyone ever seen all the support staff coming to work? How about the cooks? Who maintains the gardens? That must be an awful chore. How about the grass all around campus? Who mows it? Who rakes the leaves? Who shovels the snow? Honestly, gang, we have been incredibly naive about the actual running of this school! There must be lots of support personnel working here, all on the quiet, all out of sight."

Monique bit her lip, "Pam, that's brilliant. Of course, there must be at least a hundred workers here. We have been utterly stupid about it all. They must come to work somehow, and more importantly, they must work in some rooms somewhere, probably underground."

"So you are suggesting that the Mad Bomber is one of the staff who works here?" Kathy asked.

"It could well be a disgruntled staff worker," Pam explained, "or one of them is actually a Death Stalker in disguise, much as Dominus masqueraded as Lindsey last spring. Or it could be a student who somehow has inside knowledge of the locations of the secret, underground workrooms. One thing we can count on, I believe, is that Governor Alister has this place totally enchanted against non-staff and non-students gaining access. Look how hard Dominus had to work to get in here, if only for a day or so."

"Okay, Pam," Monique replied. "We can't go around testing every student to see if they are who they should be, and we don't even know the staff. How about approaching the problem from a different angle? How easy is it to get access to the original plans and layout of the school, the blueprints that show the rooms and the interconnecting tunnels?" She booted up her laptop. Pam did likewise.

"I'm going to go grab some rolls and tea," Emilio said. "Anyone want some too?" He ended up having to write down everyone's order. A half hour later, he finally returned laden with brunch. "Well, the dogs have been through the entire dining room. I had to wait on them to get done. No bombs in the cafeteria or the dining room. I overheard the Law men talking. Don't everyone thank me all at once," he jested.

Wolfing down the rolls, each said thanks. Pam explained, "Monique's on to something. Most definitely, there are plans, blueprints to be precise, of Bradbury's School of Magic. However, they are on file with the Board of Governors, top secret. Absolutely no other trace of them can be found anywhere else."

"That doesn't rule out the possibility that the Mad Bomber somehow broke into the Board of Governor's place and made a copy of them," Monique added. "Either that or someone on the Board of Governors for the US has leaked the information to the Mad Bomber."

"From KMAG news. I wouldn't be surprise if someone on that board was behind this bomber," Emilio added.

"So how do you figure out which one it was? A break-in or an intentional leak?" asked Lindsey, becoming even more curious as to where this line of inquiry was leading. Was someone really out to get Governor Alister fired?

"Well, you just can't walk up to the Board of Governors and ask them if they have had any recent break-ins, now can we?" Monique insinuated, a twinkle in her eye. "They would not be likely to admit it, if it had occurred—have to save face and all that. Besides, it might put all the other magic schools at risk as well."

"Yes, but no other schools have been attacked," Emilio countered, "only us."

"Guys, don't look at my computer for a few minutes. I believe I have a way to find out if there has been any reported break-ins. Only just where is the Board of Governors located anyway? Does anyone know what city?" Pam asked. Everyone shrugged, Pam said, "Never mind." She began mysteriously typing away. In fact, she hacked into her father's server in the Department of Magical Misuse, Sterling, Colorado. She clicked on the Crimes tab and began to use its search engine using the keywords of *break-in* and *Board of Governors*. After seeing the no matches found message, she tried every other conceivable variation, even to scrolling the enormously long list of simple break-ins. At last, she logged out and refreshed her screen.

Biting her lip, she looked at the expectant faces of her friends. Emilio mouthed, "Well?"

"I believe that we can say that there have been no break-ins reported. Either they have not had a break-in or they did but failed to report it or it was reported but has been removed from the databases," Pam whispered. "Just don't ask me how I know this, all right?" Monique grinned; she was exceedingly proud of Pam's uncanny abilities of Sleuthing, ever since Madam Fingers had come to Axelrod's defense in the underground chat room several years ago.

Lindsey tossed back her long hair, "Then, you are saying that we ought to concentrate on seeing if there is some traitor within the Board of Governors?"

"Precisely. We could spend years trying to prove that something did not happen, whereas it is far easier to prove that something has happened, you see," Pam stated factually.

"Well, I'll be!" Emilio exclaimed. "Darned if this doesn't sound like our latest government homework project. I, ah, don't have my notes with me, but does someone remember just what we were supposed to be doing with the Board of

Governors?"

"Such an excuse!" teased Kathy. "We are supposed to find out their names and personal bio information. I was going to use the Library this weekend, but I guess we will just have to get what we can from the Net."

"I'd like to stay with you, but I have my own homework to do," Monique replied. "Too bad you are not in fourth year. Maybe I'll see you all in the Infirmary later on." She gave Pam a hug and left.

Everyone headed up to their rooms to fetch their school work. On the way, Pam said, "I can't wait for us to learn Summon Object. It's a Grade 3 spell, so I suppose it will be in the spring."

After they congregated back in the study hall, Sandy came around and said, "You have to stay down here for a while; the dogs are now going through our dorm rooms looking for more bombs. I think it's an invasion of our privacy, but they are the Law men." She ducked out to go find others to notify. The group glared at each other. This was not very nice at all.

"Well, it *is* a murder investigation, after all," Pam justified for her friends.

Chapter 6—The Board of Governors

At suppertime, the Law men with their bomb-sniffing dogs had left. As the students filed into the dining room, they were amazed to see that all the damage had been repaired. Most all suspected it had been magically repaired. The room was just as it had been the night before the explosion. Rows of student tables covered most of the central area, the single perpendicular, and long table held the professors.

Once everyone had assembled, Governor Alister rose. "Thank you one and all for your incredibly kind assistance with our injured staff members. Thank you. I ask that you keep to your volunteer schedule at least for another night. As you know, this matter was turned over to the Department of Law, as it is a case of murder, three murders, I'm very sad to announce. However, no student was harmed in any way. We were very fortunate with that. As you are well aware, the Department of Law brought in their highly trained dogs to sniff out any further bombs that might have been set in place. I am happy to report to you that no further bombs were discovered in an exhaustive search of our campus. Tonight, you may rest assured of the safety of our campus."

"As you can plainly see, the physical damage has been repaired. However, for at least a week we will be short our dozen dishwasher staff. If some of you wish to earn some extra spending money, I'm looking for a number of temporary dishwashers. We need a dozen for the morning shift, another dozen for the lunch hour shift, and another dozen for the evening shift. The professors tell me that those of you who volunteer in this time of crisis will not be penalized in any way for missing a class during the meal times. That said, I believe it is time to dine. Personally, I'd recommend the roast duck with almonds." He waved his wand and the tables filled with food.

"Hey, we don't get duck very often!" Jim exclaimed. "Pass the duck, please."

"Hey, not until I get some first," Lindsey teased him, helping herself to a large helping.

"So who's going to volunteer to wash dishes?" Pam asked. "One of us ought to, you know. That way, you will get inside that secret room and maybe learn some key information or something."

"Not me! No way am I washing dirty dishes!" Emilio exclaimed, suddenly anything but bored.

"I'd like to, but I'm already having a difficult time keeping up," Kathy admitted. "I'd better not."

"I'll volunteer for the morning shift," Pam decided. "You cover for me in biology class."

"Okay, I'll volunteer for the lunch shift," Amanda suggested. "We'd better not do the supper shift. Becky wants to have some practice sessions after suppers. I don't want to miss those."

After they ate, Pam and Amanda went over to volunteer for dishwasher duty. Since they were nearly alone, Governor Alister asked, "Well, Pam, what do you make of all these goings on? Feel safer now?"

"No, rather the opposite, sir." Professor Cho Lin, sitting next to him, listened in on their conversation. These were, after all, her Yellow Hall students. "I should expect further bombings."

"How so? The Department of Law assures me that their dogs found no further traces of the explosives," Alister challenged her.

"Yes, they did search our rooms, rather impolite if you ask me."

"Couldn't be helped. Law trumped my authority in this matter, murder you see."

"Well, yes. Either the Mad Bomber, as we are now calling him or her, is a not-student, you know, perhaps a Death Stalker using a Morph Self into Another, the another being a student here, or the Mad Bomber is a staff member, or a morphed staff member. And of course, they found no more bombs ready to explode; the bomber isn't that stupid to go around leaving bombs in place to be discovered before they go off. He's probably got lots more hidden. I bet you didn't let the bomb sniffing dogs search all the secret rooms in the school."

He smiled, "Of course not."

"So I feel no safer now than last night. However, we can't go around testing every student and staff member to see if they are who they are supposed to be. That violates everyone's First Amendment rights or so we've learned in government class. Hence, I'm taking a different approach, looking for who is behind these attacks. All signs point to some traitor on the Board of Governors, sir."

Cho Lin nearly choked. Alister merely raised his eyebrows. "Excellent thinking, Miss Betts. I bid you good luck in your continued research. If you will excuse me, I see others wish to volunteer for dishwasher duty. We will speak more later." The two girls headed back to join their friends.

After telling her friends what Alister had said, Lindsey commented, "Well, he certainly didn't try to dissuade us from this avenue. Maybe he too is thinking along the same lines."

It was Saturday night. Most all gathered around the TV listening to the news, when the group got back to the commons. The headlines scrolled across the bottom of the screen:

Murder at Bradbury's School of Magic. Three staff were killed in an explosion. Nine are so seriously burned that they may not survive. Many are calling for the expulsion of the incompetent Governor Alister Broadwell.

Around and around the banner moved, until the group left in disgust, heading into the study hall.

Top priority: research into the Board of Governors. Internet searches continued from where they'd left off before supper. Much of it was useful for their homework project anyway. Finally, ten o'clock came far too soon, and they all headed to bed. Lindsey knew that her shift in the Infirmary would begin at midnight, so she went to bed early.

Much later, she again sat beside the heavily bandaged young woman. Deiter Cross sat across from her beside the same young man. Tonight, the two patients woke up more frequently and in great pain. Both worked hard to get their patients to sip more of the healing potion, probably laced with the sleeping drought that Lindsey had been fed last year when she was in here.

Deiter finally asked her, "Some are saying that you and

your friends think that the Mad Bomber is someone in Black Hall. Is that right?" She detected a note of anger in his whisper.

"Pam found the laptop that was used to sabotage the school's computer lying in Black Hall's garbage dumpster. That's the only connection to Black Hall, Deiter. Honestly, anyone could have dumped it in any of the dumpsters," she tried to be polite about it.

"Well, we wouldn't be so stupid as to try to blow ourselves up," he justified. "There is a huge difference from crashing the silly computer and killing three people and causing these people here so much pain. We Black Hall's are not evil murderers, no matter what you and Pam think of us."

"We've never said that you are murderers, Deiter. Obnoxious at times, nasty, and bullies, but that is a very long way from being a murderer. I think that there may be another Death Stalker around here, maybe disguised as a staff member. Who knows?" He seemed satisfied with her answer and dropped it.

Sunday afternoon, the group compared notes on their government project, the Board of Governors. Already they knew that this group was composed of twelve members who are called Governor Generals and that there was one for each of the corresponding twelve regent countries or areas. The Governor General of the US controlled all the schools of magic in the US and had appointed Governor Alister Broadwell some twenty-five years ago.

Lindsey looked over her listing for Professor Thalmus. She'd identified the twelve members, their place of residence, and their age.

Henry Albright, Denver, Colorado, US, 55
Alison Vandersol, Vancouver, BC, Canada, 36
Rao Paolo, Rio, Brazil, South America, 39
Hans Jurgens, Amsterdam, Netherlands, EU, 48
Molly Breckenridge, London, England, UK, 51
Vladimir Chevsky, St. Petersburg, Russia, 49
Run Lun Sun, Peking, China, 37
Al Zhan, Taiwan, Pacific Islands, 44

Bale Runsgore, Calcutta, India, 57
Tammy Springs, Sydney, Australia, 33
Tom White, Durban, SA, African, 54
Pina Pong, Singapore, SE Asia, 35

Lindsey's listing agreed with the list of Audrey, Pam, Kathy, Amanda, and Emilio. She then complained, "Okay, we agree, but honestly, I don't see where this gets us on finding out who is behind the Mad Bomber."

Pam bit her lip again, deep in thought. "As I see it, there are three possibilities. One, anyone or more of these have been kidnaped and replaced by a morphed Death Stalker. Two, one of more of these are totally behind Dominus Malefic and his movement. Three, one or more of these used to be an ardent supporter of Dominus and is using his comeback to further their evil ends."

"Hum, using your choice three, Pam," Amanda replied, "if we subtract say fifteen years, that would be about the time Dominus was captured. I don't think age is going to rule any of these out, except possibly Tammy Springs." She rattled off her new list with fifteen years off their ages.

Henry Albright, 40
Alison Vandersol, 21
Rao Paolo, 24
Hans Jurgens, 33
Molly Breckenridge, 36
Vladimir Chevsky, 34
Run Lun Sun, 22
Al Zhan, 29
Bale Runsgore, 42
Tammy Springs, 18
Tom White, 39
Pina Pong, 20

"How can we see if any of these have been kidnaped?" asked Audrey, confused about where this was heading. It was one thing to tell if your parents were acting very differently, but these were total strangers and scattered all over the world.

"We can't," Pam stated flatly. "The only avenue open to us now is their known affiliations and viewpoints on Dominus, that sort of thing. We need to look into the backgrounds of each of these people, in depth, mind you. Perhaps one has undergone a sudden, total change of viewpoint, suggesting he or she is a Death Stalker in disguise. We need an in depth study, mind you, going back at least twenty years. This is going to take a long time, lots of library work, foreign language translations, the works. Why don't we split this between us?"

They agreed. Pam said, "Okay, I will take the first three, Henry, Alison, and Rao. Lindsey, you take Hans, Molly, and Vlad. Amanda, you take Run and Al. Emilio, you take Bale and Tammy. Audrey, you take Tom and Pina. Let's get scientific about this. As you study these people, rank their support of Dominus on a scale of one to ten, ten being an ardent supporter. Also, take careful note if any has completely altered their viewpoint in say the last year, corresponding with the escape of Dominus last year."

"At least, I get a pretty one," Emilio replied, looking at a web picture of Tammy Springs. Pam rolled her eyes in mock jest.

"When you get your analysis done, send me the results. I'll keep them all together in one place," Pam requested. Keys hit the keyboards as the five launched into the task. However, soon they had to switch to doing their homework assignments, much to the dismay of Pam.

Again at midnight, Lindsey took her turn sitting with the recovering staff in the Infirmary. However, Doctor Caterwall told them that their bandages would be coming off on Monday. If all went well, the night nurse could handle the nine patients after that. Lindsey was glad that they were recovering so well. Besides, these midnight hours were taking their toll on her sleep.

During the week, Pam and Amanda learned how to operate the fancy dishwashing machinery in the secret room. Plus, they got to meet the various cooks, whom they had never seen before. On Friday, Pam stuck up a friendly conversation with Bertha Botts, a matronly cook, who had been working here for a quarter of a century. A few choice compliments about her cooking and Bertha became a fountain of key information!

As Pam arrived in algebra class, she whispered to her friends, "We must meet in secret really soon! I've found out some really vital information!" Since Professor Herbert began his lecture at that very moment, Lindsey had to stifle her keen curiosity until lunchtime.

Over chicken nuggets dipped in salsa, Pam began to tell her exciting news. "You should see their setup. A short tunnel connects to the enormous kitchen. Bertha gave me a tour today; she's cooked for students for twenty-five years. The pantry is connected to the kitchen area. The keen news is this whole campus is built over some old abandoned mines. You know there used to be a whole lot of mining going on in this part of Colorado. Anyway, two long shafts connect to the kitchen. One shaft leads to bathrooms and a lounge and then on down to the parking lot outside the walls. The other shaft is the one that Bertha uses every day. She lives in Telluride and that tunnel goes straight into town!"

"So there are two secret ways into the campus!" exclaimed Amanda, "Cool!"

"I'd like to see these tunnels for myself. I bet they are super cool," Lindsey added.

"I wonder if they are on that map we found last year and never got a chance to use," Amanda added. Of course, she was referring to the hand drawn map that she and Lindsey discovered in one secret closet room, full of obsolete furniture. However, there was no time to check now; that would have to wait until after supper.

Professor Arthur Thornby continued teaching them alteration based magical spells. "What is a wizard or witch without the ability to cast the Fireworks spell? Nothing at all. Today, you have a small fire pot before you. From these small flames, it is time for the Fourth of July." Indeed, everyone quickly caught on to this spell with fireworks spewing in all directions. Lindsey never had so much pure fun before in spell casting class. On Tuesday, they worked on Sound Shatter. Small crystal goblets would shatter when they created a loud sound of the right frequency. Of course, each time they were successful, they then had to cast their useful Mend spell.

On Wednesday before spell casting class, Deiter caught

116

Lindsey's attention. "Heads up, Lindsey. Today we are going to learn a very important spell indeed! A vital one, you'll see. I've been looking ahead at the other alteration-based spells. He's going in order, and this one is just super!" She smiled, but had no idea what the next spell might be. However, Deiter had never given her any warning, friendly or otherwise. Lindsey wondered what had come over this antagonistic boy.

"Class, have you found yourself too weak to lift something, you ladies, not had enough hand strength to open some of these vacuum sealed jars? Well, not any longer. Today, we are going to learn the Personal Strength Increase spell. By use of this spell, you can increase your physical strength by nearly twenty-five percent! Of course, it only lasts for an hour or so, longer as you become more skilled with magic."

Now Lindsey understood Deiter's excitement. He wanted to be physically stronger. Well, he got his wish; now he could bully even better, she thought. A set of barbells appeared before each pair of students. Professor Arthur had them adjust the weight so that they could just barely lift them. After casting the spell, the test was to see if they could now easily lift the barbells. A loud woo hoo came from Deiter, as he lifted his heavy barbells high over his head, becoming the first student in the class to master this spell.

A little while later, Pam could not resist giving a woo hoo back at Deiter, holding her barbells high over her head. He grinned back at her, and she flushed; that was not the reaction she had desired. "What's come over Deiter?" she whispered to Kathy and Lindsey; both merely shrugged.

On Thursday, the class learned the Hide by Rope spell. A variation of the ancient Indian rope trick, they conjured a rope some twenty or so feet tall. Once it went solid, the students would climb up it to the top, where a hidden room appeared that they could climb into and hide. They could even pull the rope back up so that no one could see them at all. The spell kept them hidden for about a half hour, but Professor Arthur explained that the duration would increase as they gained more experience with it. However, if one failed to climb down before the spell expired, they would find themselves unceremoniously falling to the ground. Many of the girls could not climb the rope very well, and to compensate, they made their ropes only a few feet tall. Lindsey was one of these. Her rope only went up three feet.

Finally, on Friday, they learned to magically Lock any door or object that otherwise could be thought of as having a lock. The outdoor setup looked a bit strange, a door set nicely in a frame stood before each pair. As long as the spell was not cast or not cast properly, anyone could open the door, which was the purpose of the partner. Once successfully Locked, the partner couldn't open the door, unless they used their Dispel Magic or Unlock spell. However, since the spell is permanent, many Dispel Magic spells had to be used during the course of the class period to undo each successful casting.

However, Professor Arthur's parting words brought warmness to Lindsey's heart. "That completes the alteration based Grade 2 spells. On Monday, you are to report to the Hall of Illusion, where Professor Cho Lin will be teaching you the illusion based spells." Lindsey had only the highest respect for Professor Cho Lin, who was also in charge of Yellow Hall.

Finally, after supper on Monday, the four girls had time to examine their maps. Pam had made duplicate copies for all the roommates, and she showed them what Bertha had shown her earlier. Indeed, the rooms that Pam had briefly seen, other than the dishwashing room, in which she and Amanda had been working, were on the map, roughly to scale. Only two dotted lines suggested the pair of tunnels.

"Look this means that there are at least two other ways into our campus," Amanda stated, realizing that nearly anyone could enter unnoticed by using either of them.

"Yes, but Bertha said that they are password protected. You can't enter unless you know the password, which she said is changed every year," Pam continued her explanation.

"Still, I would like to see these for myself." Lindsey's curiosity was aroused. She had her Ring of Invisibility that she inherited from her father, but that would mean going by herself. She quickly discarded that notion.

Pam continued, "We should do what the silly Law men didn't do."

"What's that?" asked Kathy.

"Check all these secret rooms for the bomb making stuff, that's what. After all, if I were the Mad Bomber, I would very likely keep the supplies hidden in one of these secret and unused rooms," Pam explained.

"But I don't even know what bomb stuff looks like," conservative Kathy protested.

Lindsey looked at Amanda, who shook her head. All three were relieved when Pam added, "Well, don't feel left out; I don't either. You guys go on down to the study hall, I'll join you in a couple of minutes." She got her computer out of hibernation and began typing away.

When Pam arrived in the commons a short while later, she found everyone glued to the big screen TV. Lindsey whispered to her, "Dominus. He's released his manifesto. It's horrible." A bit later, Pam found the Dominus Manifesto plastered all over the Internet on many sites.

The Wizard Manifesto of Dominus Malefic

Whereas wizards and witches down through the long ages of history have been cursed, reviled, even burned at the stake, I, Dominus Malefic, am ushering in a New Golden Age for we users and controllers of magic on Earth—my Golden Path.

On Earth, man is at the top of the food chain. Consider the lowly sheep that lives its life to eat grass. Along comes mother wolf searching for dinner for her cubs, thus the sheep has purpose. In parallel, long has man, by virtue of his superior mind, been at the very top, dominating, controlling, ruling all other life forms on Earth. This is how it should be.

Yet, there are two forms of man! All throughout recorded history, man has known that there are two forms: the normal man and the wizard man. Yet during this enormous time period, man still believes in the Big Lie, that all men are created with equal rights. Why has man fallen victim to the Big Lie?

We have all told small lies at one time or other in our lives. Yet, we balk at telling a really big lie because we cannot believe that anyone would have the impudence to fabricate such a huge lie. Therefore, we don't, and yet those of feebler minds then believe the Big Lie.

Just like there is an enormous gulf between the sheep and the wolf, a similar intellectual, spiritual, and physical gulf exists between the norms and us wizards. If you do not see the truth, I invite you to lay aside your wand and take a normal job as a garbage man for one day. This gap between the two, in my opinion, is sufficient to divide man into two separate species!

Call them sub-man and man, or man and superman; it matters not, save that this enormous gulf in abilities is in fact very real and cannot be hidden. This is not to say that sub-man has not evolved. He certainly has. For example, it has only taken him ten thousand years of recorded history to realize finally that some prefer gay or lesbian relationships and to allow them to choose the partners of their choice without prejudice!

We are the superman species. Yet for ten thousand years, we have had to hide our abilities from sub-man. Do you really wish to wait another ten thousand years for sub-man to finally realize and allow us supermen our rightful position on Earth?

I say no! It is time for Truth to prevail. Time to cast aside the Big Lie.

It is time for us supermen to step out of the closet in which we have been hiding for ten thousand years. Step out into the sunshine, the warm light of day. Cast off our darkness and embrace who and what we are, the true supermen of Earth!

No longer will we be content to be second-class citizens. No longer will we be satisfied to live by the rules of the majority because the majority is but sub-man on this planet. Lacking the tiniest fragment of magical abilities, these norms will finally be forced to see the Truth and recognize the true rulers of Earth.

Consider the historical and long-standing relationship between man and horse. The horse depends upon man for its food, shelter, and veterinarian care when needed. In turn, the horse transports man, plows his fields, and otherwise works for man, obeys man.

What of the true relationship between norm and wizard, between sub-man and superman? Obviously, sub-man, lacking the superior skills, abilities, and magical knowledge of superman, should be his servant in all ways, as the horse is to man. That is the Truth of the matter, not the Big Lie. All men are not created equal. All supermen are born with equal rights, just as all sub-men are born with equal rights. The two species of man are not equal in any sense of the word, just as a horse and man are not equals. Just as saying all horses and all men are born with the same equal rights is the height of folly, so saying the blanket Big Lie is folly.

Sub-man is but a horse to us supermen. Now is the time in history when supermen take over the rulership of Earth. I do hereby cast off the Big Lie forever and don the mantle of rightful ruler of Earth. I invite those of you who have been living in the closet to step out into the warm light of day and assume your rightful place.

Worry not about harming sub-man, for would you not slap a horse that was disobeying your orders? Slap them as needed to achieve your superior needs.

At this time, I call upon all of you who can see the Truth to step out of your closet and lend me a hand in setting things on the correct path, this righteous path of Truth.

To quote another who said it best, "Those who do not realize the truth or do not wish to believe it will never be able to lend a hand in helping Truth to prevail."

Your help is needed.

Respectively yours,

Dominus Malefic, Wizard Supreme

"He's nuts, that's what he is!" Emilio lashed out of his boredom.

"Mom's not a horse!" declared Lindsey flatly.

"He's insane," Kathy pronounced.

"We are all in very big trouble," Audrey whispered, becoming rather fearful. Many emotions raged a war inside her heart.

"Now we know better what to look for in the behavior and belief patterns of the Governor Generals," Pam attempted to find something useful from this diatribe of hate. "Let's get to it. I wonder who he quoted?"

"Hitler," Emilio answered soberly, "back in the World

War II era." Pam smiled her thanks.

The entire school was talking about the Manifesto on Tuesday. Many in Red Hall expressed the belief that open warfare was coming between the wizards and the norms. Not unexpectedly, Lindsey heard some in Black Hall expressing their support of the Manifesto. Between classes and during mealtimes, the Manifesto was the central topic that everyone discussed for the rest of the week.

To offset this bad news, Governor Alister announced that the canceled soccer game of last week would be played this Saturday, juggling the previously scheduled track meet into the late morning hours. Both Blue Hall and Black Hall won their respective track meets, while Yellow Hall won their soccer match. Indeed, Lindsey scored three of their five goals and thoroughly enjoyed the game with Blue Hall, so unlike her games last year.

However, everyone's attention remained focused on the Manifesto and what was happening in the world outside of the school. Nearly every student vied for a seat around the Big Screen in the commons right after evening meals. However, Pam continued to keep her friends on track with their research project of the Governor Generals; failure could only make matters worse, at least from her point of view.

By Sunday night, Pam found that this Manifesto had in fact made her research a bit easier to do. Hardly anyone in power remained tight-lipped. She found an interview that Rao Paolo gave for KBRZ of Rio de Janeiro. Of course, she had to use her Understand Language spell that she had learned last year to comprehend what he was saying. She entered a quote beside her entries for Rao: "We are all human beings, we are all different and with different skills." She marked Rio as being "Okay."

She turned her attention onto Alison Vandersol next, figuring to get the ones who were not directly responsible for Governor Alister out of the way first. Alison had given an public address in Vancouver on Friday afternoon. "Magic is a gift from God that should be used to help all mankind. If we use his defective logic, then the gifted mathematicians, genius scientists, these should become a third species. And what of our virtuoso musicians? Should we elevate them to another species as well? No, this is madness. Humans are humans, period." She went on, but Pam just noted this quote in her log and added, "Okay" after her name. Secretly, she thanked Dominus for making this task very simple.

She turned her attention to the US Governor General Henry Albright. His was an illustrious career, turning to politics when he was twenty-five. Independently wealthy, his campaign expenditures were rather large. However, he had been successfully elected to his post five times now. His current term would last another five years. "I don't condone murder. However, I am sick and tired of playing a secondary role to the run of the mill population. It's high time that we wizards wielded more power and respect in the world at large." She found this recent quote. However, he had refused to grant any interviews for some time now. She found reports that KMAG had four times requested an interview with him. He even lived in Denver, close to KMAG studios. If he was a Dominus supporter, why had he not just come out and proclaimed his support, she wondered. Pam sighed as she realized that she was going to have to spend considerable time researching his past.

Lindsey reported on her three. No doubt about it, Molly Breckenridge was on the side of Dominus. "Clearly, wizards and witches possess great power. We should be ones in charge of our governments." She reported several more choice quotes, but Pam kept only this one in her overall log.

Lindsey made a new category, On the Fence. She placed Vald Chevsky and Hans Jurgens in this new position. According to Hans, "Wizards are the power behind the future and as such ought to be afforded more rights. However, lawlessness is not the avenue to that power." According to Vlad, "The world needs more powerful wizards to help guide the world to better prosperity, but anarchy only leads to self-destruction." Pam sighed and added the new category to her list, 50-50 she called it.

Run Lun Sun of China threw his full support behind Dominus. "Do not put weaklings into positions of power. Our leaders must be strong. Wizards are the strongest men in the world and to us should rightfully befall the control of the world."

Al Zhan of Taiwan held the opposite view. "You cannot separate men based on what they can or cannot do and use that to determine the master race. Adolf Hitler tried that approach, which only led to a world war. Dominus Malefic is simply an insane criminal, who unfortunately possesses magical skills. Sad."

Bale Runsgore of Calcutta sided with Dominus. "Certainly in India, we have long recognized that all men are not born with equal rights. That is obvious if you just look at it. Would you put the lowly, starving peasant of the gutter in as your president? The foolish just might. Wise and powerful men should lead. Who is more powerful than great wizards, I ask you?"

Tammy Springs of Sydney was given an "Okay" status. "I hold degrees in biology. I have studied both the bodies of normals and those of wizards and witches. I can tell you with total and complete certainty that there is *no* difference between them. You cannot make any such arguments that wizards are a different species. Clearly, that is utter nonsense!"

Tom White of Durban, South Africa sided with Dominus. "All men are certainly not equal. Look at what happened here when the blacks were given their own country to govern and rule. Complete and utter fiasco of the greatest magnitude. With our superior skills, we ought to be the ones controlling the destiny of Earth."

Pina Pong of Singapore went into the Okay category. She explained to reporters, "This Dominus Manifesto is pure bunk, not a shred of truth in it. Notice he did not say who would be the ultimate ruler if he had his way, probably the strongest wizard. Might has never made right."

"Well, the Board of Governors is pretty evenly divided," Amanda said, looking over Pam's final summary. "Five Okay, five for Dominus, two on the fence."

"Yes, but Henry Albright is the one who appointed Governor Alister and all the other US school governors," Pam countered. "I bet you anything that he is somehow involved with the Mad Bomber of Bradbury's!"

"Sure, only now we've got to find that connection," Emilio said in his bored manner, as if this was utterly trivial to accomplish.

"Well, I need to practice all these new spells," Lindsey admitted. "Guess we've done all that we can for now." She and the others went outside to practice the lot of them, leaving Pam sitting alone in the study hall, thinking hard. She waved her wand and sent a message, but cancelled the spell before it occurred, deciding that was something she could find out for herself.

With Lindsey, satisfaction with a spell did not occur until she could cast it non-verbally and without her wand. She'd mastered all the helpful spells and Grade 1 spells this way last year, and it had saved her life when Dominus had kidnaped her. Kathy, Amanda, Emilio, and Audrey didn't mind helping her, because they found it a good review, solidifying the spells in their minds more fully. As Emilio put it, "Work on them now, and I won't have to cram on them later."

As the second week in October began, the weather took a turn for the worst. A cold, dreary rain began falling on Monday, which didn't let up all week. It was almost as if Dominus was now in control of the weather. Combined with the relentless bad news on the TV, Lindsey's spirits were gloomy indeed.

The bright spot happened when they all headed into the Hall of Illusion for their next spell casting class with Professor Cho Lin. "I'm pleased to be with such a talented bunch of young students. Today, we're going to learn a most useful spell indeed. Invisibility to Sight. Please note that this spell does not hide sounds; if you make noise, you will be likely spotted. Also, you cannot attack another while invisible; doing so cancels the spell. However, it does last an entire day and night. When you cast it, make sure that you specify the recipient. If nothing is said, it will be you that becomes invisible. If you say, "Invisible: Lindsey," then she will be the one becoming invisible. However, you do need to touch the recipient subsequently for the spell to activate. Now the wand motion is a 'Z' pattern. Remember, with all illusion-based spells, you must be convinced that your illusion is going to be believed.

This is a more difficult spell, so do not be discouraged if it takes you two days to master it."

The whole class threw themselves into the practicing of this spell with a passion! Everyone had great plans and ideas for the use of this spell, a most useful one indeed. To her amazement, Lindsey found this spell extremely easy to do. Perhaps it was due to having tried to be more or less invisible all her life, when she had no hands and was continually teased about it.

On the other hand, Deiter and Lyle found the spell exceedingly difficult to manage. Neither succeeded on Monday. However, by the end of Tuesday, everyone in the class had managed to become invisible at least once. Lindsey already had this one non-verbal and without a wand, much to her satisfaction.

On Wednesday, they learned to Cause Blindness. Under the careful watch of Professor Cho Lin, the pairs began to work this bit of magic. Once successful, she cast her Dispel Magic to remove the blindness. She cautioned them that there was a seventy-five percent chance of the spell working on normal people, but the more powerful the wizard or witch that they were attempting to blind, the lower the chances of success. "Even if you face Dominus, there is a five percent chance that this would blind him, though I suspect he would be able to dispel it in short order." Lindsey now realized the wisdom in teaching them the Dispel Magic spell first thing this year. They could rectify many adverse spells now.

On Thursday, Professor Cho Lin had them working on two spells, Blur My Image and Cause Deafness. "If you know you are about to be attacked, Blur My Image will make it more difficult for your attacker to strike you," she explained. "Deafness is often used by men like Dominus against you. Once you have been deafened, if you try to cast another spell that requires words, you face a twenty-five percent chance of it failing because you can't hear yourself speaking."

She looked at Lindsey and added, "This is why the best Dispellers always learn to cast their spells non-verbally and without a wand. Deafened, they are not at any disadvantage at all." Lindsey smiled and renewed her efforts to master every spell totally and completely.

On Friday, they learned Generate Hypnotic Pattern and Multiple Images of Self. Cho Lin explained, "The wand motion for the hypnotic pattern is a circular, spiraling one. A swirling, spinning wheel of colored lights will have a good chance of hypnotizing others, who will just stand there and stare at it until you cancel the spell. If you are doing this to normals, you can get two dozen of them hypnotized with a seventy-five percent chance of success. However, if you try this with other wizards and witches, your chances of success are naturally lowered."

She looked over at Audrey and Deiter. He was staring dumbly at Audrey's swirling colors. "Miss Lemon, would you please cancel your spell? Deiter needs to hear my instructions first. Well done on being the first student to cast this one." She repeated what she had said for his benefit, though his face was red, and he was not paying close attention to Cho Lin, glaring instead at Audrey.

"Now then, the second spell is quite useful on the soccer field, Multiple Images of Self. I believe that you have all seen that one in operation on the field. Four images of the caster appear and mimic what the caster is doing. Will the real one please stand up? That's a joke, by the way. It is designed to confuse your observer, especially useful if you are being attacked. Ladies, if you find that some unwelcome men are coming after you, cast this one and confuse the heck out of them. Be advised, however, the multiple images only last for a few minutes, but as you gain experience with it, the duration increases as well."

However, Lindsey did not like the final words from Professor Cho Lin. "Next week, you will report to the Hall of Charming and Enchantment. Professor Janice Smith will be teaching you your advance charming and enchanting spells." All of her unpleasant memories of last year came back to Lindsey. Countless times, she had been belittled with "Make sure that your wand activates." Lindsey groaned when she heard the announcement. Amanda felt sympathetic towards her friend. After all, she had been Lindsey's partner and had to deal with it as well.

On Saturday, the soccer field turned into one giant mud puddle after just three minutes of the Black Hall versus Brown Hall match. Sloshing across the field, slipping and sliding, and mud became the story of the afternoon. Yellow Hall had to deal with similar conditions last year, and they sympathized with Brown Hall players. For the spectators, it was rather amusing to watch. Black Hall won easily and without all their dirty deeds that they had used against Yellow Hall last year, such as kicking one's legs instead of the ball. There was no need to do that in this game, for the mud made a mess of everything. Everyone knew that this would be the last soccer match of the year, snow would soon be on its way, here in the high country.

Saturday evening when the four girls retired to their dorm room for the night, Pam had a package to show them. "This arrived this morning. Now we can do some real investigation." She showed them her detector.

"What is it?" asked Kathy.

"It is a C-4 detector. It detects the odor given off by the binders in C-4 explosives, you know, plastic explosives. That's what's been used in both of the bombings here on campus. Now I can go into any room, and this device will register if any C-4 is present in the room. I think it's better than the bomb-sniffing dogs, if you ask me. I just got it in the mail," Pam proudly proclaimed.

Lindsey replied, grasping where Pam was headed with this new hand-held machine, "I see. Now that we can all go invisible, and armed with the maps and the activation words, we can check out these secret rooms for more explosives! Way to go Pam!" Pam smiled appreciatively.

Amanda suggested, "We should do it in the evenings before curfew time. After all, there may be all sorts of enchantments about the school that alert our House Mother if we are out after curfew."

The four got out their maps and began to make plans. Amanda and Kathy became the invisible tunnel watchers, one on either side of the secret room to be examined. Pam and Lindsey would enter the room and check it out. If someone was coming, they would be messaged. Perfect plan.

"We can probably rule out the kitchen, panty, lounge, and the dishwashing rooms," Pam suggested, "because they are high traffic areas. The Mad Bomber would have to be mad to store his supplies in there."

"Isn't he mad anyway?" Kathy said, a bit confused by the dual use of mad.

Pam ignored her and continued. "Some of these are also not likely spots, such as the room with garden supplies, book store supplies, medical supplies, pool equipment, yard tools, library stacks, and stadium levels. We can check those last. I count four storerooms, one of which Lindsey and Amanda discovered last year, where the map was stored. I say let's check those first."

At seven p.m. on a Saturday night, very few were down in the tunnels. The four made their way down the tunnel that led to the Admin Hall. Halfway down, they located the approximate spot where the secret door must be. Kathy and Amanda moved off several hundred feet in both directions and cast their invisibility spells. Pam and Lindsey then prepared to investigate. While Pam operated her new device, Lindsey held the map and she said in a commanding voice, "Hide, Please." The secret door slid open about fifty feet from where they were standing.

Pam entered, with Lindsey right behind her. As soon as Lindsey entered, the door shut, leaving them in utter darkness. "Light!" Lindsey commanded instantly and then Pam followed suit.

"Look at all this stuff!" Pam said, forgetting that she was supposed to check her new instrument. Lindsey had to remind her. Embarrassed, Pam fiddled with her new machine and at last said that there was no trace of the explosives here. To be very sure, the instructions said, allow ten minutes for the machine to detect vapors.

While they waited, Amanda sent them a message that someone was coming. Both held their breath, hoping that whoever it was wasn't coming to the storeroom. Shortly afterwards, Kathy sent a message saying it was a just student. Finally satisfied that this room was explosives free, Lindsey commanded, "Exit, Please." They walked back out into the tunnel and the door closed. While they waited, Amanda and Kathy walked up to join them. However, Amanda, still invisible, could not resist the opportunity to tickle Lindsey. Of course, the second she did so, she became visible again.

"Shall we try the next one?" Kathy asked. "This is rather exciting. I've never done anything quite like this ever before! I wonder if we are breaking any school rules?"

"Have you seen any signs saying Please do not visit any of the secret rooms?" Pam chided her.

"Well, no."

"See, come on. Let's check on the one off the Humanities tunnel," Pam suggested. Twenty minutes later, they once more were in the approximate position.

"Hide Please!" Lindsey commanded. The door opened but was well over a hundred feet from their estimated position. All four had to readjust their positions. The two entered and cast their light spells once the door shut.

"Wow! Look at all these old clothes! The place smells like moth balls!" Lindsey stated the obvious. "Will that mess up your machine?"

"Hope not. Golly, it is blinking red. Where's my manual? I want to double check this." Lindsey held the device for her while she rummaged in her pocket, producing the crumpled instruction booklet. She flipped pages and ran her finger down one. "Yes, blinking red means definite, strong detection. How fast is it blinking, Lindsey, really fast?" Both looked, of course this was a subjective measurement. How fast is fast?

Pam moved about the room, pausing in each location for a time to see how the meter reacted. As she went to the easternmost portion of the twenty by twenty foot room, the blinking was noticeably faster. "We are getting closer to it," she announced.

Lindsey lifted up the edge of an old, outdated dress and revealed a large green army colored sack. "Bingo! What do we do now? We've found the bomb stuff!"

"Well, I can't get fingerprints from the canvas. I don't dare open it. I guess we message Alister and tell him what we've found. Here, hold the machine again for me will you?"

Pam asked. Lindsey did, marveling over how fast the little red light was flashing.

A bit later, Pam said, "Okay, let's get out of here and let Alister know about this!" Lindsey spoke the command words, but only after they extinguished their light spells. Neither wanted to open the door and let light shine outside into the tunnel. Such would not be prudent. They stepped out into the dimly illuminated tunnel and called for Amanda and Kathy.

"We found it! A whole green bag full of the stuff!" Pam announced.

"Let's get out of here! If that goes off, we'll be killed!" Kathy urged, pushing them on down the tunnel, very much frightened.

"It has to be triggered by a detonator, Kathy. It can't go off on its own, not even it you try to set fire to it. Safe stuff. I'll message Alister now. Hold on a minute." The four paused, three keeping watch. Governor Alister received a message while in his office sipping tea.

Check the storeroom on side of the tunnel from the
dorm to the Humanities Hall. Easternmost section,
beneath old dress. Large green sack of C-4. P.

He reacted immediately.

Pam received a reply seconds later.

Thank you. Well done. I assume that I am not to ask
how you came to find this? A.

Everyone chuckled when she relayed his message. She sent back that he was not to ask. The four beat a hasty retreat to their room. "We can still do a bit more study," Kathy suggested. "Besides, we ought to let Emilio and Audrey know that we found it."

"Okay, you go ahead of me. I'll be along shortly," Pam replied. "Just make darn sure that they don't tell anyone else or we may be in big trouble over this. Too many questions can be asked." That put a damper on Kathy's enthusiasm. The three grabbed their books and left.

Pam got her laptop going and fired up her Spy Cam software. Because her hard disk was far too small for extended duration recordings, she installed a trigger. The computer software would only begin recording when the room was illuminated. Finally, having done all she could think of doing, she too grabbed her books and went to join her friends. She had seldom felt so satisfied!

At ten, they all headed back to their room. While the other three headed down to take a shower, Pam rewound the cam recording. It had indeed activated while she had been down studying. She watched as Alister appeared. He too carefully lifted the dress and stared long at the sack. She suspected that he was casting a number of spells, but her Spy Cam did not have sound capabilities; those were much more expensive and required far more hard disk space than she had available. After perhaps ten minutes, he left, and the recording stopped.

It began again, though there was no way to tell the time elapsed between the two events. Alister was showing two Department of Law men the sack, which they levitated, and opened using magical hands. They verified the sack contained C-4 along with a pouch of detonators and two more timers. Pam could tell they were timers because she could see the clock faces. Then, the men left and the room went dark. However, Pam saw that there was still more recorded material, so she continued the replay.

Alister appeared again with an identical green sack, and he replaced it exactly as it had been found. Pam smiled. No way would the sack contain real explosives. Alister, she bet anything, had made a replacement sack containing fake explosives, perhaps hoping to catch the guilty Mad Bomber in the act of retrieving it. In the middle of watching this, Pam received another message.

Do not go back into that room until further notice. A.

She chuckled. She figured that Alister had certainly set a trap for the Mad Bomber. So had she, for that matter. If he returned to retrieve his stuff, she would have him recorded on her computer! She grabbed her towel and headed to the showers.

Chapter 7—Halloween

"Good afternoon students. How wonderful to see you all once more." Professor Janice's red lips mouthed the words with a fake smile. Lindsey guessed she was not at all pleased to see them again, not after last year. Pam had taken a lewd movie capture of her making out with one of her students after class. She'd threatened Professor Janice with full Internet exposure if she did not start treating Lindsey fairly. Yes, even Pam sensed the covert hostility in her voice.

"This week we are once more going to attempt to learn some key spells with which some of you at least may use to handle conflicts. If you will remember last year, I had you take up a partner with whom you were not particularly friendly. Please do so once more, Lindsey, you are with Deiter Cross this week. Pam, you are with Lyle. Does everyone understand? Good. Now get to your partners. We have much to learn, though some of you might find this difficult to do." With much general grumbling, the whole class juggled their preferred seating. Deiter made Lindsey move over to his pair of chairs.

"Now then, that is much, much better," her red lips smiled at the thirty annoyed faces staring back at her. "Open your book to page 13, the Magical Rope spell. Rope Activate is the first command. You then follow it with specific commands. Rope Encircle, Rope Tie, Rope Untie, or Rope Undo. When you have mastered this spell, the rope will serve your needs. But of course you need some rope," she waved her wand and ten-foot pieces of rope appeared before each pair of students.

"I'll go first," Deiter insisted, so Lindsey sat opposite him, waiting to become tied up. "Rope Encircle!" he commanded, but nothing happened. "Rope Encircle!" he repeated two more times.

"You forgot the first command, Rope Activate, Deiter," Lindsey tried to be helpful. He glared, but recalled Professor Janice saying so and tried that. "I think you have to really believe that the rope will obey you," she coached. Ten minutes later, the rope gave a wiggle, and he then commanded it to encircle Lindsey.

"Rope Tie!" Lindsey was bound tightly. "Ah ha. Now I have you tied up. How does that feel, eh?"

"Very good, Deiter. Now try the rest of the commands," Lindsey suggested. She did not enjoy being tied up like this at all.

"I like you best tied up," he smirked. "Hey, see if you can wiggle out of it. This spell is no good if the person you've captured can wiggle out of it."

Since he was not about to release her, she tried to get herself free, while Deiter watched her evidently amused. Finally, she cast her Dispel Magic, silently. His mouth opened as he watched the rope drop limply onto the floor. "Be careful who you tie up with this spell, Deiter," she said with a note of hostility in her voice. "My turn. Rope Activate!"

Before Deiter could react, the rope wiggled, signaling it was now obeying her. "Rope Encircle. Rope Tie." Now the tables were turned. However, Lindsey did not desire to watch him struggle against his bindings. "Rope Untie. Rope Undo." The rope dropped onto the floor, releasing him.

"How did you get out of mine so fast?" he asked finally, having experienced being tied up tightly.

"Dispel Magic," she replied.

"But I didn't hear," he started to say and then stopped. He realized that she had done it non-vocally and without her wand. "We ought to practice this some more," he said instead. By the end of the class, both were managing this spell well.

On Tuesday, Professor Janice was in better humor at the start of the class. "Today, we are going to attempt to learn a clever spell that can impact another person's memory, Forget. When you cast it, the victim will forget what has just happened during the last couple of minutes—nothing longer, I'm afraid. So when you are ready, do something that you wish your partner to forget and then cast your spell. The wand action is a sweeping motion as if you were sweeping the memory out of their heads and away from them. Just be careful what you do that they are to forget, at least until you have the spell down properly."

Before Lindsey knew what was happening, Deiter

leaned over and kissed her on her cheek. "Forget!" he waved his wand, unfortunately, nothing happened. "Forget! Forget! Forget!" he became a bit frantic. Professor Janice, watching the pair, grinned broadly, her white teeth silhouetted against the perfect red frame of her lips.

Even Lindsey now saw the humor in Deiter's frustration. "Forget!" she commanded, and Deiter stopped what he was doing and looked up at her.

"What? Whose turn is it? I think I've kind of forgotten," he said somewhat perplexed. Professor Janice gave a snickering chuckle at them, but turned her attention onto Lyle and Pam.

A while later, Lindsey felt that she was indeed forgetting something that might have been important. Then, she realized that they were doing the Forget spell and that Deiter had been successful. She felt embarrassed and definitely hated this spell for sure. She even tried Dispel Magic, but it had no effect on her memory, convincing her even more that this was not a nice spell at all.

The next class period, things got even tougher. The Sparkling Dust spell caused a bunch of sparkling, glittering mica dust to appear. For several minutes, it sparkled in the opponent's eyes. If he was lucky, they simply couldn't see out of it well at all. If they were unlucky, they were once again blinded. Many of the girls shrieked in terror when they suddenly found themselves blinded. Fortunately, the blindness only lasted a couple of minutes.

At least Professor Janice gave them an appropriate use for this spell. "If you believe that there is some invisible person near you, if you cast this spell on that area, it will reveal the invisible person as well as potentially blinding them for a short while. Now this time, I want your partner to become invisible, and then you cast it where they are sitting so that you can see for yourselves how effective this spell is on revealing the clandestine."

Now Lindsey felt somewhat better about the spell. Still, she detested becoming blinded, even if it was only for a couple of minutes. She felt very helpless when she couldn't see anything.

On Thursday, the barbells that they had used while learning the Strengthen Self spell appeared. "Today, we are going the opposite direction. The Weaken Opponent spell is very useful if you are in a combat situation. If successful, your opponent temporarily has the strength of a ninety-pound weakling! Caution, the effects only last for a couple of minutes, though as you get more experienced with it, the duration becomes a little longer. Now adjust the barbells so that you can lift them. Then, have your partner Weaken Opponent and try to lift the barbells in your weakened state."

Once more, Professor Janice was amused no end for the entire class period. "Ah come on, Lindsey, surely you can lift these little barbells," Deiter teased. Lindsey tried her best, but could not lift them. Again, she felt embarrassed and frustrated with the effects of this spell. Yet, if she could have cast this against the Death Stalker Rubius who held her prisoner last year, she might possibly have been able to escape him.

She saved the best for Friday. "Today, we will be learning a spell most useful for this coming holiday, Halloween. It is the Frighten spell. Please do not try to Frighten me. The spell is nearly useless on more powerful wizards and witches." For fifty minutes, the room was filled with terror-stricken students, trembling and shaking in fear for the five or so minutes that the spell's effect lasted. Again, Lindsey saw nothing funny with this spell at all. Deiter even dropped his own wand when she successfully Frightened him. Professor Janice snickered and smiled the entire period.

As the unsettled and annoyed students left, Professor Janice told them to report to the Hall of Divination for next week's spells. "Thank god that is all we have to have from her," Emilio commented. "I swear she gets her jollies watching us all suffer. I nearly peed my pants I got so scared there." The girls giggled; they had already done their share of screaming and just wanted to forget all about the class.

Kathy decided to change the subject, as the group walked to their next class. "Tomorrow is Halloween. Just think, next year we'll be third years and can finally go into Telluride and see the sights!" That lightened them up.

Indeed, at supper, the entire dining hall was once more

decorated for the season. Spiders hung from giant webs; bits of cobwebs draped down from the ceiling; lighted pumpkins overhead provided the illumination. Even a few illusionary bats appeared to be flying overhead, compliments of Professor Cho Lin. Of course, if you really stared hard at them, you could tell that they were just an illusion, but a believable one though.

Over dinner, Tom and Sandy were talking about their coming trip on the morrow. Sandy heard of a quaint ski shop and wanted to visit it. Jim whispered to Lindsey, "Next year, I will take you to see the sights myself!" Her face went hot, but replied that she would love to go.

The four girls went to their room to fetch their needed things; it was going to be another study session. However, Pam noticed that her computer was now flashing and paused to see what had activated. "Hey gang! Spy Cam picked up something! Wow! Someone is trying to pick up the bomb materials. This must be our Mad Bomber!" All three crowded around Pam to watch the short video. From the student's robe patch, he belonged to Black Hall for sure. He was an older boy, at least fifth or sixth year, but none of the four recognized him.

As they watched him open the explosive's sack and begin to put together another bomb, the boy suddenly looked startled and jumped up. Governor Alister had entered the field of view of the cam. "I wish we could hear what they are saying," Amanda lamented. The two were probably yelling at each other.

Then the lad seemed to crumple and all hope evaporated from his face. He glanced at the bomb materials. Pam suggested, "He's probably just found out that it is fake stuff there now." Alister took the boy's wand and tied his hands behind his back. The last image was the two leaving the room. All went black once more and the video ended. "Who is that anyway?" she asked again.

"Maybe Tom knows," suggested Amanda. Pam played the short video once more, stopping it when she had a clear image of the boy's face. Here she paused it and took a screen shot of the image. After touching it up in Paint, she then sent it to her cell phone.

"What's Tom's number?" Pam asked. Her fingers dialed

the numbers as Amanda recited them. "Tom? Pam. Say, I am going to send you a photo of a Black Hall older student. I need to know his name. We thought that perhaps you might recognize him. Okay. Call me back if you do. Thanks, bye." She punched a few more buttons and the picture was sent to Tom.

A minute later, her cell rang. "Hi Tom. Wow. Great! Thanks. Er, well, you will know soon enough. Governor Alister has just arrested him! We think he is the Mad Bomber. Don't ask me how. Yes, okay. Bye. Hank Wilkinson, sixth year Black Hall," Pam blurted out.

"Never heard of him before," Lindsey replied, typing his name into the school's website search engine. She quickly pulled up his school information. "Lives in Denver. Not much here about him really." She sighed; she didn't really expect to find much about him on the web site though.

"Hey look, Spy Cam on the gates is showing something!" Pam interrupted everyone's thoughts. Indeed, six well-dressed men and women suddenly appeared at the gates and were walking through them. Pam recognized two immediately. "Law men, they were here before. I bet they are going to arrest Hank!"

"Why would one of us blow up the school and kill the three staff?" asked Kathy. "I don't get it. I sure wouldn't want to hurt, let alone kill, anyone here."

"He must be a Dominus supporter," Amanda replied. "Guess we will find out soon enough. Come on;, we ought to go down and tell Emilio and Audrey the news."

"What? Caught the Mad Bomber? Wow!" Emilio replied.

"Can we see?" asked Audrey and Monique in unison. Both were waiting to see Pam. Quickly, she replayed the short video for the three.

"How did you get that video anyway?" asked Monique, more than a little curious of her dear friend.

Pam smiled and winked, "Little secret for now. Will tell you later on—secret for a while yet."

"Spy Cam images. Those came from a Spy Cam, Pam. I would recognize them anywhere. What I don't understand is just where that place is? Looks like a mass of really old clothes," Monique continued to pressure Pam, who did not deny any of what she said. "Well, I can see that you are not going to tell me straight out. I have to go to the Library—research paper is due next week. I just wanted to tell you, Pam, that next year, I'll take you to Telluride on Halloween."

"Hey, thanks! That will really be fun. I wish we could go now, but that's the rules," Pam replied. After Monique left, the group settled in for the evening's homework.

"This algebra is getting impossible to understand!" declared Kathy, whose math skills were not terrific. "I mean like this X-two. What is it? I know about the X-Files and the X-Men. Is X-two a mystery show or a sci fi flick?"

"Huh?" exclaimed Lindsey. "I've never heard of the X-Files or the X-Men."

Pam took charge. "Those are ancient TV shows and movies. Let's see this X-two you are talking about, Kathy." Kathy showed her the page and Pam groaned. "That's not X-two. Look it reads: $X^2 - 9 = 0$. X is the unknown, whose numerical value you are trying to discover."

"Oh." Kathy said. After a pause, she added, "Why would I ever want to do that? What good is this anyway? I'm never going to use this algebra stuff, never."

Pam thought for a moment, before answering. She knew that her answer would be critical for Kathy to understand. "Suppose that you wanted to make a skirt and that some fabulous material scraps were on sale. The ad said that the nine square feet of material was in the shape of a square and that was all that the ad said. Would you buy that material to make your skirt? Would it be big enough?"

"Well no, it would only be three feet by three feet. I guess I might if I wanted to make a mini-skirt, though," she replied.

"Great. How did you know that it was three feet by three feet?"

"You said it was square and was nine square feet, so it has to be three feet by three feet. Why?" Kathy replied, not seeing any connection to the algebra problem.

"That's just what this problem is all about, Kathy. The X represents how long a side is and the nine is the square feet of cloth. It's a symbolic way to represent the problem you need to solve. You can solve it two ways. In this simple problem, you can add nine to both sides and then have just $X^2 = 9$ and take the square root of nine to get three. But it could also be minus three, that would also work, but not if we are dealing with cloth, you see. However, we are supposed to be breaking it into factors in this chapter. So you should work it like this.

$$(X - 3)(X + 3) = 0$$

So that X can be either 3 or −3."

"Oh! Well, why didn't it say so. I think I get it. I'll do some other ones. It's lots easier if I think of this as square feet of material though." Pam smiled and went back to finishing her page of equations, knowing the she and Lindsey would soon be looking over everyone else's work.

Around nine, Pam received a message:

Pam, please come to my office immediately. A.

She quickly explained that Governor Alister wanted to see her and left the others discussing what this was about, certainly and most likely about the arrest of Hank Wilkinson.

Pam walked to the Admin Hall and found Governor Alister's office. She knocked and he opened the door for her. As Pam walked inside, she noticed that Professor Cho Lin was also here, sitting off to one side. The only other chair was directly opposite Alister's leather chair. She sat down somewhat timidly.

"Thank you for coming on such short notice. I believe that you will not need this where it was located," he handed her the Spy Cam, which she had used to capture the images of Hank earlier this evening. She smiled and tucked the miniaturized camera into her pocket. "I believe that you already know that earlier this evening I apprehended a student attempting to construct another bomb."

"Yes, sir. Tom said it was Hank Wilkinson, a sixth year Black Hall student," Pam replied. "That was fake bomb making materials that you left there, right?"

"Indeed. I wanted to personally thank you for having found the C-4 and detonators, though I believe that you had some help."

"Well, yes, Lindsey, Amanda, and Kathy helped, sir."

Pam saw no reason not to tell the whole truth.

"I took the liberty of replacing them with fakes. As we both suspected, the culprit returned to put together another bomb. I have questioned him and he is now in the hands of the Department of Law."

"Did he confess? Why did he want to murder the three workers?" Pam asked. "Is he a supporter of Dominus and his insane Manifesto?"

"Yes to the that last one. He ranted a good deal about Dominus being totally right and justified in taking over control of the world. He said that Dominus recently contacted him via email. He was told where the explosives were hidden and given instructions on how to make another bomb. He was to detonate it on Halloween, while we ate our evening meal. His target was the glass windows, rather like last year."

"So he didn't confess to murdering those three kitchen staff?" Pam asked.

"No, nor the stadium bombing."

"Do you believe him? That he isn't the Mad Bomber?" Pam asked.

"I do. However, I'm afraid that I may be the only one who does." He glanced at Cho Lin. "It seems the excitable Law men prefer to believe that he is responsible for the three deaths as well. I have a little something that you might be interested in, Pam. When he was being interrogated, he drank from this glass. No one has touched it since then. Would you like to have it?"

"Good thinking, sir! Now we can know for sure at once. Can I?" Pam asked very excited about the prospect of fingerprints.

"Yes, please do so. It would be nice if I had more sharing my point of view," Alister smiled.

Quickly, Pam took out her laptop. While it was booting, she cast a dirty spell onto the sides of the glass, bringing out the definite outlines of the prints. She found a particularly clear one, took a picture with her cell phone, and sent it to her computer. A couple minutes later, she brought up a three-way comparison: the prints from the stadium blast, the prints from the dishwashing murders, and this new one of Hank's.

"Oh my!" she exclaimed.

Alister's eyebrows raised, and Professor Cho Lin suddenly became very interested. "He's not the Mad Bomber. Not even remotely matching prints. Here, see for yourself. They are completely different. The two on the left side are the Mad Bomber's prints and the one on the right is Hank's. I don't even need to use comparison software to tell they're not remotely the same, sir. We, we don't have the Mad Bomber. He's still on the loose!"

Cho Lin looked downcast, "I was so hoping that you were wrong, Alister. We are still dealing with a maniac on the loose around Bradbury's!"

"We are indeed, Cho Lin, as I suspected. Few students know of the secret rooms, you see, very, very few. I can count them on one hand, I suspect." He winked at Pam, who grinned.

"Thank you, Pam. You are definitely becoming an excellent Sleuth indeed. My compliments." Alister meant it too.

She beamed, but had a sudden thought. "Now how are we going to catch the Mad Bomber? I mean, he must have gotten wind that the stash of C-4 was discovered. I bet he found out from someone that knew about it here at Bradbury's or from those in the Department of Law, who dealt with it after you gave it to them."

"I trust with my life those that I've told here, Pam. However, it is common knowledge that Dominus supporters have infiltrated the government. Most certainly, he has people within the Department of Law who support him. However, that will be hard to trace from here, likely impossible for us to know for sure."

"So what are we to do, Alister, just wait until he bombs again?" asked a frustrated Cho Lin. "You know as well as I do that if a student dies, they will certainly close the school."

"That is always a possibility. However, I do not believe they would close the school. Fire me, certainly, but not shut the school down. The other schools do not have the capacity to take on six hundred new students," Alister calmed her fears.

"I'm still going to try," Pam said, mostly to herself.

"Try what?" Alister completely lost sight of her intention.

"To trace who within the Department of Law might have informed Dominus about the finding of the C-4," she said. "I have other ways and means, sir. I'll let you know if I can find anything useful."

Professor Cho Lin started to protest, "But. . ."

Alister cut her off. "You are looking at the beginnings of a Master Sleuth, Cho Lin. Nurture as you would an orchid and the beauty springs forth. Pam, have you any other observations you would like to share with us concerning the so called Mad Bomber?"

"Well, as a matter of fact, I do. You see, I believe that he or she is not masquerading as a student. I know that we all thought so at first. I even had Amanda looking over Black Hall students to see if they were like Dominus was last year, when he was being Lindsey. We thought that because of the laptop we found in the Black Hall dumpster."

"Yet, no one was seriously injured in the stadium blast, so I still pursed that same notion. However, when the dishwasher room blew up, that changed my thinking. The Mad Bomber is very likely not a student for two reasons. One, our students, while some are very obnoxious, I don't believe that they could knowingly murder three people. Two, our students didn't know of the dishwashing room or kitchen, not until after the bombing. Well, four of us did, but I don't think anyone else does. Now my thinking is along the lines of some staff member. Whether they are possessed by Dominus, a morphed Death Stalker, or just a supporter, I haven't yet decided. If it was a staff member, I'm inclined to believe that they didn't intend for anyone actually to die because of the bomb. Hence, no more bombing, as they probably feel very guilty. I'm afraid I just don't know enough advanced magic to make a better judgment call, sir."

"Besides, it wouldn't be fair to all the staff to go around to each and try to see if they are the guilty party, not without some evidence of their complicity. Just because they break the law is no reason that we should."

"Point well taken, Pam. Now then, I do have one other

thing that might interest you. Hank told us that the email he received ordered him to reformat his hard disk so that no trace of the email remained. He voluntarily turned in his computer, and the Law men verified it is blank. It doesn't even boot up anymore. They left it here with me. Would you like to 'borrow' it for a time? I believe Hank's future may well be decided by his laptop," Alister hinted.

"Ha, that was a stupid order. Reformatted bah. I'll have it back by morning, sir! Emails can be traced to the sender. I will get right on it, top priority. I wonder who sent him that email?"

"Thank you. Professor Herbert Mac Elroy speaks highly of your computing skills," Alister replied. "As it is getting near curfew time, I should let you get back to your dorm. Keep me informed of your progress."

"I will sir. Great thing to hang on to his laptop!" she exclaimed, shutting down hers and packing both into her back.

"Pam, you be careful. If you need anything, let me know," Professor Cho Lin said as Pam got up to leave. Pam smiled and agreed.

At ten o'clock, Pam entered her dorm room. "Well?" all three roommates exclaimed the instant she opened the door and entered. Pam quickly went over all that had been said. By the time she finished, all four were growing sleepy. The exciting project would have to wait until morning.

"This is way more exciting that a soccer game," Pam declared early the next morning. She wolfed down some waffles and was now back in her room, but her friends were just rising. Lindsey saw all the dismantled pieces of the laptop and shook her head; this was beyond her knowledge for sure. The three headed off for breakfast.

Pam's desk, now her workbench, was littered with screws and disassembled pieces of Hank's laptop. Soon, she had his blank hard drive hot-wired into her computer. A few keystrokes later and a program from the Underground Web site to restore the drive began running. Since this would take several hours, Pam headed back down to the dining room for brunch, self-serve on Saturday and Sunday mornings.

Already most of the third year and older students had

left for their day in Telluride. The dorm was three quarters empty. It was Halloween, nevertheless, and those that were here chatted and played games in the commons or the dining hall. When Pam returned, Emilio, Fern, and Amanda were playing a game of hearts. Lindsey and Kathy were watching, Kathy trying to teach Lindsey the game strategy. After Emilio won, he suggested, "Senorita Pam, how about a game of hearts?"

All six played another game and munched on Halloween shaped candies and cakes. Sleepy eyed Audrey joined them and watched, as Pam skinned Emilio in the game. "Here, Audrey, take my place, I have to go check up on the computer program in my room." Audrey took her seat, and Pam went back upstairs. Sure enough, the hard disk was back to the way it had been prior to the format command.

After reassembling the pieces, Pam booted up Hank's computer. As part of the restoration process, she had also hacked into the system, retrieving Hank's passwords. Almost as if this were her own computer, Pam got it up and running with little wasted time. Bingo, there was the last email he had received. She sent a duplicate to her own email address. Now she had a choice to make. Should she spend time poking around his files to see if there was anything else that might be incriminating or should she concentrate on this email?

Pam decided on the email. Now the real detective work began. Using her own computer and the duplicate copy of the email, she began the tedious backtracking, from server to server, retracing in reverse the route the email had taken to get to Hank's computer. Obviously, the previous stop was the central Bradbury computer. An hour later, she finally got the IP address of the sending computer, having plowed through several attempts at forged addresses. "Got you!" she said aloud.

Next, she went to the main address directory, WhoIs, and entered the four numbers. After a bit of a look up delay, the owner of that account was returned to her. "My god!" she exclaimed. After staring at the results, she decided to be very meticulous about this and made a complete print out of the results, an electronic copy of the results, a backup copy of the original email and the results, and then made a copy of that copy. This last copy, she converted into a password protected zip file and emailed it to Lindsey, to her father, and copied it into her secret location on her father's server. Finally, she made another copy and emailed it to Governor Alister.

Lunchtime had arrived. Pam packed everything up and headed down to join her friends. None felt like doing any homework. Though the day was crisp and quite chilly, it was Halloween, a holiday. Emilio went up to his room to take, in his opinion at least, a well-deserved nap. The five girls decided to take a long walk around the campus. "Snow will be here any day," Amanda advised. True, a light dusting had already happened three times, but it had all melted quickly. From last year's experience, they knew that at this higher altitude, Bradbury's would soon be under a foot or more of snow, which would remain until the spring thaw came.

By the time of the supper celebration, all the older students had returned and were in a very festive mood. After the fancy dinner would come dance time, rock and roll time to be more precise. Traditionally, Halloween at Bradbury's was a costume dance night. Not being very creative this year, everyone simply wore the same costumes that they had worn last year.

Emilio used his Phantasm spell to make himself look like a skeleton—creepy bones walking around. Amanda dressed like an Apache princess. Pam was dressed like some movie star, and as she had last year, Amanda fixed up her hair. Kathy looked like a queen, complete with a glittering tiara. Lindsey dressed up like a fairy, complete with dainty little wings. Amanda's sister, Fern, dressed like a goblin. Jim looked like a pirate, complete with toy sword.

The lighting was dimmed; candles within pumpkins overhead provided the illumination. Whoever did the decorations had really gotten into the spirit of play. The back wall contained tables with hundreds of different kinds of snacks, many in special shapes as befitting the season. The music was provided by a magical console, and it took requests. Six hundred students filed onto the floor, along with the House Parents and all the professors and staff.

Lindsey noticed that many of the fourth, fifth, and particularly the sixth year students were paired and dancing close together in the center of the floor, just as they had last year. She spied Sandy and Tom dancing so close that mere inches separated their lips. She looked away.

Monique from Red Hall came over to Pam and whisked her off to the dance floor. Monique was once more dressed as a woman impersonating a man, a bit strange, Lindsey thought, but both appeared to be having a good time.

"Ah ha. The old pirate has captured the fairy queen. Now you have to dance with me!" Jim captured Lindsey. She giggled, and he pulled her out onto the dance floor. Lindsey still didn't quite get this style of dancing. Last year, she had learned to waltz, but the formal dance was not until May. Soon, however, she forgot about being self-conscious and began just to have fun with Jim.

Before she knew it, Governor Alister announced, "It's nearly ten o'clock. Here comes the last dance of the evening." Jim pulled her very close to him as they danced. For some reason, Lindsey didn't resist either. She felt as light as the fairy she was dressed to be.

Laughing and chatting, the students headed back to their respective dorms. Because of the festivities, everyone had completely missed the evening news. Pam remembered and suggested that something might be on about Hank Wilkinson. They turned on Hugo and KMAG; none expected what they heard.

Hugo was saying, "I repeat, the Mad Bomber of Bradbury's School of Magic is dead tonight. Hanged himself in his jail cell. Earlier today, Hank Wilkinson, a sixth year student at Bradbury's was apprehended while making yet another bomb. He was taken into custody this morning, along with ten pounds of plastic explosives. The Department of Law now suspects that the deadly bombings on the campus were carried out by this student, acting with a grudge against the school. His murderous rampage has now ended. Guards found his body suspended from his cell bars just an hour ago, an apparent suicide. So ends the tale of the Mad Bomber. After the break, KMAG has some exclusive footage of today's exciting events."

"Oh my god, he's dead!" Kathy cried.

"But he was innocent! He's not the Mad Bomber," Pam protested.

All four headed to their room. Pam had to send a message to Alister about this. While she did so, Lindsey asked, "Why would he hang himself? He didn't do it. He wasn't a murderer."

"Some people freak out when they are put in jail, I've heard," Kathy tried to think of a plausible explanation.

Pam booted up her laptop once more and typed a long and furious email to her father. "Are you coming to bed?" asked Lindsey a bit later.

"No, I am hoping my dad answers me right away," she said. Ten minutes later, she read her father's reply.

Dear Pam,

Terrible tragedy, this Hank Wilkinson business. Got your prints. I have no authority in Denver, but I know Thaddeus Tomlinson well. I have sent him a confidential email on this matter. You were wise to use the Secure Email system; normal emails can be intercepted, especially in these dark times. I share a bit of hope with you: Denver is using the A9000 system. (He inserted a specific URL for her to click on here.) Check it out. More when I know more. Keep up the stellar work, dear.

Love,

Dad

Smiling, she clicked on the URL her dad gave her. It took her to the Able Security Monitoring Company and their new jail video monitoring system. Specifically, the page contained some specifications. Pam read: "The video feed is sent to the monitoring station and recorded on disk. However, a secondary feed is sent off site to an undisclosed location in case of tampering." Pam realized what her father was trying to suggest. While whoever killed Hank in his cell had probably wiped out the primary recording or tampered with it, it was highly unlikely that they knew about the duplicate copy that was fed to some off site location and recorded there. If only the Denver Department of Magical Misuse would pursue this matter, justice might prevail, Pam thought as she turned off her computer and crawled into bed. As she relaxed, her thoughts drifted back to the dance and Monique, gorgeous Monique.

Around three in the morning, Pam awoke in a sweat. What if nothing was done? What if no one believed it? Quietly, Madam Fingers logged into the Underground website. Pam bit her lip determining how best to phrase her request. She typed a private message for Dingo.

Dingo

Got a project for you. Need a copy of the last six months' worth of incoming and outgoing emails using this IP address. (She entered the four numbers.) They have been 'removed' from the server, but I still want them. Use extreme caution. Check WhoIs first. If it is too risky, let me know, and I'll understand.

Madam Fingers

Satisfied, she sent the private message and turned off her laptop. Within a few minutes, Pam was sound asleep once more.

Chapter 8—The Blast

Sunday morning, Audrey pleaded, "We have got to cram on biology all day today! Remember, we have the final exam over the entire plant kingdom on Monday!"

"Does that mean we will be done with plants?" asked Emilio, who was ready to be "done with plants" the second day of class.

"Yes, but only if you pass," Pam pointed out. "If you flunk, then you have to take the whole plant section over again. You have to pass it to get your high school degree, you know." Emilio's spirits sank.

"I think I need help, Audrey," he begged. She giggled, and they began reviewing. The others joined in, since none wanted to repeat plants.

By 8:30 a.m., Audrey had finished her biology test, but hung around outside the room for her friends. One by one, the others finished and joined her. Emilio was the last to exit, but only after the bell rang, ending the test. He looked glum.

"I am resigned to having to take plants a second time," he said morosely. "I didn't even finish the last two questions."

Later after PE, they all headed to government class. Today, Professor Jerry Thalmus had a surprise for them. "In light of what has been happening in our world, we are going to put your learning to good use." He handed out copies of Manifesto of Dominus to each student.

"Look at the first paragraph, which reads in part," a most serious tone in his voice, "Whereas wizards and witches down through the long ages of history have been cursed, reviled, and even burned at the stake—okay, let's analyze just this much. Is there any truth in this assertion of his? Yes, Deiter?"

"Sure there is! The Salem Witch Trials. They burned them, though often they burned the wrong people," he stated factually.

"In the late nineteen hundreds, anyone worshiping magical things were dubbed Satan worshipers and treated as if they were somehow insane or crazy people," Peaches added. Quite a few more examples were mentioned, primarily by those in Black Hall.

"Ah, so there is truth in the opening line of Dominus," Jerry concurred with them. "I believe that it is absolutely critical to also ask why. Why would a normal feel this way towards one who can use magic? Ideas? Miss Betts?"

Pam's hand eagerly shot up almost before he finished his question. "Fear, sir. Some normal people fear us."

"Yes, indeed, but why should a normal fear us?" Jerry probed further. "Let me give you something to ponder. Suppose at this very minute Dominus Malefic and his band of Death Stalkers appeared in our class, right here where I am sitting on my desk. How would you feel? You are all wizards and witches are you not? How many of you would feel just a little bit afraid of what might happen? Show of hands, please." Those in Red Hall shot their hands into the air, while most of the students in Black Hall slowly raised their hands.

"Why? Why would you be afraid or scared of Dominus? After all, you are wizards and witches too," Jerry hung that admonition in solidly.

"He's so much more powerful than I am," Peaches timidly replied. "He could kill me, and I wouldn't stand a chance!"

"Right, some say he can just speak one word, and it'll kill a person!" Audrey added.

"Sure, look what he did to Lindsey last year in the restroom," Amanda added. "Stunned her, cut off her hands, and sewed her mouth shut. She couldn't do a thing to stop him. He's just too powerful."

"Excellent, excellent." Jerry wrote on the board: Greatly more powerful => afraid, scared, fearful. "Is this right?" The class was strangely silent; Pam's hand shot up into the air once more. "Miss Betts?"

"No sir. Look, if you suddenly brought Governor Alister in here, would anyone in here be the least bit afraid of him?" Many heads shook "No." "He's way more powerful than any of us, but we are not afraid of him."

"Astute observation, Miss Betts. While I will not get into

a debate over whether Dominus is more powerful than Alister or vice versa, I think that we can all agree both wizards are immeasurably more powerful than any of you students. Yet, if Dominus were here, you would feel scared and afraid, while if Alister were here, you would feel safe. Do we need to amend our conclusion on the board?"

Audrey hazarded an answer, "Alister wants to help people, while we all know that Dominus has murdered many people and hurt or harmed lots more. He's pure evil, while Alister is pure good." She spoke from her convictions.

"Let's not use the terms good and evil. They are relative terms. Audrey has given us another way to look at these men: helping people versus harming people. Let's amend our statement here to read thus: Greatly more powerful and has been harming people, not helping people => afraid, scared, fearful. "Can we all agree on this statement?" Indeed, he had everyone's agreement on the statement.

"Notice that this rule applies to us wizards in our world, as well to those in the normal's world. Yet, it also applies to interactions between the normals and us, does it not? Is Professor Herbert or Professor Jasper, who are normals, afraid of Governor Alister or even you young witches and wizards? How about Dominus, are they afraid of him?" Everyone in the class got his point. It made no difference who you were; the statement on the board held true universally.

"Now then, let's consider the second paragraph of Dominus, which reads: 'On Earth, man is at the top of the food chain. Consider the lowly sheep that lives its life to eat grass. Along comes mother wolf searching for dinner for her cubs, thus the sheep has purpose. In parallel, long has man, by virtue of his superior mind, been at the very top, dominating, controlling, ruling all other life forms on Earth. This is how it should be.' Is man at the top of the food chain?"

Everyone agreed completely. Jerry continued, "What makes man at the top of the food chain? Elephants are larger and stronger. I would not like to have a confrontation with a tiger or lion. Even rattlesnakes can be nasty with their poison. Guard dogs can be awfully vicious."

"Man has a mind and can think and solve problems,"

ventured Lindsey.

"Yes, if the elephant's watering holes dry up, he is in very big trouble from drought. Yet, man would simply set about digging a new well, knowing that there are often underground streams that can provide all the water he can use. Okay, so do we all agree that there is truth in what Dominus has asserted in this paragraph?" Once more, he had complete agreement.

"Now we come to the crux of Dominus's argument. His next paragraph must be examined line by line. It reads: 'Yet, there are two forms of man! All throughout recorded history, man has known that there are two forms: the normal man and the wizard man.' Let's examine just this much. I know you have all just finished your comprehensive test over the plant kingdom. True, you have not begun your studies of the animal kingdom, man in particular. However, I believe you already know enough to analyze this portion. What makes an oak tree a different species than algae? What is used to place a given plant within a particular species? Why are men and wolves different species?"

"A tree has leaves and branches and algae don't," Emilio finally had a simple enough question about biology that he could answer.

"A man walks upright, has opposable thumbs, can use his hands for all sorts of things. A wolf walks on all fours and doesn't have hands and cannot make tools, and he has very big canines," Audrey added.

"Ah, different physical body parts, is that what you are saying?" Jerry asked. Most agreed. "Now then, if we are separating species by physical differences, which is what is used to classify into species, then what different body parts do you all have that Herbert or Jasper doesn't have? Do you all have a third arm? A second brain? Two heads? A tail? Special internal organs? Come on; what is the difference between a wizard's physical body and that of a normal person?"

Slowly, he got everyone to see that there was indeed no differences at all. It was just the ability to use magic that was different. "Okay, now I happen to know that Miss Lemon here is quite the plant expert." Audrey blushed, as all heads turned to look at her. They knew she had finished the big test in less than a half hour, and most considered her a plant genius. "Mister Lopez, I happen to also know is anything but a plant genius. How well do you think you did on your plant test?" All headed now turned to Emilio.

"Well, er, ah, maybe I'll have to take plants over again," he admitted. Many girls giggled, while his face reddened.

"Okay, then if we follow the logic of Dominus, we have just discovered two new species of man. Plant woman and non-plant man." Everyone laughed at this absurdity. Jerry, however, was not finished. "I happen to know, as many of you also know, that Miss Betts here is a computer genius, a whiz, and has won the Microsoft Top Computer Student of the Year three times in a row before she ever came to Bradbury's." Pam's face went bright red. She never told this fact to others, though the knowledge was readily available, if one looked at her biography on the Internet. "Mister Cross, would you care to challenge Miss Betts to a computer duel?"

All heads turned to Deiter. His cheeks turned pink. He replied after a cough, "Er, no sir! She'd skunk my butt! Everyone knows that she is hot with computers."

"Ah, then if we again apply the principles of Dominus, we now have two more species of man, the computer geek and the rest of us." Everyone again laughed at this silliness.

"Mister Cross, would you care to race against Miss Whitewater or Miss Barron here? Class, would you care to place a bet on who would win such a race?" Fortunately, Deiter did not have to answer, for the whole class roared with laughter.

"Ah, then we have yet another species of man, the talented athletes and the rest of us poor sots, eh? My, but the principles of Dominus are creating a whole lot more species of man, are they not?" Jerry punched his analogy in hard.

"Okay, how many species of man are there really?" Jerry finally asked, once the laughter died down. The entire class agreed that there was only one species.

"You see, the basic premise of Dominus is completely false. However, notice that he began with several premises that were completely truthful. Then, he slides his false one in there, pretending that one is also true. Let's see what Dominus next presents: 'Man still believes in the Big Lie, that all men are created with equal rights.' Notice this Big Lie thing comes immediately after his own big lie! Clever, he throws your attention immediately upon this one, not on his, classic misdirection. All men were created with equal rights. That is a founding principle of our country, is it not?" All heads nodded. "Flunk! Flunk! Flunk!" Jerry shouted. "That line in our constitution means: All men were created with equal rights *under the Law*!"

"Equal, definition of: the same as, same in the amount, size, number as. Okay, Mister Cross, to be equal, you are going to have to let your hair grow several more feet, start wearing cherry red lipstick, and, oh yes, you will need to either take female hormones or get some breast implants soon so that you are equal to Miss West here. Lindsey, you are going to have to cut your hair very short and start taking steroids to beef up your biceps, if you are to be equal to Lyle here." The class roared with laughter.

"I don't know of two human beings who are truly equal. Even identical twins are not wholly equal. They frequently have different personalities." Heads nodded in agreement.

"Our constitution is talking about our *rights* as human beings! Now natural rights are universal rights inherent in the nature of people and not dependent upon human actions or beliefs. A natural right exists even when it is not enforced by the government or society. On the other hand, a legal right is specifically created by a government for the benefit of those it represents."

"Okay, then let's see what kind of rights you all have, whether inherently or legally. Does Miss Barron have the right to wear her hair as long as she desires, Mister Cross?"

"Er, yes," he replied.

"And what about Miss Peggy West, does she have the right to wear whatever color lipstick she chooses?" Everyone agreed.

"Ah, but does Miss Barron have the right to kill Mister Cross here, just kill him right now?" Everyone agreed that she didn't.

"We all have the right to live out our own lives as we see fit. Where do our rights terminate? When we take actions that are more broadly harmful to others. When we steal from a store, or shoplift a tube of lipstick instead of paying for it, or killing another person unjustly, then we cross over the line from basic human rights into a violation of other's rights. Law steps in at that point. Thus, it is not a Big Lie. All men are created with equal rights, usually interpreted as being rights under the laws of our country and international law, which precludes harming others without just cause."

"Remember the Four Inviolate Laws.

1. Thou shalt not use magic to injure or harm another unjustly.

2. Thou shalt not use magic to kill another unjustly.

3. Thou shalt not use magic to steal from another that which is not yours.

4. Thou shalt not use magic to force another to do something against their will unjustly.

These are set up to help protect everyone's basic rights on this planet. Take out the word magic and they apply equally to normal people as well."

"So you see, the Manifesto is itself a Big Lie. Let's skip down to the ending, where he reveals his master plan for the organization of the world. I quote: 'What of the true relationship between norm and wizard, between sub-man and superman? Obviously, sub-man, lacking the superior skills, abilities, and magical knowledge of superman, should be his servant in all ways, as the horse to man.' If we follow his principles, then Mister Cross should get down on his knees and do anything that Miss Whitewater or Miss Barron tells him to do, for are they not his superior in athletics? Mister Lopez, you should be on your knees and do whatever Miss Lemon asks of you, for is she not the plant genius? And as for the rest of you, the whole class ought to get onto your knees and do whatever Miss Betts asks of you, for is she not the computer genius?"

"Some of you have a mother or father who is a normal human being. Do you really consider them as your horse or dog, subservient to your every whim? Hardly. In fact, had you behaved in such a manner, the school Seekers would have definitely *not* selected you to come here to Bradbury's!"

Just then, the bell rang, ending the class. On their way out, Pam said, "Boy, Professor Jerry was sure all fired up about the Manifesto!"

"Well, I sure learned some things today," Emilio replied.

Peggy West teased Deiter, as they walked out, "Deiter, want to borrow my lipstick?"

For once, he was not antagonistic. He grinned, "Sorry, we are not *equal*. We just have equal *rights*." Both laughed.

The week in Professor Mary Ann Thronby's Hall of Divination was also interesting. Her appearance had not changed since the last time this group of students was here in her classroom last year, while learning how to identify magical properties of items. Her hair was disheveled and appeared to be flying in hundreds of directions. Her clothes did not match. Her eyes darted and flittered around the room, as if searching out some terrible presence. The bell rang, signaling the start of the spell casting class. Her eyes finally seemed to focus on the here and now.

"It is so good to see you all once more. This week, we are going to be learning several new divination spells. In order, they are Determine Malevolent Intent, Detection of the Invisible, Understanding Personality, Locate an Object, and Read Other's Thoughts. Sometimes as you walk down a street, a person comes close to you. For your own safety, it is wise to be able to Determine Malevolent Intent of that person. The wand action forms a question mark in the air. Break up into your usual pairs and learn to cast the spell. When you believe you have mastered it, then you are to come up here and cast it upon my dog here." She pulled back a covering to reveal a large, vicious looking Doberman secure in its cage. It growled loudly, and she quickly covered his cage.

"Don't need any magic to know that dog is vicious," Emilio muttered. After a number of minutes, most believed they had this easy spell mastered. However, none could detect any real malevolent intent from their partners.

Emilio decided for once that he would go first, since

obviously her dog was quite malevolent indeed. Professor Mary Ann used the kennel blanket to hide them from the view of the class. She also cast a silence spell so that no one could overhear them. "Now then, Emilio, cast your spell."

He did as instructed; only he looked perplexed at the result. "Something must have gone wrong, Professor."

"Why do you say that, Emilio?" she probed.

"Well, cause it's not showing any yellow halo around the dog, and the dog is obviously malevolent!"

"No, he is not malevolent. He is my guard dog, here to protect me, but he has no inherent evil intentions toward you. He is just warning you not to harm or threaten me, Emilio. Now, see that card on my desk? Do *not* under any circumstances *touch* it. Cast your spell on the card, please."

"Gosh, it is glowing bright yellow, malevolent indeed!" he replied shocked at his spell.

"Correct, Emilio, pass. It is a *cursed* card. If you touch it, very bad things will happen to you. Now return to your seat and help others learn this spell. Do *not* tell them about the dog or the card please." He did as told.

The next day was just as interesting. The Detection of the Invisible became a fun game for the students to play. One or more cast their invisibility spells, and then the others tried to find where they were at in the room. Everyone had an enjoyable class period.

On Friday, Lindsey was forced to remove her father's ring and pin, because they totally blocked anyone from using the Read Another's Thoughts spell on her. At first, everyone thought this would be a very cool spell to learn. However, as they cast it on their various classmates, their opinions rapidly changed. Lindsey discovered that Audrey thought that she would look good wearing some lipstick. Deiter thought that she was still inferior to him. Pam discovered that Lindsey was bothered by her relationship with Monique. Deiter was upset to find out that Lindsey really thought that he was nothing but a spoiled brat. In short, everyone got a good dose of just what the others really thought about themselves. After the class ended, Lindsey was very glad to put her father's ring and pin back on. Now, no one could read her thoughts.

The next week of spells was taught by Professor Huan Su Sung in the Hall of Invocation and Evocation magic. None had ever had him before, though Lindsey adored his wife, Cho Lin.

Suave, but harsh, was how Lindsey described her impressions of Huan after Monday's class. His appearance was definitely svelte, yet he was very demanding of them. Spells must be done correctly. A blanket of snow covered the grounds, as they met outside the Hall to learn to cast an offensive spell, quite similar to the one the Death Stalker had used on them, when their bus had broken down on the way to Bradbury's back in August. Called Ball of Flames, the caster created a ball of flames a yard in diameter and which could be rolled along like a beach ball by the caster. Today, great clouds of steam rose as the many flaming balls rolled across the snowy landscape.

Next, they produced Clouds of Nauseating Gas, designed to render nearly helpless those in its path. More than a few students, who caught a whiff of the vapors, vomited. Finally, on Wednesday, they learned how to cast the Wall of Giant Spider Webs spell. Great masses of the thick, sticky webs filled large areas outside the Hall. Professor Huan had each student experience being caught in the webs as well, learning how to deal with them to escape.

Lindsey noted that the wand motions for these three evocation spells were quite similar, an out-rushing gesture, paralleling the idea of a great evocation. On Thursday and Friday, Huan also taught them a conjuration spell, which nearly every student practiced keenly, Missiles of Acid. Similar to their Magical Missiles in nature, these missiles struck much like an arrow, but additional damage occurred as the missile's acid caused burns upon exposed flesh as well as damaging clothing. Pam had identified this spell during Cho Lin's testing of her Sleuthing skills last year. Now she proudly could cast it in her defense.

What bothered many of the Yellow Hall students was Huan's announcement that next week they were to report to the Hall of Necromancy and Professor Delius Dogs, who was also the Hall Monitor for Black Hall. While Deiter and his group were very excited about this, Lindsey and her friends were not.

On Monday, the group of thirty students headed for the Hall of Necromancy, the dark arts. The building was entirely black. Stone serpents climbed up the walls on either side of the doors. Human skeletons were carved into the stone walls at periodic intervals. Lindsey whispered to Amanda, "This place gives me the creeps!"

Indeed, walking the halls to their classroom only added to the mystique. Skeletons, zombies, and other tortured, demented creatures adorned the walls they passed by. Delius Dogs was an imposing man, probably around forty. He had a dark complexion and an antagonistic stare. "Welcome to your first exposure to necromancy, that branch of magic devoted to the magic, spells, and enchantment, often with the dead. It is sometimes called the dark arts, which comes from the root of the word, nekros, Greek for dead body, and niger, Latin for black. Some of you will never successfully learn these dark spells, never." He looked at most of the girls in the class. Lindsey felt a cold chill come over her.

"Yet, do not worry about any failure to cast necromancy based spells. They aren't required for a passing grade in spell casting. Indeed, I would expect only a quarter of you here today to be successful with these spells, though I will try my best to teach you how. Later on in the spring, you will be back here with me again to attempt to learn the appropriate Grade 3 spells. However, the first spell I am to teach you is not technically a necromancy spell, but a summoning based spell, Summon a Swarm to Your Defense."

"When you are in dire trouble and need some assistance, you can summon a swarm of creatures to come and fight to protect you. These can be various insects, centipedes, various biting bugs, spiders, bats, even rats and mice. However, this time of year, the swarm that will answer your summons is very limited. Only mice, rats, and bats are still around. Many students are quite frightened of a mass of thousands of spiders and bugs, so that is why we teach this one in the winter. I hope you can deal with rats, mice, and bats."

Lindsey didn't care for any of these and wished the class

were already over! Many girls shared her opinion as well. However, some, like Peaches, seemed to revel in this spell! "The wand motion is like this," he explained. His wand made motions as though he was beckoning someone to come over to him. "Now listen carefully! What I'm about to say is of the utmost importance for your safety. When you summon them, you're to direct them to appear over there in that large empty space by the wall. Do not direct them out here into the main portion of the room! If you do, they will begin eating your fellow students! Do I make myself perfectly clear?" he bellowed antagonistically. Lindsey again wished the class were done.

"You go first," Amanda suggested to Lindsey, when they were supposed to start practicing.

"No, you go first. I don't like this spell at all!" Lindsey replied. The two argued for a couple of minutes before Amanda finally agreed to start casting, but only because Delius gave them a cold stare first.

Ten times, Amanda tried to cast the spell with no luck. Deiter and his group were already being successful. Hordes of rats and mice crawled around the empty space, sometimes trying to eat each other. Lindsey felt rather sick at her stomach. Delius Dogs now stood behind Amanda, making her even more nervous about this spell. "You have to really intend for the rodents to come to you. You have to want them to come, Miss Whitewater. I detect that you do not truly want them to come to your defense. Imagine Dominus is standing there in that space." He waved his wand and an image of Dominus appeared there, staring out at the class. Several girls screamed until others told them it was only an illusion.

It looked real enough to allow Amanda finally to call a hundred mice to her defense. Then, it was Lindsey's turn. She decided that of all the creatures to come to her, she disliked bats least. "Summon Swarm: Bats!" she commanded. On the eighth try, a hundred bats appeared fluttering around the designated space, some making dives upon the mice and rats below them. Soon, there was an enormous battle between the bats, rats, and mice! Delius merely dispelled all the magical summonings and asked the class to continue. Lindsey found this whole spell very disgusting indeed, praying for the ending bell to sound.

The next day's spell was even worse, the first true necromancy based spell, Ghostly Hand. "With this spell, you are extracting a bit of your own life force and placing it in a ghostly image of your hands. You control the hands and can use them, for example, to strangle your opponent. Again, I do not expect that many of you will be able to master this spell, but you must try," he stared straight at Lindsey when he uttered this last. She glared back at him.

After two days, Lindsey finally gave up. Here was the first spell that she was not able to cast nor had even the remotest wish to cast either! After two days of trying, Audrey managed to cast it—a pair of ghostly hands moved around at her will. Likewise, Pam managed to conquer the spell. The rest of Lindsey's group was unable to cast this one. All the Black Hall students learned to perform this spell on the first day, however.

Lindsey was more than happy to return to Professor Jerry Thalmus the following week. As Thanksgiving approached, Professor Thalmus announced, "You have now covered all your Grade 2 spells. The next two weeks are practice sessions. As last year, you will be given forty-five minutes to cast all the Grade 2 spells that you can in that time period. When you return from Christmas vacation, we will begin learning Grade 3 spells. Unlike last year, I do not care whether you speak the command activation words or whether your wand activates." He glanced at Lindsey and smiled at her. "When you feel you have had all the practice you need, let me know, and I will give you your test. As soon as you have completed your final test, you may then have a free period in place of this class, until we resume after Christmas vacation."

He winked and added, "That's an added incentive for all of you to hurry up and take the test, you see. Free time? Nah, you don't need that, now do you?" he teased. Many groans went his way.

In order to accommodate all the varied spell casting, the class met on the third and top floor of the Hall of Abjuration, on the far west side of the pentagram campus. The room had large windows, and the view from here was spectacular. Snow covered the grounds and, just beyond the wall, the Dark Woods looked spooky with its branches covered with snow leaves. Beyond the woods, the snow covered slopes of the mountain rose majestically. However, when they were to cast the damage causing spells, they simply went up the stairs to the roof.

Today, Lindsey had gotten through all her spells, excepting the two necromancy ones, one of which she still had not learned nor wished to do so. She and Deiter were near the windows assisting their partners with their Create Darkness spells. Professor Jerry was at his desk, also by the windows. From his seat, he could easily observe all his students hard at work and could remedy any disasters as they arose.

Lindsey suddenly felt the rabbit's foot jumping around in her pocket, very annoyingly. It took her a moment to realize what this meant. Then, she caught a glint of light flashing from outside the windows and turned to see what caused it. The rabbit's foot was going berserk! Deiter, seeing her turn toward the windows, also turned his head to see. At that instant, both saw a blinding flash of magical energies, followed by the strangest explosion either had ever heard. With the bombs that had been triggered on the campus, they were violent outward explosions. However, this one exploded inward, or so it seemed to Lindsey. Like a giant vacuum, the explosion hit the side of the Hall of Abjuration. All the windows shattered; the shards were sucked outside in a flash, falling harmlessly to the ground. However, the suction of the blast was so strong that Lindsey, Deiter, and Professor Thalmus were also swept off their feet and pulled outside the building.

So strong was the jerk and pull that all three lost their wands, which were pulled out of their hands as if by some super-humanly strong hands. Three stories up in the air, all three began falling like heavy rocks. Deiter screamed, but Professor Thalmus was temporarily stunned, hitting his head on the side of the window frame as his body was forcefully pulled out by the blast. "Gentle Fall!" Lindsey silently commanded and her rate of fall became quite gentle. She saw that Deiter had lost his wand and Professor Thalmus was unconscious; she acted without thinking. "Gentle Fall: Deiter! Gentle Fall: Thalmus. Margarete: Come to me!" she thought, but did not vocalize her words. One can think far faster than one can speak. This Lindsey knew well.

She landed on her feet, staring at the origin of the magical attack. Something was flying, hovering to be more precise, just over the Dark Woods. Her staff of power came flying into her hand, and she commanded again without thinking, "Lightning Bolt: that flying thing." Deiter landed, wondering how he had not been killed. He saw the staff flying into her out-stretched hand and saw her pointing it towards the strange hovering thing that had attacked them. He saw the bolt of lightning streak out from the staff towards the thing and strike it solidly. As they watched, the flying thing began to billow smoke. Almost at once, the thing began to descend, wildly out of control, though its operator was most definitely trying to get it on to the mountainside and out of the woods.

"How did. . ." Deiter fumbled for words.

"Gentle Fall. I cast it on you too and Professor Thalmus. Gosh, he is bleeding from his head!" Deiter picked up his wand and Lindsey's too, handing hers to her. Just then, Amanda came Gentle Falling down to them.

"Are you okay, Lindsey? I saw that flying thing. Magical energies are streaking from it. Someone bombed us again! Bastards!"

"I'm fine. Did you see where it landed?" Lindsey asked. Pam set down beside them, asking the same questions.

"Yes, come on. I think it is still within the walls. I can follow its magical energy trail. It's as clear as a jet trail in a blue sky," Amanda replied, anger burning within her.

"Pam, get help for Professor Thalmus. We're going to get this bomber fellow before he can get away!" Lindsey called out. "Warm!" None was wearing their outdoor clothing. It was cold, and the snow was up over their ankles.

Ignoring the weather, both girls began to run towards the downed machine, though not fast in the slippery white stuff. Just as angry, Deiter took off after them, two steps behind them. "You're not going to leave me behind!" he called ahead to them. He was right. The snow slowed the distance runners enormously, and he could keep up.

Though they had to take a roundabout course through the woods, slipping and sliding on the rough terrain, Amanda continued to guide them unerringly. The magical energy trail was unmistakable to her senses. Whoever this was, Amanda wanted them to pay dearly for this unprovoked attack on her school and her classmates.

"What in the name of. . ." Deiter exclaimed, as they came upon the downed machine. Unlike anything that they had ever seen, the crumpled mess lay smoking on the ground. Bleeding heavily, a bearded man, wand in hand, came crawling out of the wreckage.

"Ultralight," Amanda stated, recognizing what was left of the craft.

"Surrender!" Lindsey screamed at the man, who had gotten to his feet. Instead of surrendering, he whirled his wand. Instantly, Lindsey recognized that wand motion. He was about to shoot a ball of fire at them. "Suck It!" she exclaimed; the man's spell arced into her staff.

"Missiles: man!" Deiter fired off his spell, sending several magical missiles to the man. They bounced harmlessly off him.

"Dispel Magic: Man!" Lindsey ordered from her staff, but to make doubly sure, she also cast it herself, silently, Dispel Magic: Man. Magical energies flashed around the man.

"Missiles: Man!" Amanda let lose her volley, while Deiter realized that whatever had been protecting him had now vanished. Her missiles hit him, and he staggered from their unexpected strike.

"Kill!" screamed the man, waving and pointing his wand at Lindsey.

"Suck It!" she screamed back, hoping her staff would do as she ordered. The deadly magical energy again arced into her staff.

"Missiles of Acid: Man," Deiter shot his next spell and watched it burn a hole into the man's chest.

Alister, Cho Lin, and Blake Smith suddenly appeared beside the trio of students. "Disarm!" commanded Alister.

"Bind!" commanded Cho Lin, one second after Alister's

spell knocked the man's wand from his hand.

"Golly, you didn't leave anything for me to do," Professor Blake complained. "First real battle in ages, and I didn't have time to get a spell off. Ah well. You kids all right?"

"Yes sir," Lindsey replied. "We stopped him from making a getaway. Who is he and why did he attack us?"

Governor Alister looked at Amanda and asked, "Miss Whitewater, do you detect any magical alterations coming from him?"

In the fury of the confrontation, she had not looked. Now she stared at the still bleeding man carefully. "No sir, just from the ultralight."

"Agreed. You are looking at the Death Stalker known as William the Bold. We don't know his last name, however. Blake, how about gagging him for the time being? We don't know if he can cast non-verbal, non-wand spells. I don't want to take any chances with him. Then, levitate him and transport him to the gates. The Department of Law folks will be here any second. Kids, I suggest that you return to your dorms. All classes have already been cancelled for the rest of today. Oh yes Lindsey, Professor Thalmus sends you his thanks. He is resting in the Infirmary as we speak."

"Was anyone else hurt?" Amanda asked.

"Bumps and scrapes, nothing serious I believe. I will chat more with you later on. Oh yes, I almost forgot." He picked up a piece of metal from the remains of the ultralight and pressed the fingers of William onto it. "Here, take this to Miss Betts. I'm sure she will know what to do with it," Alister said to Lindsey.

Slowly, and with many Warm! spells, the trio trudged through the slippery snow, retracing their steps. Once on solid ground and out of the forest, they began to chat.

"Thanks for coming with us, Deiter," Lindsey said. "With your help, we held him until Alister got there. Warm!"

"Thanks for saving my life. I thought I was a goner. The ground was flying up at me! I was mad at him too, you know. Warm! It felt good actually to fight one of these Death Stalkers, though without your staff, we would have been dead I'm sure. Now I'm truly sorry that I made fun of you and your wand activation last year, Lindsey. Say, what did your staff absorb anyway?" Deiter asked.

"I recognized the wand motion for a ball of fire. That was the first one. Warm! I didn't like the sound of the second one, Kill, so I had Margarete absorb that one too. I don't know what it was."

"Well, we made a pretty good team, didn't we?" Amanda commented. "Warm! We actually got to him and held him, though I think we may have had to kill him, if Alister and the others had not come when they did. We don't know how to disarm someone. I see that as a critical step, don't you Deiter?"

"Absolutely. Without a wand, you can't do anything," he replied and then became extremely red faced. "Er, most can't do anything. Lindsey is amazing. I don't know how she can do all these spells as she does. Warm!"

"Me either," Amanda chatted away, "but I have a theory about it. Warm!"

"You mean how I can cast these non-verbally and without a wand?" asked Lindsey. "Warm! You've never told me about it."

"Well, it's kind of embarrassing for you. Warm! But you grew up without hands and began using magical energies long before you even knew what it was. I just think that has somehow given you a stronger connection to the magical energies, somehow."

"Well, I don't recommend experimenting with that theory! I was miserable all my life until I came here, you know. Warm! Hey, there's Pam waiting on us." Indeed, Pam, Emilio, and Kathy were standing by the main southwestern entrance to the dorms.

"Are you all right?" asked Pam worriedly.

"Yes, we three got him!" Amanda proudly pronounced. Pam looked at Deiter, who smiled a satisfied smile back at her.

"Glad you are fine," came the voice of Tom, from behind the three. "Get inside pronto, Alister's orders. We are on lock down. There could be more bombings." Hastily the three entered and went their separate ways.

Amanda rapidly told Tom what had happened, before they got to the two separate stairs. He gave her a hug and then led Emilio back up into the men's quarters, while Pam led the others to their room. "Alister wanted me to give you this," Lindsey remembered the bit of metal. "He put William's fingers on it and said you would know what to do with it."

Pam's eyes gleamed! "You bet I do!" She dashed to her computer and began scanning in the image, after dusting it with black dirt.

Meanwhile, Lindsey received a message from Jim, asking how she was. She blushed as she read it and quickly sent him a silent reply. For once, she was grateful that she had learned how to cast a Message spell silently. While she was occupied, Amanda related the details to Kathy and Pam. Both Pam and Kathy had only gotten a couple of bruises, as they went flying into some chairs. Kathy explained that nearly all the students got minor bruises, nothing more. Only the three closest to the windows got sucked out by the blast.

"Darn!" exclaimed Pam, thoroughly disgusted. All eyes turned to her. "He's not our Mad Bomber either! I'd better message Alister at once." She proceeded to send him a short note.

"Come on; let's get a hot shower and cleaned up," Kathy suggested. "We've all been waiting on you two to get back." The four headed down to the showers.

Jim was waiting for Lindsey when the foursome went down to the dining room for supper. "You sure you are all right?" he asked Lindsey. "I heard about it from Tom, though we all heard the blast. Did you really help Professor Thalmus and Deiter?"

"Yes, he was knocked out. I think he hit his head on the windowsill. Deiter lost his wand, so did I for that matter. Amanda was cool though; she came down to check on me and got us to go after the Death Stalker. I wouldn't have, if I didn't have my staff with me, though. I think he tried to kill me with a spell."

"Excuse me. I know you are all having a good discussion about the latest bombing," Governor Alister spoke up, and the room quieted down. "Yes, a Death Stalker, William the Bold, flew a magically enhanced ultralight plane here and tried to bomb us again. The blast, which I'm sure you all heard, took out a section of the windows on the third floor of the Hall of Abjuration. The suction from the blast sucked Miss Barron, Mister Cross, and Professor Thalmus out of the window. Yes, the professor is all right. He hit his head on the windowsill and was knocked out. Miss Barron had the foresight to cast Gentle Fall on both of them. Miss Whitewater, Amanda, that is, forgive me Fern," he eyed Fern, who blushed, "came down to check on them, and they saw the ultralight fleeing. Miss Barron shot a lightning bolt into it disabling it. The three of them then charged across the Dark Forest through the snow without their winter clothing and apprehended the Death Stalker. I believe they shot several spells to subdue him, by the time that we arrived to take him into custody. However, the bad news is that William is not our so-called Mad Bomber. He is in the custody of the Department of Law at this time. Now then, shall we dine?" He waved his wand, and piles of food appeared as usual.

During the next days, the professors piled on the homework. However, they all knew what was coming, the final exams, just before the Christmas holidays. Thus, Lindsey took the spell casting test sooner than she would have desired. There were four spells she had not yet learned to do non-verbally or without her wand. However, she passed nicely, but did not even attempt the necromancy spell. With her newfound free hour, she worked hard on her algebra, which only seemed to get more difficult with each passing day.

Thanksgiving came and went. With all her friends having passed their spell casting tests, they helped each other, cramming for the finals coming shortly. Loaded down with schoolwork, no one had any time to conduct any further investigations.

Two weeks before the holidays, the group was in the study hall as usual. Someone began asking about their plans for the holidays, and they all chatted away for a time. Finally, Lindsey, who noticed that Audrey was rather silent, asked her, "So are you going home for the holidays, Audrey?"

"No, I'm staying here," she said quietly.

"How come?"

"I've no home to go back to anymore. When I came

here, I left the last foster home for good. I'll figure something out for the summer when it comes," she said putting on a brave face.

"Well, that's no good. Why don't you come to my house and stay with me over the holidays? We are next door to Amanda, Fern, Tom, Jim, and even Sandy. We'll have lots of fun," Lindsey offered.

"But what will your parents say about bringing a homeless waif home? Won't I just be in everyone's way?" Audrey asked.

Lindsey rummaged in her bag for her cell phone and punched the button to dial her mother. After a brief conversation, Lindsey explained, "All set Audrey. Mom's making up the spare bedroom for you. You must come now. She won't take no for an answer. You will like her, you'll see." Audrey beamed, thanked her, and gave her a hug.

Later that same evening, Lindsey got an unexpected cell phone call! The four were up in their room, preparing to hit the sack, when her phone rang. Quite surprised, her phone hardly ever rang, Lindsey picked it up and said, "Hello."

"Miss Lindsey Barron?" a man's voice said.

"Yes," she replied.

"Ah good! I'm Mr. Fred Betts, Pam's father. Pam gave me your cell number. Is this a good time to talk?"

"Who is it?" whispered her friends.

Holding her hand over the phone, she whispered, "It's your father, Pam!"

"Yes, it's fine." Lindsey replied, unsure what to say to him.

"As you probably know, events are becoming a bit unwieldy, what with all the trouble Dominus and his men are causing, especially here at the holiday season. I have been forced to put in long hours at work, as you may well imagine. Because of my position, it is becoming increasingly unsafe for my family. I wonder if we may impose upon you and your mother this holiday season."

"I'm not sure what you mean, sir."

"There is no easy way to ask this, but do you suppose that your parents would mind hosting my wife and Pam over the holiday season? I can probably get away on Christmas Day and perhaps New Year's Eve and join everyone. We simply cannot afford to have extra Department of Defense men watching my family and house over the holidays. They are already stretched very thin up here in Sterling."

"Wow. Cool! That would be great! Probably we'd best check with mom and dad first, though."

"Of course, I wanted to touch base with you first. I know Pam thinks very highly of you, her best friend she says. Since you approve, can you give me your mom's number, and I'll call her tonight." Lindsey did and he said thanks and goodbye.

"What did dad want?" Pam asked the second she hung up. Of course, Amanda and Kathy were all ears, sitting on the edge of their beds waiting her reply.

"He wanted to know if it would be okay with me if you and your family come and spend the Christmas holidays at our ranch. Something about being shorthanded in the Department of Defense and your place not being safe."

"Whoopee! Wow! Incredible." Pam was elated about this news. She had not yet said anything about the concerns that her father had voiced to her about the security of their home. Such were the liabilities of being the head of the Department of Magical Misuse.

Just like last year, the last week before the Christmas holidays little schoolwork got done. Everyone was excited about going home for the holidays. Surprisingly, the Blake professors conjured a huge Christmas tree in the dining hall, and Professor Janice decorated it beautifully. All that week, the dining room was festively decorated. Even their evening meals contained treats for the season. Lindsey particularly loved the chocolate drop cookies shaped like tree ornaments. Amanda preferred the ginger snaps, which looked like Santa Claus. Emilio was not particular, helping himself to all kinds of cookies as frequently as he could. "Growing boy," he explained to the girls, who giggled.

As last year, the only "un-holiday" actions were all the final exams in algebra and government classes, along with the magical theory ones.

Chapter 9—The Holidays

Lindsey remembered to notify their House Mother that Audrey and Pam would be traveling to her family's home for the holidays; that way the school bus schedules could be planned in advance. She also did her shopping online, ordering presents for her friends and family. However, she was uncertain what to get for Pam's parents and decided to ask her mother for help with that when she got back home.

The only unexpected news came from KMAG. It seems that William the Bold had escaped. Once again, Dominus and his men had broken one of their members out of jail.

"What's the bloody use in capturing them alive?" Emilio commented.

"They deserve a trial, but honestly what has become of our Department of Law anyway?" Pam replied.

"Some are here with us on the bus," Lindsey replied. They were on the school bus heading home for the holidays. Each bus now had four Department of Defense wizards riding along, in case of further trouble.

"Well, I passed my Grade 0 spells, Lindsey," Fern changed the subject. "I got every one of them done with a few minutes to spare."

"Well done Fern," Lindsey praised Amanda's young sister.

"Yes, good going, sis," Jim added. He was sitting beside Lindsey here at the back of the bus.

"This is going to be a great vacation," Pam added. "I never dreamed we would have nearly a month together."

"I hope I'm not an imposition," Audrey said solemnly, for about the tenth time.

"No way. Honestly, before I met you last year here at school, I had absolutely no friends at all. It was just my mother and me, no one else. Only now do I realize how much I missed. Everyone just made fun of me all the time, you know, no hands and all that. So this is going to be such a special Christmas!" Lindsey was truly happier than she'd ever been.

"We're only five miles away," Fern explained to Pam. "Actually, we are their nearest neighbors. Usually, we just ride over to her ranch."

"Don't worry, Audrey. One thing that mom has is horses. She still believes in farming with horses, not tractors. Actually, she's quite right about that," Lindsey explained. "For a small farm or ranch such as ours, the cost of a tractor and its upkeep greatly exceeds the money mom gets for her crops, but if she uses the horses, almost all is profit. That's how we've survived all these years, being very frugal. Now, things have changed, mom's remarried, Lloyd Compton, a Department of Defense man, and I have gotten my inheritance from my dad, so now the pressure is off her. Still, she likes to farm with the horses. I do hope you two know how to ride."

"I've seen a horse at the zoo once," Audrey said lamely.

"Don't worry," Pam explained. "I never rode much either, but Lindsey's horses are real tame. It is very easy. Will there be much snow on the ground?"

"At our old place, about this time of year, there might be six inches. By the dead of winter, maybe a foot or more," Lindsey answered. "Is that about right at our new ranch, Jim?"

"Yes, ought to be a bit of snow now. We can all go sledding down the arroyo. Dad has this big bobsled that seats four at one time. It's a blast. Whoosh!" Jim replied, making a hand gesture indicating great speed.

The bus stopped to let Emilio and his brother off in Pueblo. "See you all later. Happy Christmas everyone," Emilio called out as he climbed off the bus. Everyone waved to him.

"We're the last stop," Fern explained to Audrey and Pam, who had never been on this particular bus. Pam's bus took a more northerly route, while Audrey's came directly from Denver, fully loaded at the start. A half hour later, it was just the Whitewater clan, Sandy, Lindsey, and her two friends left. "Not long now. We're all supposed to get off at Lindsey's place. Mom and dad are meeting us there."

"Right," Tom added. "They say things have gotten a bit rough or rowdy these past few months. I guess we'll soon see what they mean."

"Well, I'm glad that I didn't volunteer to work at the

casino over the holidays this year. It can get rather rough in there," Sandy added. "I'm going to just relax. Honestly, gang, the courses just keep on getting harder and harder. Fifth year is a royal pain! I've hardly had any free time at all!" Tom gave her a tight squeeze, and she smiled at him.

Jimmy, their bus driver now decked out in holiday clothes, called out, "Barron Ranch. Merry 'is'mas everyone." He still had not gotten his two missing front teeth replaced, making it hard to understand him. The giant yellow bus appeared before the front porch of her new ranch house. Quickly, everyone climbed off the bus and fetched their large duffle bags from the cargo hold beneath the seating level.

Their breaths froze in the chilly air. Indeed, a half foot of snow covered the ground, but the snow on the grounds before the ranch house was hard packed from constant traffic. As the group threw their bags over their shoulders, the front door opened, Lena called out, "Welcome, come on in before you freeze. Everyone's inside waiting. Hot cocoa all around." Lindsey grinned; she was very happy to see her mother again. Playing host to so many had rekindled a spark of life that had gone out of Lena many years ago. Lindsey could never remember her mother looking so happy.

The large group tromped inside, depositing their bags just inside the door. Pam's mother was there, as well as R. B. and Luci. Lloyd stood beside Lena as the introductions flew. "Mom, dad, this is Audrey Lemon. Audrey, this is my mom, Lena, and new dad, Lloyd Compton." To Audrey's surprise, Lena gave her a warm hug, something an adult had never done for her. Even Lloyd gave her a friendly hug as well.

Lindsey continued, "Audrey, this is R. B. and Luci Whitewater, well actually, Running Bear and Lucinda Morning Dove. R. B., Luci, this is Audrey, the plant genius who got us all past biology class this fall!"

Fern added, "Mom, she is a true genius with plants! I have to show Audrey my flowers in my room really soon!"

"A wise person knows their plants," R. B. pronounced with some importance, which escaped Lindsey.

Pam then did her introduction, "Everyone, this is my mother, Polly, and my dad, Fred. He's head of the Department of Magical Misuse in Sterling. I didn't think you'd be here this soon," she added, giving them both a big hug.

Polly was a slightly portly woman, distinctly not particularly attractive, yet she had that personality that made you feel completely at ease around her. She was also a witch, who loved to make quilts. Fred was rather short, with a well-trimmed, small black moustache. His beady eyes took in everything around him. Around Fred, one had the sense that he knew absolutely everything that was going on.

"Well, Pam, I wanted to at least greet you, but I will be very honest with all of you. I came today to ask that you give me a full account of what has been happening at Bradbury's. Pam's told me about the recent bombings, but I need to hear it from those who were there. I know this is not quite what you young folks may want to do the first instant that you are home, but this Dominus business is becoming a major problem."

"Well, they cannot talk without some warm cocoa and cookies," Lena suggested. She and Polly went to get them, while Lloyd and Fred conjured sufficient chairs for everyone.

"We could talk in private if you prefer," Fred suggested.

"It's okay with me. I'm sure that R. B. and Luci and mom and dad and Polly all want to hear it first hand as well," Lindsey replied. "Oh by the way, R. B., it works really well." The old inventor smiled at Lindsey and nodded. Since everyone else had no idea what she meant, she took out her rabbit's foot. "I'll explain it later on."

For the next hour, everyone sat spellbound as the girls related what had happened, starting with the bus breakdown on their way to school in August. Even though Lena had almost no idea of the magical things, she did realize that her daughter had saved people's lives and had helped capture the latest bomber, and that pleased her immensely.

Eventually, Lindsey got to the latest bombing. "There I was, along with Deiter, standing by the windows on the third floor. I was helping Amanda with her spells. Professor Thalmus was sitting on his desk also by the windows, watching all of us. That's when the rabbit's foot began jumping around wildly in my pocket."

R. B. interrupted her, "See, Luci, I told you it would

work. Gave her some warning, it did."

"Dad, can I have one too?" asked Amanda.

"Me too," put in Fern.

"Don't forget us," Jim and Tom added.

R. B. just laughed. "So now *you* want one of your old dad's inventions, do you?" he teased them. Everyone chuckled. Lindsey continued with her story, aided by Amanda.

Amanda explained, suspecting that her parents would be very worried, "You see, I figured with Lindsey having her Staff of Power with her that we could take down this bomber person. That's why I decided to go after him. I was right. Her staff is powerful."

Lindsey had watched Fred as they told their tales. His eyes confronted all three girls in turn, never missing a word. Though he wrote nothing down, Lindsey had the sense that he could quote back precisely what had been said. He exuded confidence.

At last Fred spoke, "I can see that Governor Alister is precisely correct. Pam, you are rapidly becoming a powerful Sleuth. There is no doubt about that in my mind any longer. In these dark times that are coming, we need all the Sleuths we can get. I'm proud of you, daughter. There is also no doubt, R. B., that your daughter, Amanda is a natural born Tracker. I've only known a few wizards who could spot the magical traces that she does and at her young age. Lloyd, Lena, there is certainly even less doubt that Lindsey is taking after her father, becoming a Dispeller. In fact, I have searched the records that are confidential, mind you, and found that there has *never* been a student yet who casts non-verbal, non-wand in their first year. Lindsey may well develop into the world's greatest Dispeller of magic."

"Don't let my praise go to your heads, girls. You are only in your second year, and you have so much yet to learn. However, I wanted to verify these things for myself. I will let you in on a little secret. Governor Alister is a keen judge of people and their skills. In fact, he has been allowing each of you three to tackle what he feels you can actually master. If he thought for an instant that you couldn't have taken the bomber or that the bomber might have harmed either you or Deiter, he would have acted sooner. I suspect Alister arrived when he did to keep you three from actually killing the Death Stalker, though in hindsight, it might have been better had he let you, seeing how Dominus broke him out of jail. I'm telling you three this so that you can trust him fully."

"It has been my great pleasure meeting all of you at last. I must get back to work, but I will try to be here on Christmas Eve. Lena, thank you ever so much for putting up with us over the holidays." He kissed her hand, and Lena blushed, feeling happy that she could share her home with his family. Then, he put on his coat and simply vanished.

Pam whispered, "Teleport spell." Lindsey smiled, that was one spell she wanted to learn.

"Okay kids, before you do anything else, here are the rules," Lloyd explained. "R. B. backs me one hundred percent on this. No traveling anywhere beyond the main buildings of either homestead without going in groups of four. There has been a good deal of trouble brewing between some local ranchers, the whites in Arapahoe, the gamblers, and the Indians on the reservation. Nasty stuff, this Dominus Manifesto thing. We parents figure that four of you together ought to be able to handle any nasty business that should develop. Understood?" All nodded.

"Good. Other than that, there are no rules, except help around here as you can. Have fun; it's Christmas!"

"Okay, kids, time for us to head home. Grab your things and hang on to your mom and me," R. B. said. Lindsey had no idea what he meant, so she watched the Whitewaters gathering their coats and duffle bags.

A round of goodbye's, see-you-later's, and email-me's ensued. At last, all of them, including Sandy, were touching their parents, who held hands. R. B. said one word, and they all vanished, arriving in their front room in the next instant.

"Well, then, Audrey, Pam, let's show you where your rooms will be, and Lindsey can show you around the place. I figured you girls would want to bunk together, so you all are in Lindsey's room. Polly is in the guest room. Make yourselves comfortable. Lunch is in an hour."

Lindsey took her friends into her room. Sure enough,

Lloyd had conjured two more beds, creating a triple bunk bed. "I'm on the bottom, those are my blankets, and so you two can fight over who wants to be on top." They giggled, but Pam wanted to sleep on the top bunk. Lloyd had also conjured two small dressers and added two more chairs around Lindsey's table. Now they had a place to operate their laptops and store their things.

"Your parents are so cool, both of yours, I mean," Audrey gushed, as she stowed her few possessions. "You two are very lucky to have such wonderful folks, and Amanda's are great too, only they really are Apaches aren't they? I've never known any real Indians before. They're just like regular people."

"Wait til you see their unusual home, designed and built by R. B.," Pam added.

"Say, there are only three of us here. How are we supposed to travel over to the Whitewaters, if we have to go in fours?" asked Lindsey. As if someone were reading her mind, her computer beeped, indicating an incoming email had arrived.

It was from Jim. She opened it.

Hi,

I've learned my Teleport spell. When you three want to come over, Message me and I'll come over and bring you, either by spell or by horse. Horse is more fun; spell is faster. If I am not here, Tom or even Sandy can get you.

Love,

Jim

She blushed at the closing, but relayed the answer to how they would travel the five miles back and forth.

Once they had unpacked, Lindsey took them on a tour, mostly for Audrey's benefit, since Pam had been here during the summer. Over lunch, Lloyd suggested, "Say, after lunch would you three like to come lend me a hand getting our Christmas tree? I found a really nice pine growing on the southeastern fence line."

"You are not going to cut down a real, living tree are you?" asked Audrey, rather shocked.

"Oh no, no, no. I'm bringing it roots and all, in a big pot.

After we are done with it, I'll put it back into the ground so it can continue to thrive. I'm just changing its location for a short while. Only the norms cut down the trees, a rather barbaric practice, but then they really have no choice if they want a real tree. I know many prefer the artificial trees, but there is no comparison to a real live tree, not in my book." Audrey was very relieved to hear this.

After lunch, he told them to bundle up. It was quite cold outside. He and Lindsey harnessed up old Arthur, Lena's draft horse, a light brown Percheron, to their buggy. The girls loved the three mile buggy ride through the snow-covered landscape. They watched fascinated as he worked his magical spells, leaving a huge hole where the tree's roots ran deep. Even more interesting was the extra-dimensional pot in which he placed the tree. The pot appeared as if it was barely a foot tall, yet fully supported the tree. With their help, he secured it to the rear of the buggy, and they rode back home. To Lindsey, the cold, fresh air felt fabulous.

The rest of the afternoon, the girls decorated the tree, sometimes using a bit of magic, other times, making old-fashioned paper ornaments. After a warm supper and helping with the dishes, the three retired to Lindsey's room. Interestingly enough, Pam spotted a piece of paper Lindsey had left on her dressed last summer when she left for school. It bore the names of the Rat Pack members.

Having nothing to absorb her attention, Pam stared at the paper.

Samuel Rabnor, Dispeller

Able Monument, Tracker

William West, Eliminator

Mabel Pruit, Diviner

While the other two began listening to music over Lindsey's old radio, Pam doodled. R a b n o r was then rewritten B a r r o n. Clever, she thought to herself. Suddenly, she remembered something that Lindsey had shown her, the letter from her father. "Lindsey, can I see that letter from your father, please?" Lindsey retrieved it from her jewelry box, where she kept the few things that were most precious to her, one of which was her dad's letter to her.

Pam skimmed to the bottom, and read: "PS. If the world goes bad again, seek out Able and Bill. We all did the same with our names." That was it! Their names. They scrambled the letters of their real names. No sense messing with Mabel; she had been brutally slain by the Death Stalkers. She started with Able, writing out the letters: a b l e m o n u m e n t. Now came the hard part, rearranging them.

"What are you doing?" asked Lindsey, when she saw Pam writing letters and then crossing them out.

"We all did the same with our names. Rabnor becomes Barron. I am trying to figure out the other two," Pam said excitedly.

"Golly, I wish you had a Scrabble set," Audrey suggested. "That would make this lots easier to do."

"We've got one somewhere," Lindsey replied. "I'll go ask mom." A few minutes later, she returned with the worn set. "She and dad have been playing it quite a lot." Pam took out the necessary letters for Able, while Lindsey took out those for Bill.

"I think I need lots of help, Audrey." Her friend also took out the same set of letters. "Gosh, there sure isn't much you can make from West, is there?" Lindsey said, becoming frustrated quickly.

"Well, Able isn't easy either," Pam replied. The three played with the letters for some time.

Audrey suddenly said, "Say, you can at least get Wilma out of it, though that doesn't help much, I mean Bill is a guy."

"True, if you take out Wilma, what's left anyway?" Lindsey commented, fiddling with the letters. Let's see, w e s t l i. What can you make out of that anyway? W e l t s i."

Pam let out a screech, quickly covering her mouth. Lindsey nearly knocked over her letter holder. Both stared at Pam. "That's—that's—that's my Aunt Wilma. You remember, you met her last summer. Wilma Weltsi. What a coincidence indeed, shocking. Better keep on trying though," Pam suggested.

Audrey, having given up on Bill's letters, looked over Pam's shoulder. "Say, you can make Tumble out of it. What goes with Tumble anyway? Strange for a last name, Tumble."

"Oh no!" exclaimed Lindsey. "Wasn't R. B.'s sister's last name Tumble? We met her last summer too."

"Weird coincidences! Yes, Tumble, but her first name was a strange one, Indian probably. What was it?" Pam fiddled with the remaining five letters. Shortly, she exclaimed, "Monane."

"Right that was it, Monane Tumble. Why?" Lindsey replied.

"Able's letters spell Monane Tumble," Pam declared. "This is really too weird, too spooky!"

"Tell me about it. In all those pictures of the Rat Pack, Bill and Able were most definitely guys, not women," Lindsey said.

"But wasn't Dominus being you, Lindsey, last year, I mean?" asked Audrey.

Pam stared at Lindsey, who stared at Pam, mouths open wide. Lindsey spoke first, "Both of those two women insisted on hearing all about everything we did last year, remember? They sat there on the couch and made us tell them every detail! You don't suppose?"

"No, it is more like some strange coincidence, that's all. I haven't got any real problem to work on, and my mind is going off the deep end," Pam conceded.

Lena poked her head into the room. "Hey, are any of you up to playing a game of Scrabble with us older folks?" The rest of the evening was spent in the front room. The girls found the three adults more than a match for them, especially Lena, who kept coming up with the strangest words that made quite a lot of points.

After Lena skunked them three times, Polly commented, "Lena, I would never have expected a rancher woman to have the incredible vocabulary that you possess. The way you pull those words out of the hat is amazing. You are one mean Scrabble player." Everyone chuckled.

Lena's answer did not surprise Lindsey. "When you live alone out here on the High Plains, with no neighbors for miles, a dictionary is comforting, especially if you have to home school your daughter."

"I didn't know Lindsey was home schooled," Lloyd

commented.

"She had to walk to school, no buses. When the snow got too deep, starting around this time of year, I'd home school her until the spring thaws came. Actually, it worked better for her; she had no hands at that time and had an awful time in school. It nearly broke my heart everyday she had to go the Plano school. They picked on her and teased her something horrible."

"What an admirable thing to have done for her, Lena," Polly replied. "You've done such a fantastic job with her. Well done indeed!" Lena smiled. Until this instant, no one had ever complimented her on her six years of home teaching.

The next morning bundled up against the cold, Lindsey took Audrey and Pam on a tour of their ranch buildings. While doing some of the chores so her mother would have more time with the guests, Lindsey showed them her horse, Betsy, and the other dozen that they now had. Her mom had acquired four more horses during the fall, and she had to examine them herself.

"This place is huge," Audrey commented, never having been on a real western ranch before.

"Oops," Lindsey exclaimed, as a paper message appeared before her eyes.

Aunt Monane is coming for a visit this afternoon. She wants to speak with you and Pam. I'll come get you three at noon. Okay? J.

"Strange coincidence," Pam suggested, as Lindsey relayed the news. "Wonder what she wants?"

They had just finished eating when Jim knocked on their front door. Lindsey dashed to let him inside. Lena called out, "Hi, Jim. We're just finishing lunch. Want some?"

"No, ma'am. My aunt is coming for a visit and wants to talk to Lindsey and Pam. What time do you want them back?" Jim replied formally.

"Suppertime," Lena answered.

The three girls grabbed their coats and bags and stepped outside. Audrey blurted out, more than a little excited about this novel adventure, "This is exciting. I've never been teleported before. How does it feel? What do I have to do? I've heard it can be dangerous."

"Just hold on to my hands," Jim said reassuringly. "True enough on the simple Teleport spell you will learn next year. If you land low, your feet may be under ground; that's gotta hurt. However, I always aim a little above ground; that's infinitely safer. You ready?" All three took a deep breath and held it, as if they might have to hold on for a long time.

"Why are you holding your breaths?" Jim asked, as they arrived just outside his family's front porch.

"Oh! We're there! I didn't feel anything," Audrey commented, letting out her breath. Lindsey felt a little silly as well.

"Hi all," Amanda said, coming outside, bundled up as well. "Welcome to the Whitewater ranch. This is the house."

"But it looks like a pile of dirt. Where's the roof? That sloping ground?" asked a confused Audrey.

"Yes, everyone does a double take. Dad built it out of natural materials. The walls are three feet thick and most is underground. The roof really is earth with prairie grass growing on top. It's cool in the summer without air conditioning and warm in the winter. Quite a cozy nest, once you get used to it. Come on. I'll show you my horse and the barn. Oh yes, all the bits of junk you see out here aren't junk. They are dad's magical inventions." They walked to the barn. Jim snuck his arm around Lindsey's waist as they walked, and she blushed, joining hers to his.

"That there is a snow depth predictor of dad's," Fern came running up to them. "It tells you how deep the snow will get when there is a snow storm. See those rusty milk cans all around? Those are enemy detectors. If someone sets foot within the perimeter, an alarm goes off in the house." Fern was having fun chatting with Audrey, who kept looking utterly amazed at each new item.

"If you are here in the summer, we can go for long horse rides," Amanda suggested.

"Have to watch out for snakes though," Fern added.

Just then, Tom and Sandy appeared beside them. "Hi all," Sandy said. "Tom just came to fetch me. I get to spend the night with you, so whose room will I be sharing?" she teased.

"Mine of course," Amanda quickly added.

"Why not mine?" Fern broke in, slightly annoyed with the decision.

"Come on. Let's see if mom's still got the hot cocoa on the stove," Tom suggested. The group headed inside.

"Wow!" Audrey continued to comment as Amanda took her from room to room. "So much space; you wouldn't think so from outside. Really cozy!"

Finally, taking Audrey by the arm, Fern pulled her into her room. "What do you think of this?"

Audrey's mouth dropped. All along one earthen wall, a ledge had been carved. Now plants of a dozen varieties grew in the ledge. "I've got living walls," Fern proudly proclaimed. Audrey fell in love with Fern's room and while the others chatted in the living room, she and Fern went to work on her plants. Audrey spotted a bit of mold here and had all sorts of suggestions to help the plants become healthier than they were.

At one o'clock on the dot, the gong sounded, announcing the arrival of someone near their front door. "Tom, get that will you? It's probably your aunt," Luci called out from the kitchen. "I'm whipping up some snacks for them."

"Hi Aunt Monane," Tom said as he let her in. "Oh hi. You're Pam's aunt, right?"

Pam heard her aunt's voice saying, "Yes, Wilma, Wilma Weltsi. Tom, right?"

Tom took their coats and led them into the front room, where everyone was sitting around the various sofas. As usual, the place was a mess. Papers, magazines, an old pizza box, and soda cans lay where they had been left from the night before. "Ignore the mess, Aunt Monane, we sort of had a welcome home party last night. Slept in today," Jim hastened to explain.

Having heard her aunt's voice, Fern brought Audrey with her to meet them. Soon, it was introductions all around. Luci entered floating a large tray loaded with Christmas goodies. "What would you like to drink?" she asked Monane.

"Dear, could we have some of your special peppermint tea? I've been telling Wilma here about how fabulous it is, you can't beat home grown plants." Rather pleased with the compliment, Luci dashed back to the kitchen to brew a pot. The children all had hot cups of cocoa.

Once more, Lindsey guessed that Wilma, R. B, and Monane were in their late thirties. Wilma was very fit, strong boned, a no nonsense type of woman. She still wore her brown hair short, in an easy to care for style. Wilma's piercing eyes seemed even more so that last summer. As before, Wilma's handshake was firm and solid. Monane was an Apache, with long, black hair and darker skin, very similar to Amanda's appearance. She too was quite fit. Again, Lindsey noticed that her eyes did not miss a thing. Like Wilma's, she greeted her with a solid shake.

After a bit of pleasant conversation, during which Jim and Tom continued to vanish the trash that they had left here from the night before, Audrey and Fern went back to their plant doctoring. Monane said, "Well, it's time that we had our private chat with these three girls. Would you mind seeing that we are not overheard or interrupted, Tom?"

Despite his unbridled curiosity, Tom knew that his aunt meant what she said. "Sure thing. Come on, Sandy. This is an open invitation to come to my room." Sandy flushed, but eagerly rose to follow him out. Shrugging, Jim left as well, leaving the two older women alone with Pam, Lindsey, and Amanda.

Monane began quite serious, "Girls, things are going quite bad in the world around us, almost as bad as fifteen years ago. Never has the school been bombed nor the bus attacked. Please tell us all about it, all the details, starting with the bus attack in late August."

Once more, Lindsey and Amanda related what had happened. Pam told about the bleachers and the bomb there. Soon, the three found themselves relating nearly everything that they had done, including the latest episode with the strange bomb and their capture of the Death Stalker.

"That is the strangest bomb that I've ever heard about," exclaimed Monane, very perplexed. "Did Alister say anything about it?"

"No, it was, well, different, you know," Pam tried to

explain. "The other two bombs—they were C-4 explosions, but this one didn't so much explode as it sucked out everything, like an implosion. I ought to have been researching this one, now that you mention it. I'm slipping in my detective work." She looked a bit forlorn. She'd been overlooking a significant clue, she thought.

Wilma whispered, "Pam, while you are researching it, try the key words magical and implosion. That ought to get you on the right path." Pam looked very grateful for the tip.

That reminded Lindsey of the weird coincidence they found last night with the letters of their names. "Monane, Wilma, you won't believe the strangest coincidence we uncovered last night; well mostly it was Pam's doing. You see, my dad changed his last name when he went into hiding, r a b n o r to b a r r o n. We've been looking for clues to the other Rat Pack members, you know, Able and Bill. In my dad's last letter, he suggested that, 'If the world goes bad again, seek out Able and Bill. We all did the same with our names.' Well, we fiddled with the names, Able Monument and William West. You'll never guess what else can be spelled with those letters! Monane Tumble and Wilma Weltsi. Weird, isn't that?"

Wilma waved her wand. In the air between the girls and the two women, the names appeared in glowing scarlet letters:

Able Monument and William West.

Below them appeared the letters:

Monane Tumble and Wilma Weltsi.

She said softly, "Cat's out of the bag. Bright girls, Monane."

Monane replied, "At your service, girls. How may we help you?"

"You, you, you are Able and Bill, the Rat Pack?" Pam had a difficult time putting her words together.

"None other," Monane answered. "You see when we formed our little group in secret, your dad, Lindsey, gave us the idea. He said that for our own safety, we two should be disguised, particularly so, because we're women. Sam came up with the plan. He acquired many samples from two homeless derelicts. Mabel brewed up a large supply of Polymorph Potion. After all, this world would more readily accept Able and Bill in the roles we wanted to play, than they would accept two women. In the end, Sam's idea saved our lives, because no one other than our group knew the identity of Able and Bill. After Mabel was murdered, we all went into hiding. Your dad changed his name, following our lead."

Wilma took up the story from here. "You see, after I subdued Dominus and his men, we wanted to continue our work and round up the remainder of the Death Stalkers, and then go after those in high places who were supporting and aiding Dominus and his men. However, we underestimated the men's influence, and they managed to get our funds and authority withdrawn, saying that Dominus was captured and the rest didn't matter. Ha! The heck it didn't matter! Now here we are right back where we started, only we don't have Sam anymore."

"Without Sam, a Dispeller, we don't stand much chance of apprehending Dominus. Worse, without Mabel to give us a clue where he may strike next, we are nearly powerless. A double whammy, so to speak. However, girls, you three are showing incredible promise, simply amazing. Lindsey, you are so like your dad in many ways, and yet you are so far ahead of where he was when he was in his second year. He didn't start going non-verbal until late in his fourth year!" Wilma explained.

"That's true. Girls, we've decided that you three need more protecting while you are at school and around here," Monane continued. "After his encounter with you, Lindsey—in the cabin last year, where you disrupted his plans for the rod, while handless and with your mouth sewn shut—we suspected that you finally got the attention of Dominus. It would have certainly gotten our attention. However, we only had suspicions, but this latest attack on you specifically, Lindsey, suggests to us that Dominus has his eye on you. While he probably doesn't consider you a real threat, as methodical as he is, he will still try to eliminate you, though it certainly isn't his top priority."

Monane continued, "Lindsey, I see you are still wearing your dad's ring and pin. Continue to do so; this is very important. Whenever you need us, Message Able Monument first. As a Tracker, she can follow the magical energy trail left by your message to her and find wherever you are, so you don't have to reveal where you are located. Send the message silently. With the ring and pin on you, no one else can overheard or read your thoughts and will not know what you are doing or asking in the message. This is critical for our safety as well; without Sam, our Dispeller, we are quite vulnerable to Dominus and his men and their combined spells."

"Only this time around," Wilma broke in, "I will spell to kill! I've had enough of this leniency to these evil men!"

Though still in awe with this discovery and in the presence of such powerful witches, Pam still had a thought, "Who else knows about you? I mean that you are *the* Rat Pack survivors."

Monane answered, "At this time, most have retired from public service or have passed away. However, there is still one who knows how to contact us, though he doesn't know our identities. We still trust him, as we have always trusted him, Governor Alister Broadwell."

The three gasped. "Well, that makes sense," Pam replied first, before the others could.

"There are still a number of good men in the government. Pam, your father is one of them. As time goes on, expect to begin seeing the true colors of many of our so called public servants," Wilma added sarcastically.

"Someone ought to document those who are on the side of Dominus. After he gets captured, they'd know who also to arrest," Pam said, more to herself than the others.

"Get proof positive, undeniable proof. They will try to weasel out of nearly anything. Then make sure it cannot be stolen or destroyed or compromised. Once they know it exists, they will definitely go after it, trying to confiscate, steal, or destroy the proof, to say nothing of you," Wilma stated flatly.

"Wilma, you are scaring the poor girl," Monane complained. "Just be careful if you do this, dear." She softened the harsh reality that began to dawn on Pam. This was not some fun puzzle to be worked out, rather a life and death matter. "Our advice to you three is keep your eyes peeled for a really hot Diviner and a good Eliminator. The odds are that none are at Bradbury's or we would have heard about them already. Alister is pretty good at spotting native talent."

Amanda asked, "Aunt Monane, do you have any idea who the Mad Bomber might be? He's tried it twice now. We don't know if it is the same one who caused the bus breakdown. Should we suspect he will blow up more things?"

"No clue, dear. That's where Mabel was invaluable. She could predict with good certainty where they would strike, though not always accurately on the time of their strike," her aunt replied.

Lindsey began to see the larger picture. "So Pam can Sleuth and find out things after the fact, where as a Diviner predicts future events."

"That's right, dear," Monane replied.

"Well, then wouldn't having both a Diviner and a Sleuth on the team make it even better?" she asked.

"Absolutely, but finding them is the challenge. There are three Dispellers currently active in the world, but none are anywhere near as good as Sam was. We know of five Diviners, but they are not very accurate, and three are of questionable ethics. We know ten capable Trackers personally. No offense, Wilma, but Eliminators are the easiest to find; they just have to be fast and furious on their attacking spells, creatively using them to entangle or kill their opponents. But don't get me wrong, it's not easy being an Eliminator."

"Often, you find yourself facing down ten wizards, anyone of which could easily kill you, if they got off the right spell in time. Eliminators have an uncanny sense of how fights go. With spells going in all directions, the Eliminators just know what to cast and at whom and at the right time. That's tons easier than trying to figure out how to keep us alive amongst all those flying spells. Sam was brilliant at it. Lindsey, we both miss your father too. We were all very close, dear friends." Both women reflected for a minute, as if their loss had only just happened, yet it had been so many years ago.

Once more, Lindsey felt her great grief and sorrow over the loss of her father, but she also saw tears welling in both women's eyes. No longer was it just Lena and Lindsey morning

Sam's death. Two others had loved him as well. She took strength in this knowledge.

After a moment of silence, Monane said, "Amanda, when you finish school, I'll personally train you as a Tracker, teaching you everything that I know. For now, your job is to stay alive and graduate from Bradbury's." Amanda grinned, quite pleased.

"I know that you don't know anything about Dispellers, but I would love to know more about my father, as a wizard. I have my memories when I was little, but he had forsaken magic then," Lindsey asked.

"Dear, he had not forsaken magic. He did what he had to do to take the heat off Monane and me and to stay alive himself. He was one of the few people that we've ever known that could face down ten wizards and witches, know somehow what spell each was about to cast, and handle that one spell keeping us in the fight."

Wilma sighed, her old memories coming back to her. "We were all in school together, Bradbury's. Oh, Sam, he was a rogue, a jokester, loved to do silly things, like the children's cartoons on TV. What's that rabbit's name? Oh, yes, Bugs Bunny. He fancied himself Bugs, always going around doing what ought to be impossible, yet silly things. That's how he got his nickname, Looney, you see. He even got Mabel to try smoking cigarettes, Remember, Monane, how green sick she became? Almost fainted. That's how she got her nickname, Green, for green sick. Sam never let her forget that episode."

"Ah, those two were quite a pair—always thinking up new ways to create a little mischief, they were," Monane replied, remembering their early school days as well. "You remember how they got old Delius Dogs?"

"Yes, I still laugh about it sometimes," Wilma reminisced. "Delius can be so dark and humorless, you know. Well, one day when we all arrived in his classroom, just as Delius was about to start lecturing to us, why, up popped this skeleton with fake, cherry red lips. Before anyone could do anything, the skeleton said, 'I love you, Delius!' and kissed him on his lips, transferring the red lipstick. Immediately after that, the skeleton disintegrated into a pile of dust, while saying, 'Brought to you by Looney and Green.' The whole class roared. Delius never did figure out who Looney and Green were."

"Golly, Monane, look at the time. I had better get back before I am missed," Wilma said. "Again, dears, if you ever need some assistance, Message Able Monument; Able and Bill will come to the rescue," she winked at the three girls. Hastily, the two women went to say goodbye to Luci, promising to return during the holidays.

A while later, Jim asked, "Well, what did my aunt want with you three anyway?"

Amanda replied, "They told Lindsey and us some stories about her father, Sam, when they were in school. He really got Delius Dogs a good one. I'll tell you about it later."

Before he could protest, R. B. came into the room. "Ah, still here, good, good. Pam, Amanda, I have these for you." He handed them each a rabbit's foot. "Keep them on your person at all times. If trouble is about to strike, the foot will jump around warning you. I figure that you two need them as much as Lindsey."

"Wow! Thank you, R. B.," exclaimed Pam, awed by the gift of a magically enchanted item.

"Thanks, dad!" Amanda gave him a big hug.

"What about me?" Jim said.

"You aren't in any danger, excepting possibly flunking your math class," R. B. teased his son. Jim knew better than to call him on this one. He was struggling in math.

Tom and Sandy came into the living room. Tom suggested, "Hey, why don't we all go make a huge snowman. It's the season for snowmen."

"But the snow is dry. It won't pack," protested Fern. She and Audrey had finished caring for her plants and had come to see what the others were doing.

"Use your Warm spell on the snow and then it packs nice. Come on," Tom insisted. Everyone bundled up, going outside to play and to build the giant snowman. When they finished, he stood ten feet tall, as though he was guarding the Whitewater ranch.

As they stood around pooped but satisfied with their

handiwork, the three rabbit's feet of the girls began to jump around in their pockets. "Trouble coming," Lindsey called out, as the sounds of three snowmobiles grew louder, coming their way rapidly. Suddenly, the three machines came sliding around the group, circling them, before the drivers stopped.

A tall, thin boy, probably eighteen, climbed off and walked up to Amanda. "We're here to warn you, Amanda Whitewater. You lay off hurting Death Stalkers or we're going to hurt you!"

"I'd be careful what you say, Lone Wolf. You're just a big coward," Amanda swore back at him. Lindsey guessed Amanda must know him, since he was definitely another Apache. Lindsey kept her eyes moving from man to man, trying to sense what they might do. Tom, Jim, and Sandy already were forming a barrier between the three and the younger girls. If the three tried anything, they would be greatly outnumbered. Lindsey guessed that this was what was going through their minds.

"You watch your back, Amanda! We have your number. Dominus rules!" Lone Wolf threatened.

Just then, R. B. came out of the house, actually using a magical door, so that he appeared in front of his daughter. "Freeze!" he commanded, with a startling wave of his wand. All three men froze, unable to move. "Forget! Confuse! Flee!" he did three more quick flashes with this wand.

Lone Wolf said, "Huh?" and looked around, wondering where he was. Hastily, he gunned his engine and roared back toward Arapaho. His cronies followed him.

"Stupid idiots!" R. B. muttered, as he stepped back through his door into his workroom.

"Whoa! Now *that* was cool magic! Your dad is *really* hot!" Pam exclaimed.

"Well, I was hoping for some fireworks, some real damage," Jim replied, slightly disappointed.

"No, this was better. They don't remember what happened, only that they were spooked off the ranch," Amanda countered.

"Who were they?" Lindsey asked.

"Local thugs," Sandy answered. "They have been

causing trouble in town and around the casino for years now. One day, they will go too far and get what's coming to them. Things have been going downhill all year long."

"It will only get worse, until Dominus and his gang are captured again," Luci said; she'd come out to see what the trouble was. "Why don't you all come inside and taste one of my new recipes. I got it from a relative in the Midwest. It's called pumpkin bread. Let me know if you like it." Everyone loved it.

Christmas morning, just as everyone hopped out of bed, Fred Betts finally returned, looking rather haggard. He'd been up all night long, but department business was all that he would say. Overnight, the pile of presents beneath the tree had grown. However, Lena insisted that everyone have Christmas breakfast before tackling the presents.

She and Polly served up a scrumptious breakfast, bacon, eggs, and waffles with real maple syrup. With the dishes magically cleaned and put away by Polly, faster than Lena and the girls could bring them into the kitchen, Lloyd announced, "Time for presents. I wonder if you have all been good girls this year? Will Santa be good to you?" Everyone chuckled at his tease.

With so many staying here, the pile was enormous. Hence, Lloyd took the expedient approach. He used a bit of magic to sort out the presents, making a small pile before each person. Eagerly, the girls tackled theirs first, while the parents watched and took some photos.

Some of the presents directly affected their lives. Pam opened the large present from Lindsey. Her eyes nearly popped out of her head. "This is a *real* fingerprint kit!"

"Yes, it is the real thing, an official CSI portable fingerprint lab. It has a mini-gas chamber for the super glue thing, a mini-scanner, the works," Lindsey replied.

"There are enough powders to take a thousand prints!" Pam exclaimed. "Wow! Thanks, Lindsey." Pam also had some idea of its cost, several hundred dollars, so it wasn't a cheap present.

Lindsey had given Amanda a magical ring that would store three spells of her choosing. Of all the presents Lindsey gave out this year, this one was the most expensive. With Amanda risking her neck, she wanted to give her something in the way of a backup. A Staff of Power was terribly expensive, but this ring would really help her out.

Audrey opened her small box from Lindsey. She also gasped. She had not really expected to receive significant presents, perhaps some socks, that sort of thing. Her hands held a tin of wild flower seeds, extremely rare seeds! She knew that a tin of this size with these very rare plants was very expensive indeed. Tears clouded her eyes, as she hugged Lindsey, who said, "You can plant some on our ranch, if you can't find anywhere else to plant them."

Lindsey gave Emilio a very expensive and very appropriate handheld calculator, in hopes that it would alleviate the many math errors he constantly made. She gave her mother a new sewing machine. Luci had made her another one of her special Indian blankets turned into a sort of serape with hood. Amanda had a closet full of them and couldn't see why all three wore theirs every day of the vacation. Polly gave everyone a handmade quilt, each with different patterns. Lindsey's had various colored Dutch windmills on hers. However, Polly explained to everyone that she, with R. B.'s help, had enchanted the quilts. Each one would automatically adjust to the temperature of the person sleeping beneath it, either warming them or cooling them as needed. Lena could not get over how fantastic a gift this was.

Pam's father gave her a very special gift. All the information was typed nicely on a paper. Located within the secure Department of Magical Misuse, Sterling, Colorado, and alongside the department's huge servers was Pam's new personal server computer. It came equipped with one hundred terabytes of disk space and was accessible via her laptop. She had been given her own personal login to the department's network, and from there, with triple security walls, she could get to her server. The heightened security virtually guaranteed that no one but Pam could get to her machine. Lindsey guessed that Fred had known just how often Pam had "borrowed" the department's server and was now giving her one of her own, along with legal access to the department's server.

Jim gave Lindsey a birth stone ring, set with a magnificent Moonstone. Her mother gave her another stylish prom dress and a large collection of hose and some designer shoes with little heels to match. Lloyd gave Lindsey a very special gift. Inside an unbreakable box were four potion bottles, each containing a healing draught, similar to the potions that Dominus had drunk to save his life last year. A tiny note said, "Use these wisely." She gave him a big hug and kiss.

Pam gave Lindsey three more books on the art of Dispelling, two of which were quite rare and expensive. However, when Lindsey opened the small present from Audrey, tears came from her eyes. She held in her hand a hand carved, beautifully crafted, wooden doe. The expression on the doe combined with its body position expressed pure love, pure affinity. It was an incredible work of art!

In fact, Audrey's new friends received a similar carving, each suited to the personality of the person. "This is incredible, Audrey! It's so beautiful! I can feel the emotion from it!"

Audrey flushed. She had almost no money, never did have. Hence, she gave from her heart instead. Lindsey now understood those in Brown Hall far better. Audrey had captured emotions and efforts in wood. She was a virtuoso wood carver. Lena's was a draft horse, and she cried, so great was the emotion that she saw in the horse. Amanda's was a lean wolf. Pam's was a sly fox on the prowl.

Fred's was a black bear, rearing on its hind legs, its great teeth bared. Choked with emotion, he told Audrey, "Thank you, Audrey. Do you realize the incredibly high quality of your work? If you wish to market these, each one would bring at least a hundred dollars, maybe more. I have some connections, if you wish to pursue a venture with these. You could even be anonymous if you desire. These are perhaps the best carvings that I have ever seen. In fact, Audrey, they are so well done that they are even enchantable! If so, you could probably ask closer to five hundred to a thousand dollars a carving."

Audrey's mouth dropped. "You, you, you're kidding

me?" She just could not believe what she was hearing. They were just simple wood carvings, in which she tried very diligently to place the emotion and effort of the image. Fred took Audrey aside, and they chatted for over an hour. When they were finished, she appeared very pleased indeed.

Sometime later after all the presents had been opened and examined, Lena and Lloyd rose. He cleared his throat so that everyone looked at the two of them. "We have one more present to give out, a very special one indeed. It's for you, Audrey. Fred has told us of your particularly unique circumstances. What with the world going off its rockers at this time, we want to do something for you. Lena and I have decided that we want to give you a permanent home for as long as you desire, here with us. Whenever you are not away at school, we want you to come here and live with us, sort of like we have adopted you as our second daughter. Mind you, if you accept, you will have to do your share of the chores around here. We know that as of the start of school this fall, you have no home to back to when summer comes. We want you to consider this your home for as long as you desire. What say you, Audrey?"

In her nearly thirteen years of bouncing from unwanted home to unwanted home, virtually no one had ever shown her unrequited love. Suddenly, here it was being handed to her. She could only bawl in response, so overcome with emotions that she could not control, hardly ever having experienced them. Everyone had the decency to allow her time to recover. At last, she wailed, "Thank you!" and hugged them both tightly. There was not a dry eye in the room.

A bit later, Lloyd explained, "While you are all back at school, Lena and I will simply add on another bedroom for you, we want you to have your own room as well." Audrey just continued to cry for some time. At that moment, something deep within her clicked into place.

That night as the three girls lay on their beds chatting about their presents, Audrey quietly said, "I'm sorry Lindsey. I, I have sort of a confession to make. I sort of felt or knew or something that something good would come if I made everyone one of my wood carvings. I, I had no idea what, only that I ought to do it. Now, I sort of feel like I've rather bribed my way into your family. I'm sorry."

"You have not bribed your way, Audrey! Forget that! Mom and dad had already decided that long before you gave them your presents. I know them both. They didn't give this to you because of your presents. I honestly think that they rather like you and want to help keep you safe. You are one of the good guys, you know. So many are going over to Dominus's side these days. We good guys need to stick together."

"You're sure that I didn't somehow charm them into letting me stay here?" Audrey asked, still not convinced that she was not somehow responsible.

"Yes, you charmed them, but not the way you are thinking. You are a kind, warm, loving, gentle, terrific person, who is in dire need of a helping hand that they can easily give. In these times when evil is growing, my folks want to help as they can. Mom knows nothing about magic, but she is a great judge of people. She would not have made you the offer unless she really felt strongly that you were more than worthy of her help."

Audrey sighed; she felt very relieved at last. "I do love it here, and I've only been here less than two weeks! Your mom and dad are great." Lindsey smiled, that, she knew.

"I've managed to stay alive because I somehow know just the right thing to do at the right time, you know," Audrey admitted.

Pam's eyes opened wide; she knew that Audrey's statement was profoundly important, but just not what it meant or implied. Now she had another riddle to ponder. That night, she slept with her CSI kit beside her pillow, a prized possession.

Chapter 10—Avalanche

"Morning, Mrs. Compton," Audrey softly said as she wiped the sleep from her eyes the morning after Christmas. Pam and Lindsey were still sound asleep, though it was now nearly seven o'clock. Lena was up at dawn, as she did every day, fixing breakfast. The smell of coffee brewing filled the kitchen, though she already was sipping her peppermint tea.

"Please, just call me Lena, Audrey. What will you have? Bacon, eggs, toast?"

Audrey flashed her a smile, "The others all wanted to be called Mrs. this and that. Well, if it isn't an imposition, could I have all three, please? Thanks for having me stay with you and your family, Lena. I admit that I rather put where I was going to spend this summer kind of out of my mind, figuring to worry about that in May. Pam's father, Fred, he is going to help me set up a storefront from which I can sell some of my carvings. If he is right and they do sell, for the first time in my life I will have my own source of income, and I will use some to help out around here this summer."

"Dear, that's a grand plan," Lena replied, slipping three slices of crispy bacon onto the whole wheat bread, which had just popped out of the toaster. While she cracked two eggs into the skillet, she added, "It's important for everyone to contribute as they are able. Around a ranch, there is always a lot to do. What kind of wood do you need to have to carve? Maybe we have some scraps that you could use." She placed two sunny side up eggs onto the toast and gave it to Audrey.

Just then, the front door opened; a blast of cold and snowflakes showered the front room as Lloyd dusted himself off. "Going to be a blizzard today, I reckon. I've done as you've asked, Lena, got rope lines to the barn and house tied nicely. Do you really think we will need them?"

"Best to be prepared, Lloyd," she replied. Seeing the confusion on Audrey's face, she explained, "Sometimes out here on the high plains, we get some strong blizzards. Can't see a foot in front of you. Yet, we still have to take care of our animals in the barn. Horses must be fed and watered, chickens fed; even the barn cats need some assistance in the dead of winter. Yet if you go walking toward the barn in a blizzard, you're likely never to find it or find your way back to the ranch house. Hence, we string a rope between the two. Now a blind man can move between the two buildings."

Polly joined them, "I heard the morning weather report, though I admit it was for Sterling. Morning, Lena, Lloyd, Audrey."

"Blizzard coming? Bacon, eggs, toast?" asked Lena.

"Please, you are a dear! Bless you. I'll fix the lunch," Polly volunteered. "Yes, they say it is going to be a very nasty one this time. Bit unusual for late December, but not unheard of or so they say."

"What's unheard of?" asked Lindsey, wiping the sleep from her eyes. She and Pam came wandering into the dining room, joining the others. Polly explained about the blizzard.

After breakfast, the girls headed out to the barn to do the many chores, relieving the adults from this burden. Already the snow was coming down heavily, but visibility was still good, as they made their way to the barn. Pam learned how to milk cows by hand. The eggs were gathered, and the many animals were fed and watered.

Then, Lindsey showed Audrey the scrap woodpile. Audrey found both Osage orange posts and an old 4x4 mahogany post. The three, following Audrey's orders, used their spells to cut them into foot long chunks. "Can you see the images lying inside here?" she asked. "This one holds a fox; this one, a bear; this one, a tiger; and this mahogany block has a rhino inside, just begging to be released."

Try as they might, neither Pam nor Lindsey could see what Audrey saw in these blocks. Nevertheless, they helped her carry them back to the ranch house. They used the ropes for the return trip; visibility had dropped considerably while they had been in the barn. As they started walking, the ranch house was not visible any longer, a whiteout.

No sooner had the three entered the front door than the electricity went out. "Figures," they heard Lloyd's voice call out from the black room. "Light! Oh, hi kids. Power's out. I'll start up the generator now. Go give your mom some light, Lindsey; she and Polly are in the kitchen."

Quickly, the three cast their Light spells and headed for the kitchen. "Hi dear, power's out," Lena called out, having already lighted one oil lamp so they could see. Polly finally had her wand out and was casting Permanent Light spells around the ceiling for Lena. "Golly, in times like these it pays to be surrounded by witches," she jested. The girls giggled and helped them with other lanterns.

Lena placed one lantern in each room, along with a supply of matches. "Now then, as you know, magic can be, ah what's your word, oh yes, dispelled. So I've got a nice oil lantern in each room, just in case. I would expect the power to be off until long after the blizzard is over and the roads are cleared so the power company trucks can get through to repair the downed lines. Polly says that the blizzard may last for a couple days. Lloyd is cranking up our generator, which will power the furnace so we won't freeze. Plenty of LP gas for the stove; plenty of food in the pantry. Nothing to worry about."

"Let's go check on the weather," Lindsey suggested, and the three headed into their room and the old radio. While Pam continued to conduct her research and the establishment of her new server, Audrey worked quietly in one corner, carving her wooden blocks. Lindsey kept an ear on the weather news, while she emailed Emilio and Kathy, and then chatted on her phone with Amanda. Shortly, Fern and Amanda came over to spend the day with them, compliments of Jim and his spell. R. B. kept his sons busy around their ranch, preparing for the two feet of expected snow that his gauges told him was on the way.

Now with lots of free time, Pam finally began tracking down the clues that her father had suggested. All the video feeds from the jails were sent as well to another site. Via her father's computer, she watched the tampered video that had been used to suggest that Hank Wilkinson had committed suicide and that William the Bold had overpowered a guard to facilitate his escape. Now she needed to find the secondary storage facility, which may yet contain the unaltered video, since only the installer and few others knew even existed.

Her reasoning went thus: cabling to another off site

location would be prohibitively expensive. It had to be wireless. Sure enough, looking over the details of the installation parts, she found a relay transmitter that used a strange frequency, 850 MHz. This was just outside the assigned frequencies for a mobile to base transmission from a popular company that provided wireless connections. Pam then determined just where the transmitter had been installed, typically on the building's roof. From the GeoSat web page, she zoomed in on the building, found the tiny dish, and carefully measured its position in three dimensions.

Armed with this and the knowledge that the transmission behaved rather like light beams in this frequency range, Pam began to explore possible receiver locations. She picked the Denver Municipal Jail, where Hank had been held first. Using the maps of GeoSat and armed with the alignment of the transmission dish, she began laying out her line of sight path. An hour later, she zoomed in on the rooftop of ABC Satellite Services, near the outskirts of Denver.

Now came the hard part, she needed full access to those video logs! While she could ask her father, that was not prudent. It would alert Dominus to the fact that there were unaltered videos around. Hence, she logged into the Underground once more. Madam Fingers had a private message waiting for her.

Madam Fingers. Your order has arrived. Dingo.

Pam opened a new window to her PayPal account and transferred some funds to the Service U Company. Next, she completed a fake transaction in which she apparently purchased three hours of computer servicing, which transferred those funds to the service technician who had performed the work, Dingo.

Now she replied to his message, and a private chat request was his reply.

M.F. Pleasure working on your computer. Thanks, helpful this time of year. D. Simultaneously, a lengthy file transfer began, as he uploaded the information from his computer to hers.

Pam sent:

Need total computer access to ABC Satellite Services,

Denver. Admin login. Can get?

After a pause, she received the replied she expected. He would have it for her by this time tomorrow. Once the file was received, both logged off the Underground network. Pam opened the large, compressed file, entering the proper password, which Dingo had used to protect it from others who might intercept it. There was no need for the regulars of the Underground to mention explicitly any passwords; they all knew that it would be their handle, Madam Fingers, in this case.

Pam now had five hundred sixty-three emails to and from Governor General Albright. First action: send the file to her new secure server, just in case anything happened to her laptop. Second action: begin reading them, discarding those that seemed normal. Near suppertime, she had ten key email messages left, one of which was the original of the one that she'd recovered from Hank's laptop. The other nine were highly incriminating, though at this point, she was not positive just how they tied into this mess.

The last action she took before logging off was to save a copy of the Privacy Act Versus Email. This legal document outlined the international laws regarding any expected privacy when sending any non-secure emails. In essence: none. This Pam and all grade school children had already been taught. Nothing about the Internet was in truth "private" with the sole exception of secure transmissions, those with SSL, and the very few secure safe email systems, and even these could be mishandled, though not likely.

At dinner, she explained to the others what she had found thus far and in turn discovered everyone else had just left her alone to "do her investigation thing." Audrey had six carvings in progress; Fern had been helping her, learning how it was done. Amanda and Lindsey had spent the day reading their new books and helping around the house.

Lloyd commented, "Well done, Pam. It seems conclusive that the Governor General is behind Hank Wilkinson's attempt at bombing. The trick will be tying Albright to the Mad Bomber and to the Death Stalker William the Bold. I've made you up a folder containing what is known about Dominus and the Death Stalkers. Perhaps some of this information may be useful to your investigations."

Pam's eyes sparkled. "Way cool! Thanks Mr. Compton! This is invaluable to us. Have you ever heard of a Simon Mac Fludie? I've got a strange email from him to decipher."

"Thanks, dad. We ought to know all we can about these Death Stalkers," Lindsey added.

"No, Mac Fludie. Sounds Scottish, well sort of. I guess you can MagGoogle for him," he replied.

As the girls began to clean up the table, Jim, Tom, and Sandy appeared near the front door. Lindsey's heart skipped a beat as she saw the trio arriving. "Hi everyone," Sandy spoke as the Teleport spell brought them to the Compton's home. "We thought you all might like some company on a blustery winter's eve."

Jim added, "Mom sent along all sorts of goodies too." The large group played Scrabble until the ten o'clock news came on the radio. The weather report sounded grim! The storm was standing still over south central Colorado, dumping feet of snow in the higher elevations. Power was out to all but the larger cities. All roads were impassable, and a state of emergency had been declared. However, the many ski lodges were becoming quite blessed with the snowfall; a most promising start of the new year for them was at hand.

The next morning the blizzard still raged, however, the many animals had to be serviced. Lloyd pointed out the problem. "Gang, what with the drifting, why, the snow is up to our waists in many places on the way to the barn."

"Shovel time?" Lena suggested.

"No, Lena, you have three young witches here and me. I think it is time we used a little magic on the snow. Girls, get your wands and coats. To the barn we go, yo ho ho." A few minutes later, the four were on the front porch facing the huge drifts, which completely covered the steps and very nearly the rope line leading from the porch pillar to the barn doors.

"Wow! Cool! Look at this snow!" Pam exclaimed. She'd lived in the city and had never seen snow like this. She could see perhaps five feet in front of her, but no more. "How do we get rid of it?"

"Well, you all don't yet know the Dig spell, so we will have to make do with what you can do," Lloyd suggested. "I'll dig a small trench following the rope. You three come after me and see if your Clean will remove and enlarge the path. It will probably take hundreds of those spells. Let's get cracking. It'll only get worse the longer we wait." All three watched as his magical shovel appeared and began digging out the steps and then a narrow path along the rope line. Then, the three began to follow, wands waving like mad.

An hour later, they arrived at the barn, and a four-foot wide trench led back to the ranch house. All four were now completely white, a snowman and three snow girls, as they stomped into the barn. Numerous Warm and Dry spells flew for a couple minutes. Then, the four handled the necessary chores. "You know, there is so much more to do each day on a ranch than back home," Pam commented. "I mean, if I was in Sterling, why, I'd just be working on my computer all day with nothing else to do, except perhaps catch a bit of TV or some video rentals. This is way more interesting, Lindsey."

After lunch, Pam transferred another sum and received the login she desired. Indeed, once into the ABC Satellite Services computer system, she found it fully automated, ready to replay the Law men's requests. Simply pick the location, date, and time span and video would be queued up automatically. Indeed, this site, she guessed was little more than a computer system running on automatic. Pam entered the information for Hank Wilkinson and then set the playback speed to 5X normal. Images flew by of the jail holding cell.

Now she saw a young boy being held in this facility and slowed the playback down to only 2X normal. Then she saw a horrifying sight. A man in wizard robes entered the cell, probably using the Unlock spell. She watched as he strangled the boy and then made it look like a suicide. When she stopped the recording, she discovered that the site software allowed her to make an official copy of a section. Dutifully, she made a copy beginning with the appearance of Hank in the holding cell through the cover-up and departure of the wizard. Once the capture was specified, the software asked her to specify locations where this official excerpt was to be sent. Pam specified the Department of Law, Denver, and the Department of Magical Misuse (both Denver and Sterling). Additionally, she had it sent to her secret server and to Governor Alister at Bradbury's School of Magic. Finally, the program asked when the video was to be sent, so Pam indicated an hour from now.

Encouraged with her find, though not unexpected, she then looked for the video surrounding the escape of William the Bold. This video excerpt was much shorter, revealing a guard secretly handing William his wand. The guard's face was very visible in the snippet. She had it sent to the same locations. Finally, she logged out of the system and held her breath. Would this server actually send the requested video to these locations?

She logged into her own secret server and began to monitor incoming feeds. Sure enough and right on time, the video feed came to her system as a giant mp4 file, which she immediately encrypted and stored in her ever growing data base. Once both were safely on her server, she went to get her friends and Lloyd.

"Look what Sleuth Pam has uncovered," she said proudly. "It's gruesome to watch Hank get murdered, but maybe Lloyd can recognize who did the deed." The five watched the grim video and the much shorter one where William was given his wand back so that he had the means for an escape from jail.

"Well, the Law department will have their hands full when they get these!" Lloyd commented, grinning from ear to ear. "Can I see the face of the one who murdered Hank again? I think I recognize him." Pam replayed the video and froze it when she thought his face was best visible.

"Calvin Tomlinson, Death Stalker. That sure looks like him, Pam," Lloyd replied.

Pam rummaged through the package of information he'd given her on the Death Stalkers and found a photo of Calvin. The girls compared this older image with that on the video image. The likeness was good, though the photo had been taken at least a dozen years ago. Pam decided to identify the murder as Calvin for now.

The blizzard finally ended, and everyone helped with

the digging out process. Indeed, the ranch looked like a winter wonderland now, with drifts many feet deep in places. With this unseasonably large snow, the Whitewater toboggan became heavily used. Daily, the kids congregated at the Whitewater ranch to sled down into the arroyo. Too soon came the end of the vacation. On Sunday, all bags were packed, and the whole bunch stood on Lindsey's porch awaiting the arrival of the bus.

"Do you think it can get through all that snow?" Lindsey asked Jim. Her long drive was entirely buried under feet of snow. Before he could answer her, everyone heard the telltale popping sound of the bus materializing before them. "Er, I guess it can," she answered her own question. Interestingly, the bus left no tracks in the snow down their long road to their ranch. Lindsey also noted that this time four Department of Defense men got off to inspect them. She did feel somewhat safer with four instead of the one who had been protecting them last fall.

Lindsey, Pam, Amanda, and Audrey were very excited about returning to school. This term they would be learning Grade 3 spells, many of which were quite powerful attacking spells, such as the Ball of Fire and Lightning Bolt spells. Typical of nearly all students, these particular spells seemed to them to be the epitome of magical use, the conjuring of massive flames or electrical arcs. On the other hand, Jim and Tom were looking forward to the track Nationals in May, hoping to do better than their third place finish last year.

Slowly but surely, the bus picked up all the other students on this route. Emilio and Kathy at last joined their friends. All began chatting rapidly in an attempt to make up for the three-week absence. The bus now moved into its long haul portion of the run, crossing the snow covered south central Colorado and then on up the nearly deserted road toward Telluride and Bradbury's School of Magic.

Lindsey felt a little uneasy. The bus had just past the location on State Road 145 where they had been attacked last fall. Here, the road was named San Juan Skyway. To her left, the heavy snow covered mountains loomed in their white majesty. Ahead lay Lizard Head's Pass, some ten thousand two hundred feet above sea level.

Boom! Boom! Boom! Avalanche cannons fired just ahead of the bus. Everyone turned to stare at the steep, snow covered mountains to the left. In slow motion, the enormous snow pack began shifting, sliding down, gaining speed and momentum as it fell. "Avalanche!" many students screamed. Sitting ducks, thought Lindsey as she watched the wall of white thundering down all along the left side of the road.

"Seat belts on; brace for a collision!" yelled the magnified voice of Tom, the lead Defense man in charge. As he drove the bus, poor Jimmy could see no way to avoid the avalanche. The entire side of the mountains was coming down on them; it didn't matter whether he speeded up or slowed down.

"Wha' do I do?" Jimmy yelled frantically to Tom.

"Stop the bus now. Men, throw a force field around the bus, overlap with mine. Now!" called out Tom. From the very rear of the bus, Lindsey watched the magical fields begin to surround the shell of the bus.

"Are we going to be all right?" Amanda asked her brothers.

"Maybe. Without the force fields, the avalanche will tear this bus to shreds in a second," Tom said very worriedly, holding onto Sandy tightly.

"They should be trying to levitate the bus up above the avalanche," Audrey quietly commented to Pam. Lindsey merely sent a message to Alister and continued to watch the ever growing wall of white coming at her. She felt helpless to avoid it.

Just as the leading edge of the roaring avalanche reached the bus, the bus began to rise in the air. However, it failed to rise fast enough, and the wall of snow struck its bottom, causing the bus to begin to spin counterclockwise. The roar of the snow was deafening, and the spinning disoriented everyone, as up became down became up, repeatedly. Screams of terror filled the bus, while Lindsey waited to hear the tearing and wrenching of metal, which would signal the disintegration of the bus itself.

It didn't come. Instead, the spinning subsided along

with the roaring of the sliding snow. At last, the bus stopped altogether in an upright position on top of a giant mound of snow. For a minute no one moved or spoke; shock had set in on everyone. At last, the door opened and the kindly face of Governor Alister appeared. "Is everyone all right in here? The carnival ride is now officially over." Only Alister could bring a touch of levity into the panicked disaster.

Moans and groans came in reply. Alister added, "Floor Monitors, check your students. Department of Defense men, please step outside and set up a defensive perimeter, please."

Jolted into action, Sandy began checking those around her. "Hold your hand on your nose, Audrey; it looks like a nose bleed, nothing worse." One by one, the students were checked. Up front, several had broken arms; while at the rear, bloody noses were the norm. Lindsey felt herself and discovered nothing was hurting, a good sign. Pam had a bruise on her cheek where a flailing arm had cracked her a good one. Jim also had blood streaming from his nose, but used his handkerchief to stem its flow.

Tom opened the rear emergency door and gratefully, Lindsey and her friends were the first ones to step out and onto the snow pack, under which somewhere lay the road. While they were trying to get their bearings, Lindsey saw the dark shape of a man far off in the distance, just before the beginnings of the avalanche zone, high on the mountainside. Evidently, Tom had also spotted him, and she watched as three of the defense men decided to check on the man.

"He's out of spell range," Jim explained to his small group. "Looks like they are going after him anyway." Three men vanished from their location and appeared near the man on the distant southern ridge line. Lindsey spotted a few flashes of light and a bit later, the sounds of small explosions echoed over the stillness, raising concerns for additional snow slides.

Professor Cho Lin and the Blake's, who had accompanied Alister, now had all the injured sorted out. Ten broken arms needed immediate attention, which they reported to Alister. "Okay, the bus is sound. Let's use the bus to continue the short distance to the school grounds," Governor

Alister commanded. He added, "Cho Lin, you are in charge. I want to keep Pam, Lindsey, and Amanda with me for a time. I will bring them back myself. Message me when the bus arrives and keep me posted on the condition of the wounded children, please."

"What's up?" Pam asked Governor Alister, as the rest of the students now re-entered the bus, casting long glances at the trio, who were remaining behind.

"More on the job experience. Come. We must assist the Defense men. I believe they are in trouble up there. Hold my hands please." Quickly the three did as he asked and were teleported up to the ridge where the men were now located. "Ah, Tom, what's happened here?"

"Shot two of my men, forty-five caliber, if I am not mistaken. He's minus a hand now. I got the gun hand and gun," he pointed to the bloody remains lying on top of the white snow. "An avalanche cannon is over there. Seems to be a deliberate attempt to wipe out the bus, Governor. My men are wounded, but not seriously. Culprit took off already, though he is probably bleeding badly. I have already requested backup. What are these three doing here?"

"Ah, my helpers. Mind if we look for some clues?" he asked politely.

Considering Tom was more concerned with making his wounded men more comfortable until help arrived, he merely nodded. Because of the blood on the hand and gun, several fingerprints were quite visible. Pam quickly took several photos with her cell phone.

Amanda said, "Not much in the way of magical traces here, except for two teleport spells and one disintegration beam."

"Right, this was a non-magical attack, and darn effective, I might add. I'm glad that Lindsey had the cool head to message me in time for me to get here and levitate the bus," Alister replied. "Audrey had a very wise idea for the bus. Come on; let's see what else may be found." He teleported the trio down to the road just before the avalanche zone.

Pam said, "You know, just before I heard the cannon fire, I heard a smaller noise near the bus." She tried to recall that fleeting sound before the chaos erupted. "Can I walk along the road a ways?" she asked.

All four spread out, covering the two-lane highway. Beginning at the edge of the avalanched covered road, they retraced the route the bus had traveled coming up to the disaster zone. About a mile back, Pam spotted something. "Hey. Look at this." All four stared at what appeared to be pieces of a firecracker on a stem. Bits of what appeared to be the remains of a photoelectric cell were also visible.

"Wow! Way cool. Can you all see this!" exclaimed Amanda. Pam and Lindsey looked dumfounded at her, having no idea about what Amanda was talking. "Look, there is a magical aura around those pieces, whatever they are. Then there is this beautiful, thin, straight line of magical energy running from here straight up there to that avalanche cannon. It's way cool. Can't you see it?"

"Er, no," Pam admitted, wishing with all her might that she could see what her Apache friend was seeing. Lindsey shook her head, though she tried to imagine what Amanda was seeing.

"Allow me," Alister spoke up, waving his wand, he commanded, "See as Amanda." He touched both Pam and Lindsey lightly on their shoulders. Suddenly, both girls found themselves looking out of Amanda's eyes!

"Holy cow! I'm you," exclaimed Pam. "I see it! I see it! Oh, is this what you are seeing, Amanda? I mean the magical energies?"

"Oh this is strange! I feel like I have six eyes now!" Amanda replied, blinking in surprise. "Oh, yes, see it? Isn't it really cool, nice and straight, a line from here to way up there."

"Wow, Amanda. This is incredible! You can see stuff like this? Wow," exclaimed Lindsey.

Alister cancelled his spell, "We don't want Amanda to go cross-eyed." All three girls chuckled.

"Well, that can only mean that this stuff here was meant to signal the firing of the cannon to start the avalanche to wipe out the bus," Pam declared. "I wonder if there are any clues in these remains." She began a careful inspection of the various bits. One piece of the photocell looked large enough to hold a fingerprint, so Pam deliberately Dirtied the piece. Her CSI kit was back on the bus, unfortunately. Again, she took a cell phone photo of the index fingerprint. Then, Alister magically gathered all the pieces, putting them into a plastic baggy and sealing it.

Just then, a message appeared before Alister. "Cho Lin reports that the bus is pulling into the parking lot. Shall we join them now?" It was more of an order than a question. Seconds later, all four were standing beside the bus as the hundred children began exiting. Sandy, along with the other monitors and older students, helped the ten who were in great pain. Already, they had their arms mostly immobilized with makeshift splints. These ten were rushed to the Infirmary.

Alister and the three professors saw to the transportation of all the student bags to their appropriate rooms. After thanking him for allowing them to investigate, the trio joined their friends, heading to the dorms. Several Department of Law men met Alister, and Pam saw him handing over the bag of evidence they had collected. Emilio, Kathy, Audrey, Fern, and Jim wanted to know what the trio had done with Alister, and Amanda was very keen to relate all that they had seen. Pam was more interested in getting to her room and laptop!

Ten minutes later, while Kathy, Amanda, and Lindsey set about unpacking their many bags, Pam booted her laptop and transferred her cell phone photos to it. A minute later, she was eagerly comparing fingerprints. "Yahoo! That was none other than our Mad Bomber at work again!" she declared loudly. At once, the three came over to look at the finger print comparisons on her screen. Pam sent a brief message to Alister with her findings.

"Well, at least the Mad Bomber is now missing a hand. That ought to make him lots easier to find," Amanda replied hopefully.

"Yes, but it can be regrown in a few days," Lindsey countered.

"True, but where?" Pam countered. One just did not walk into norm's hospitals and ask for a hand to be regrown. He would have to use a wizard hospital. None of the girls knew anything about such places, if they existed. They only knew that it could be done here at the school Infirmary, though they had heard of it being done elsewhere. Pam decided she had yet another research project to handle. She wondered if Governor Alister was aware of this, and perhaps even the Department of Law would be on the lookout for him as well.

Next, the four headed to the Infirmary intending to help their injured classmates. However, Doctor Caterwall already had tended to the ten. All were on the mend and due to be released in the morning. Instead, they chatted with the injured, one of whom was Deiter Cross.

"I'd sure like to get my hands on that man who did this," Deiter growled. He was no longer in any pain, and his bone was healing rapidly, thanks to the potion the Doctor had given him. His anger, on the other hand, had only increased. "I swear to you, Lindsey, I'm going to work doubly hard at spell casting this spring! I'm going to be the meanest, nastiest Eliminator this world has ever seen!"

She smiled, "Well, I think Dominus and the Death Stalkers are going to be very hard to eliminate. I certainly don't have the skill to take them on. Good luck on learning the spells. I know we're going to learn good ones this spring. I'll help you as much as I can." He smiled, and his anger began to subside.

"Thanks for coming to see how I was doing, Lindsey. You know, this is going to sound strange, but you are the first girl that I can really talk to—I mean about *important* things." Deiter flushed, but Lindsey merely smiled, not knowing just what to make of his pronouncement.

On Monday, classes resumed. Biology began with a study of single celled animals. Algebra only got harder. In PE class, Lindsey got a surprise. This spring they would learn swimming in depth: nine different strokes and life saving techniques. Until now, she only knew of the single pool located on the grounds above the Infirmary. Yet, an Olympic sized pool was underground, beneath the one above ground. Worse, all of her classmates already knew how to swim, using at least one type of stroke. She did not, having never been swimming—being a child with no hands precluded it. Lindsey found herself way behind the others.

In Government class, they took up the principles of the normal's version of governing. Professor Jerry naturally assigned a paper on this first day back: List the major problems facing the norm's governments on earth. Lindsey knew next to nothing about this topic.

Later in the day, Professor Jerry Thalmus introduced Grade 3 spell casting. "This spring, we tackle your Grade 3 spells, some of which are extraordinarily powerful. This week, I will be teaching you three abjuration-based spells, at which point, I will turn it over to Arthur Thornby, who will spend many weeks with you on the numerous alteration-based spells. Yes, the Ball of Fire spell will come in late spring, when the weather is warm enough to be outside."

"Sometimes, a wizard or witch may need to protect others, such as normals, from harm. The Protection spell does just this. This is an old, old spell. One traces out a circle on the ground, and all those within are then protected from harm. Well, at least it offers them some protection. Ruffians will tend to be repulsed from harming those being so protected, possibly doing them less harm than they otherwise would. Other times, the Protection from Flying Objects can be useful, as it nullifies strikes against your body from flying objects, such as knives, stones, and bottles. It does nothing against magical attacks, such as Magical Missiles. Yet, in street brawls with normals, it is useful for a witch or wizard. The last spell I have, Mind Block, will help you counter the Mind Reading spell you all learned last term." The class went to work on these three spells, knowing that next week they would have Professor Arthur for many subsequent weeks.

Of course, the next day, Professor Cho Lin reminded them that they would each be giving a concert to their fellow class members later in the spring. She urged them all to spend one hour each night practicing on their instruments. Nearly everyone had more or less forgotten to practice all that much during the fall term. Lindsey now realized that she was diligently going to have to put in that hour each night.

Since they all spent their evenings studying together, the group agreed to spend the hour from six to seven practicing their music. At seven, they would then congregate back in the Yellow Hall study room. Poor Pam, she had so many extra-curricular projects to investigate now that she completely ran out of time to do them all. One of her plans she cancelled at once, that of trying to fingerprint every student at Bradbury's. She had been planning to take a job as the evening dishwasher and confiscating one glass from every tray, cataloging its fingerprints. However, since the Mad Bomber had lost a hand during the avalanche attack, she quickly decided the Mad Bomber could not be a student. No one reported any returning student who was missing a hand.

As the days passed rapidly, spell casting only got more and more interesting, if not more difficult. Besides learning how to Speed Up One's Actions and Slow Down Another, they learned how to Breath Water, which Lindsey really appreciated, since she was still struggling with learning how to swim. This one spell she worked with diligently, until she could easily do it non-verbally and without a wand. Only then did she feel more comfortable in deep water. They learned to create strong Wind Gusts, which would even blow clouds of noxious gasses away. Another useful spell was Shrink Item, which would shrink any non-magical item to less than a tenth of its size, until needed.

As the weather improved, they learned to Fly. This spell rapidly became the most enjoyable spell for everyone in the class. Pam found the Create Secret Page an incredibly useful spell, because it allowed her to create a secret page in her notebook on which she could jot key information that others could not see.

Before anyone was aware of it, Valentine's Day arrived! Again, this was one of the days in which the third year students and above were allowed to venture into Telluride for a day of fun, a brief escape from their studies. Just after breakfast, Pam received a large bouquet of red roses from Monique. While Pam conjured a vase in which to put them, her roommates teased her a little, though not much. Lindsey saw at once that she was just a bit embarrassed by the attention.

However, Lindsey received a box of chocolates from

Jim, and then to her complete surprise, a single red rose came. "Who's it from?" Amanda asked. Lindsey shrugged—no card, no note, just the rose. Jim denied sending it, though he wished he had thought of that. "Lindsey's got a secret admirer!" Amanda teased her, which only frustrated her more. She had no idea who sent it to her, though it smelled nice and looked pretty.

Since they had the day off, Pam at last had some time to work on her backlogged investigation projects. She decided to examine the old mine maps that Monane had sent her. This whole area of Colorado had been heavily mined in the distant past, silver primarily, though some gold was found. Much of the hillside had abandoned mineshafts dug into them. First, Pam scanned in the map that Lindsey and Amanda had found last year, on which Looney and Green had marked in many secret rooms and tunnels. She added the few additional entrance tunnels that she had uncovered after the dishwashing room had been bombed.

Now she scaled the maps Monane had given her to about the same scale as the school map—her best guess of scale anyway. She began to look for any matching patterns. Her reasoning was simply that, when building Bradbury's, it would be easier to reuse abandoned tunnels than to carve new ones through the granite bedrock. An hour of trial and error matching yielded a result! She found the two long tunnels that the staff used: the one into Telluride and the ones that went to the parking lot matched known existing tunnels, long abandoned!

However, something struck her at once. There was a third tunnel that very nearly came to the campus, but not quite, ending shy of the secret staff lounge, behind the dishwashing room. Long she stared at this pattern on her monitor. Somewhere, somehow the pattern seemed familiar, though she could not place it.

Amanda and Lindsey came into their bedroom, chatting over the flick they had just seen with their friends. "Gosh, can you believe that someone would spend so many years digging an escape tunnel to get out of prison?" asked Lindsey.

"It sure seemed an impossible task," Amanda replied.

"Oh, hi Pam. Getting anywhere on your detective work? You missed a good flick, Count of Monte Christo."

"Yes and no. Ever had a time when you are sure you have seen something somewhere before but you can't remember where or when or whatever?" Pam answered disgusted with her lack of memory. "I've been staring at these tunnels all morning, but I can't place something."

"Send yourself an email to remind yourself," Amanda teased her roommate. However, she got a completely unexpected response.

"Eureka! That's it! An email!" Pam declared. She brought up her email system and began pouring over the ten special ones that she had retrieved from the Governor General. "Bingo! No, double bingo. Here, look at this one," she said triumphantly. Both girls moved in close to Pam to see what she was pointing out.

They saw a crude diagram showing a huge L-shape with a diagonal line coming obliquely toward the corner of the L, but not quite touching it. "Now, look at this overlay," Pam said as she switched to the map overlay image she had been studying. "Here is our map of Bradbury's, and it is overlaid with Monane's old mine tunnels in this area. Can you see it?"

"Looks like another old tunnel comes close to Bradbury's," Amanda commented.

"It doesn't quite connect," Lindsey offered, unsure of what Pam was concluding.

"Look, suppose that you wanted to make a new, unknown, and secret way into Bradbury's. Would not this old tunnel be just perfect? It ends so darn close to the staff lounge room that it ought to be easy to join there. I will bet anything that this is how the Mad Bomber comes and goes! He's constructed his own private entrance! I've got to get this to Governor Alister at once!" Pam put her computer into hibernate mode and headed off to find him. The others went down to lunch.

Halfway through their lunch Pam returned with a satisfied look on her face. After helping herself to the buffet meal, she joined her friends. "Well?" Lindsey asked.

"He thought this was an incredible discovery! He wants

us to join him in searching there after lunch! Gang, we get to play detectives! Let's hurry up and eat!" Pam gulped her chicken nuggets rapidly.

She need not have rushed for it was a half hour before Alister joined them. "Are you ready, Miss Betts?" he asked politely, a twinkle in his eyes.

Pam could scarcely contain her enthusiasm. Lindsey and Amanda joined her, while Fern and Audrey watched them leave, following Governor Alister down the stairs to the tunnel complex below the dining room. He led them to the dishwashing room, commanding the newly made secret door to open for them. Inside, he greeted the five dishwasher staff. The rest was also off in Telluride for the day. He led them down the back tunnel, which led to the staff lounge. None of the girls had been here before.

The room was about thirty feet square. Four large couches, six soft armchairs, and one long table with a dozen chairs lined the walls. A giant coat rack was affixed to one wall. Many magical lights permanently affixed to the stone ceiling provided the illumination. Several decks of cards lay disheveled on the table, along with numerous teacups and coffee mugs.

"We are looking for a secret or concealed door somewhere in this room, in all likelihood," Governor Alister explained. "It could be located anywhere. Let's get searching. A chocolate bar for whoever finds it first," he teased. All four began diligently searching. He began tapping lightly along the walls. Pam realized that when he encountered the hollowed area behind the secret door, the tapping would change in pitch. The others followed suit, tapping in various likely areas around the room.

A half hour later, Amanda gave up in disgust. No one had found any trace of a secret door anywhere. She lay down on the couch, which was extremely comfortable, and stared up at the ceiling. That's when she noticed the faint outline of magical energies in the shape of a square near one corner of the ceiling.

"Look at that. Why would there be magical energies there in that blank portion of the ceiling?" she asked absentmindedly.

"Ah, our Tracker has once more proved her worth," Governor Alister said softly. "There is indeed a secret door there in the ceiling. I would not have thought to look for one up there, though now that I see it, what better place for one, eh?" He levitated upwards, followed at once by Pam and then the other two girls, Amanda suddenly becoming un-bored.

He used an Open Door spell to open it. A panel slid off to one side, revealing a black hole that led off to the northeast. "Well, well, Pam you have solved the riddle that has perplexed me all year. Here is undoubtedly how our Mad Bomber comes and goes."

"Cool! Now we need to lay a trap to catch him," Pam declared, eager to catch the man responsible for the bombings and the murder of the dishwashing staff.

"We best not install magical detection spells," Governor Alister thought aloud. "If I were the Mad Bomber, every time I came here, I would use my detection spells to see if my secret entrance had been discovered. If I place any such enchantments here, our Mad Bomber may well detect them and beat a hasty retreat."

"Sir, I can use my Spy Cam," Pam volunteered. He gave her permission to proceed, and Pam quickly installed one, hiding it behind one of the magical light sources, positioning it so that it would clearly capture the image of anyone coming through the hole in the ceiling.

While she was busy with this action, Alister closed the secret door and placed his own clever enchantments onto a distant couch, where the Mad Bomber would not likely be looking for such. "I would ask you three to keep quiet about our little trap here. Who knows what ears the enemy may have within the school?" Lindsey knew that some students tended to support the ideas contained in the Manifest of Dominus, particularly those within Black Hall. Again, he thanked them, and the four left.

A bit later, Pam spent a few minutes programming her laptop to be activated by the Spy Cam. Finally, they all headed to the study hall for a long afternoon of study catchup. None of the group could keep their minds on their schoolwork. The

Valentine's Day dance was right after supper, when the older students returned from their outing in Telluride. Lindsey closed her books, "I can't keep my mind on this stuff. I'm going to go take a shower and get ready for the dance." Everyone else took this as a good excuse themselves and abandoned their attempts to study today.

"What are you doing?" asked Lindsey, who was watching Kathy making faces in her mirror in their room. All four had cleaned up and were getting ready for the dance. Dinner was not for another half hour.

"I'm practicing flirting," Kathy answered. "Maggie over in Red Hall gave me some tips to try."

"But why?" Lindsey asked, wondering why anyone would want to do that.

"Well, you've got to be able to attract your fellow. You have to keep his interest in you or his eyes could wander to some other girl. You've got to get his attention and all that, you know."

"Er, I didn't know any of that," Lindsey admitted, wondering what else she knew nothing about.

"Oh yes. First, you see a fellow you are interested in; next, you have to attract his attention to you. Then comes the hard part: to get him to want you too. After that, you have to continue to keep his attention, rather like Sandy does with Tom, hanging on his arm and all that—make the fellow feel important that he has you, you see. Boys have such egos with girls, haven't you seen that? Anyway, I'm practicing. Is this more attracting or like this when I tilt my head so?" Kathy asked.

"I've no idea," Lindsey admitted, "I think they both look, well okay." Amanda simply threw a pillow at Kathy. Kathy immediately returned the toss and a full-fledged pillow fight ensued, ending when all four were laughing too hard to continue.

Amanda suggested, "Doesn't all this merely make you into an object and not a person, you know, an ornament worn by the guy, his trophy? I don't think that I want any part of that, personally."

"Well, this is a male dominated world, Amanda.

Women are supposed to be pretty and look nice," Kathy countered.

"So where does that leave me and all the rest of us who are not remotely pretty?" asked Pam, her tone turning very serious indeed. That put the kibosh on the joviality of the foursome. Embarrassed, Kathy had no immediate response.

"Beauty is in the eyes of the beholder," Amanda answered her friend. "Personally, I am after love. He should love me as I am, and vice versa. I don't intend ever to be anyone's object of lust and desire. That sounds more like a slut or something."

"Yes, we are all after love, Amanda," Kathy defended herself. "But women are not as powerful as men, you know. We have to use our wiles to get men to do what we want. Look, here is a good example of what I mean. Peggy West gave these clips to me. They are from an ancient comedy flick called *Fierce Animals*, staring Kathy Lee and John Cleese. Here watch how she flirts perfectly with him to get him under her total control." Kathy played the excerpts Peggy had made for her.

The four watched the clips, and all agreed that she was a master of flirting to control men. "See, that's what I mean. It is another tool that we can use in life." Kathy continued to insist.

"The only time I've ever seen mom do anything like that," Lindsey replied, "was when she and Lloyd were about to go to bed—I think to make love or something. Mom never uses it like Kathy Lee was using it, not in real life."

"Right, Lindsey. My mom flirts with dad only when they are in a playful mood and going off to make love in their bedroom. I think that thought and reason make for a better relationship. I won't marry anyone who has to be controlled by flirting instead of reason," Amanda sermonized.

"That's why I like Monique so much," Pam ventured her opinion. "She treats me with love and respect, and she loves me just the way I am. No one has ever treated me as she does. I remember one boy back in sixth grade, Henry. He said that I ought to get my teeth fixed so that I would look like the Barbie doll that we had in our classroom."

"What happened then?" asked Kathy.

"I slapped him and told him that I wasn't a Barbie doll. Ugly people have feelings too, you know."

"Good for you!" Amanda replied.

"Mom's not pretty either," Pam continued. "She always told me to find someone who would love me as I am and for who I am. Monique is the first person to do just that, love me for who and what I am. She makes zero demands on me."

"But I don't understand, Pam," Lindsey finally felt brave enough to say what she wanted to ask. "Monique is a girl. I mean, well, how can you have a family and all that?"

"Oh there are lots of ways to have children, if and when we might want them. Honestly, aren't we all searching for someone to love wholeheartedly, with no reservations and be loved likewise in return? Isn't that what is really important in the final analysis?" Pam replied.

"Well, Pam, you won't get any argument from me on that one," Kathy proclaimed. "But I haven't found the right person yet, though I have eyes on Emilio. When I do, I want to be sure that I can get him to want me just as much; that's why I am practicing. I'd just die if I fell in love with some boy and he didn't love me back. That'd be about the worst thing I can imagine. Wouldn't that just be awful?"

Lindsey had never given that any thought, but she had to agree with Kathy, that would be an awful situation. "So flirting with him—that would get him interested in you?" she asked, trying to see how such a one-way relationship could be changed.

"Well, I don't know, but it certainly could help it along, I suppose," Kathy admitted. "It's part of our arsenal. You've never seen boys flirting with us now have you? No, they strut and act as if they are super cool, mega-important. They brag and act downright silly to attract our attention."

"Yes, but Jim has never done any of those things to me," Lindsey thought aloud.

"That's why we are all in Yellow House," Amanda explained. "We don't let our emotions control our actions; thought prevails. I prefer it that way, personally." Lindsey now had another appreciation for the separate halls. Already she had seen personality differences between them. "Hey, it's time to eat. I'm starving." The four headed down to dinner and then the dance afterwards.

Chapter 11—A Long Winter

After Valentine's Day, the class met with Professors Mary Ann and Cho Lin for spell casting. Outside the snow continued to fall nearly every other day, making this a long winter indeed. Listen from a Distance and See from a Distance turned out to be very vital spells, though difficult to master. Professor Mary Ann continually reminded her students, "Remember to believe it will work. These spells depend upon belief."

After two day's dismal attempts, Lindsey finally got both spells to work. With the first spell, she could hear whatever sounds were present at some distant location, far from her. She only needed to be familiar with the location. She chose, naturally, her barn back home and was quite startled to hear all the animals and even her mother chatting to them as she gathered the eggs! The second spell allowed Lindsey to see whatever was visible at some distant location. Now she could both watch and hear what was going on in her barn hundreds of miles away. "Wow! This is one of the most incredible spells ever!" she exclaimed to Amanda.

"No, useful, very useful," Pam corrected her. "With this, I can see what's happening anywhere that I know about, without having to be there. This is an incredible sleuthing tool!"

Professor Cho Lin taught them how to create Invisible Writings, how to make all objects around the caster also become invisible, sort of a Mass Invisibility. However, the Ghost Form spell captured everyone's undivided attention. With this spell successfully cast upon oneself, one's body and all possessions were turned into a ghostly form, invisible to normal eyes. In addition, while one could move around normally, he or she also had the ability to slide through tiny openings, such as keyholes! Additionally, Professor Cho Lin added more details to their currently known phantasm spells. In short, it was a most profitable week.

Of course, the following week with Professor Delius Dogs was a nightmare for Lindsey. She hated necromancy even more. First, he tried to teach them how to Hold Undead Creatures. He animated several skeletons and some corpses, which he turned into zombies, and then had the class practice their spells. Mostly the girls shrieked in terror. More than one zombie and skeleton was smashed by various spells when they moved too close to frightened students, who were unable to cast the necessary Hold spell and had cast destroying spells on the undead.

Lindsey hated the Touch of the Vampire spell and refused to have anything to do with that one. Delius dutifully explained that when one was wounded, by casting this spell and touching another person, the caster was healed of some wounds, while his or her wounds were transferred to the other person. Even Pam wanted nothing to do with this spell. Peaches, on the other hand, reveled in this spell, as did Deiter and most all the Black Hall students.

On the last day with Professor Delius, Lindsey finally consented to learning the next spell, Fake Death. With this spell, the caster appeared to be quite dead, his body completely lifeless. In the back of her mind, Lindsey thought that in some dire circumstances, this spell might prove useful, though scary.

Although March had come, the snow pack still had not begun to melt. Nevertheless, the class found themselves on the roof of the Hall of Evocation magic. Professor Huan Su began teaching them the spells, which every student just had to learn, the spells that they considered actually made them official witches and wizards, the power attacking spells.

They began by learning how to cast the famous Ball of Fire spell. Deiter and many other boys really excelled, casting giant flaming spheres very quickly. By the end of the first day, thirty giant, flaming balls arced out over the snow packed grounds, sending up clouds of steam. The class, on Deiter's suggestion, had all cast the spell at the same time, a time honored class ritual, Lindsey learned later. Professor Huan Su merely smiled as the class cheered. He had been one hundred percent successful today.

The next day, he taught them how to cast Lightning Bolts. For some, this spell was slightly trickier, in that more than a few were slightly afraid of electricity, whereas none had any back off from fires. After that spell was mastered, Professor Huan Su expanded into related spells, teaching them to cast five Flame Balls; each was a foot in diameter when it exploded on the indicated target. "This spell is particularly effective if you are attacking a mob of normals, where a fire ball would be total over-kill. Plus, it allows you to direct an effective attack at five separate targets simultaneously," he explained.

He followed this spell up with another variation, the Flaming Arrow. With this spell, the caster conjures a magical arrow, much like the Magical Missile spell. However, it becomes a flaming arrow, whose flames cause substantially more damage. Many rotting pumpkins were torched by this spell during the next two days.

The following week, he taught them far less exciting spells, beginning with Phantom Horse, which brought a large horse into existence to carry the caster as though it were a real horse. Further, as they gained experience with the spell, their "horse" would be able to travel over water as if it were solid ground.

Next, he taught them the Safeguard Page spell. Once cast upon a page, if anyone other than the caster ever read the page, the tiny magical symbol that the spell created would activate, striking out at the reader. If it successfully touched the reader, the reader was instantly put into a state of suspended animation for up to five days, allowing the caster to deal effectively with the spy. Lindsey, Amanda, Kathy, and Audrey saw absolutely no use for this spell. Pam, however, thought it would be perfect to help protect her secret writings, and she made sure she really had this one mastered. Of course, a Dispel Magic would undo the suspended animation.

"The final spell is not required for a passing grade, just as the necromancy based spells," Professor Huan Su explained. "Summon Creatures to My Defense spell does just that, calling forth between two and eight creatures to come and defend you from hostile attackers. Whatever creature comes will be at least as effective in combat as a normal man, but not more. You have no control over who or what answers your summons, however. It could be giant rats, wolves, coyotes—whatever happens to be the closest to you. I would suggest that you use this spell sparingly." In the end, Lindsey refused to learn two of the necromancy spells and this Summon Creatures spell. She had not the heart to cause other innocent animals to fight her battles.

The following week, the class returned to Professor Janice, who Lindsey still did not like. Her red lips with their fake smile greeted the class, "Welcome to the last week of Grade 3 spell casting. We have two most useful spells to learn, very difficult ones at that, and your wands must activate for these to work properly." She smiled covertly at Lindsey as she uttered this last.

"Now the first spell is called Suggestion. With this spell successfully cast, you can make a simple suggestion to your victim, and he or she will obey it. However, you cannot suggest that they harm themselves, for that will break your spell. So Lindsey, forget trying to suggest that Mr. Cross jump off the roof." She remembered the incredible hostility between those two during their first year in her spell casting class. "You can suggest that someone does something that might embarrass them, but you must make it sound like a reasonable thing to do."

"Allow me to give you an example," she continued. Lindsey already had been told to remove her ring and pin. Afterwards, she wished that she had not done so. "Miss Barron," Professor Janice waved her wand and said "Suggestion: kiss Mr. Cross." Instantly, everyone in the class became fully alert! They all knew how antagonistic these two students had been all last year. Kissing Deiter would be the last thing that Lindsey would do. Lindsey felt a powerful surge of magic and a strong urge to kiss Deiter. This she resisted completely. It wasn't something she'd ever considered doing.

"You see, while I didn't ask Miss Barron to harm herself, I tried to suggest that she do something that her mind wouldn't rationally conceive of doing. Now watch this second attempt." She waved her wand and said, "Suggestion: Miss Barron, Deiter is a most handsome young boy. You are drawn to his charming face. I do believe that he is in love with you.

Go ahead and give him just a little kiss."

The concatenation of plausibilities struck Lindsey solidly, as each seemed so true. She leaned over and kissed his cheek before she realized what she was doing. Of course, the whole class roared with laughter, including Professor Janice. Deiter, however, did not. His face reddened and his anger grew. Once more, Lindsey realized just how important wearing her fathers' ring and pin were to her survival. Had she been wearing them now, Professor Janice would not have been able to embarrass her with her Suggestion spell.

As she often did, Professor Janice then divided the students into pairs, partnering each with someone they disliked. As usual, Lindsey found Deiter was now her partner. He whispered, "I'm sorry about that Lindsey. Professor Janice went too far!" She smiled, grateful for his concern. By the second day of practice, the class had uniformly gotten the spell well learned, opting to suggest rather silly things for their partners to do, such as kiss one's shoes. Some of those in Red Hall actually had their partners putting on their red lipstick, accompanied by numerous giggles in response.

However, Deiter held a grudge. This wasn't the first time the Professor Janice had made him into a fool before the whole class. Near the end of the class period, when Professor Janice was occupied trying to give Pam and Loyd a hassle, he slipped quietly up behind her and cast, "Suggestion: Professor Janice. Look at Lindsey. She's very lovable, isn't she? Why don't you give Lindsey a loving hug for having done so well in your class?"

Everyone in the class suddenly stopped and stared at Professor Janice, who had a foggy look in her eyes. She moved over to Lindsey and gave her a long, loving hug. When she stepped back, the spell was broken, and the class roared with laughter. Her face became as red as her lips, but only for an instant. Fortunately, the bell rang, and the class rushed out before she could react.

On their way to dinner, Deiter said, "Well, I got a small revenge on her for us, Lindsey. Maybe she will think twice before picking on you again."

"Thanks, that was rather cool. You took an awful

chance, Deiter. What if she now comes hunting for you?" Lindsey replied.

"I can handle her now. She only can charm people. I think that we're now more powerful than she is."

The next day, apparently Professor Janice had forgotten all about the incident. "Today, we are going to learn how to stop a person dead in their tracks. It's called Hold a Person. When successfully done, the person will become immobile for a couple of minutes. Now this spell is an area of effect type spell, not an individual type spell. It affects all people in a twenty-foot by twenty-foot area, but only up to four people, never any more. Of course, each person has some chance of throwing off the spell's effect upon them, much like the Dispel Magic spell. Normally, we would go outside to cast this spell, but since the snow is still so deep, we will just have to make do in the classroom."

Of course, trouble ensued almost at once. Every time one student was successful at casting the spell, not only was his partner affected, but also many of the nearby students. Hence, it took four days to get everyone through this spell.

"Now next week you are to report back to Professor Thalmus. It is review time. Again, I remind you that soon you will be given forty-five minutes to cast all your Grade 3 spells. Unless you are very diligent in your practice sessions, some of you may not pass and will have to repeat this course again." Everyone groaned.

It was now late April, and still the spring thaw had not even begun! "This is making our track and soccer meets a complete mess!" complained Becky just after supper. She had called her team together for a brief meeting. "As you know, we go to Nationals again this year, on the seventh of May, that's barely a month from now! We are supposed to have another track meet against Blue Hall and a soccer match with Black Hall before then. Yet, there is supposed to be a track meet between Black Hall and Brown Hall and a soccer match between Brown Hall and Red Hall before then as well. I don't see how we can get four events done in three weeks. The field is still underneath a foot of snow!"

Just then, Professor Blake came over to the nine. "Good

news, your track meet will be on Saturday, April 21. We will schedule the Black versus Brown meet on Sunday. I guarantee the track will be ready for you. The following Saturday will be the Brown versus Red soccer match and the next Saturday will be your soccer match. Got that?" Becky nodded, writing down the revised schedule.

"But we cannot even practice yet," Emilio complained. "The track is still buried!"

"Look, forget about the local competitions," Becky suggested. "As soon as the track is usable, let's work out for the Nationals, like a big run every couple of days. I know how exhausted I was last year during our last meet. We need to get into really good shape this year."

Indeed, it was a slow race on Saturday. The outside temperature was barely above freezing, though as promised, the track was clean and in good shape. Yellow Hall won, but their winning times were substantially longer than their race last fall. Yet, all nine knew that the Nationals would soon be upon them. They knew just how grueling running four complete races in one day had been last year, excepting Fern; this was her first year.

During the week, many staff members spent hours clearing away the snow from the soccer field, in preparation for the first soccer match on Saturday between Brown Hall and Red Hall. However, Friday night, Pam noticed that Governor Alister was not at the professor's table as he always had been. After eating, she went to see Professor Cho Lin, thinking he might have gotten a cold or flu.

"This is a disaster!" Pam exclaimed to her group a short while later. "Governor General Albright has forced Governor Alister to go to Denver. He's trying to get Alister fired from his job here. Even Cho Lin is worried about it."

"Yes, but what can we do about it?" asked Lindsey, who had come to depend upon the lovable, but capable old wizard. Bradbury's just would not be the same without Governor Alister in charge. All were so upset by the ill news that no one got any studying done that night at all.

Chapter 12—Teamwork

Pam fretted all night long. This was not right. The safety of all the students was Alister's prime concern, and he had always been there for them, until now. What if the Mad Bomber struck once more? What if someone came in through the secret door in the staff lounge? True, all had been completely silent there for months now. Pam tossed and turned. How could they fire Alister?

Saturday morning, Pam spent on her computer, researching the bylaws of the Board of Governors. While each Governor General was authorized to hire any magic school governor of his choice, only by a majority of the entire Board of Governors was one fired. That much she knew from her government class last fall. She wanted something more, some other rule that she could somehow use to rescue Alister.

Amanda came bursting into their bedroom, "It's all over the news! The Board of Governors wants to meet to discuss firing Governor Alister!"

"I figured so. I've got to find a way to help him," Pam declared and continued her research. Amanda went back down to see if anything else developed. By now, word of his absence and threat of being fired was all over the school. Pam was sweating, a nervous sweat, as she scrolled the seemingly endless bylaws of the Board. Just as her stomach growled for lunch, she came upon something.

"Eureka! Darn them anyway! I will do it!" she declared with a vengeance. Just then, she received another email message from Monique. The underground fellow, who had hacked into Governor General Albright's email system, was asking for Madam Fingers. Quickly, Madam Fingers entered the Underground and opened a secure, private chat. After a brief minute, some funds exchanged hands, and Pam downloaded another batch of emails and logged off the site.

Very carefully, quoting section and paragraph numbers of their bylaws, Pam composed the most important email message of her life. She re-read it five times, making sure that there were no misspelled words, that she had quoted the precise lines with the correct section and paragraph numbers. Finally completely satisfied, she sent the email message. It went to fourteen recipients: the twelve Governor Generals, Alister, and to the Department of Magical Misuse, Sterling, Colorado.

She carried her laptop and went down to grab some lunch before the big soccer match. While the others brought her up to speed on the news, much of which was probably lies or exaggerations, she ate hurriedly. Pam explained, "I've gone and done it, gang. I am sticking my neck way out here, but I cannot sit by and let Alister lose his job. None of it is his fault."

"What do you mean?" asked Lindsey.

"According to their own bylaws, any interested party, who has key information regarding the conduct of a Governor of a magic school, and who is not able to travel to the main Board meeting, is allowed to call a special session of the full Board of Governors and is allowed to present their evidence. I did it. I invoked my right to call for a special session. I'm going to show them all the evidence I've got so far."

Her group gave her a round of applause. "Terrific! Great thinking!" Lindsey replied.

"Go get them!" Emilio added.

"Well, now I have a whole lot of preparation work to do. I have to get everything properly organized so that even an idiot can see the whole picture," Pam explained.

"Don't worry; we'll all cover for you in all the classes," Amanda added an encouraging note, knowing how much missing classes meant to Pam.

"Thanks. I'll go up to my room and get to work right away. You may as well go watch the soccer match with everyone else. If I need anything, I'll message you," Pam declared with renewed enthusiasm.

A while later, Lindsey sat on the Yellow Hall section of the stadium bleachers, while Professor Blake began the soccer match introductions. Jim sat on one side of her, while Amanda was on the other side. "Keep your eyes on your counterparts on the field, Lindsey," Jim suggested. "See if you can pick up any tips. I'll be watching my counterparts."

Back in their room, Pam began sifting through this next batch of emails from Albright's server. Having already made a backup copy, she began deleting those that did not seem relevant. She heard the distant sounds of a few stadium horns; the soccer match was underway.

Wonk! Wonk! Wonk! Suddenly, Pam's computer sounded a loud warning tone. Pam jumped, so startled that she spilled her can of soda on the floor. She opened the computer's window. It was her Spy Cam window that had sounded the alert. She saw a fuzzy outline; the secret door in the ceiling of the staff lounge was opened. She saw a flash of magical energies and watched as one of the dishwashers collapsed on the floor. Immediately, the intruder's invisibility spell was cancelled. He had attacked while being invisible, which automatically cancelled the spell.

To Pam's horror, she saw that the man carried a green army backpack, a detonation fuse was clearly visible. It was a satchel bomb! Pam immediately messaged all her friends.

In front of Lindsey, a message appeared.

Mad Bomber has entered the staff lounge! Satchel bomb! Help! P.

Lindsey acted instantly. "Margarete: Come!" She dashed down off the bleachers and began running for the dorms. Amanda was right behind her, followed by Jim, Tom, and Emilio. Deiter Cross, seeing Lindsey's staff coming flying to her and seeing them all running, dashed after them, casting a Haste spell on himself so that he could catch up. Meanwhile, Kathy messaged Cho Lin relaying the news.

"What's up?" yelled Deiter as he caught them as they raced into the dorms.

Dashing down the stairs two at a time, Lindsey yelled back, "Mad Bomber has just broken into the staff lounge carrying a large satchel bomb! We have to stop him before he blows up a whole lot of students! You had better get to safety. This is going to be dangerous!"

He's still in the lounge, tinkering with the bomb. P.

The group reached the secret door to the dishwashing room. As they arrived, she hastily said, "Hold on a second. Let me cast a Skin of Stone on us all, just in case. Oh, and a Globe of Protection too." As fast as she could, she commanded her staff. Spell after spell shot forth onto her friends. At last, with everyone's wands at the ready, she called out, "Help Please!"

The secret door opened wide, and they entered, looking around for the Mad Bomber. The dishwashers were absent, their work done. Most had gone to watch the soccer game. "This way," Lindsey said, leading them down the long hallway to the lounge. Partway down the corridor, Lindsey saw a flash of magical energy. Without thinking she yelled, "Suck It!" Her friends saw a Ball of Fire begin to materialize but then become absorbed into her staff.

Jim, Emilio, and Deiter fired off a round of magical missiles back at their opponent. A shocked look appeared on all three faces. The missiles simply bounced off the Mad Bomber, who now shot another spell at them. However, a wall of force now blocked them from the bomber, who steadily began pushing them back down the hall.

They retreated into the dishwashing room, where they could spread out and individually attack him. Shortly, the man appeared, still carrying the bomb over his shoulder. He still kept the impenetrable wall of force between himself and them. "He's using a Wall of Force," Jim called out. Lindsey had tried three times to dispel the wall, but nothing had happened.

"I'm on it," Tom called out. "Needs my new spell." Waving his wand in a peculiar manner, he called out, "Disintegrate: Wall of Force." The magical energies collided and the wall was gone. However, at that instant, the Mad Bomber darted through the open doorway into the tunnel beneath the dorms. Lindsey shot off another Dispel Magic and thought that something had happened with the Mad Bomber, though she could not tell what.

He slammed the door shut on them and cast another Wall of Force, preventing the group from leaving the dishwashing room. "Now what do we do?" asked Amanda, furious at being penned in like cattle.

"This way," Lindsey called out and raced down the hall connecting to the kitchen. Dashing past two startled cooks, she opened their door and raced out after the bomber, whose footsteps could be heard dashing up the stairs.

Everyone raced up the steps after him. "We've got to somehow contain him," Lindsey called out, fearing that he would set off his bomb in the stadium. That worry entered all their minds as they cleared the dorm and headed outside.

Jim saw him racing just ahead of them and cast his wall of force in front of the man, who ran head long into it, jarring him and causing him to hit the ground hard. A volley of Flaming Arrows hit him next, from Emilio and Deiter. Amanda shot an Acid Missile at him. From his wrenching, they all knew that Lindsey had eliminated whatever spell he had been using to protect himself.

While sitting on the ground, he waved his wand and shot off two spells in rapid succession. Before Lindsey could command her staff, she was hit by a powerful blow that sent her sprawling backwards. Because of her protection spells, she was otherwise unharmed. Likewise, Tom was hit with the same spell and sent sprawling as well. Lindsey realized that the man was no fool. He was taking out his most worthy opponents first: the sixth year Tom and Lindsey with her Staff of Power.

Deiter and Amanda shot another round of Flaming Missiles at him, while Emilio tried something different. The Mad Bomber dispelled both of the missiles coming at him, but didn't catch what Emilio was casting in time. His spell lobbed a large pile of sticky webs all over the man, pinning him to the ground.

Lindsey struggled to get to her feet. The wind had been knocked out of her. Off to her right, Tom also struggled to regain his feet. A flash of magic and the webs were gone. Before Amanda and Deiter could send forth another volley, he shot another Ball of Fire their way, hoping to catch all them in a mass of flames. "Suck It!" Lindsey's voice fairly screamed. Just as the flames reached Deiter and Amanda, the spell dissipated, sucked once more into her staff. Because of the onrushing flames, Deiter, Amanda, Emilio, and Jim all four ducked, protecting their heads, giving him time to cast additional spells.

A giant cloud of poisonous gas appeared moving towards the group. Hastily, Tom conjured a huge gust of wind, blowing the vapors off to their far left, out of harm's way. While he was concentrating on getting rid of the gas, another spell hit Tom, and he froze, motionless, being held by the Mad Bomber. Likewise, Jim was also immobilized; it was an area of effect spell.

Lindsey had to make a choice. Did she waste time trying to dispel that magic or go after the bomber? She used her staff to dispel the Hold Other Persons spell, releasing Jim and Tom, hoping that Amanda, Emilio, and Deiter could survive, while she was freeing these two. Luck was on their side for this instant. The Mad Bomber cast a powerful volley of a half dozen magical missiles at the three, two missiles to each one of them. While the three cringed, expecting great pain, the Globe spell that Lindsey had cast upon them completely nullified the missiles, much to their amazement.

However, their delay allowed him to get to his feet and try other tactics. Suddenly, the grasses beneath the feet of Deiter, Amanda, and Emilio began to grow, twisting and entwining about their legs, riveting them to the ground as if they had been somehow glued to the spot. While they three were confused, he shot a Blindness spell at all three. Amanda and Emilio shrieked in shock, yelling that they couldn't see. Deiter somehow shrugged it off and was unaffected. Meanwhile, the Mad Bomber began moving around the wall of force.

Off towards the stadium, Lindsey saw the mad rushing of students, all heading for the safety of the dorms! Hundreds of students were unknowingly running right into the middle of the battle! "Ah, this is even better," the Mad Bomber yelled. "I'll get the whole lot of them in one blast!" He began fiddling with his explosives satchel.

Lindsey shot another Dispel Magic on him and saw another of his protections evaporate. Deiter saw his chance. Even though he couldn't move his feet, he could still cast. He waved his wand and commanded, "Lightning Bolt!" He pointed to the fleeing bomber and watched as the bolt arced out to him. Lindsey watched as the bolt actually struck the Mad Bomber in his back, sending him flying through the air.

Tom, now on his feet, called out, "Entangle!" followed

immediately by "Web!" The Mad Bomber hit the ground and became doubly entangled; growing grasses entangled him as well as a mass of sticky webs.

Lindsey finally cast a spell at the bomber, "Hold: Bomber." Unable to move to dodge her spell, he froze. While Tom raced to the man, Lindsey began undoing the spells on her friends. At that instant, the professors, leading the mass of students, arrived on the battle scene. Professor Cho Lin took charge, casting three more Hold spells on the man. Her husband, Huan Su, carefully removed the satchel bomb pack from his back. Professor Black confiscated the man's wand and broke it in half, guaranteeing the Mad Bomber would have no chance of retaliation.

"Are you kids all right? What's happening here?" asked Cho Lin, while the nearly six hundred students encircled the battlefield, chatting like mad.

"Yes, we are fine," Lindsey replied, as Pam came running up behind her.

"You got him! Good!" Pam declared. "It's the Mad Bomber, we think. At least he has a bomb. I'll confirm his identity in a minute." She had brought her CSI kit and her laptop with her, though they were currently magically minimized. While she set to work obtaining his fingerprints, Tom, being the eldest and the Floor Monitor, explained what had happened. He never had such a large, attentive audience before!

Pam took a photo of the prints on her cell phone and then transferred them to her laptop. Many nearby students crowed around her, looking over her shoulder. She brought up the comparison view. "Yes, we definitely have the man who has been bombing our school. He is the Mad Bomber!" A loud round of applause erupted, even Cho Lin smiled in relief.

"Bomb's disabled," Professor Jasper Jones announced. "Completely harmless now. He could have killed half the students this time."

"Well, look here!" Professor Blake pointed out. "I was going to tie up his hands, but he's only got the one hand! His other hand is an illusion!"

"He probably could not risk getting it regrown just

now," Professor Janice observed. "Alister has had everyone on the lookout for someone trying to get a hand re-grown." This, Lindsey had not known, but Pam had strongly suspected Alister would have done so.

"We need to check him out further, before we release our spells that are holding him," Professor Cho Lin cautioned. "Mary Ann, have a look see, please." The rattled professor of divination magic cautiously approached the entangled, but held man, as if he might somehow attack her. She cast her spell silently and began studying him.

"Ah, good thing you did not try to apprehend him. He has a contingency spell in effect here. I believe it is a teleport spell. Allow me." She waved her wand and cast Dispel Magic, not once, but ten times in a row. Only then was she satisfied that the Mad Bomber had no more surprises in store for her. "Now you can arrest him, though the world might be better off if we killed him. Lord knows, Dominus will simply come and free him, as he has done with his other captured Death Stalkers."

"Okay students, wands at the ready. We will free him and take him into custody. However, if he tries anything, you all have my permission to hit him with your magical missiles. It is unlikely he could survive being hit by six hundred magical missiles. Not even Dominus could survive that," Professor Cho Lin said, mostly for the benefit of her prisoner. She released the magical bonds, and Professor Blake Smith helped him to his feet, tying his arms behind his back with a piece of conjured rope.

"Students, shall we all march our Mad Bomber down to the Admin Hall, where the Department of Law men shall be shortly arriving?" Professor Cho Lin asked. Pam immediately saw what she was doing. By having all the student body taking a small role in the capture of the man who had been terrorizing the campus all year, she was allowing each student to take a measure of relief and self-pride, a psychological boost to everyone's morale.

Once at the gates by the parking lot and Admin Hall, she had three professors stand guard over him along with ten sixth year students. "Now then, shall we all return to the stadium and let Brown Hall and Red Hall finish their soccer match?" It was not really a question. Cho Lin wanted things to return to normal as soon as possible.

She had Lindsey and her group remain behind with her, however. The other students gaily headed back to the stadium with everyone talking about the exciting events. Soon they heard the sounds of the stadium horns; the campus was back to normal.

"You all reacted faster than I did," Cho Lin commented when they were finally alone, mostly anyway. "Alister left me in charge and in control of his advance alert spells. Honestly, I didn't know what to believe for a few minutes there. Yet, Alister was right all along. We are very powerful when we all act together."

Deiter smiled. He had his first taste of a real battle, and he loved it! "Imagine Black Hall and Yellow Hall working together. I would never have thought that was possible," she said. "Well, done, Deiter, Lindsey, Amanda, Pam, Jim, Tom, and Emilio. Incredible job indeed!"

Just then, a dozen Law men and women arrived and walked up to the group. "We give you the Mad Bomber of Bradbury's," Cho Lin announced. "Check his fingerprints. We already have done so. He's responsible for all the real bombings this past year, including causing the avalanche that nearly crushed a school bus loaded with students."

"Here's his satchel bomb," Jasper added. "I've taken the liberty of disarming it."

"Hank Bertoni, Death Stalker, so you have been behind all these bombings," the lead Law man said, recognizing their prisoner. Pam took note of his name. Without further discussion, the men teleported the prisoner and bomb away. Everyone but Pam headed back to the game. Pam returned to her email studies, more determined now than ever to find a connection between Hank Bertoni and Governor General Albright.

As they walked back, Lindsey said, "Thanks for helping Deiter. You really sent him sprawling with your lightning bolt, allowing us to capture him. If he had gotten away, he could have blown up half our classmates."

"First time in my life, I have done something truly useful and important. Gosh what a rush!" Deiter was elated. She smiled. "But we all had a strong hand in it. You saved our lives from several spells there. That I can swear to!"

"You bet she did!" Jim added. "Kind of goofy command word, for a girl I mean, Suck It?" Everyone chuckled. It most definitely had been her father's staff, most masculine. "We would not have gotten past square one if Tom had not used the Disintegrate spell on his Wall of Force, though. That spell is a sixth year spell. I can make a Wall of Force now, just learned it a few weeks ago, tough spell to master. I can't wait until I can learn Disintegrate."

"Well, little brother, that is a tough one. I took nearly a week to get it working right. You get to eliminate rotten pumpkins left over from Halloween," Tom explained.

"Hey, how come those magical missiles didn't hurt us?" asked Amanda. "I thought I was a goner when they came flying at me."

"First Globe of Protection," Jim replied. "You will learn it next year. I hate to admit it, but I completely forgot about using it. Thanks, Lindsey for bestowing it on us all." They arrived at the stadium, and Deiter sat beside Lindsey and her friends, instead of rejoining his Black Hall group. "Hey, wonder who's winning?" Jim asked.

Pam, now armed with far more data than before, knew precisely what she was looking for in the mountain of emails. An hour later, she found what she knew had to be there, three incriminating emails in fact. Such a satisfied look her face had never had before. Now she set to work trying to work out the best means of presenting her case.

After supper, Pam checked her email once more. Sure enough, there was a reply from the Board of Governors. She read the preliminary "blah blah blah" about how unusual her request was, how inconvenient, but the bottom line read. "We shall convene on May 2 at Bradbury's at precisely ten a.m. You have exactly thirty minutes to present your case." Additional warnings about this being a hoax or not worth their time followed, which she ignored.

She sent a message to her friends, telling them what she

was doing and when. No sooner had she sent them than she received a message from Governor Alister. He had returned and wanted to see her in his office. She smiled and felt calm at last. She headed for his office.

Chapter 13—The Board of Governors

Pam had but ten days to prepare the defense of her lifetime. From her point of view, everything depended upon her presentation being positively perfect, with no loose ends, no holes that could be utilized. Alister had asked her if she knew what she was doing, did she realize the ramifications of her email request. She had said that she had, and now she had to live up to his expectations. No, that was not exactly correct. She had to live up to her own expectations.

Limited to thirty minutes, Pam needed to present every key piece of evidence along with supporting legal documents. Yet, she knew from their earlier studies of government and the Board of Directors explicitly, that half would be Dominus supporters, looking to find any way to shoot down her presentation.

She cut all her classes for the entire week, something utterly unheard of for Pam. True, Lindsey, Amanda, Emilio, and Kathy were taking copious notes for her. Still she knew that she would have a next to impossible task to catch back up in the short weeks that remained, but she knew she had to do this properly and correctly. Kindly, her friends left her alone, rarely distracting her from her work.

By Saturday morning, she had finally pieced together all supporting legal documents, proving various assertions that she would be making. Now she began playing back her presentation, looking for logical flaws, looking for anything that might be jumped upon and used to invalidate her conclusions.

Over lunch, she sighed, "Now to get it in the right order." That was all she said.

"You can do it. If anyone can, you can," Lindsey encouraged her. She had unlimited faith in Pam. A half hour later, Pam was back at it once more. By suppertime, she was finished. Her presentation ran for barely fifteen minutes, well under the allotted time limit. She fired off copies to her secure server and her father's server as well. Taking a deep breath, she messaged Alister, asking for his help in setting up the display for the morning session.

Alister personally walked her to the Admin Hall. They went to a fancy meeting room on the second floor, filled with plush chairs and a giant flat screen display monitor. She downloaded her presentation onto the small computer and then played it through, satisfied that all was as good as she could make it. Alister, however, had stayed out of the room while she played it back. According to the rules of the Board, he was not allowed to view her presentation or to assist her in any way. Since she didn't trust anything to chance, she made a backup copy onto a DVD and hid it in the room, just in case someone got to this little computer before her presentation and tried to destroy it.

Finally, Alister walked her back to the dorms. "You will do just fine tomorrow. Relax and enjoy it," he suggested. Pam didn't know how she could possible relax, let alone enjoy it. Yet, Lindsey came to her rescue in part.

"Come on; shower time." She took Pam to their showers and gave her a long water massage in their fancy Jacuzzi, which did the trick, loosening muscles Pam had not known were so cramped.

"Per the rules, I'm allowed to bring along one supporter. How would you like to come, Lindsey? You don't have to do or say anything, just give me support," Pam asked.

"Cool! I'd love to. Thanks for asking me," Lindsey replied, very eager to hear firsthand what went on in the meeting.

By the next morning, Pam was almost too nervous to eat breakfast. Wisely, Lindsey had Pam eat a turkey sandwich along with some orange juice and a large milk, hoping the turkey and milk would relax and calm her friend. Together, they walked down to the Admin Hall and went to the second floor room. Per her instructions, she was to wait outside until called.

"No matter what happens, Pam, we are all incredibly proud of what you are doing," Lindsey whispered to her friend. At last, the door opened and someone beckoned them to enter. Pam walked determinedly into the room and went to the front, beside the small computer. She fired it up only to discover that someone had deleted her presentation. She caught a snicker from somewhere behind her, but this she ignored. She leaned over behind the computer, retrieved her DVD, and inserted it. While it was loading, she finally turned to face the full Board of Governors. Alister was sitting at the side of the room; Lindsey, beside him.

Around the table sat the twelve Governor Generals. A name placard identified each person. The culprit, Henry Albright, Denver, Colorado, US, sat on her immediate right. Beside him sat Molly Breckenridge, London, England, UK. Next came Run Lun Sun, Peking, China. Bale Runsgore, Calcutta, India, and Tom White, Durban, SA, Africa, were beside them. These Pam knew were supporters of Dominus Malefic. On her left sat Alison Vandersol, Vancouver, BC, Canada, who was the current chairwoman of the Board. Next to her sat Rao Paolo, Rio, Brazil, South America, followed in turn by Al Zhan, Taiwan, Pacific Islands, Tammy Springs, Sydney, Australia, and Pina Pong, Singapore, SE Asia. The two on the fence men sat at the very end of the table, Hans Jurgens, Amsterdam, Netherlands, EU, and Vladimir Chevsky, St. Petersburg, Russia.

Alison Vandersol spoke clearly and decisively, "This special session of the Board of Governors is now in session per article forty-seven of our bylaws. We are here to hear Miss Pam Betts speak on behalf of Governor Alister Broadwell of Arthur Bradbury's School of Magic. Let the records show that he is present as is Miss Betts and her representative, Miss Lindsey Barron. Miss Betts, you have thirty minutes to make your presentation. Start now."

"Thank you for allowing me to speak. I will first make a short video presentation that outlines the precise and succinct details that I wish this Board to know. I will then entertain any questions you might have." With that, she hit Play and stood aside, allowing the twelve members to watch.

First, she showed the legal standing on expected privacy of emails: none. They were in the public realm, no privacy expected, legally. Only on the rare secure email systems could one expect privacy. With this documented, giving the exact legal clause and location, a series of emails to and from Governor Albright appeared on the screen, along with Pam's short commentary on each. An initial email from Dominus requesting he find a way for Alister be fired from his position, suggesting that he use an avenue of incompetence. A follow up email showed the abandoned silver mine shafts and their relation to the existing staff tunnels of Bradbury's. Pam had highlighted the tiny distance that the shaft had to be extended to connect with Bradbury's staff lounge. This was followed by photos of the secret entrance made in the ceiling.

Next came another series of emails directing the Death Stalker Hank Bertoni actions, along with specific instructions concerning the attempt to sabotage the school bus and the initial bombing of the stadium. Pam presented a short description of each action event and its outcome. She showed on the screen the fingerprints that she had taken and that the Department of Law now had on file.

Little by little, Pam connected each email with the resultant action on the part of Hank. Then, she showed the coercion of Hank Wilkinson, the sixth year Black Hall student, and what his orders were. After showing his fingerprints did not match those of the Mad Bomber, she showed two short clips of his apparent suicide, the second clip showed what had actually happened. Just as a furor was about to erupt over where she could have possibly gotten this real video, her documentation appeared on the big screen, complete with the official time-date stamp and seal of legality from the security company involved.

The next round of emails showed clearly that Governor Albright then ordered the ultralight attack on Bradbury's, attempting, if possible, to kill Lindsey Barron, if the opportunity arose, which it did. Her video then showed the results of that attack along with fingerprints that did not match those of the Mad Bomber, rather those of William the Bold.

Then two more short clips of William's miraculous escape from prison appeared, the second one showed the guard giving him back his wand. This brought even more hushed comments. Another round of emails appeared followed by the latest attack. In fact, Albright had shipped the explosives to Hank Bertoni. Pam had the order and shipping lists to back that assertion. Her video then relayed the results of the latest attack. Finally, she produced the official fingerprints now on file with the Department of Law for Hank Bertoni and showed the side-by-side visual comparison, yielding positive proof that Hank was the Mad Bomber.

Pam listened to her closing words. "In short, what you have just seen is a criminal attempt by Governor Albright to try to get Governor Alister fired. Additionally, he is responsible for the murder of the three staff members and the horrible burns suffered by the other nine. Because Governor Albright has violated numerous criminal codes (here she outlined the precise penal law codes), I will therefore be sending a copy of these documents to the Department of Law immediately upon the ending of this presentation. Said documents have now been dutifully sent. Thank you for your time." Her presentation ended. Pam moved in front of the screen and said shyly, "I will now entertain any questions you might have."

"How were these documents just sent? I mean you are standing here before us, and there is no outside computer contact," asked Hans Jurgens from Amsterdam.

"My laptop sent them from my dorm room. I knew that you were a very punctual group, and I simply timed my presentation. I assure you that they have been sent."

"You can't honestly believe any of this! This is preposterous!" yelled a very upset Governor Albright. "It's all a pack of lies."

"Are you telling us that you let other people use your own private secure computer that is dedicated solely to Board duties?" asked an insinuating Pina Pong.

Albright refused to answer that one. He was trapped no matter how he answered that one. Instead, he yelled, "You ugly bitch. I'll get you!" He waved his wand and started to cast a spell. Quietly, Lindsey cast hers first, non-verbally and without a wand. "Hold: Albright."

He had paid no attention at all to Lindsey, who sat quietly beside Alister. Besides, without any visual clue that she was also casting, he was not prepared for her spell. Her spell activated before he could finish his casting. Governor Albright merely froze in position, unable to move a muscle. Alister, who realized what Lindsey had done, merely walked over to him and removed his wand, handing it to Alison, the Board Chairwoman. "You may release him now, Miss Barron." Lindsey smiled and canceled her spell, silently.

Several Board members grabbed a hold of Albright, while the others stared at Lindsey. They had not seen her do anything at all. Her wand wasn't even out of her dress pocket!

"You bitch!" Albright screamed at Lindsey. "Dominus will hear about this, and you are as good as dead!"

"Governor Albright, if you cannot hold your tongue and foul language, I will be forced to silence you," Alison threatened.

"Your days are numbered," he started to threaten Alison. She waved her wand and silenced him. Albright's mouth worked, but no sounds came forth.

"Now then, that was an impressive bit of magic, Miss Barron," she said politely. "Non-verbal?"

"Yes, ma'am. Non-verbal, no wand," Lindsey said softly. "I was watching him and expected him to try something, and I was ready for him."

While the Governor Generals were impressed with Lindsey, they were more impressed with the masterful presentation by Pam. "Just how did you come by those emails?" asked Tom White, a Dominus supporter.

"Everyone should know that when you send an email, the electronic version is public domain. Copies of the emails can be found all over the Internet, as they travel from sender to receiver. That's why the law says there can be no expectation of privacy when you send one." Pam knowingly dodged a direct answer to his question, knowing that he was in league with Dominus.

Alister spoke up, "Excuse me, but a group from the Department of Law have just arrived in our parking lot, requesting to be allowed access to Governor Albright. Will you excuse me while I fetch them?"

"Certainly, Governor Alister. You may take Miss Betts and Miss Barron outside with you, but do have them remain near the door, in case we have further questions of them," Alison replied.

Pam and Lindsey followed him outside the room. Once the doors closed, Pam said, "Thanks, Lindsey, you saved my butt! He was going to kill me!"

"Indeed he was, Miss Betts. If you two will remain here, I will bring the Law men." Alister opened a magical door and stepped through it.

"Gosh, when are we going to learn that cool spell?" Lindsey asked.

"Next year, Lindsey. It is a Grade 4 spell," Pam replied. "I peeked into a third year student's spell book. Do you know what spell he was going to use on me?"

"Er, not really. I figured it must be something very nasty. His only hope was to kill you so that he could then claim everything you said was a lie. Anyway, that's what I thought."

The magical door opened and ten Law men and women, faces exceedingly stern stepped into the hallway, followed by Alister. He winked at the girls and led the others into the meeting room. The girls would have loved to see what happened inside, but didn't dare peek. Pam wished that she had installed one of her Spy Cams in there, though.

A couple minutes later, the Law people came out, dragging a protesting Governor General Albright with them. He was securely bound and even gagged, but he still glared hatred at the two girls as he was led away.

"What really bothers me," Pam said, "is that sooner or later, Dominus is going to break Hank and Albright out of jail. Then, he's going to come after me."

"I know, Pam. We just have to learn all the magic we can and help each other. Look at the positive side: now even Deiter is on our side. I never, ever though Deiter would be with us in going after Dominus and the Death Stalkers. We are strong, as long as we all work together, just like Governor Alister says," Lindsey waxed philosophical. Pam squeezed her hand, grateful for her support. "Besides, we are a team!" Both girls smiled.

A bit later, the door opened, and Alister stepped out. "You can come back in now. They have all gone." The two quickly went back inside, only the placards remained as a memento of the meeting. "You may keep the placards, Pam. I thought you might like them." She grinned and began collecting them.

"As far as the outcome, Pam, Governor General Albright has been arrested. The Board voted to expel him from the Board of Governors. An election will be held late this summer to elect a new US Governor General. I would say that you were entirely successful with your project. I will see to it that you have an automatic A for your government class. One less course for you to have to catch up on, I believe."

"Wow. Thanks. That helps, but I'm afraid that I've missed an entire week of classes," Pam said exuberantly.

"You are entirely welcome. I would like to ask a favor of you, Pam. May I replay your presentation for the entire school this evening at supper? I would like the whole school to know the entire truth of what has been happening around here this school year."

"Sure, can the dishwasher staff watch it too? I mean they suffered the most from Albright's attacks."

"Absolutely. Thank you. I will keep your DVD a little longer then. By the way, you two have most certainly made a solid, long lasting, and impressive impression on the Board of Governors. This is, as you know, both good and bad. It is good in that you have gained perhaps five strong allies. Yet, it is bad in that Dominus is now keenly aware of Miss Betts as well as Miss Barron, once again. I will speak with your fathers." Pam began to worry about her parent's safety. Would Dominus hurt them to get back at her?

"On the brighter side, Pam, I have been here for nearly a quarter of a century. In all these years, never have I seen a better job of sleuthing nor such a perfect legal presentation. I would not be surprised to see the Department of Law attempting to hire you as soon as you graduate. Please accept my thanks for a job exceedingly well done." Pam grinned from ear to ear.

"Now I think that you should return to your friends. I believe they are most anxious to find out the results." The two lit out for the dorms, eager to tell the others that Alister would not be fired.

"Arrested? Incredible!" exclaimed Amanda, as Pam related the news to half of Yellow Hall, who was waiting their return in the commons.

"Cool, Pam! I knew you could do it!" Jim added.

Tom merely lifted Pam up into the air and swung her around, while everyone cheered her, much to her embarrassment. Pam hated being in the limelight. "Now tell us all about it! Was it scary being with so many powerful wizards and witches?" Tom asked.

Pam spent a half hour going over what had happened. Everyone gasped when she told how Albright drew his wand and began to cast a killing spell on Pam. Of course, they cheered Lindsey when they heard that she had actually cast the Hold Another Person spell on him, ending any possibility of the Governor General's escape or attacks. "Governor Alister is going to show everyone my presentation tonight at suppertime. So you all can see just how guilty Albright really is. Now, where are all those notes you took for me? I have an entire week of work to learn in only one afternoon!" Pam declared, suddenly realizing that she had missed a whole week, and tomorrow she would be utterly lost in all her classes.

Pam was standing off to the side of the big screen in the dining room. Alister had moved the unit here from the Admin Hall meeting room, and Pam had given the entire student body a very brief explanation of what she had done to force the Board of Governors to assemble here at Bradbury's to hear her testimony, saying as little as possible. She was more nervous now than when she was standing before the Board of Governors. She played the fifteen-minute presentation. Her final words replayed and the monitor went blank. Pam turned it off. Utter silence filled the otherwise noisy dining room.

Off to her right near the conveyor belt system stood the dishwashing staff. They had come to see it as well. One of those men who had been so badly burned began to solemnly clap. At once, the other staff eagerly joined him, followed by the entire student body! Pam's face turned beet red, and she couldn't wait for tomorrow to come, tonight to come, any significant period to elapse so she would be out of this center stage!

When the applause died down, Governor Alister allowed her to go sit with her friends once more. He then explained what had happened after her presentation, including the role that Lindsey had played, preventing Albright from doing any further harm or escaping.

"Finally, I believe it is entirely fitting for us all to acknowledge the incredible actions, which prevented yet another bombing, possibly harming hundreds of you. Will the following students please rise? Deiter Cross, Jim, Tom, and Amanda Whitewater, Pam Betts, Lindsey Barron, Emilio Lopez. These students risked everything not only to stop the Mad Bomber from striking once again, but also to capture him alive. Let's give them our thanks." Once more, the room exploded in loud applause and cheering. In fact, the Black Hall students whistled and cheered Deiter, who enjoyed this attention. Finally, it was time to dine.

A while later sitting with her friends in the commons, Pam asked, "Okay, what all have I missed?"

"Well, we won the soccer match, five to three. Lindsey and Amanda scored twice each," Emilio replied.

Pam giggled, "Great. Sorry I missed it, but what I meant is school work."

"Oh, well, Professor Herbert is reviewing everything to prepare us for the big test," Emilio answered, "though I don't think it is a review. I swear I've never seen the stuff before."

"I'm with him," Kathy added, "I'm sure we've not seen it before." Naturally, Pam did not believe either of these two and collected all the notes that everyone had taken for her.

"Of course, it's a review," she said after looking through the dozen pages. She began explaining how it was just a different, more concise way of defining the problems. Pam had the feeling that she was going to be spending a lot of time tutoring these two.

"Oh, we are covering the human reproductive system this week," Audrey announced, "in biology, I mean. Honestly, how complex can it be?" Pam's face reddened slightly. It promised to be an interesting week.

After looking over all the notes, Pam finally found a

very useful bit of information. Because of the upcoming Nationals next weekend, the professors were staggering their final exams over several weeks. This she began to work to her advantage, drawing up a study schedule such that she would be fully prepared for each test.

"Okay, gang. Here's how we do this. First, we all get through our spell-casting practical this week, yes, all of us this week. Then, next week we hit math hard. I have a pass on government, but I'll help you all through it. The following week, we hit music, English, and history hard, dealing with those tests. That leaves us with the last two weeks to finish off the two magic theory classes. Let's get to work."

Chapter 14—The Nationals Again

May 6 came. The whole school assembled in the Stadium, just as they had last year, giving their team a rousing send off to the Nationals. The sun shone brightly in the morning sky, drying the dew upon the green grass. Governor Alister presided over the big send off for the Yellow Hall track team. "It is with the greatest pride that Bradbury's School of Magic sends these fine young athletes to compete in the Nationals. Last year, they raced to third place. This time may they bring home the first place trophy!" The crowd cheered and yelled for a minute.

"As I call your name, please step forward, and I will place your official ribbon around your neck. Captain Becky Salinos." She walked slowly and held her head high, Becky had high hopes of leading her team to victory. Sally was introduced next, followed by Jake and Tom. Alister was going in age order. Next came Jim. Lindsey, Amanda, and Emilio were next to be brought forward, while Fern was last. After a loud round of cheering and yelling, Governor Alister explained, "Today, they travel to Des Moines, Iowa. Tomorrow, they compete. Sunday, they return. Let us all root and hope that they can bring a trophy back with them!" They received the largest applause yet, and they walked off the field.

Near the field, they picked up their small backpacks with a change of clothes, their track outfits, and their wands. Because of tight security, they were allowed to bring little else. Hank and Betsy, the coaches, were the last to board the bus in the parking lot.

Professor Cho Lin accompanied Hank and Betsy, since she was the Yellow Hall Councilor. Though the bus was nearly empty, Amanda and Lindsey went to their usual seats in the very back and on the top level. Fern and Jim joined them. Jim explained to his little sister, "You don't want to miss the view. You can see much better from up here."

As the countryside sped rapidly past them, they gazed in awe at the spectacular Colorado Rockies, which soon gave way to their homelands, the high plains. However, once they entered Kansas, the scenery rapidly became incredibly boring. Like last year, they dozed off for a time. Around lunchtime, the bus came to a halt outside a giant stadium that dwarfed their own. "Wake up sleepy heads, we're here," Jim called out to everyone. "Come on. Lunchtime."

Just like last year, here in the bus parking lot, Lindsey saw dozens of other school buses. She wondered just how many other schools were competing. She failed to find out last year and vowed to ask about it this time.

Hank led them into the large dining hall. A man asked for their school name and pointed out a banner. Hank said, "Hey, we are over there. See that big Bradbury's School of Magic banner? That's us. Come on."

A waitress came to take their lunch orders, and, while they waited for her to return with their orders, Hank opened their schedule card and read it to the group. "Okay, we are up at ten in the morning. Because we were trophy winners last year, we get a break on the very first race. We get the second set at ten, not at eight in the morning, and we go against a weaker team this time. If you remember, last year our first race was against the New York City School of Magic, very tough competitors. This year, our first race is against the Twin Cities School of Magic."

"Where's that?" asked Fern.

"Minneapolis-Saint Paul, Minnesota," Hank replied. "Sixteen schools are competing in elimination style. If we win, we move on to join the next eight. This track supports four simultaneous team races. Half of the sixteen schools race at eight in the morning, the other half at ten. If we win, then at one p.m. we race one of the other winners and move into the quarter finals. Like last year, if we get into the quarter finals, we are assured of a trophy. If we are incredibly lucky and win that race, then we race in the final race for first place, after the two losers race for third place, at two p.m. The final race is at three p.m. There is a banquet at five and then, first thing the next the morning, we head home."

Hank smiled, "Ah, here comes our food."

Later, they were shown to their rooms, and they

changed into their track outfits. Hank and Betsy led them down to the track for a practice session. Many other students from the other schools were also on the field doing trial runs, getting the feel of this new, fabulous track. Lindsey thought that the running surface was the best yet. Their hopes high, The team had dinner and went to bed early, but many were very nervous, however.

Finally, around 9:30 in the morning, they went to their warm up positions at the side of the track. Near them, the Twin Cities group was also warming up. Lindsey looked at her competition. Most all the racers were at least forth year or higher. She saw none that was her age or even Fern's. Lindsey tried to keep in mind that this team was probably not the stiffest competition that they would be facing, if Hank's analysis were correct.

Becky took her team aside for a final word. "Remember how exhausted we were last year during the third place race. Let's be smarter this year. Don't try to set new track speed records on our first race, just beat them. Save our strength for the later races. Got it?"

"And here comes the Arthur Bradbury's School of Magic, Colorado," the announcer said enthusiastically over the loud speaker. Lindsey saw that there were thousands of people in the stands, and her stomach really gave a lurch, just as it had last year. After they were announced, the race began. One minute later, a smiling Sally walked back; she'd won her 100-meter dash by a foot.

Becky, Jake, Fern, and Emilio went to their starting positions for the mile relay race. Meanwhile Amanda, Lindsey, Jim, and Tom took theirs for the twenty-mile relay race. As before, Lindsey would lead off, passing to Jim after five miles.

Amanda sent her a Message, a paper floated before her eyes until she read it.

Keep our pace. Ignore the other runner. Watch us as you go by. A.

The paper vanished, and Lindsey smiled back at Amanda. She took her position beside the tall Twin Cities boy who was a fifth year student. He gave her a sneer, which she ignored.

The announcer gave the countdown, and the two sprinted from the starting line. He tried to egg her to speed up, but Lindsey watched her pace, concentrating on bringing to mind her racing Apache style pace. As she passed Amanda, she got a thumbs up sign and knew she was on the right pace. Here, the track was double the size of the one at school. Hence, the runners only needed to make five passes around the track. Hank located himself half way around so that he could signal his runners, when they were beginning the last half mile, at which point they would pour on the speed.

Lindsey had been running all her life at the higher elevations of Colorado. After last year, she knew that this was a benefit. At this much lower elevation, she didn't feel as winded as she maintained her pace. At last, Hank's whistle brought her out of her mechanical run, the last half mile. As they had practiced, Lindsey slowly increased her pace, passing her competitor! Now she spied Jim begin his warm up run, matching her speed ready for the handoff. As she passed the finish line, Jim snatched smoothly the baton from her hand, and she began to slow down.

At last, Lindsey could just relax, catch her breath, and cheer for Jim, Tom, and Amanda. "Oh, we won," Fern came up to her, grinning broadly. Lindsey shook her hand.

Finally, Amanda flew across the finish line, victory went to Yellow Hall and Bradbury's! Time was a spectacular 106:33! While this was a minute less than their first race here last year, they had not expended so much effort, hoping to save some for the trophy race.

As they ate, Becky pointed out to Fern, "At least we are in the best eight schools in the country." Fern beamed, very glad to be a contributing member of the team.

At one p.m., they had to race Chicago's School of Magic. They had raced against them at this time last year, Lindsey remembered. Again, all the team members were much older; none was less than fifth year students. Their competition looked terribly fierce indeed.

Lindsey walked to the starting line and looked at her competitor. He was tall and thin, nearly a foot taller than she was. "Hi, I'm Fred, sixth year."

"Lindsey, second year," she replied. "I remember you from last year. Say that was not me that you talked to after the race. It was Dominus Malefic impersonating me. Sorry about that."

"Wow! We heard some rumors. Can we chat later? Good luck, Lindsey." She agreed and wished him the best as well.

Then the race began, Lindsey sprinted out of the block and immediately found her pace. All the running with her Apache friends over the summer was paying off. However, she noticed that Fred decided to pace her, just as he did last year. Like well-oiled machines, she and Fred continued to speed down the long track, admiring how great the track felt beneath their feet. Minutes later, Hank sounded his whistle, and she slowly increased her speed to the best she could manage. Just like last year, Fred, her competitor, was keeping pace with her, though he was straining his utmost. Lindsey pushed all the harder, and then concentrated on making a perfect handoff to Jim. Finally, she slowed down to cool off and catch her breath. Fred was right beside her. They had been in a virtual tie the whole five miles, exactly like last year.

"I thought I had you this year, Lindsey," Fred gasped. "You, good runner indeed. Tied me again! Good job."

She grinned back. "What do you mean? You tied me." He grinned at the tease, "You are good too! Going to be a close race." A while later, she joined the others. Becky reported that Sally won her heat, but her group lost. Thus, everything depended on this last race. Lindsey gave Sally a big hug. On cloud nine, Sally had now won two sprints in a row.

"Man, this Chicago team is good. Jim's in a tie as well!" Becky exclaimed. Sometime later, Becky moaned, "Still a tie. I can't believe Tom's only tied. Come on Amanda! It's all up to you." She, of course, could not hear him. She was facing a sixth year, veteran runner, who at last pulled ahead of her. Unwilling to break her pace, she allowed him the advantage, saving herself for that final sprint. As they got the final whistle for the last half mile, he was already several hundred feet ahead of her, just as his counterpart had been last year.

Fred, who was now standing near Lindsey, commented,

"This is a repeat of last year! How do you women do it?"

"Apaches," Lindsey teased him. Fred grinned. Both watched their team members flying down the last few feet. Amanda increased her speed once more, drawing on her inner strength. Faster and faster, she flew down the long straightaway. She caught up to him and crossed the finish line two strides ahead of him!

The whole team yelled and cheered. Soon the scoreboard displayed their time: 106:40. Just as Lindsey suspected, unlike last year, they were conserving their strength and had only slowed a little from their first race, a very good sign indeed.

Fred commented, "Amazing, Lindsey, you've knocked us out of the finals two years in a row. Incredible. I'll see if I can meet with you after the banquet tonight. I'll be rooting for you in the next race. Good luck." He shook her hand.

However, they only had two hours to eat and rest up before the next race against the Sam Houston School of Magic. As they looked at their competition, Lindsey saw that they were up against an entire team of sixth year runners! She remembered how they were beaten last year by the Los Angeles team, also composed solely of sixth year students.

"Okay, we can do this," Becky instilled some heartening words. "I think that this race will be won by our Apaches, who have been running all summer. Let's do it!"

Sally lost in short order, but only by a fraction. A little while later, the four milers lost theirs, again only by a few feet. Lindsey, warming up, made a decision. They had to win this race or be satisfied with third or fourth place, just like last year. She recalled how badly they had been beaten by Los Angeles with their four sixth year runners. "I'll take second place," she whispered to herself, making the decision. Then, the race began. Lindsey found her usual pace, which was easily going to be matched by her long legged competitor. Instead, Lindsey pushed just a little harder, giving it her all on this run, knowing that she wouldn't have anything left for another race. Yet, if she could just somehow give her friends a lead after this first five miles, maybe they could hold on to it. Amanda, then Jim and Tom, tried to signal her that she was going slightly too fast. She ignored them and continued to push herself to the limit. When she finally handed off to Jim, she had managed to give Jim a hundred foot lead over Houston.

When she finally got her breath after nearly collapsing, she explained to Amanda, "We have to win this race. I shot myself to get us a lead. If you can hold it, then we race for second place. I know I will be slow if I race again today, but it will be worth it if we can take home second place this year."

Jim held his own, refusing to break his pace and training pattern as had Lindsey. He realized why she had done what she had done, however, and hoped her change of strategy would pay off. When he handed off to Tom, the Houston runner had begun to catch up, his lead was down to seventy feet. When Tom handed off to Amanda, their lead had dropped off to thirty feet; the Houston runners had been forced out of their racing strategy and were giving it all they had to try to catch up.

As Amanda raced along, maintaining her usual pace, even though she felt herself tiring, she had a lead and was determined not to lose it. If she did, she knew that they would most likely lose and only get fourth place, Lindsey would not be able to hold her own in the next race. However, Lindsey's strategy had thrown a monkey wrench into Houston's game plan, forcing their runners to play catch up, throwing them off their usual game pace. As she passed her fourth mile, her competitor had closed the gap to a mere ten feet. One more mile, she just had one more mile to hold on to Lindsey's incredible lead.

As the two runners came down the final straightway with the race on the line, Amanda knew that she had him beaten. Forced to run faster than normal the entire way in an attempt to catch up, the Houston lad was shot. Amanda did not have to pour it on as she normally did; she coasted across the finish line, a few feet ahead of the other runner. They had done it! They would be racing for first place!

Everyone yelled, cheered, and then headed for the showers to cool off and try to recover as much as possible. Unlike last year, they would now have a full two hours recovery time before the championship race against the Miami

School of Magic. Their time was still hovering around the 106 minute mark, due almost entirely to Lindsey's effort.

Drinking energy-boosting drinks, Becky and her long distance runners began to work out a strategy for the final race. Lindsey said, "Well, I won't be worth a darn in the next race. I'll be lucky to hit seven minute miles."

"True, any ideas how we can work around this?" Becky asked.

"We could switch Amanda and Lindsey around, see if Amanda can give us a lead and hope that Lindsey could somehow hold on to it," suggested Jim.

"Yes, but they always put their best runner in the last position, as we do with Amanda. He'd be sure to catch Lindsey," Tom pointed out.

"I think that the best thing to do is to keep to our game plan," Amanda suggested. "We have all worked at longer distance running all summer. I don't see any way around all of us breaking our running pace, giving it our all."

Jim commented, "I see what you mean. If we let Lindsey run first and that gives them a big lead, then we have no choice but to break our pace and try to close the distance, just like we did to Houston. If we reverse our order, we can likely keep our pace and maybe stay with them until Lindsey races last, and at that point, she falls way behind. Personally, I would rather work out on trying to catch up than coast along and let Lindsey take the fall for us."

Everyone agreed, and no changes were made. Lindsey's sacrifice had gotten them into the championship race. Now they would have to see if they could deal with it. A little later, they watched as St. Louis School of Magic took third place over Sam Houston. Then, with a great fanfare, the championship game was announced, and they took their positions once more.

Sally lost by three feet this time. The miler's lost by ten feet; exhaustion was taking its toll. Once more, everything depended upon the long distance runners. As Lindsey began, she discovered her legs were aching, and she couldn't hit her usual pace at all. Instead, she just did her best to get through the five miles. When she handed off to Jim, Miami had a hundred fifty foot lead over them.

Lindsey had not realized that the Miami team was also exhausted. Hence, they were only a little behind. Now everything fell upon the Apache runners, who had to catch up by breaking their own racing paces. Jim cut into Miami's lead, leaving them only a hundred feet behind as he passed off to Tom. When Tom passed off to Amanda, he had also cut their lead another fifty feet.

Amanda realized that she too had a choice to make. Since her brothers had been able to cut into Miami's lead, she ought to be able to do so as well. However, if she did so, she would have nothing left for the final sprint to the finish line, so unlike her normal race. On the other hand, she doubted that she could pull out enough to catch up fifty feet in the last burst of speed. She was too tired to do that. Hence, she decided to do as her brothers had done, give it her all to close the distance from the get go.

This was what a championship race was all about. Amanda, like her brothers, managed to close the distance. Two runners flew down the finish line, very nearly neck and neck. Miami won by a mere foot! The noise of the crowd drowned out conversation for a while, giving Amanda time to cool down a little.

Even though they took second place, the Yellow Hall team hugged each other, as if they had won first place. Indeed, they had won second place and very nearly first as well. Lindsey's strategy had ensured them of a better finish than last year. This they celebrated. Their time was 110:12, fully ten minutes faster than their last year's final performance.

"Just wait until next year," declared Tom with a passion.

Next, came the team presentations. Lindsey and Amanda's legs felt like butter, and they could barely walk onto the field. Even Jim and Tom felt utterly exhausted as well. Becky, who was in the best shape, grandly accepted the very tall second place trophy amid the noisy cheering. Emilio and Fern also helped her hold it high in the air.

Amanda was leaning on Lindsey, as they both waved at the cheering mass of people. Just then, Amanda spotted the telltale magical energy beam coming from high in the stadium crowd. It was heading straight for the two of them! Without thinking, she shoved Lindsey forward, falling down on top of her. In the next instant, the disintegration beam struck the track behind where they had been standing, carving a three foot hole into the ground, sending a shower of debris over the other team members.

Several seconds elapsed while the stunned crowd tried to grasp what had just happened. Lindsey felt so helpless. She could not see her attacker to retaliate. Should they run? If so where? Becky screamed, and she and Emilio put the trophy in front of the two girls, hoping to turn it into some kind of protective barrier. They all felt naked, helpless without their wands. Only Lindsey could cast spells, but she had no idea what to cast. At last, she cast her area invisibility spell, hiding her entire team.

They watched as mass pandemonium broke out. Amanda whispered that she saw another flash of magical energies and suggested the assassin had likely teleported away. Alister and Cho Lin suddenly appeared in front of them, wands at the ready. Betsy and Hank moved in behind them. Security men flooded the area where the attack had originated, but as Amanda suspected, they found nothing. However, the crowd was in a panic, many racing for the exits, completely out of control. The Nationals had never before been the scene of a magical attack, let alone an assassination attempt as this clearly had been.

"Good move Lindsey," Governor Alister spoke softly, while not looking directly at them. "What I want you all to do is to grab hold of everyone's hand. Let me know when everyone is holding on to another, chain like. I'am going to teleport you all out of here." A minute later, Lindsey landed back in their hotel room, along with everyone else in a big jumble on the floor.

"Thanks! Someone tried to kill me," Lindsey exclaimed. "If it hadn't been for Amanda's quick thinking and shoving us out of the way, I'd be dead now."

"Yes, Amanda was brilliant. Very well done, Miss Whitewater," Governor Alister replied. "I think that you all should, as you say, hit the showers. I know your bodies are exhausted. I know mine is just having watched yours today. That's a joke by the way. Congratulations on winning second place. Darn impressive, very well done."

Cho Lin appeared in the room. "Ah, whoever it was, they got away. Security forces are now dealing with the panicked crowd. Are you kids all right?" She looked very worried indeed.

"Yes, we're fine," Becky replied for her team. "Amanda spotted it just in time and got the two of them out of the way. Honestly, I felt so helpless without my wand. The only thing I could think of doing is putting the giant trophy in front of Lindsey as a barrier. Then, Lindsey made us all invisible, but still I felt so helpless." The others nodded. She had expressed just how they felt as well.

"You all handled yourselves superbly! Well done," Cho Lin replied. "Hank and Betsy are trying to meet with the officials. They are going to bypass the banquet unless they can get some guarantees of our safety." That sounded good to everyone, and they returned to their connecting rooms and hit the showers.

After the hot shower, Lindsey laid down on her bed and nearly fell asleep. At last, a starving sensation forced her awake. "Come on, Lindsey; time to eat," Fern called out to her.

"My legs are like putty again," Lindsey complained.

"So are all of ours," Jim consoled her.

"You can lean on me," Emilio suggested. Amanda leaned on Fern, Tom on Betsy, and Jim on Sally. The group headed down to the banquet arena, which was under extremely heavy security. Lindsey saw almost as many security men as participants!

After choosing the roast duck, Governor Alister and Professor Cho Lin both magically examined all the food and drinks on their table. Hank explained, "They are looking for poisons, bombs, and other bad things." Lindsey wondered who would poison their food. It seemed an awful thing to do.

The fancy dining hall was, as last year, all decorated in the colors of the top four winning teams. "Pretty cool, eh?" Emilio commented as Lindsey looked around.

After the meal, the officials gave several speeches, and each of the four winning team members rose and were presented a pin. Once the little ceremonies finished, they all headed to their rooms. Amanda, stiff and sore, could barely climb the stairs. "On the bright side, I'm not as sore as I was last year, but I think we need to run even longer this summer, gang."

After the dinner was done, Fred, from the Chicago team, came over to Lindsey. "Hi Lindsey. That was some racing you all did today, to say nothing of the attempt on your life." She smiled and introduced her team members to Fred.

"Say, can I ask you something?" She nodded. "In the third race, the one you took from Houston. Did you purposely break your normal pace?"

"Er, yes," she replied. "Last year, we kept our pace and lost. I figured that if I could get us a lead by overrunning myself, we would be in the running for at least second place. It worked, but I just had nothing at all for the championship race. I will do better next year."

"I thought so. I could tell you were running differently in that race. I've been watching all your races—that's how I could tell. Smart tactic, got your team into the championship race, good move." She smiled, but was a little amazed that someone else had spotted her shift so easily.

"What I don't understand is how Amanda, is that your name?" Amanda nodded. He continued, "How did you see that assassination spell coming? It was definitely a disintegrate beam that he shot at you. Darn fast reactions too."

"Er, I saw the magical energies coming our way. No time to do anything but shove her out of the way," Amanda answered truthfully. "Then Lindsey made us all invisible so it would be harder for him to attack us a second time, and Becky put the trophy between us as an additional barrier."

Fred looked at Amanda and then at Lindsey. "But you didn't have a wand with you, did you? It's against the rules for us to carry our wands in the race."

"Non-verbal, no wand casting," Lindsey said rather shyly. "Amanda is training to be a Tracker; she can see magical energy traces." She attempted to put the emphasis onto her friend and off herself.

"Then it's true, the rumors we have been hearing in Chicago—that you are in training to become a Dispeller?" he asked, eyes wide open.

"Well, yes."

"Cool! Way super cool! Oh darn, that's my coach waving for me. I guess I have to go. Here's my email address. Let's chat by email, okay?" He handed her a scrap of paper with his address on it. Lindsey had no time to give him hers. His coach was very insistent that he leave now.

At last, deserts finished, Alister escorted everyone to their rooms once more, and then he cast a number of protection spells on their doors. Amanda observed all the magical energies surrounding all the doors and windows and tried to explain them all to Lindsey and Fern. In the end, everyone fell asleep almost at once, however.

At breakfast the next day, the dining room was once again under very heavy security. Alister and Cho Lin once more cast numerous spells on the food they were about to eat. He was taking no chances at all, though Lindsey suspected that there was more to it than that. Perhaps he was sending a message to those that ran the Nationals.

After eating their fill, they gathered up their things and stood in line to leave the hotel and enter their bus. Standing in the huge lobby, Lindsey watched as fifty security men surrounded the Miami team and their coaches. As one large body, they marched out to their school bus. Only when the bus was underway did the men march back to the lobby. One asked Alister if he was ready, and the men surrounded the Bradbury group, escorting them safely to their bus. Then, they were on their way home.

The long distance runners slept the whole way back, their bodies very exhausted from the running. When they arrived, the entire student body was waiting for them in the stadium. Becky and Emilio proudly carried the huge trophy into the center of the field to the yells and cheers of the six hundred students. Lindsey, standing there before all her classmates, realized that this was Becky's finest hour, her proudest moment. She had captained her team into second place in the Nationals. She would treasure this moment for the rest of her life. Becky would be graduating in a few weeks and moving out into the world. Thus, this was her shining moment to remember always.

Once the celebrating was done, Governor Alister stood and outlined what had happened during the trophy presentation ceremony, describing how someone had tried to kill their team. Again, Lindsey realized his wisdom. News of the attack would soon, if not already, be all over KMAG news, Alister wanted the students to know what had really happened there.

"Wow. You nearly got killed, Lindsey," exclaimed Pam. They were back in their dorm room, stowing their few things. "Amanda, you are a super Tracker already! You've saved her life! Good going! Did they find out who did it?" Pam asked what interested her the most, who had done it.

After they said no, Pam added, "Well, I guess there would not be any real clues, if he teleported away immediately. But wait, maybe he left his fingerprints or DNA on some snacks. He must have watched the whole track meet, picking the right time to attack. I wish I had been there to investigate." The two girls chuckled.

The large study group followed Pam's schedule. During the week, all took their various exams, and all passed their practical spell-casting. Lindsey had them all down with the exception of the necromancy-based spells. Deiter Cross was the only student who got all the Grade 3 spells cast in the allotted forty-five minutes. Once again, he took his strategy from Lindsey's suggestions from last year, organizing them in the right order to minimize wasted time. When he was successful, he actually sent Lindsey a thank-you email, which surprised her immensely.

Chapter 15—The End of Term

Lindsey passed the music of the world test easily. Essentially, each student listened to some excerpts and had to identify the culture and era of the music. In fact, everyone in the class passed Cho Lin's test. The many recitals followed. Theoretically, each student had been practicing all year and now had to give a short performance before the class.

Lindsey decided to be brave and give her recital first. She had fallen in love with the ancient harpsichord, but in all honesty, she had only barely begun to learn how to play it. Professor Cho Lin transported the beautiful instrument into the classroom and Lindsey announced, "I am going to play *The Spanish Pavan* by John Bull, rather slowly though. She did her best with it, at least enjoying her own music playing.

Amanda gave her Native American song cycle, which Lindsey found interesting. Emilio joined her on drums on two songs, and then he did a fancy drum solo bit. Unfortunately, few others appreciated her music. One by one, the others gave their brief recitals. Some of those working on rock and roll songs sounded halfway descent.

Kathy played a simple flute song, passably well. Pam's rock and roll sound on the acoustic guitar was a hit, reproducing the old Jethro Tull sound from the 1970's. She was the only student who got a loud round of applause for her performance. Audrey chose to play the medieval pipe and drum so that all by herself, she could make a full, rich sound with percussion and melody. She did rather well and Lindsey enjoyed her music, which sounded rather Celtic.

By Monday of the last week of May, all their tests were finished, and the students were now officially done, free time for the final week. Unlike last year, the grades came out on time. Monday morning, the group compared grades and discussed their next year's classes. Lindsey received an A in all classes except biology, in which she got a B. Pam, of course, had straight A's. Amanda had A's in all but biology, algebra, and government, in which she had B's. Audrey had B's in algebra, government, and history; the rest were A's. Emilio had his usual C in algebra, with B's in all the other traditional subjects. He had A's in the three magic classes, however.

Fern was elated and just had to show her sister her report card: all A's! She also had cast all of her grade 0 and 1 spells perfectly and was quite proud of her achievement.

That afternoon, the group began working out what classes they would be taking next year, as third year students. Quickly, they realized that they had one actual elective course! Their schedules worked out as follows:

```
 8:00 Chemistry
 9:00 Algebra II
10:00 English/US History
11:00 Physical Education
12:00 lunch hour
 1:00 Spell Casting—Grade 4
 2:00 Evocation Theory I
 3:00 Illusion Theory I
 4:00 Study Hall/Elective
 5:00 Dinner
```

"Well, this is cool," Pam stated as she examined the printout of her next year's schedule. All had the same classes together as they had for the last two years. Lindsey was very glad of that, since each helped the others out—a scheme that had been highly successful thus far. "I wonder what we can take as an elective."

"It's tailored to your unique needs," Emilio pointed out, proudly. For once, he knew something that Pam did not. "I asked about that already," he hastily admitted. "I am taking Desert Survival Techniques. I thought that sounded interesting, though I probably ought to have taken Study Hall."

"Oh. Cool. No, Emilio, you would just sleep right through Study Hall. It's better that you take something educational," Pam pointed out. "How did you find out?"

"Just go see Professor Cho Lin," Emilio replied, "that is, if you don't want a Study Hall."

"Well, I am taking a Study Hall. I need it," Kathy stated flatly.

"Me too," Audrey added.

Pam, Lindsey, and Amanda trotted over to see Professor Cho Lin. They had to wait a few minutes. Several other students were there ahead of them. "Welcome, I assume you are here about your electives?" she asked politely.

"Yes, Emilio is taking Desert Survival, but I would like something more suited to me, if that's possible," Pam spoke for the trio.

"I believe that I would bean you if you said you wanted to take Desert Survival, Pam," Cho Lin jested. Pam grinned. "Actually, I am prepared for all three of you. Pam, how does Sleuthing Theory I sound to you?"

"Wow! There is such a course?" Pam asked, her eyes nearly bulging from her head.

"For you, there certainly is. Amanda, how does Tracking Theory I sound to you?"

"You're kidding? A real course in Tracking? Sign me up!" exclaimed Amanda.

"Lindsey," Cho Lin began.

Lindsey interrupted her, "You have a Dispeller Theory I course for me?"

Cho Lin grinned, "You bet. Shall I put you three down for those?" The trio raced back to the dorms to tell the others the fabulous news!

"Now we are really getting down to business!" exclaimed Pam. She was ready for the fall term to begin right now! "It is such a waste that we have to wait three whole, long months before we can begin!" she lamented. Emilio tossed a pillow her way, missing her head, however.

Now armed with their schedules, the group headed for the Bookstore to acquire their new textbooks for the fall. Lindsey, who was now used to covering two grades of spells each year, stared at the equally thick Grade 4 spell book. "These must be doubly harder to learn, since we only get one grade of spells the whole year," she noted. Pam concurred, after leafing through several pages.

Kathy lamented, "When will the math ever end?" She hated math as much as Emilio did.

With their books stowed in their rooms, the group

decided to take a walk in the formal gardens. However, as they began, Pam's cell phone rang. It was her father. The group moved away from her, giving her some privacy, though everyone was curious about the call. Seldom did their parents call here; usually the students called home on the weekends.

Pam's face was electric as she rejoined the others. "You will never guess what that was all about! Lindsey, I get to spend the entire summer with you and Amanda! Dad says that there have been some threats made against us and our home. Some minor vandalism happened last week. He thinks that it would be safer for mom and me to spend the summer on the Compton ranch. Isn't that the greatest news?" Lindsey gave her a big hug, as did Amanda. Emilio felt a little left out, as did Kathy.

That night, Lindsey called her mother, who told her about Polly and Pam coming to spend the summer. Lena hoped that this would be all right with her. Lindsey was elated and told her mother how excited she was about having Pam stay with them all summer. The end of term was turning out to be the best ever.

On Wednesday, Governor Alister messaged Lindsey, asking her to come to his office at once. Lindsey arrived, having run there from the dorm. "Is something wrong?" she asked, assuming the worst, though she didn't know what that might be.

"Oh no, no. Quite the contrary. I have a favor to ask of you. Next fall we are going to have another Special Needs student coming here. She is a transfer from the Twin Cities, I believe. Because of your background, I believe that you are the single-most student qualified to help her. That means that you would be appointed a Yellow Hall Floor Monitor, so that you can assist her as needed. She will be a third year student, as you are. However, I would like very much to have her room with you. I have spoken with Kathy a moment ago, and she is willing to move into the room next to yours to help out our new Special Needs student. Will you accept this additional responsibility? Of course, Sandy will also be a Yellow Hall Floor Monitor and can help you with anything you need. Will you accept this additional responsibility?"

"Sure, I certainly needed lots of help when I first came here. It is only right that I have an opportunity to return the help to someone else. Only I don't know the spells that Sandy uses to move all our things up to our rooms."

"Oh, that is not a problem. If you accept the responsibility, you will be taught that spell yet this week. It is not a difficult one."

"Great. I was wondering how the Floor Monitors were chosen and when. Sandy will be a sixth year student this fall, so we all expected some more Floor Monitors. Does this mean that I have to return a week early to help all the first years too?"

"Yes, on returning early, but mostly your task will be to assist our new Special Needs student. If you have extra time, I'm sure Sandy would love to have some help. Sandy is one of the best Yellow Hall Floor Monitors we've ever had."

"She sure is. Yes, I'll do it gladly."

"Thank you. I will warn you up front that this Special Needs student may be a bit of a challenge for you. However, now that you have accepted, I will also let you know that she will be staying at your ranch this summer. Your mother has graciously accepted boarding her this summer, subject to your accepting this added responsibility. Honestly, she has nowhere else to live, and your mother has a generous heart indeed."

"You, you mean all this was arranged before you spoke to me?" Lindsey asked, just a little perplexed with the whole business.

"Yes, but it all hinged upon whether you were willing to accept the added responsibility of the Special Needs student. If you were not, then other arrangements would have had to be made. Frankly, Lindsey, if you had not accepted it, I really don't know what else I could have done for her. I'm so grateful that you willingly stood up and accepted this added responsibility. I thank you, and I do owe you a favor, Lindsey. Thank you. You should go straight to Professor Cho Lin, who will teach you right now the new spell that you need to do your job effectively. Oh yes, by the way, her name is Ashley Stokes." His phone rang, and Lindsey left, heading for the Hall of Illusions.

An hour later, Lindsey had the spell down pat. "Move This To Cho Lin's Desk!" The book immediately moved from its position on the floor over to her desk. Lindsey grinned.

"Good girl. Now, let's see if you can do it without your wand," Professor Cho Lin suggested. A half hour later, Lindsey had that mastered and turned her attention on to doing it non-verbally. This was trickier, as it required her undivided attention. If her mind wandered, the book ended up in crazy locations about the room. Two hours from the start, Lindsey felt completely confident that she could cast this special spell easily. She also thought that she could teach this one to Amanda and Pam as well. It would give them something to do, besides packing.

On her way back to the dorm to tell everyone about her new position and her new spell, her mother called. "Hi dear. I'm so glad that you accepted the responsibility of looking after Ashley while she is at school with you," Lena said.

"It gives me the chance to repay all the kindness others gave to me when I came here. It is the very least I can do. Besides, I like helping people. Are you sure you're not going to be overwhelmed with so many staying with us now? I mean we have Audrey and Pam and Polly and now Ashley."

"No dear, Polly and I have taken a strong liking to each other. Besides, I discovered that I hate the empty nest syndrome."

"Huh?"

"It was terribly, terribly lonely around here when you went off to school, and I was all by myself. I don't know what I would have done if Lloyd had not been here. Someday after you have raised a family and all your children leave home, you will know what I am talking about, dear. Trust me. I'm looking forward to having all of you here, even if it is only for the summer."

They chatted a bit more. Lindsey was now convinced it was okay with her mother and rushed to tell the others the news. "What did Alister want?" asked Pam, her voice full of concern, suspecting some dire trouble had arisen. In fact, all of her friends had feared the worst when she dashed off to see him.

"You're now looking at your Yellow Hall Floor Monitor for next year. I have accepted the responsibility of helping out a new Special Needs student. Audrey Stokes. She will be a third year student, just like us. I'm so sorry that you are being forced to move next door to us, Kathy."

"What? She is moving? She knew about this and didn't tell us?" asked Amanda, a bit annoyed that Kathy had said nothing all these hours.

"Sorry, Alister told me not to say anything ahead of time. It all depended upon whether Lindsey would accept the position and would want to help her. I will be next door—that's not a big thing. I'm more than happy to do such a small thing to help a Special Needs student. After all, Lindsey was a Special Needs student when she came here, and we all helped her," Kathy explained.

"Thanks Kathy. She is going to come to live with us on the ranch this summer as well. I guess that we will be meeting her soon enough," Lindsey replied. "Oh, I almost forgot! The reason I was gone so long was that Cho Lin taught me a new spell: how to move our things into our rooms! It was an easy spell, actually. I thought that since we have lots of free time, I could try to teach it to you too."

"Woo hoo!" exclaimed Pam, eager to learn a new spell. Even Kathy was pleased to get the chance to learn this one. Moving objects was an incredibly valuable spell, as far as these four were concerned. By the end of the afternoon, all three now knew this spell. Pam had hundreds of uses for it, as did Kathy.

The next day, the girls began preparing for the Formal Dance, which would be held after the fancy dinner on Friday night. On Saturday night, graduation would be held and then on Sunday, everyone would be heading home for summer vacation.

"Oh my," exclaimed Lindsey. She had put on her new sky blue gown, made from silk, long and slender, with a deep leg slit. However, her bust line had grown substantially since her mother had made the dress for her last fall. In fact, all four girls had the very same problem. During the year here at school, they had not paid much attention. Now that they were trying on their prom gowns, all four discovered that their bodies were definitely maturing rapidly.

Kathy had the most sewing experience and, with measuring assistance from Pam, began to alter all four dresses accordingly. Lacking patterns and any real gauge of size, Kathy went by trial and error. By Wednesday evening, she finally had all four gowns properly altered. The four, wearing their gowns, examined each other's fit. All were quite satisfied now.

Pam spent Thursday in the Library, doing a bit of light reading. The others took long walks around the campus. Jim accompanied Lindsey all around. The flowers were in full bloom; the grass, bright green. Birds were everywhere, a perfect time of year here at the school.

Friday morning, long lines developed in the girl's restroom. By afternoon, the four girls were finally getting themselves dressed for the big dance. In contrast, Emilio, Jim, Tom, and several others were having an impromptu soccer game.

"Honestly, Kathy, don't you think that your dress is revealing too much?" asked Amanda. The low arcing cut revealed just a little too much she thought.

"No, it is supposed to be this low, to attract attention. After all, we are supposed to be attractive and all that. I learned that in biology," Kathy replied. Amanda sighed; no way would she reveal that much of herself.

"How do I look?" asked Lindsey. She had slipped into her new silk, full length gown that her mother gotten her for a Christmas present. The necklace that Kathy had given her adorned her bare neck, and she wore the bracelet of gold and turquoise that Emilio had given her last year.

"Wow, stunning. It's the latest style too. I think it looks even better than the one you wore last year." Pam complimented her.

"Yes, and your slippers match, Lindsey. You are finally getting a sense of fashion. If you all want, I can loan you some of my teen glamor and fashion magazines. They show all the latest fashions and how to accessorize properly," Kathy suggested. Indeed, she had a stack of magazines.

She went on, "You know the latest craze is to wear real

nylons, not pantyhose. You have to have a garter belt though." She pulled up her long gown to show off her newest acquisition.

"Now that is sexy," Pam commented, totally surprised with the frilly look.

"See, everyone finds them incredibly attractive," Kathy replied, more certain than ever that she had made some wise fashion decisions.

Finally satisfied they were properly dressed, the four began working on their hair. Lindsey decided just to brush hers out as normal, long brown hair down her back.

Kathy, with her short, curly brown hair, chose to wear a light brown prom style dress, which had just a hint of glitter in it. Amanda's dress was a light yellow, also full length with a wide walking slit, falling like a tube below her waist. Like Lindsey, she just let her long black hair lay down her back. Pam's prom dress was a light shade of red, gleaming and silky looking, though not made of silk as Lindsey's was. All year, Pam had allowed her short black hair to grow, secretly emulating that of Lindsey and Amanda, though she knew hers would never be as thick and silky looking as Amanda's. She snuck glances at those two and arranged her hair similarly.

Finally, it was time. First, everyone was to rendezvous in their commons, meeting up with their dates. Next, they would all dine together. Once the meal was finished, the dining hall would be turned into the grand ballroom. After a flurry of "How do I look's," the four girls headed down the stairs to the commons.

As soon as they entered the commons, Jim spotted Lindsey and came up to her. "Hi Lindsey. You look terrific!" As last year, he gave her a corsage, pinning it to her shoulder. He wore the same brown western suit, suede perhaps with dark thread highlights and a string necktie.

Henry Waldorf, the same boy who dated Amanda last year, came up to Amanda. As before, he looked like a perfect businessman, Lindsey thought, in his impeccable grey suit and black tie and highly polished black shoes. Henry was still slightly taller than Amanda was. "You look stunning, Amanda!" She beamed and took his arm. Lindsey took Jim's arm.

Lindsey looked around to see if Pam's date was here. She spotted them. As always, Monique Blackburn from Red Hall was dressed like a very well dressed man, a tuxedo as before. She wore her hair in a tight bun, but her red lipstick dispelled any notion that she was a man. Lindsey again observed that Monique was taking on the role of the gentleman this evening, escorting Pam, who looked radiant.

Jim escorted Lindsey to their table, held her chair for her to sit. While they chatted, Lindsey noticed that many of the older girls wore heels, and she decided that next year she should too. Indeed, this was the night of the school year when all the girls felt special, and they looked it.

The professors and faculty entered equally elegantly dressed, and Governor Alister gave a short welcome address and waved the food onto the tables with his wand. Monique and Pam sat next to Lindsey and Jim. "Doesn't Pam look fabulous?" Monique went on, chatting while they ate. Lindsey watched the two, and it was very evident that Monique was very taken with Pam, who felt very comfortable with the attention of Monique. She wondered if they really were in love. This was one thing about which Lindsey had no experience.

Before long, the delicious meal was finished. Like last year, Governor Alister announced that the chairs would be disappearing. It was a subtle hint to the shyer boys that they needed to dance, not sit around. All the tables and chairs then vanished.

The same musicians were here just like last year, she noted, and soon the stately music began to play. With Jim leading her out into the middle of the hall, now decorated in candlelight with gold and silver fluttering reflecting ribbons, Lindsey's heart raced. This year, she didn't have to concentrate on remembering how to dance as she had last year. She and Jim quickly became one with the rhythm and music. Time flew by.

Before long, it was intermission time. Audrey in her brown dress, eyes glowing, brought her date over to introduce him to her friends. Bill Williams, a third year Brown Hall student, was a shy lad, but was well dressed. From the way that he clung to Audrey, Lindsey saw that he really liked her. Pam insisted that Tom and Sandy use her cell phone to take a picture of the five couples. Grinning, all ten of them squeezed in, while Tom and then Sandy took several snaps. Only after Pam reviewed them, did she allow the group to move from their positions. She then took some of Tom and Sandy for them.

Once more, the music began. Jim led Lindsey elegantly into the middle of the room once again. Before long, the lights were dimmed and Alister's soft voice announced, "Last dance of the ball." So soon! How did it get to be ten p.m. so quickly, Lindsey wondered. Only a minute ago it was six. This same time distortion happened to her last year as well!

Jim pulled her body close to his as they danced this last one. Before long the music ended. Jim leaned over and he gave Lindsey a kiss on her lips and said, "Thank you, Lindsey for a yet another fabulous evening I will never forget."

She flushed, "I don't want it to end. How did time go by so fast?" Jim smiled and led her to the stairs. One by one, the four girls entered their room, feeling as if they were floating.

"This is so much fun! I wish we could do this a dozen times each year, not once," Lindsey exclaimed, still dancing to soundless music around their room.

"I agree. Henry really likes me; that's for sure. He's asked me to accompany him to Telluride next year. We are all going to be old enough to take the day trip off-campus, you know. I accepted," Amanda explained rather starry eyed.

"Emilio has really fallen for me. Did you see the way he was fawning over me all night? He kissed me at the end too!" Kathy spoke up. "He's going to take me into Telluride next year too. Say, how did the time fly so fast anyway?"

"Isn't Monique something else? She makes me feel absolutely pretty!" Pam volunteered. "I do think that Monique is in love with me. She's already volunteered to escort me to Telluride next year. Maybe we could take up a petition to have more formal dances. If we had enough signatures, maybe Governor Alister would schedule more of them."

It wasn't until around midnight that the four finally undressed and put away their formal dresses. Lindsey wished that she had many more opportunities to dress up like this, like once a week, maybe. Like last year, it made her feel so utterly different, extremely special.

The next morning was packing day for all six hundred students. The Awards and Graduation Banquet would be tonight, and early the next morning, the buses would take the students home for the summer. All bags had to be packed. "I keep getting more stuff," complained Lindsey, who had to make a quick trip to the Bookstore to purchase two more duffle bags.

After lunch, the track team met in the dining room, Becky's orders. "As you know, it is time for me to pass the baton of our team on to another. Sally and I are graduating."

"Second Place at the Nationals! Woo hoo!" Sally had to interject, totally proud of their achievement and trophy. Everyone grinned.

"Yes, so now it is my final responsibility to nominate your next team captain. As you know, if you later decide you don't like or want my choice, you can change it. I think it ought to go to Jake or Tom, both of whom will be sixth years this fall. It was a hard choice, and I want you all to know that I have discussed it with both of them. They both agree with my choice. I want Tom to take over as Yellow Hall team captain."

Everyone clapped and Jake spoke up, "Listen, I figured it was only fair for Tom to step into the limelight. Half our team is the Whitewaters, so he ought to have the chance."

Amanda gave Jake a hug, "Thanks, Jake."

"Well, you will need to find two new team members by the fall," Becky added. "Over the years that Sally and I have been on the team, that has been the single biggest problem, getting new team members. So few students are really interested in track and field, you know."

"Say, Becky, I've been wondering what you and Sally are planning to do after tonight's graduation," Lindsey asked.

"I've been offered a position on the Houston Rockets, playing goalie, second string, to start with," Sally replied, very proud of her new position. "The pay is very good, and if it works out, you may be seeing me on the national wizard TV sports channel. It's great that I have landed a job doing what I love doing the most, playing wizard soccer."

Becky explained, "I've accepted a scholarship to the USA Olympics Training School. If it works out for me, I may well have my dream come true, running in the Olympics! Of course, it would be incredible for me to win a gold medal. I'd be happy just to compete there, along with the best of the best in the entire world. I promise you that if I win a position on the US team, I'll send you an email to let you know." The group chatted about the long-range plans of the two girls. Then, it was back to packing.

At five o'clock, Governor Alister clicked his cup with his spoon, getting their attention. All chatter in the dining room stopped at once. "Here we are once again at the end of another fine year at Bradbury's, more eventful than most, if I do say so myself. Tonight we are gathered to celebrate our new graduates and present many special awards. However, first, we must all eat, so let the final diner of this school term begin." He waved his wand and the tables were covered with hundreds of steaming, hot dishes.

Now sitting beside Lindsey, Jim gallantly said, "My Lady Lindsey, would you join me with the duck with almonds?" He did a fine imitation of a waiter. Gaily, the group feasted on some of the finest food served here at the school all year long. It was designed to be a memorable meal for all the graduates, for this was their last meal and last night at Bradbury's.

As last year, the chocolate pies were a big hit at desert time. A bit later, their tables magically emptied, and numerous teapots appeared before them, along with fine china cups. Lindsey poured a cup for Jim and herself.

"Now it is time for the awards presentations. As you all know, this year Yellow Hall track team went to the Nationals and brought us back this fine trophy. At this time, I would like the nine members who worked so hard to earn this magnificent second place trophy for our school to come up here and receive a special Bradbury award. Becky, would you bring your team up here. Let's give them a hearty welcome."

While the students clapped, the nine, led by Becky, walked up beside their trophy. One by one, beginning with the oldest team members, Alister presented each with a sash and a ring, shaking each student's hand personally. Then, all the team members held the hand of the member next to them and raised their hands high in a victory celebration, while the students clapped loudly. Once they had returned to their seats, Alister began once more.

"Now it is time to hand out the diplomas. I am very pleased to announce that this year all one hundred sixth year students have passed both the State of Colorado High School Exams and Bradbury's Magic Exams. I give you one hundred, full-fledged wizards and witches." A loud round of cheering and clapping ensued.

"While I am handing out the diplomas to these most deserving students, I want you who are graduating and leaving Bradbury's to think about this. You are now considered adults, but not ordinary adults, wizards and witches. You are special people, and as such, you now don a very special responsibility that is denied those of our world who do not possess magical abilities. You have great powers and skills. Now you have the obligation and responsibility to use them for good, use this power wisely and for the good of all mankind, not just for your own personal ends. I wish to remind you of your oath to obey these inviolate laws.

1. Thou shalt not use magic to injure or harm another unjustly.

2. Thou shalt not use magic to kill another unjustly.

3. Thou shalt not use magic to steal from another that which is not yours.

4. Thou shalt not use magic to force another to do something against their will unjustly."

"Now please withhold your applause until all one hundred have received their diplomas, otherwise we will be here all night long, and I will be forced to make the cooks work overtime to prepare yet another feast. That was a joke, by the way." Several chuckles echoed in the room. Lindsey realized that this was nearly the same speech he had given last year.

One by one, each of the sixth year student's name was called, and he or she walked proudly up to receive their diplomas, along with a final handshake with Governor Alister.

A half hour later, a thunderous round of applause was given to all these students.

"It is with the greatest of pleasure that I announce that this year, Bradbury's is again making some additional awards. As you all know, our school was targeted by Dominus Malefic. Through the complicity of ex-Governor General Albright, our school was bombed, our computer system hacked. During these terrible times, seven of you students displayed remarkable courage, valor, bravery, and wit. These seven students, at great peril to their own lives, solved the many riddles, captured the Mad Bomber, and brought Governor General Albright to justice. They acted not out of selfishness or some desire for great fame, but on behalf of all the people of the world. They are a shining example of what it means to work together to defeat the evil that is running rampant in our world today. It is with the greatest honor that I present these seven the Bradbury's Distinguished Service Medallion."

"When I call your name, please step up here so that I may present to you your medallion. Pam Betts, Lindsey Barron, Amanda Whitewater, Emilio Lopez, Jim Whitewater, Tom Whitewater, and Deiter Cross." The seven walked tall and proudly forward, standing beside the tall Governor. One by one, Alister shook their hand and hung a golden medallion around their neck. Then, Alister began clapping, and the entire student body joined in, whistling and cheering as well.

"As the hour is getting late, I will stop my chatting. You all have a bus to catch first thing in the morning. I hope your summer vacation is a profitable and enjoyable one, and I anxiously await your return to Bradbury's in the fall. Good night." The professors all got up and left with Alister, while the students began filing out, heading to their rooms.

The next morning, Sandy caught Lindsey at breakfast. "Congratulations on becoming a Yellow Hall Floor Monitor, Lindsey. During summer vacation, I'll go over everything with you. It's not hard, just time consuming. Very rewarding, too. Have they taught you how to move the student's things to their rooms for them yet?"

"Thanks. Yes, Professor Cho Lin taught it to me already. I really don't know what all I'm supposed to be doing. As I understand it, I'm to help out our new Special Needs student."

"Cool. You'll do fine. I know it. Come on. We better hurry up—bus to catch."

A half hour later, Lindsey and her friends were once more sitting in the rear of the bus as it flew across the south central portion of Colorado. Pam was with her, coming to stay all summer long. Lindsey felt incredibly happy; life was cheerful and fun. Hope for the best summer yet beckoned.

Chapter 16—Changes

The bus pulled up at the front porch of the Compton ranch. "What's happened to your house?" asked a shocked Audrey. Everyone stared at what was left of the ranch house. It was half torn down; new construction was ongoing just to its left.

"We'll be over as soon as we unload," Amanda replied.

"Yes, give us a couple minutes," Jim added.

Pam, Audrey, and Lindsey stepped off the bus, accompanied by the four security men and Jimmy. He quickly helped the girls get their numerous duffel bags out from the cargo bay. "Cu in 'he fall, girls," he smiled his toothless grin. Jimmy climbed back onto the bus, and, poof, it was gone, stopping at the nearby Whitewater ranch.

"Hi girls," Lloyd called out, stepping out of the front door. "Welcome home. Bit of new construction going on. We didn't quite get it all done. Why don't you put your things in your old bedroom, and I'll give you a quick tour. Your mom's got lunch waiting for you too."

"Watch this," Lindsey gaily called out to her stepfather. "Move: my room." Her six duffle bags disappeared, reappearing in her bedroom.

Lloyd grinned, "Cool! Now I can have you help us move things," he teased. Pam and Audrey followed suit, moving their many bags into the same room they shared with Lindsey. "Oh goodie, I'll have to put you two to work as well!" All four laughed as Lloyd led them inside.

Lena came rushing out of the kitchen to hug Lindsey, and then she gave Pam and Audrey a hug as well. "I bet you are starving. Polly and I have whipped up a hearty lunch for you. Have a seat. Lloyd, why don't you tell them what's going on with the ranch house." Lindsey saw her smile at him and figured she was shifting the responsibility to him.

"Yes, what is going on around here?" Lindsey asked, pretending to be annoyed. They sat down at the table.

"Well, your mother and I have decided, for a number of different reasons, to make a much larger ranch house."

"So each of us can have our own room?" Lindsey speculated.

"Yes, that is a factor, but not the only one. After spending the winter here, we now know just how energy inefficient this ancient ranch house actually is. R. B. has had a lot to do with it as well. Lena compared our utility bills with his, and frankly, we both were shocked. Your mom said that it doesn't make sense that we continue as we have been. Then, there is the matter of security for you girls and the rest of us. Times are getting bad again, really bad. I don't want to scare you, but Pam, your dad will be along at supper time. It seems that some Death Stalkers have ransacked your home. He'll brief you on it when he gets here."

"Darn!" exclaimed Pam. "I knew I was bringing doom on my folks." Tears swelled in her eyes.

"Pam, you did the right thing. Your folks are extremely proud of what you did. They are behind you one hundred percent! Wipe those pretty eyes of yours right now. We good guys have to stick together, if we want to have any hope of surviving these hard times."

"Now then, oh yes. We are building a new ranch house based on R. B.'s designs. It will be energy efficient, very large, and totally secure. Plus, R. B. is adding some extra features that you girls are undoubtedly going to love. You will see it in operation after lunch, when R. B. returns to our construction site. It's an automatic teleporting device that connects his front room to our new front room. This way you kids can come and go whenever you like, and we adults won't have to worry about your safety."

"Wow! Now that is cool! I didn't know something like that was possible," Lindsey replied, seeing immediate uses for this invention.

"I've read about these things, very advanced magic," Pam added. "Now we can visit Amanda any time we want to without having to get four of us together to make the trip. Is it safe though? I've heard basic teleporting can sometimes be very dangerous."

"Totally safe. Nothing can go wrong. Ah, here's lunch. I advise you to eat up, because we are going to put you three to some real work this afternoon," he teased. Lindsey couldn't tell if he meant it or not.

Polly and Lena brought in lunch: thick, meaty soups, freshly baked breads, and milk for the growing girls. While they ate, Lena said, "I sure hope you like our new home. It is supposed to be finished today, though I don't see how. Then, nearly everything about our new home I haven't seen how. Six bedrooms, huge kitchen, three studies, two workrooms, a family room, dining room, pantry, living room, and six bathrooms. I remember when it was just three rooms for us, dear. Anyway, now there will be plenty of room for everyone."

"The inside dimensions are two hundred feet by one hundred feet, but those are magical enhanced measurements. On the outside, it will be forty by twenty only," Lloyd attempted to explain. All three girls looked at him completely baffled. He scratched his head.

Polly came to his rescue, "Yes, it is modeled after the Whitewater's home, only greatly enlarged. When you see it after we eat, you can readily see the five to one ratio, because the roof has not yet been added. However, every time I look at the overall construction, I get completely dizzy myself. If it happens to you, my advice is to focus entirely on the inside, as I and your mother do, or entirely on the outside."

They ate quickly and Lena told them to go take a tour instead of helping with the dishes. Lloyd took the three out for a view. As they approached the front door, Lindsey could see both the outside and the inside. Her lunch nearly came up, so crazy was the spatial distortion. "Egads! She's right," complained Audrey. "Look at the inside only!"

Pam, her head spinning with the never-before-felt sensations, continued to stare at the whole thing. "Way cool, Lloyd. What a weird feeling. Kind of like falling off the top of a spinning Ferris wheel or something."

"Okay, focus on the inside. Here is the front door. Let's step inside a ways. There now, focus on the inside. To your right is the huge living room, while to your left is the coat closet, a small storage space for things brought out of the weather, and in the back there, a bathroom so we can clean up from doing the chores without bringing mud and the like into the whole house. That was your mother's idea. Then, straight ahead is the main hall, two hundred feet long, or nearly so." As they walked down it a bit, he continued. "On your left is the family room. I hope you don't mind, but I am installing a fancy big screen and my entertainment center in here. Just down on your right is a study, probably Polly and Fred's."

They walked down not quite halfway. "On the left is the kitchen and panty to the far left of the kitchen. Polly and Lena have designed this room and its layout themselves. On your right is our large dining room." They moved further down the hall. "Work rooms on either side. One of these will be for Lena and me to repair tack and stuff. The other we figured Audrey can use for her carvings, as well as you girls if you have need of a workroom. Now let's walk all the way down to the end of this hall."

It seemed weird walking along a hallway with the hot, bright sun shining on one's head, Lindsey thought. She didn't dare look up, although Pam kept doing so. "Here at the long hall's end, it tees. A back hall marks the very back of our house. There are five bathrooms along the whole back wall. Six bedrooms, three on either side of the main hall, are accessed from the side halls. Lena thought it would be convenient if you could go directly from your bedroom into a bathroom. I like it because all the plumbing is in one spot, except for the sixth one way up at the front of the house."

"The bedrooms are huge, dad," Lindsey observed.

"Yes, about twenty by twenty, plenty of room. We have not yet quite worked out the bedrooms. We designed them to hold at least two beds along with dressers, closets, and the like. We didn't know if each one of you girls wanted your own private room or if you would prefer sharing with one other girl. Lena believes that you, dear, ought to share your room with the new, Special Needs girl, Ashley."

Lindsey remembered her childhood when she had no hands and how much she had depended upon her mother for the simple things of life. Although she didn't know what special needs Ashley would have, she said, "Yes, I agree. Ashley ought to room with me, dad."

"Well, Audrey and I can bunk together," Pam added.

"Well, that helps a lot. Polly and Fred, when he is here, they can take the far right bedroom. Your mother and I will have the middle right one, leaving the other right side one available for guests. On the left side, that will also leave one spare bedroom. Looks like you can easily have Amanda and Fern over for a sleep over." The three giggled; this was precisely what Lindsey had in mind!

"Hi! Ho! You in there?" the deep voice of R. B. called out, from way up front.

"Yes, we're in the back. Just showing the girls the layout. Coming, R. B." Hastily the four walked back to the front, where the entire Whitewater clan waiting for them. After a long round of "Hi's," R. B. suggested that Lindsey take his children on a tour, while he and Lloyd decided on the next construction actions.

"Golly, your house is going to be at least a third larger than ours!" Jim said enthusiastically.

"Yes, and I can have you over for the night. We have two spare bedrooms now," Lindsey replied.

Now the work began again. Lloyd and Jim continued on the woodwork on the inside. Lindsey saw that they were cannibalizing the wood from the existing ranch house, though adding many new pine boards where needed. R. B. and Tom began the construction of the roof. Polly, Luci, and Lena put the three girls to work helping them. Their task was to finish moving all the existing stuff from the old house into the new rooms. Arranging rooms and furniture—the interior decorating appealed greatly to all three women, who put the five girls to work, carrying out their grand plans.

With so much help, things moved along incredibly rapidly. By the middle of the afternoon, the old house stood vacant, making the final removal of usable wood far easier. The five girls now got a lesson in interior decorating. The three women began making lists of just what else was needed. After they finally agreed on a room, Luci wrote down what was needed for that room.

Audrey asked if she could have one of the bedrooms with the earthen outside wall. Everyone knew that she, like Fern, would be planting flowers along the outer wall. Lindsey decided to take the middle bedroom. By suppertime, little remained of their old ranch house and the four-foot thick earthen roof was in place over the new house. Lloyd took the three girls to the front door. "Beneath the floor boards is a gold sheet." He showed them its location and dimensions, just inside the front door and square, ten feet by ten.

"You stand on it and say, 'To the Whitewater's Home' and you will be instantly teleported to their front room. R. B.'s invention. Now let's all do it. Luci has a stew waiting for us all in her kitchen. The entire group gathered around and with two trips, everyone was piled into the Whitewater's home. The teens thought that this was the greatest invention of R. B.'s ever! He was pleased.

Over dinner, he explained more fully, "You see, unless I'm entirely daffy, things are going to get much rougher in the world. Our two ranches adjoin, and I want to make a small safe haven here, where we can have some resemblance of safety. Already this spring, I put an enchanted nail in every fence post around the Compton's square ranch. If anyone crosses into your acres with malice toward you, the alarm will sound in many places, giving you all advanced warning, much as it does around here."

"Our families are close, and there is safety in numbers. Polly already knows this. So now, we rather have a mutual defense network going between our two ranches."

Just then, an alarm activated and a disembodied voice announced, "Fred Betts has arrived."

Indeed, he walked in the front door. "Sorry I'm late. Official business is getting nastier every day. I had to arrest two for magically trying to paint the sides of the Department of Law with defamatory graffiti and just at quitting time. Hi everyone."

Polly fixed her husband a bowl of the hearty stew, and he joined them. "Pam, I didn't tell you the whole story about our home in Sterling. I didn't want to upset you while you were at school. You know how important your schooling is. Anyway, here, you kids can scan through these video clips. It shows you what those supporting Dominus will do." He handed a DVD to Pam. Amanda magically pulled her laptop from her room onto the table so that they could all watch it.

"My, you've learned the special Move spell, I see," he complimented her.

"Yes, Lindsey learned it because of her new position as Yellow Hall Floor Monitor. She taught it to all of us," Amanda explained.

"Highly useful side spell. I have argued that it should be included in the Grade 2 spell book, but I keep being vetoed. Good stew, Luci."

The group of children decided that they could not all watch it on the laptop, so they took it into the living room and played in on their TV setup. By the time it finished, Polly and Fred had walked into the living room, hoping that Pam would not be too upset.

"They trashed the place!" Pam exclaimed.

"Yes, mostly juvenile vandalism," her father explained. "I got two separate sets of fingerprints. However, they are not on file. One day, they will be, and we'll have justice."

Polly added, "When I heard them breaking in the front door, I simply teleported outside and messaged your father. The damage was done, and they had fled by the time he arrived. It was a mess as you can see; however, no real damage was done."

Fred continued, "We've packed up all your things, ours too, and I'll be bringing them here as soon as Lloyd and R. B. have the house ready. We are contributing much of the new furnishings that are needed. I can't spare the time to help with the construction. We each contribute as we can. Your mother is making all the new bedding quilts and such. Until this whole Dominus situation is resolved, we'll be graciously living with the Comptons, Pam. Polly and I will be keeping our new location here a secret. I know that it will be a bit hard on your mother to be separated from her friends, but she is willing to teleport to Sterling when she needs to do so. This way, we believe that our family will remain safe during these nasty times."

"What about Aunt Wilma and her family?" Pam asked, knowing who she really was.

"Oh they are quite safe. I believe that their home is

heavily fortified against undo intrusions. However, Lena and Lloyd have told her that they are welcome to come here if things get rough in Sterling."

"What about Monane?" asked Amanda, who wanted to know about the other remaining Rat Pack person.

R. B. said, "Oh, your aunt is fine where she is, for the time being. If it gets bad, she will be coming to stay with us, as she did some fifteen years ago." Amanda relaxed; it would be wonderful if Aunt Monane, the Rat Pack Tracker, was staying here with her. There was so much that she could teach her.

Luci added, "Tomorrow, Polly and I will go into town and get the rest of the furnishings, Lena. I believe that we should equip one room at a time, don't you think? We can send the stuff for each room as we get them. You and the others can then set to work on the installations. How does that sound to you?" Lena liked the idea. After all, it was her new house, and she wanted it decorated the way she and Lloyd desired. The extended family group chatted well into the night. At last, the Comptons and Betts, along with Audrey, took their leave, returning to their new home.

A short while later, an exhausted Lena turned in. Only Lindsey sat up with her stepfather in his new study. Both were sitting in their old armchairs, which were likely to be replaced in the morning. Lloyd said, "Lindsey, I'm glad you're so accepting of all these changes. We're trying our best to create a safe haven here. While Polly could just teleport away when trouble came her way, your mother cannot. We both love her deeply, and I must do everything I can to keep her safe from harm. I need to tell you a bit more about this new home. It is designed to be entirely self-sufficient. Worst case scenario: utilities go out. I have a solar powered rig that I'll be assembling tomorrow, capable of running all our electrical needs. Thanks to R. B.'s house design, a simple heat pump will provide all the heat we could ever need in the winter and no air conditioning is needed and no maintenance either—no walls to paint or siding to keep up."

"We've put in three magical fireplaces. Just say 'Fire: Start' or 'Fire: Stop' and they will activate accordingly. I already have worked on the water wells. We have two: one for

the three circular fields, and one for domestic use. The only
thing that we are going to need to survive will be food. Your
mother has already been planning on this line. She has planted
an extensive garden, and one of the fields will be a wheat field,
so that we will have our own flower. The pantry is huge, and
I'll slowly begin stocking it up, just in case. We have all the
fresh milk and eggs we could possibly use, though Lena is
expanding that to help supply the Whitewater family as well."

"What about fresh meat, dad?" she asked.

"I'll lay in a supply. However, R. B. claims that we need
not worry much, if you like fresh game, that is. There are many
antelope around, along with rabbits and such. He will provide
meat, if times get that bad. I guess what I'm trying to explain,
dear, is that these two places, ours and R. B.'s, are being setup
to provide a safe haven for our families and anyone else in dire
need. We can easily put up many more people here, using the
studies and work areas if need be. We all know that with
Alister running the school, all of you will be as safe there as
anywhere, no matter what goes on in the world around us. We
must also guarantee your safety when you are here part of the
year."

"This has happened before, you know, the last time
Dominus ran wild around the world. Many of us banded
together. My folks joined with two other families to create a
safe place for us. Now it is my turn to do so for others."

"Thanks, dad. It means everything to us, especially to
Pam. She went way above the call of duty in getting Governor
General Albright brought to justice. Yet, that has made her a
bitter enemy of Dominus, rather as I think I've become. She
wouldn't talk much about it, but I know that she was petrified
that Dominus would retaliate against her family. Now she can
forget that fear."

He smiled, "Yes, what Pam did is absolutely incredible.
Alister played her fifteen-minute presentation for the six of us,
the Betts and the Whitewaters. Polly was in tears; she was so
proud of what Pam did and so grateful for your saving her
from being killed by Albright there at the end, I might add. It
is bonding our three families tightly."

Spontaneously, Lindsey got up and sat on her dad's lap,

hugging him. He held her tightly for a time. "Honey, there is something that I ought to tell you about all these magical spells. When you graduate, you will have learned through Grade 6 spells. However, there are three additional levels of spells beyond those, spells of great power. These, few can learn and many spend much of their lives working to gain the skill to cast them."

"Dominus is one of these. Alister has not told you this yet, but Dominus knows and is famous for using several Grade 7 spells. The one he hit you with is particularly nasty, the Stun spell. Yet, he also has the ability to cast a Minor Restricted Wish; that is the one that Alister goaded him into casting when he was trying to steal the rod from Alister. He knew that once he had cast that one, Dominus was then vulnerable. However, we also suspect that Dominus knows at least one Grade 9 spell and perhaps one or two Grade 8 spells."

"Now not to worry. I just want to put this all into perspective for you. R. B. himself is a master of several Grade 9 spells. Your lucky rabbit's foot is the recipient of one of his Grade 9 spells, you see. I dare say to make all the magical inventions of his, he must know quite a few Grade 7, 8, and 9 spells. Myself, I only know a few Grade 7 spells. I believe that Fred knows quite a few more of them than I do, but neither of us knows any Grade 8 or 9 spells. What I'm trying to say, dear, is that R. B. is a most vital ally. When you girls are finished with school, I'm sure that R. B. will want to educate you further, if you are interested in learning from him."

"Wow. I had no idea. I wonder if Pam knows about this. Can I tell her about these things?"

"Sure, knowledge is critical. The more you know, the better off you are. I suspect we ought to get some sleep. Tomorrow we are going to be run ragged around here."

That turned out to be an understatement! Polly and Luci were extremely good, effective shoppers, wasting very little time acquiring all the furnishings they had all agreed upon for each room. As planned, they sent home an entire room's set of items at one time. Curtains had to be affixed to the windows and doors, and the fabric hung. Tables, chairs, beds, mattresses, towels, various linens—the list seemed endless. The girls were kept constantly busy moving things around, positioning items, making beds, and so on. Occasionally, Jim or Tom was needed for heavier work, such as screwing up the brackets for the curtain rods. When they were not needed indoors, they worked outside with the men, filling in what remained of the old ranch house. By the end of the day, smooth dirt marked the location of the old home. Next, following Lena's suggestions and with the assistance of Audrey and Fern, another garden was planted here. This one was half flowers and half vegetables. The flower patch was where Audrey planted her very special, rare flowers.

If this wasn't enough activity, Fred brought his family's key possessions to their new home. These items, Pam personally arranged, moving them into reasonable locations. She knew her parents well. Her dad even brought her most of her own personal items as well, which Pam stored in her new bedroom.

R. B. continually fiddled with the various light fixtures around the house, enchanting them with what he called "proper magical operations." Lloyd came along behind him working out the new electrical wiring, which tied into his fancy solar energy generation system that Tom and Jim had to assemble on the sod roof. "Yeow! It works!" Jim exclaimed, flapping his burned fingers to cool them off. He had touched both ends of the power transmission wire coming from the solar panels, discovering that they indeed were generating electricity.

Next, the men hung all the many doors. Lindsey marveled at their unusual construction. None had doorknobs. Instead, about a foot above the ground was a sliding bar with a wooden dowel that allowed one to slide the bar into place, keeping the door shut. "We've got foot operated doors now," Lindsey commented to Pam. "I guess doorknobs have gone out of style?"

Pam scratched her head, "Er, no I don't think so. I shall have to investigate these a bit." Interestingly enough, both girls failed to ask R. B. about them.

The last outside construction project was to rebuild the front porch. Lena loved to sit on the porch of an evening, viewing the land around her. Late in the afternoon, Lloyd and the boys began to use the scraps of the old porch to make a new, even larger one. At the same time, Fred reconnected the phone line to the house, making sure their telephones once more worked. Finally, he hooked up the wireless Internet connection that would permit access from anywhere on the entire ranch. He knew his daughter would be demanding Internet access quickly.

Even Sandy lent a hand. Lena put her in charge of obtaining groceries to begin to fill up the pantry. Fred had opened an open credit line at the small grocery store in Arapahoe, another of his contributions to the group. During the day, Sandy made ten trips to the store and back again, carrying as much as she could, using her teleport spell. With each visit, she carefully stored the groceries in their designated locations. Lena and Lloyd had placed small placards on the shelves denoting what went where. The perishables went into the two magical refrigerators, built by R. B. of course.

Finally, at suppertime, everyone gathered at the Whitewater ranch, as Sandy made her last trip of the day into town. She brought back ten Dominos pizzas and several packs of sodas, the Whitewater children's favorite food. "I've got blisters!" complained Jim.

"Shows that you have done an honest day's work," Lena explained. He faked a smile, but didn't appreciate the sore hands.

Lloyd announced, "Well, the house is finally done. Tomorrow night, we will be having a special house warming party. You are all invited. I know that Fred will miss it; he has to get back to Sterling tonight, but I expect the rest of you to show up at six. Dancing is not optional."

"Huh?" said Pam.

"A little birdie told me that you girls love dancing. Can't get enough of the formal dancing at Bradbury's or so I'm told. Might I suggest that you all dress up a bit? We will have a fine time indeed." Pam wondered about that detail, but Lindsey was all smiles.

"We can wear our fancy dresses again, show our folks how we look," Lindsey suggested, eager to have another opportunity to dress up.

"Oh no! Does that mean we have to wear our suits?" Jim faked a moan.

Tom punched him, "Of course, I want to be absolutely dashing for my fair maiden, Sandy." She giggled, but appreciated his sentiment.

Lena added, "However, girls, during the day tomorrow, I have lots of ranch chores for you to do. We have been neglecting the normal ranch work these past few days. The gardens need weeding, the fields need tending, to say nothing of the many animals. I hope that you will not be too tired to dance." She was teasing them a little.

Indeed, Fern and Audrey proved to be excellent gardeners, and the two took over full responsibility for the several vegetable patches Lena had going. Lindsey and Pam handled all the animals, including cleaning out their stalls, a rather smelly job. Lena and Fred rode off to examine the main fields and to activate the three giant irrigation wheels that provided water to the three one-mile in diameter patches of crops. One of these was a wheat field for their own use later this year.

Around five, everyone hit the bathrooms to clean up and then to dress up for the party. Lindsey noticed that her father had disappeared, rather mysteriously she thought. She asked her mom, but Lena would only say, "Sh. It is a surprise." This only made her more curious.

By six, everyone was dolled up in their prom-style dresses, looking their best. The monotone magical voice announced the arrival of the Whitewater clan, and Lindsey rushed to meet them. Jim was wearing his fancy western suit that she liked. Tom led Sandy by her arm. Even R. B. escorted his wife, who wore a gorgeous white dress. As they gathered in the living room, Lena and Polly looked even more mysterious. Why was everyone waiting in the living room, not the dining room? Already the odors of a delicious meal beckoned many hungry stomachs.

Just then, the monotone voice announced, "Lloyd and Monique are arriving." Pam let out a squeak of total surprise, quickly covering her mouth with her hand.

She peered out at the front, and there was Lloyd in his nice business suit. Holding his hand was Monique, dressed as she had been at the Formal Dance, a couple nights ago. Her eyes darted around at her new surroundings. Pam rushed out to hug her and greet her. "Wow, what a cool place you have, Pam!" Monique exclaimed.

After a quick round of introductions, and Pam escorted Monique to the dining room, which Polly had fancied up, party style. Once they had finished eating, Lena asked Pam to show Monique around the house. Hastily, Polly and Luci handled the dishes, while Lena put them away.

Lloyd then started up his entertainment center, and formal dance music spread through the entire home. "May I have the pleasure of this dance?" he said formally to Lena. The two waltzed off into the living room. One by one, the others followed suit. Audrey and Fern decided to dance with each other, while Polly watched and prepared tea and other refreshments.

Lindsey and Jim caught a few whispered words between Monique and Pam. "I was so worried about you, Pam. I heard your home had been burglarized on the news. Was it bad? Did you lose anything?"

"No, mom got away safely just when they broke in."

"Good for her. I like this new place. It is super cool. I will sleep better each night now, cause I know that you will be safe here. I was *so* worried about you, Pam."

"I know. I was worried about my folks too."

"I was really surprised too when Lloyd Messaged me about coming tonight. Lindsey's new dad is really an all right fellow, isn't he? I mean thinking enough of you to ask me to come tonight. Not many parents would do that you know."

"I know. I'm so glad that you could come, Monique. Maybe you can come for more visits this summer. I'll ask if you are interested."

"Love too. Has to be on the weekends. I've taken a job at a flower shop to make some extra money this summer."

Once again, time seemed to fly away rapidly. At ten, Lloyd ended the dance. To Lindsey, it seemed that only minutes had passed by. Monique gave Pam a goodbye kiss, and Lloyd took her home. He returned a minute later, just after the Whitewaters had left.

Pam went up to Lloyd and said, "Mr. Compton, thank you very much for inviting Monique and bringing her."

"My dear, you are entirely welcome. It seemed proper that she be here for the dance. She seems like a wonderful person. Now you had best get some sleep. Many chores lie in wait for you in the morning." She smiled and walked, as if on cloud nine, down the long hall to her room.

"What exactly are we doing?" asked Pam. It was nine o'clock the next morning. She and Lindsey had harnessed the largest horse that Pam had ever seen to this strange looking machine, which had spikes that could be lowered into the ground.

"Cultivating the corn patch. Most folks use very expensive tractors, but on a small ranch such as ours, it really is not at all profitable to do that. Mom is very old fashioned. This is Dandy, a Percheron, a draft horse. He knows what to do. This is an antique cultivator, in use something like two hundred years ago. You sit on the seat there and lower the lever when I tell you. I will walk Dandy to the starting point in the field. As he pulls it along, the machine digs up the ground between the rows, and gets rid of many weeds. We only have to do this square mile of corn. Mom has the other patch in soybeans, but those we have to do by hand later on. Trust me; this is the easier of the two."

An hour later, they had the corn patch cultivated and led Dandy back to the barn. Next, they put on some gloves and took a machete each. When they got to the bean field, Lindsey showed Pam what to do. "We walk along each row and hack out the weeds that are growing up. Simple, but it gets tiring. We need to have it done before lunch; otherwise, it gets terribly hot doing this in the afternoon."

Both girls had a ravenous appetite at lunchtime. They had finished the needed chores. Now they could relax and work on arranging their rooms better. Audrey, with the help of Fern, who had become her constant companion, had weeded the various garden patches. Now, Audrey began working on her carvings, Fern watching her every move. Pam chided herself for not having followed the news for ages and began monitoring the Mag News. Lindsey finished arranging her room the way she wanted it. As far as she was concerned, this promised to be the best summer vacation ever.

Chapter 17—Ashley Stokes

Wednesday morning, Lindsey received an email from Governor Alister regarding the new Special Needs student, Ashley Stokes. Lindsey read it several times, quite surprised at its contents.

Dear Miss Lindsey Barron,

Again, thank you for accepting the responsibility of Yellow Hall Floor Monitor and our new Special Needs student, Ashley Stokes. There are some details about this third year student that you should know. Usually, I would send along her school records to the Floor Monitor, so the monitor can have a better understanding of her needs. However, as I again read her files sent to me from her previous schools, I have a feeling much of it may not be entirely truthful or it may be somewhat of an exaggeration. Therefore, I am not going to bias your initial opinion of Miss Stokes by sending them along.

I will give you her basic background. She is your age and was born in Chicago. Her parents, a wizard and witch, were killed in an automobile accident when she was barely two years old. It seems they were following a semi carrying steel beams, and the beams broke loose smashing into their car. She survived, but the beams sliced off her arms at her shoulders. That she survived was called a miracle by the newspapers at the time.

Her aunt and uncle, both normals, cared for her for three years after the accident. However, they used up all of her insurance money paying for her hospital care. By age five, there was no more money left that they could obtain for her care. That coupled with her "strange" behavior, which they saw as threatening to their own children, caused them to turn her over to the State of Illinois.

During the next seven years, Miss Stokes went from foster family to foster family. I'm not sure what the actual truth is during those years. I suspect that the foster parents were not skilled or equipped to handle this Special Needs student.

298

There was never any doubt about her inherent magical abilities. The Chicago School of Magic accepted her on a full scholarship her first year. Apparently, she didn't get along too well there, and the Twin Cities School of Magic picked up her scholarship for her second year. The Governor there contacted me about her this spring, and he was very eager to transfer her to Bradbury's.

I believe that it is safe to suggest that she had been mistreated most of her life, that now she has developed quite a temper, and is most likely very bitter. In your handling of her, keep in mind that she is extremely independent, fiercely so by all reports.

I have total confidence in your ability to assist Miss Stokes. Again, thank you for assuming this extra responsibility.

Yours truly,

Governor Alister Broadwell

Lindsey reread the email several times. "Mom, did you know that Ashley doesn't have any arms?" she asked. If her mother didn't, Lindsey felt that she had just made her mother's life miserable.

"Oh yes, that nice Mr. Broadwell explained it to us some time ago. We thought that you also knew about her physical handicap." Lena replied, suddenly wondering if Lindsey had not known all this time. "Should we not have accepted her, Lindsey?"

"Oh no. Nothing like that, mom. I was worried that you didn't know about it. I just found out about her now. Alister sent me an email about her."

"That's why we modified all the doors in here. It was R. B.'s great idea to help Miss Stokes," Lena replied.

"Duh. Well, now I see. I'd better let Audrey and Pam know about Ashley."

"By the way, she is due to arrive later this afternoon. We have our new home done just in time, it seems. Lloyd says she will arrive with Jimmy on the school bus. Do you want to meet her first and then introduce all the rest of us?"

"Good idea, mom. She will probably feel more comfortable around us, I think." Lindsey dashed off to tell the others.

"Well, now the doors make sense," Pam noted. "I ought

to have reached the proper conclusion. I must be slipping."

"No, they just forgot to tell us," Lindsey consoled her.

"Well, she can't be helpless," Audrey observed. "She has passed the first two years of magic school. Somehow, she must be getting her wand to activate."

"Good point," Pam complimented Audrey. "You are right. It's been tough these last two years, far harder than norm's schools. Since she is the same age as us and is also a third year student, she must be able to cast spells and do what we do, though I can't imagine how she could manage."

"We should go tell Amanda and the Whitewaters," Lindsey suggested. All three went to the front entrance and spoke the command words, arriving in Amanda's front entryway. Quickly, they related the news. A little while later, Amanda and Fern accompanied the three back to Lindsey's house; both wanted to be here to meet her when she arrived.

"Gosh, how can Ashley possible manage to do any spells?" Fern asked. The group sat on the porch, sipping sodas, waiting for the bus to arrive.

"Well, I've only had an hour to do any research," Pam defended herself, "but it seems that they use their feet as we use our hands. At least, that is what I have found out so far."

"Still, it must be awful," Fern felt terribly sorry for Ashley, and she hadn't even met her yet. "Maybe Doctor Caterwall can regrow her arms, like he did for Lindsey."

Pop! The familiar school bus materialized before the porch—actually the old porch. Jimmy had to move the bus another twenty feet. As he hopped off, he said, "Has your house moved? I' seems 'o no' be where i's supposed 'o be."

"New house, Jimmy. Mom and dad have made us a new energy efficient house," Lindsey replied.

"I can see. Jus' like 'he Whi'ewa'er's house. Unusual design. I like i'. Oh, here is Miss Ashley S'okes, delivered safe and sound. I'll ge' her bags." He opened the bottom and pulled out one duffle bag.

As he was doing this, Ashley stepped off the bus. She was short and thin, with very short light brown hair and hazel eyes. Her lips were full, and she had a very black and blue bruise on her left cheek. She wore a badly mended Twin Cities school dress. Everyone noticed her wand in a leg sling, firmly affixed to her left leg. Her shoes were slip ons, and she wore no socks. Both knees were also bruised.

Jimmy awkwardly handed Ashley her duffle bag, unsure just how to present it. "Hold the strap loose," she said domineeringly. Ashley stuck her head through the loop and carried her bag. "Honestly, Jimmy, you should get your front teeth fixed. You are terribly hard to understand," she chided him.

Jimmy grinned, revealing his missing teeth. Lindsey thought that he smiled on purpose, just to show off. "See you in 'he fall, Miss Lindsey." He climbed back aboard, and the bus disappeared, leaving Ashley standing before the front porch and the pack of girls waiting for her.

"Hi Ashley. I'm Lindsey Barron, Yellow Hall Floor Monitor. I'm supposed to help you with whatever you need. This is our new house—just got it done a couple days ago. I'm so glad that you are going to stay here with us this summer." Lindsey felt slightly awkward. Ordinarily, she would shake hands with someone she was meeting. Even when she had no hands, she still tried to do so, but Ashley had nothing she could shake. There was nothing there past her shoulders, which seemed smaller than normal, since the arms were entirely missing. She decided to do the next best thing. Lindsey leaned forward and gave Ashley a welcoming hug. To her surprise, Ashley's right leg came up around her back, adding some pressure of her own to the hug.

"Thanks. I guess you will do. I've had far worse floor monitors," Ashley replied.

"These are my dear friends. Miss Pam Betts, Miss Amanda Whitewater, Miss Audrey Lemon, and Miss Fern Whitewater." In turn, each followed Lindsey's lead and gave Ashley a welcoming hug.

"How did you get so bruised up?" Pam asked, after giving Ashley a welcome hug.

"Got into another fight at school a week ago. Gave the guy a pair of black eyes and kicked him hard in his private parts. You should have seen him keel over in pain. Bastard!" Anger seeped out of Ashley, but it evaporated quickly.

"What a weird house you have! Looks like the old sodbuster's houses we read about in our history books. Are you all really backwards out here? I mean this is in the middle of absolutely nowhere. I figured they wanted to punish me, which is why they sent me here to you. I couldn't even find this place on the map without using a magnifying glass." She exaggerated a little. Arapahoe was on most maps, albeit a very tiny town.

"Actually, Running Bear, R. B. as we call him, Amanda's father, designed it after his house. He is a powerful wizard. It has all sorts of magical enchantments on it, and it is so energy efficient that we don't even need to heat it in the winter or cool it in the summertime. Pretty incredible, but the main thing, Ashley, is that we are reasonably safe here, what with Dominus Malefic and the Death Stalkers roaming around causing big trouble," Lindsey defended her new home.

"Actually, Pam and her family are also staying with us now. Her house in Sterling was attacked by Death Stalkers," Lindsey added. Ashley gave both Lindsey and Pam a queer look. "Come on; let's introduce you to everyone else, and show you your room. You are sleeping with me, unless you want your own private bedroom."

As they stepped inside, Ashley's eyes opened wide, "Wow! It is so huge in here."

"Magically altered space," Pam announced. "It is really two hundred by one hundred feet inside, but only forty by twenty feet outside."

Polly and Lena stood just inside, waiting for the girls to enter and to meet the new guest. Lena said, "Well hello. You must be Miss Ashley Stokes. So pleased to meet you at last. I'm Lena Barron Compton, Lindsey's mother and your host." Lena just gave her a motherly hug, without waiting on Ashley. She felt the young girl start to resist her for an instant, but then allowed the hug.

"We've only just gotten our new house completed. Still ironing out the bugs, so to speak. We did make one change on your behalf, Ashley. The doors have no knobs; foot sliders take their place. R. B. and I thought that would make getting around in here easier for you."

Ashley glared at Lena, but held her tongue. "And this is Polly Betts, Pam's mother. The Betts are staying with us because their house in Sterling isn't safe any longer. All these bad men continue to cause trouble. Out here on the High Plains, you and everyone else ought to be safe and sound."

Polly also gave Ashley a hug. She stated, "Yes, after Pam got the vermin Governor General Albright arrested for murder, Dominus's thugs raided our house, tore up half the furniture. Nasty business. My husband, Fred, is head of the Department of Magical Misuse in Sterling. He is really busy these days, but he will be dropping by, probably on the weekends."

"Yes, my husband, Lloyd, is out tending the fields today, where I ought to be," Lena explained. "He said I should be in here to help you get settled in, Ashley. If there is anything that you need, just let us know. Alister didn't mention that you were so pretty," Lena added, intending to compliment her.

"I'll manage well enough, but you must be drugged if you think I'm pretty," Ashley retorted.

"My, the House Mother in the Twin Cities should be ashamed of herself!" Polly quickly stepped in, changing the subject. "Dressing you up in utter rags. Shame on her. Lindsey, after you get her settled in and familiar with where everything is, please bring her to me. We just *have* to get Ashley some descent clothes! What is your favorite color, dear?"

Ashley growled, "I don't take charity!"

Lena stepped in, as Polly was quite startled by her reply. "And you won't find any charity around here, Ashley. Everyone has to shoulder their share of the chores and duties. Arms or no arms, you will be working. Polly will merely take the cost out of your wages. Now then, if you have no preference for colors. . ."

"Blue," Ashley hastily interrupted Lena. She saw that the ranch woman evidently meant every word, and Ashley certainly didn't want any pink clothes, which so many of her foster mothers had forced her to wear.

Lindsey, followed by the other girls, led Ashley down the long hall, showing her what each room contained. "This place is deceptively large," Ashley commented, becoming more impressed with each room.

"Here are the bedrooms and the bathrooms. The adults are sleeping there on the right, and we have the bedrooms on the left. We have five bathrooms so there shouldn't be any long waiting lines, like there used to be. Our room is this first one here on the left corner. Audrey and Pam have the back one, because Audrey is raising flowers in the earthen walls of her bedroom. She is taking after Fern, who first figured out that you can raise flowers in your bedroom walls. Pretty unique, I think. Here we go. My bed is on the right, yours is on the left. If you want a private room, you can have the bedroom between us."

Ashley walked in and sat down on the bed, wiggling out of the strap of the duffle bag. Lindsey added, "I just want you to know that I understand your situation at least a little, Ashley. I was born with no hands and grew up that way. Only at school last year, Doctor Caterwall re-grew hands for me. Actually, he had to do it twice, because Dominus cut my new hands off when he captured me. You may have heard about that on the MagNews. You see, I have some idea how awkward some things can be for you."

Ashley was torn between two conflicting emotions. She wanted to curse Lindsey out for throwing sympathy her way, insinuating that Ashley had problems. Yet, she was intrigued that here was another girl who apparently had arms but no hands and had to survive nearly much as Ashley had. Further, this business with Dominus caught her interest more than anything else. Last year, she had heard all manner of wild stories on the MagNews about a girl, Dominus, and some rod relic. Could this be the same girl?

Ashley compromised, "If you call me a Special Needs student just once, Lindsey, I will kick you until you wish you never heard of those words. I'm just as good as anyone else is, better in fact, because I'm not utterly dependent upon those silly arms that nearly everyone else has. You all are stupidly lazy, wasting your feet like you do."

"I, I promise I won't. Honestly, Ashley, I could never get the hang of using my feet. No one ever told me that I ought to use them. Perhaps that would have made things easier for me.

I was so utterly embarrassed every time I had to go to the bathroom. Someone would have to help me. God, I hated meal times. I felt like a baby because someone would have to feed me. I was teased and taunted every day at the grade school here. Sometimes, I just wanted to run away and hide forever. It was awful. Going to Bradbury's was a godsend for me, because there everyone, well nearly everyone, allowed me to do what I could do and only gave me help when I asked for it. I got back my self-respect. Are you the same way? I mean hating everyone sympathizing with you all the time and not letting you do what you can?"

"Yeh, that's pretty much it. They have some stupid, crazy, insane ideas that I'm an utterly helpless cripple. Let me tell you right up front, Lindsey, I'm anything but helpless. I think most arm people are the helpless cripples."

"Cool! How about a bargain, Ashley? I won't do anything for you unless you ask me to. Except I know that I was sometimes too embarrassed to even ask for help, so how about a secret sign, just between the two of us, a sign that you want just a little assistance with something. That way you actually won't have to ask verbally." Lindsey thought her plan was a good one.

"You are pretty cool, Lindsey. Okay, I like that. How about if I move my head so, towards something? Can you pick up on that?" Ashley suggested.

"Perfect! Why don't you get unpacked now?"

Lindsey watched as Ashley used her feet as if they were hands, slowly unpacking her bag. Mostly the bag contained her schoolbooks from the previous two years. Her laptop was old and mostly worn out. She had one other change of clothes, but they were in even worse condition. The only personal item was a framed picture of her deceased parents, which she carefully placed on her dresser so that they would be looking down at her as she slept.

"I can see that you are in need of a better computer, that's for sure. Part of the Bradbury scholarship is a new laptop and fancy cell phone. I'm going to email Governor Alister today and see if we can get you your new laptop now, before orientation week. Probably you won't need the cell phone until then."

"Cool. You mean every student gets a computer like yours?" Ashley asked curiously.

"Yes, Pam, she's the computer genius, she says that these are state of the art. I just find that they are useful. Everyone gets one during orientation week."

"Duh. Well at Chicago they gave me one worse than this one, which they gave me at the Twin Cities." She paused, thought a moment, and added, "I admit that I did a little Net searching when I found out that I was being transferred to Bradbury's School of Magic. Apparently, Bradbury's is the most exclusive magic school in the USA."

"Well, I've never seen other schools, but I love Bradbury's. Come on; mom and Polly want to make you some descent clothes. Mom sews my dresses by hand. She knows nothing about magic at all, by the way. She is the only normal one around here, but she is incredibly kind and understanding, really she is. I know she'll take great pride in making you some clothes. Actually, they are sometimes better than store bought ones. Come on."

Lena measured Ashley for some clothes. "Ashley, as you know, blouses and dresses always have arms and sleeves." Ashley glared at Lena, but said nothing, wondering what insult she was about to receive.

"I've been thinking about this aspect, and I have an idea. What would you say if I designed these especially for you and make them appear not ever to have had sleeves or arms? These clothes would be especially for you, not looking as if someone has 'altered' them."

"You can do that? It certainly is an interesting idea. I hate pinning up sleeves. They get in the way. It makes me look weird, when in fact it is you who have arms that look weird to me."

Lena smiled. "Good. I have enough blue material around to make one top. If it meets with your approval, we can get more. Polly has enough blue jean material to make a pair of shorts. By this evening, you can be more comfortable than wearing your old school uniform."

"Thanks. This thing is pretty much falling apart. I keep

Mending it, but it's getting more difficult to keep it together."

Ashley wandered out to the spacious living room, where the girls had gathered, drinking sodas and chatting. Pam blushed, as she had just done a MagGoogle on Ashley Stokes, attempting to find out more about her. "I see you are finding out about me," Ashley said antagonistically, as she entered the room. Pam crimsoned even more.

"Yes, we wanted to know more about you," Pam volunteered the truth. "I mean you are so unusual."

That did it. Ashley exploded, "I'm *not* unusual! *You* are the weird, unusual ones! You can't even use your God-given feet!"

Lindsey jumped in trying to smooth the tense situation. "Yes, Ashley, we are the unusual ones. Pam here—she is already a Sleuth. Amanda is a natural born Tracker. I'm already doing wonders as a Dispeller. Audrey knows just when and where she should be for good things to happen to her; she is a master carver and has her own Internet Web store, selling her creations. And Fern, Amanda, me, and their brothers, Jim and Tom—we all just won second place in the National Track meet in Des Moines a few weeks ago. Yes, we are all the unusual ones."

Lindsey's outburst mollified Ashley. In fact, her anger turned into just as intense curiosity. "Really? You aren't just making fun of me?"

"No, here have a coke. I used to use a straw when I had no hands, but you probably don't need one," Lindsey said, sliding the coke over to Ashley, who had plopped down in one of the older sofas. All the girls watched as she slipped off her shoes, popped the top with her toes, and brought it up to her mouth for a sip.

"Cool!" Pam acknowledged. "I certainly can't do that!"

Ashley calmed down, in part because she was really showing off a bit to these girls, showing them that she was not helpless. "Tell me about all these things. I mean, we heard all sorts of weird things on the news. I didn't believe much of it, though."

"We ought to start at the beginning, Lindsey," Amanda suggested. "Otherwise, things won't make much sense. It started when Lindsey first came to Bradbury's. She had no hands and was there on a special full scholarship."

They took turns relating the many adventures all had had during their first year, complete with Lindsey being kidnaped and tortured by Dominus. Amanda proudly described how she had followed the magical energies, bringing the Department of Law people to the cabin to rescue Lindsey. Lindsey described how she had no choice but to cast her spells without a wand and non-verbally. After all, Dominus had cut off her hands and sewn her mouth shut so she could not give Rubius, the Death Stalker guard, any trouble.

They then went through all that had happened this year at Bradbury's. Pam eventually played her fifteen-minute video, which she had played for the Board of Governors. Even Fern flinched along with Ashley when Pam told how Albright had whipped out his wand and began to cast a spell that would kill Pam outright. Lindsey had cast her Hold spell, again, non-verbally and without a wand, leading to Albright's capture.

Amanda also described their various track meets. She told of their winning third place last year and second place this year. Pam brought up Audrey's new web store. She panned through the dozen magnificent photos of Audrey's carvings that were for sale.

Pam insisted on ending with, "Finally, you should know that Lindsey's father was really Samuel Rabnor, the famous Dispeller who, with the Rat Pack, helped capture Dominus some fifteen years ago. Now you can see why Dominus is after all of us." Pam had not forgotten that Ashley had angrily called her weird. She added, "Yes, we're unusual, but I don't think it's weird."

"I'm, I'm sorry. I didn't mean to say you were weird in that way. I mean you're weird because you depend on your silly arms. Who needs arms anyway? They just get in the way." Ashley was still being defensive, but her tone had definitely softened. "I, I should tell you this. I was very pleased to hear that I was being expelled and being sent to Bradbury's School of Magic. I knew it was the very best thing that could happen to me, only I didn't know why, just that it would be so."

"You'll just have to forgive us a little, Ashley," Lindsey

explained. "You see, none of us has ever met someone like you. For us, it's so unfamiliar, and we're naturally very curious. When I had no hands, everyone kept staring at me trying to see how I managed things. I was strange and unusual to them. It is such an awful feeling when they all stared at me, but I realized early on that they were mostly just curious, never having been around someone without any hands. I will say this, that after a while, everyone got comfortable with me and stopped staring."

"Yes, it hurts," Ashley finally admitted.

Pam hastily changed the subject. "What we are all dying to know is all about you? Where you've been, what's happened to you and all that. I guess it's all right if you don't feel like talking to us about things; after all, you've only just met us." Pam wanted to give her a safe way to avoid telling about herself, though her curiosity was highly aroused.

She sipped her coke and said, "Well, compared to you, my life is positively dull. As you probably know, when I was two, my parents and I were in a car accident, or so I'm told. I don't remember any of it, not even my mother's face. Steel angle beams or something broke loose from a truck and smashed into our car, killing my parents and slicing off my arms. I don't remember any of it, but I have some dim memories of being in a hospital later on undergoing some surgeries to remove the remnants of the arms. I think that they eventually took the balls out of the sockets—that's what I think happened after taking biology this year."

"I had an aunt and uncle, on my mother's side, who took me in for a few years. They were all norms, and I continually got into fights with their son and daughter. I kicked out his teeth when he called me helpless. They kicked me out, and I was made a ward of the state. I was told that all my parent's insurance money had been spent on my medical bills and that I was penniless."

"They sent me to live with foster parents after that. Each year, sometimes twice a year, I was kicked out of one house and moved into another. I don't take anything from nobody. I've been in so many fights that I've lost count. Boys, mostly. They tease me once, and I kick them where it hurts. I tried to run away three times, but that only made things worse. I had no money and nearly starved each time."

"Yet through all of that mess, I always knew just what was coming and was prepared for it. Spooked norms though, telling them that if they did such and such, they would be in an accident. They ignored me and ended up in an accident. Spooked them. I was only trying to help them, but they kicked me out, calling me a freak or worse. Of course, when they did that, I attacked them. Remember, kick the boys and men in their privates first, then you got them where you want them, at your mercy."

"I was on the streets of Chicago, having run away again from my foster parents, when the Chicago School Seeker found me. She told me about magic school and that I had a full scholarship to the Chicago School of Magic. Although I knew instinctively this was what I should be doing, I thought anything was better than how I was living at the time."

"I got teased and ridiculed a lot there, but I was determined to show the bastards that I was more than capable. I passed all my Grade 0 and 1 spells, better than many other Yellow Hall kids, but I knew it wasn't the right place for me, so I got into a lot of fights with other students, and they transferred me just to get rid of troublesome me. Twin Cities took me on this past year."

"I knew at once it wasn't the place I should be at either, but I stuck it out, determined to learn all that I could before striking out on my own. I don't know about you all, but I hated the necromancy spells and flatly refused to learn them. I even kicked the professor in his privates when he tried to insist that I at least try. I told him to flake off. I don't take crap from anyone, not even professors. Heck, they should know better. I wish I could have been there when Pam blackmailed your slut of a professor, what's her name, Janice? I'd of done far more than blackmail her! One thing I've learned on the streets and in the slums is that you don't take nothing from nobody! Besides, I knew I wasn't supposed to be in that stupidly cold city anyway. Do you realize their main city streets are under a foot of ice in January? Darn snow doesn't melt, and the mosquitoes are thicker than the air up there in summer. Nasty place to live."

"Then, as I was being kicked out of my second magic school, I learned that I was coming here, and I just knew that this was the right place, the place I'm supposed to be at, though I don't know why. So here I am. I guess there was one nice professor back in Chicago, Gillian was his name; he made me my wand sheath to fit on my leg. No one else has really been very nice to me. They all think I'm a thing to be pitied or something. I think they are the ones to be pitied!"

"Wow, Ashley. You have ten times more guts than I have," Amanda exclaimed. "I'd never dream of kicking them like you do. Bet they deserved it and didn't mess with you after that."

"No, they generally are scared of me after that," she admitted. "I hope I don't get kicked out of Bradbury's, though. I know I'm supposed to go to school here."

"One thing that fascinates me," Pam inquired, "is this prediction thing you mentioned. I figure out things after they happen. Do you figure out things before they happen?"

"Strange way to put it, but I think that is a way of saying it," Ashley replied. "Why? Oh!" Suddenly, Ashley's face went white. "Someone's in trouble, outside. I see a field, some kind of watering machine. Something's fallen on a man. He can't get free."

"Dad! Come on," Lindsey exclaimed. She raced out of the house, followed by the rest of the girls. Amanda and Fern kept pace with Lindsey's incredibly fast run. Pam, Audrey, and Ashley made no attempt at that, just jogging behind the three.

The three girls found Lloyd pinned beneath the heavy irrigation pipe that he had been repairing. His wand had fallen way beyond his reach, and he couldn't lift the heavy pipe pinning him to the ground. "Help!" he whispered, unable to breathe properly with the weight on his chest. "Levitate: Pipe," Amanda said with a wave of her wand. She was faster on the draw than Lindsey, who was in a bit of a shock seeing her father pinned to the ground.

The pipe rose enough for Lindsey and Fern to pull him out. "Thanks! Silly pipe nearly got me." Pam, Audrey, and Ashley jogged up.

"Are you all right?" asked a nearly out of breath Pam. "Ashley predicted you were in trouble, and we all came at once."

"Just in time. Thank you all. Bit of a surprise—pipe falling on me. I'm not a tenth the rancher that Lena is, I'm afraid. Oh, hello, you must be Ashley Stokes. Pleased to meet you." He held out his hand and then hastily extended it to give her a hug, which she accepted.

"Thank you for sensing I was in trouble, Ashley. I'm very glad to have you staying with us. I only hope we don't need your skills again. One accident is more than enough," he grinned.

"Now that you are all here, mind giving me a hand getting these pipes back into working order?" The group, though they didn't know what was needed, followed his orders and soon the water was flowing across the field once more. They then headed back to the ranch house.

"Say, Ashley, do you like to ride horses?" Lloyd asked.

"Er, I've never seen a horse, sir," she replied. "Are they dangerous? I mean they are really big. I've seen pictures of horses."

"Lloyd, call me Lloyd. Sir sounds far too formal. I get enough of that at the office. I'm with the Department of Defense, Denver branch, on assignment here. No, our horses are very tame. Even the city slicker Pam managed to get Dandy to cultivate the corn field yesterday, as I understand it."

Lindsey replied, "We haven't yet had time to show Ashley the whole ranch, dad. We probably should do it now." While Lloyd entered the house to clean up, Lindsey took Ashley to see the barn and the large corral. "This is my horse, Betsy. She is quite docile. I used to ride her when I had no hands. This is Dandy, a draft horse. I know he is positively huge, but he is as gentle as a lamb." Dandy towered over the girls and began sniffing at Ashley.

"What's he doing? Is he trying to eat me?" asked Ashley, more than a little concerned.

Lindsey giggled and answered, "No, he is smelling you. I think he likes you. Normally, we pet him on his nose or sides." Not to be left out, Pam bravely demonstrated how, having done it yesterday.

Lindsey then showed her the other ten horses, the chicken coop, the two ducks, the six sheep, and the six cows. "Each morning, I get to milk the cows. That way, we always have fresh milk for breakfast."

"Hey, fresh eggs too," Pam added.

Just then, Jim, Tom, and Sandy appeared. "Hi everyone. We finally got away from dad so we could come and meet our newest student," Jim called out.

"Hi, I'm Jim Whitewater," he said, holding out his hand, before he realized Ashley had none to shake.

"Hug, give her a hug, silly," Amanda advised her brother.

Jim gave her a good hug, but was surprised when her leg went around him, adding her side to the hug. "I much prefer hugging such a pretty girl as you, Ashley."

"Don't patronize me or I'll kick you in your privates," Ashley retorted.

"Hey, I'm not patronizing you, Ashley. You are quite cute, so there. Besides, if you try it, I will be forced to chase you around the ranch tickling you to death," Jim teased.

"Careful, Ashley," Fern advised her. "He will. He's a relentless tickler. I ought to know!"

"Hi, I'm Tom Whitewater and this is my fiancé Sandy Rains. We are also your Yellow Hall Floor Monitors, though you are to use Lindsey first, us if she is not available. We're sixth years now and are going to get married when we graduate."

"Congratulations! We didn't know about this," Lindsey exclaimed.

"Of course, you didn't," Sandy replied. "He only just proposed to me a while ago. We came over to tell you all the news and to show you the ring he gave me. See, it's gorgeous." Sandy proudly displayed her new diamond ring.

While the girls hugged Sandy and wished them the best, Ashley stared at all them. "You are all Indians aren't you?" she suddenly said. "Real Indians."

Jim chuckled, "Golly, I didn't know there were fake Indians." Amanda smacked him a good one with her boot in his rump.

"Yes," Fern replied. "Full blooded Apaches, and Sandy is full blooded Arapaho."

"Wow. Do you live in a teepee and ride painted horses?" asked Ashley.

They laughed. Tom explained, "I think that you have been watching too many old western TV movies, Ashley. Our house is similar to Lindsey's new house, because dad helped build it, but we do ride horses. I think everyone out here on the High Plains rides. I promise you to take you horse riding soon, if you are interested in going for a ride. There are many cool places to ride out here, between our ranch and Lindsey's ranch. Then there are the arroyos. Say, when are you going to bring Ashley over to visit our place?"

"We've barely shown her around here," Lindsey protested. "Okay, maybe after supper."

Tom grinned. "Honestly, Ashley, mom and dad really want to meet you."

"Why? Haven't they ever seen an armless person before?" Ashley was immediately on the defensive.

Tom cleverly countered, "Come to think of it, Ashley, I don't think any one of us here has ever seen an armless person before, but that's not why they want to meet you. That would be a really dumb, stupid reason. I think that they want to meet you just to see who you are. After all, we are your neighbors, and half of the time you are all over at our house, and the other half we are all over here."

Ashley seemed mollified for the moment. Just then, a message appeared before Ashley's eyes. She flushed, unused to receiving messages. "Er, your mother wants me in the house right now. Back in a few minutes." Ashley didn't say anymore but headed to the ranch house.

Tom and Jim looked at Lindsey curiously. She explained, "Mom and Polly are making her some new clothes. Honestly, all she has are two torn up school dresses."

A while later, Ashley rejoined the large gathering. She wore a silky blue top that looked very form fitting, no trace of armholes or sleeves were visible, as if they never were part of the blouse. Her new denim shorts also fit her properly, showing off her well-formed legs and her wand sleeve tied to her left leg.

"Wow! You look positively super!" exclaimed Jim. "You are one hot neighbor."

"Cool it Jim, or she'll kick you in your butt," Amanda cautioned him, though Ashley did appreciate the compliment for once.

"Now I see how you carry your wand," Sandy added. "I was wondering how you managed that. Good design. Whoever made that one was thinking of you."

"Personally, Ashley, I love the way the blouse is made. It really fits you well," Audrey volunteered, running her hands over her shoulders and down her sides. "Incredible look. You are a knock out." Ashley actually flushed slightly, highly unused to so many compliments on her looks.

"Hey, almost forgot. We were supposed to come get you two. Mom's got supper ready," Tom butted in. "Lindsey, bring everyone over after supper, please. If not, R. B.'s going to have a fit."

They all walked back into the ranch house. As they walked, Ashley whispered to Lindsey, "Why doesn't Tom and Sandy just teleport them home?"

"Because it is easier and safer to use R. B.'s latest invention. He's made a permanent teleportation system between our front room and theirs. This way we can go back and forth safely." Lindsey did her best to explain the device, though she had no idea how it worked.

As they walked in the front door, they saw Tom, Sandy, Jim, and Fern vanishing before their eyes. Amanda gave Ashley a hug, "Great meeting you. Come over after dinner, please. Bye for a bit." She gave the command word and also vanished. Ashley looked at the wooden floor but saw nothing out of the ordinary.

"Dinner's up," called out Lena, and they washed up in the little bathroom off the main entrance. Ashley moved a stool over to the sink and then washed off her feet. Lindsey watched carefully, both out of curiosity and to see if she needed any help. She didn't.

Ashley realized that this first meal together with the

whole family would be embarrassing for her. She expected either everyone would be asking to help her with everything or else just staring at her. However, she knew intuitively that she belong here somehow and vowed to restrain her temper this one time.

As everyone gathered around, Lena explained, "Left overs made into a stew tonight. Ashley, you must forgive us. We have no idea what your needs are at meal time. Please tell us if any arrangements are needed."

Ashley didn't expect this, but replied honestly. "It is a whole lot easier if I had a stool to sit on. I need to be higher up." Lloyd brought in a bar stool from a side room. Ashley said it was perfect. Indeed everyone watched a little as she efficiently began helping herself using her feet, as if it was as simple as eating with your hands.

However, the novelty soon wore off, and everyone began chatting. Lloyd was grateful for Ashley's timely warning that he was in trouble. Lena asked about what other colors Ashley liked and asked Lindsey how many outfits were needed for school. When the meal was finally done, Lena said, "Okay, kids, you are on dishwashing duty. As soon as you are done and the dishes put away, we are supposed to go over to the Whitewaters for the evening."

A bit later, Pam took charge. "Division of labors here. There are four of us. What's the most efficient way to handle this pile of dishes? Ashley, what's the easiest part of the operation for you to handle?"

"I have a mean Clean spell. It's a bit hard for me to carry the dishes in here or to put them where they go, but I can sit here and clean away, if you feed me the dirty ones."

Audrey and Pam brought the dishes into the kitchen, while Lindsey fed them to Ashley, who sat on her stool and, using her wand, cleaned each as she was handed them. Then, Pam and Audrey began putting them away—at least where they thought they went. No one was sure where the dishes went—things were too new. In less than a half hour, the dishes were done, and they reported that they were ready to go.

Lindsey and the girls stood on the proper location just inside their front door. She said, "To the Whitewater's Home."

Instantly, they appeared in a similar location there. "We'd better move into the room. They will be right behind us."

"Hi, come into the living room," Amanda was the first to greet them. They had barely moved out of the way when the adults appeared behind them. By the time that everyone got into the large living room, which the boys had been ordered to clean earlier this afternoon, Luci and R. B. arrived as well.

"Ah, this must be Ashley. Come here; let me see you," said a jovial R. B. His hair was a bit disheveled. He'd just come in from his workshop, having tried to get a bit more done between supper and the arrival of his guests.

Resistance grew in Ashley; obviously, he could see her well enough right where she stood. However, she felt a strong pull from him and walked over to the tall Indian. "My, you are a pretty one. I am Running Bear, R. B. for short, Ashley." He gave her a big hug. She found herself adding her leg to his hug as well, though she had not intended to do so.

"I do so like your blouse. Highlights your form just perfectly. My compliments to the seamstress." Lena smiled; it was her handiwork; Polly had made the shorts. "Oh, I am shirking my duties. Ashley Stokes, this is my lovely wife Lucinda Morning Dove, Luci for short."

Luci gushed, "Very glad to meet you at last. The kids have been telling me about you. Why, you are even prettier than Jim suggested. Come here; give let me give you a welcome hug to the Whitewater home." She gave Ashley a strong hug. "You are welcome to pop in anytime, dear. Kids are always coming and going around here." Ashley actually smiled, though she had not intended to do so, but she was not certain why.

R. B. then said, "Ashley, will you accompany me into my workshop? This won't take but a moment. I promise all of you I won't monopolize our newest guest," he teased the others who were finding seats.

He put his arm around her waist and guided her out of the room to his workshop. Once inside, he shut the door and looked long at her. Ashley felt a little uncomfortable. At last R. B. spoke, "Ashley, I want you to tell me why I have asked you to come into my workshop, please."

This was not at all what Ashley expected, though at the moment, she was not even sure what she had expected. She found herself replying without thinking, "Oh, you want to give me something." She wondered why she had said that! She'd only just met this strange Indian.

"Precisely, spoken like a true Diviner. I suspected so when my daughter explained what you did for Lloyd this afternoon. These are dark times that we are enduring. Many out there intend us harm. Here is a little invention of mine. It looks like an ordinary rabbit's foot. Keep it on your person at all times. If ever someone is about to cause you harm, the foot will begin dancing a jig. The more it dances, the closer the danger actually will be. I have given one of these to Lindsey, Amanda, and Pam as well. You may ask them how well it works."

"Er, thank you," Ashley replied, thinking that this might just be a hoax, a rabbit's foot, luck charm.

"Should I put it in your pocket for you?" R. B. asked.

Her defenses rose. "No, I can do it for myself, thank you." She sat down, took the foot between her toes, and inserted it into her new pants pocket.

"Excellent, I see that you aren't lazy either."

"What do you mean by that?" Ashley said rather antagonistically, as she struggled to get to her feet.

"You insist on being totally independent. I have known many who have lost limbs, mostly during war times. So many of them allow themselves to be dependent on others. I like your spirit, Ashley. Now then, may I examine your wand sheath? Perhaps I can improve upon it for you."

"Well, I am independent! It's you folks with arms that are the lazy ones. You don't make hardly any use of your legs and feet, except to walk around," she replied still slightly antagonistically. "Why? Why would you want to improve it?"

"Because in these dark times, we need to stick together, to band together. There is strength in numbers. Alone, the dark forces are stronger; united, we are stronger. If I can improve it a little, it may one day be of immense value to you."

She allowed him to examine it. "Would you please show me how you retrieve your wand?" Ashley sat down and slipped off her shoe again, retrieving the wand with her toes.

"Too slow, too inefficient," R. B. muttered. Ashley bristled, though she knew well he spoke the truth. It was always slow and awkward for her to retrieve her wand. "Do you need to be seated to use your wand? I mean can you also cast while standing?"

"Er, yes, but I usually sit. It's more comfortable."

"Good, good. Well, you've given me a whole lot to ponder. I'm an inventor, though I suppose my kids have already told you that. Let me see what I can devise. We'd best head back to the others or Luci will be all over me about monopolizing our guest. You are quite lovely, by the way. I mean it, lovely indeed. Ah, but I see this is something that you do not see. Ah well. Here we are. I told you I wouldn't keep her long." They joined the crowded living room.

They decided to hold a Scrabble competition with the winner to get a free pizza. To make things fairer, the adults played against the adults, the kids against the kids. Then the two winners would duke it out. Meanwhile, everyone got to chat up a storm. While they were setting up the two boards, Amanda and Fern took Ashley on a quick tour of their house. Fern desperately wanted to show Ashley her flower garden growing in her bedroom walls. Indeed, Ashley was impressed, never having seen anything like it, which pleased Fern.

Lindsey spied R. B. moving the letters around without using his hands or his wand. He saw her looking at him and smiled. The other adults were very familiar with his antics, claiming he was just trying to intimidate them. Not to be out done, Lindsey began to move her letters around as R. B. had. Soon everyone was laughing at the two show-offs. Even Ashley found this funny as well.

A while later, Amanda complained, "This isn't fun. Pam, you are too darn smart for us! What the devil is rhizopus anyway?"

"Yes, is it even a word?" Ashley aired her frustrations too.

Didactically, Pam said, "It is the fungus or mold that grows on bread and potatoes when they rot." Jim moaned.

Sally snickered. "What's the matter, Jim? Upset because

a fourteen year old girl is beating the pants off of you?"

"Careful or I will tickle you," Jim replied.

"Oh, I will need my big, tall, handsome protector. Tom, save me from this wild tickler." Everyone roared.

Pam won rather quickly. Among the adults, the only real competition was between Lena and R. B. Already, Lloyd and Polly knew that Lena was a mean Scrabble player. Now they saw that with R. B., Lena had nearly met her match. They continued laying down all sorts of unusual words; only a few points separated them. Finally, Lena laid down predella, ending the game.

"Wait one little minute. What the heck is predella?" asked R. B.

"The platform on which churches place their altars, usually some kind of base or stone platform. Let's see, looks like I won, R. B." Lena smiled, having had the best challenge in Scrabble in years. R. B. shook his head, though grinning.

Now everyone crowded around Pam and Lena as they mixed up the letters. "Come on Pam," Lindsey cheered her friend. In fact, the audience was more excited about the match than the two players were. Amanda saw more words that she didn't know appearing than ever before.

Lindsey explained to Ashley that Pam was the brains of their class, while Lena had studied the dictionary while home schooling Lindsey part of each year. Now the duel made more sense to Ashley, who found herself rooting for Pam. Normally, she would be detached from others playing games. Life was not a game for her. It was deadly serious, had been all her life. Finally, Pam finally won using the word vinology, which she had to explain meant the study of wine making.

"I'll take sausage, cheese, mushrooms, and avocados on my free pizza, please," Pam teased. A little later, the Domino's delivery wizard appeared at their front door with six pizzas and two packs of sodas.

While they were eating, Jim said, "I liked the dancing night better. What say we hold a big dance one night real soon?"

R. B. looked at Luci, who grinned back at him. "Well, how about Saturday night we hold a dance again?" Luci suggested.

"Only if we hold it in our new living room," Lena insisted. "After all, it is our turn to host all of you. Yet, you better bring the music because I'm not sure if we are setup to play the music like you had here." That settled, the group headed for home, which now only took a minute.

As Lindsey and Ashley prepared for bed in their bedroom, Ashley quietly said, "R. B. gave me this rabbit's foot. He said it would warn me of danger. Is he pulling my leg? Does it really work?" Lindsey showed her hers and told her just how well it did work. Ashley was even more impressed.

The next morning at breakfast, Polly asked, "Ashley, would you like to accompany me into town to pick out some material for more of your clothes? We should also get you some more shoes."

"But how am I going to pay for them?" she asked.

"From your allowance," Polly was quick to reply. Ashley couldn't counter this and agreed. "However, per Fred's orders, we are supposed to always travel in groups of at least four of us. Pam, Lindsey, Audrey, would you three like to accompany us? Perhaps do a little shopping of your own?"

"Mom, I need to do some research. I'll pass on the shopping trip." Polly gave her daughter a strange look. It was not like her to avoid going shopping, not unless something important had come up. Pam hastily asked, "Say Ashley, do you know what your mother's maiden name was?"

"No, I've no idea, sorry." A while later, holding hands, Polly teleported the three girls away with her, taking them to her favorite fabric store in a suburb of Denver. Pam booted up her computer and began her research.

Around lunchtime, they returned loaded with packages. Audrey had purchased several new carving knives along with some clothes. Ashley insisted on carrying her own packages, which they tied together with a long piece of scrap cloth using it as a shoulder strap. She had two new pairs of shoes and quite a lot of material and accessories: zippers, matching thread, buttons and so on. Polly had insisted she get some proper undergarments as well.

After lunch, Pam invited Ashley into her room—alone,

she insisted. "Ashley, I've been doing a bit of research on your parents."

"Why? They are long dead," Ashley replied, a bit annoyed.

"Well, they were wizard and witch. Lindsey's father, while obviously an exception, did leave her an inheritance. I figured that since both of your parents were users of magic that they would have had some kind of magic account somewhere. It only makes sense that they would have. I checked on your father, but that was a complete dead end."

"I remember the governor in Chicago looking up dad. I think he may have had a similar idea, now that you mention it. He didn't find anything either," Ashley sighed.

"Well, he isn't me. I traced back your dad's line, the Stokes of Chicago. Problem is, there are no other Stokes in Chicago that are related. Your aunt and uncle are on your mother's side. That is one of the things that bothered me. He just rather appeared on the scene, so to speak. He graduated from Bradbury's."

"How do you know that?"

Pam task switched to another opened window, the school's web archives. "See, there are his records, graduated over twenty-five years ago."

"Say that is cool! I'm going to school where my dad went to school. Yes, that looks like a younger dad than my picture. Can you email me this URL so I can get to it on my computer?" Ashley asked, elated to have another photo of her father. Pam did so at once. She continued, "Now, look at the fine print. He was actually from Denver, Colorado. It must have been after he graduated that he moved to Chicago. I'm still looking for that connection. Now, look at this page," she switched to another web page.

"See, it lists Samson and Bertha Stokes as having a son, Joshua Stokes. I pulled up his birth certificate, and it appears to be in order. Now look at this newspaper article." Ashley read the short notice in the Denver Chronicle. "See, it says that upon graduation from Middle School, Joshua Stokes went to Bradbury's School of Magic."

"How did you ever find this tiny article?"

"My skills. Now do you know what this means?"

"Er, no."

"You have two grandparents, that's what! I have their address written down. I think that we ought to pay them a visit sometime. After all, they probably do not even know that they have a granddaughter! However, there is a whole lot more here. That's all I've got on your father, so then I began looking at your mother's past. Her name was Lisa Billings, but she went to school in Chicago, which is probably where she and your father met."

"Well, I guess that all makes sense, though I didn't like the Chicago School of Magic at all. Maybe mom didn't either. Ah well."

"I did a bit more searching, Ashley. Look at this page. It's the Mag Mercantile Bank web site."

"Hey, there's mom's name. What's that mean?"

"That means your mother still has an open bank account at this bank, that's what! I have no way of finding out what is in the account, not without the account number. However, I emailed them, and they said that, if we bring in a death certificate and your DNA proves that you are her daughter, they will transfer the account to you. Who knows, maybe there is nothing much in it. After all, she had it before she got married. At least, I think it is worth a trip to check it out."

"You really think that there is money in her old account?"

Pam just shrugged. "No way to know unless we check it out. I've asked Lloyd to take us there as soon as you are willing to go—now, if you feel up to it."

As if reading their minds, Lloyd stuck his head in their door. "Anyone wanting to make a quick trip to Chicago?"

"Pam's found an old bank account that my mom may have had. It probably has nothing in it, but I guess it wouldn't hurt to check it out. I hate to bother you, sir."

"Lloyd, not sir. Do I really look that old to you?" he teased. Both girls giggled.

"Come on. I'll tell Lena where we are going. Since Lindsey is your Floor Monitor, I suppose that she should come along with us, so we are four in number. House traveling rules, you know, always in fours."

Lindsey grabbed her Staff of Power and made sure she had her rabbit's foot in her pocket. "Honestly, dear, do you really think we need your staff? We are only going to a bank," Lloyd said.

"I'm responsible for Ashley now, dad. I feel better having it with us, though you are probably right, just a bank." The four held hands, Lloyd placing one of his on Ashley's shoulder, and he waved his wand and spoke clearly. The four stepped onto the concrete sidewalk just outside a very tall building in downtown Chicago. The girls stared up at the incredibly tall skyscrapers.

"This way." Lloyd led them into the Mag Mercantile Bank and asked directions for the archival verification unit. A beady-eyed older man looked up from his desk as the four approached. He stared for a minute at the figure of Ashley, who was wearing her new form-fitting top, which did anything but hide her missing arms.

Lloyd explained, "Here is the death certificate of Lisa Billings, who married Stokes. This is her daughter, who wishes to inherit her mother's old account."

"Ah, I see." He took the certificate, entered its number into his computer and verified it matched what he was seeing. "This is in order. I need a DNA sample. Which young lady is the daughter?" Ashley stepped forward. "Kindly open your mouth so that I may take a swab." Ashley complied, though she thought this was a bit icky. He placed the swab into his machine.

"This will only take a minute." He waited patiently, though he looked incredibly bored. His computer made a beeping noise and he looked up. "Ah yes, confirmed to a ninety-nine percentile match. Now then, let's see what that old account has in it. It has not had any activity for over sixteen years now, quite some time. Ah, well, there is a balance. If she was going to leave the funds for such a period of time, I would have recommended a savings account, pays a much higher interest rate." He printed out a statement of her account and handed it to Lloyd, since Ashley had no hands to take it.

"What does this mean?" Ashley whispered. She had never seen anything remotely like a bank account statement before and didn't know what it said.

"Your mother left a small amount of money in her checking account. Over all these years, the bank has added interest to it. Today, you have ten thousand one hundred sixty-three dollars and fifteen cents. You have quite a lot of money, Ashley."

Ashley's mouth opened, but she couldn't speak. She had five dollars once. Usually she only managed to have a dollar or so in her tiny moneybag. The man with the beady eyes asked, "Will madam be wishing to convert this account into her own checking account or perhaps you, sir, would prefer to withdraw the funds on her behalf, considering her, well, her condition."

If they had been any place else, Ashley would have kicked the man in his privates, but right now, she was staggering with the significance of the whole experience; it was surreal. She nearly fainted.

"I believe that she would prefer to transfer it to her own private checking account, sir. How do we handle this?" Lloyd spoke for Ashley, who nodded.

"Ah, very good, but I will need her signature on this form, where the X is located. Plus, she will need to sign this checking account master form, plus she will, of course, need to sign each check that she writes." Ashley now realized that he was trying to be polite in suggesting that without arms, this was a futile action to be taking.

Ashley slid her chair into a better position, sat down, took off her right shoe, picked up his pen, and slowly and carefully signed her name, Ashley Stokes, beside the X. The little man's eyes nearly popped out of his head. Suddenly, he was anything but bored. He slid the second form over to her so she could sign it as well. "Very well. On behalf of the Mag Mercantile Bank of Chicago, permit me to welcome you as our newest customer. If you will fill this form out, your checks and monthly bank statements will be sent to you. I will have some temporary checks for you in a minute."

He slid a lengthier form in front of her, while he typed

rapidly on his computer. "Lloyd, I need help with this. I don't know what to put down." He told her their address, going slow enough so that she could write it down. By the time that she had filled the form out, his machine made another noise and a small package arrived, her new temporary check book.

"Now then, could she withdraw a little money before we leave today, sir?" Lloyd asked.

A few minutes later, they walked out of the bank. Ashley had one hundred dollars in small bills tucked safely in her pocket. "While it might be nice to stroll Chicago, now is not the proper time," Lloyd said. A minute later, they arrived back at their ranch.

Ashley, now nearly white and still in somewhat of a shock, whispered, "I, I am rich!"

"What's this?" asked Lena.

"Mom did have an account. I, I have ten thousand dollars. This can't be real. I feel faint. I have to sit down. I can't believe this is happening to me!" Pam helped steady her as she nearly collapsed into the nearest sofa in the living room. Audrey raced to get her a glass of water.

Ashley even allowed Audrey to hold the glass to her lips so she could drink easily. "Someone tell me I'm dreaming, please."

Lloyd replied, "Yes, her mother had a small amount in her checking account. Over these sixteen years, interest added to it. She has a little over ten thousand dollars now. Incredible."

Audrey let out a loud cheer, which Pam and Lindsey echoed. Ashley, recovering a bit, also got up, and the four girls danced wildly around the room. "I'm rich! I'm rich! I can't believe it, I'm rich!"

The adults allowed Ashley and the three girls to express their excitement until they calmed down. At last, Ashley recovered. Getting very serious once more, she said, "Pam, I don't know how to thank you for what you've done for me. No one else discovered mom's old account. If it had not been for you, I never would have found it. I owe it all to you. How can I ever repay you for what you've done for me? All of you, you have been so kind to me. No one else ever has. I can't believe my incredible good luck. I just knew that it was right for me to come here, but I had no idea why. Pam, I want to hug you to death!" She moved over to Pam and gave her a hug anyway, using her leg to pull Pam up tightly to her. Pam's arms went around her as she returned the hug. Tears came to Pam's eyes as Ashley pulled away.

"It's, it's what I do, sleuthing. I'm so glad for you, Ashley. Honestly, it might only have been a dollar in that old account," Pam tried to be honest with her new friend.

"I know, Polly, how much were all those supplies we bought today? I want to write you my very first check to pay for them!" Ashley begged her.

Polly knew better than to refuse and told her the total. Everyone watched as Ashley slowly wrote out her very first check to Polly Betts. The bored banker had written in the current balance, and Lloyd explained to Ashley how to write the check into her checkbook and to debit the amount.

Lena then showed Ashley the new sky blue top that she had just finished while they were off to the bank. She asked, "Ashley, do you have a formal prom dress for the fancy end of term ball at Bradbury's?" Lena already knew, via Lindsey, that she didn't. "Well, then, you and I need to look over some patterns." She whisked Ashley off to her new sewing room.

Lindsey said, "Pam, very, very well done!" She gave her a big hug as well. While Lindsey and Audrey began helping Polly in the kitchen, Pam went off to continue her research. Perhaps there was more to be found, she thought. Pam would not stop until all avenues had been explored. Though she worked on it for another couple of days, Pam found no other traces.

The next day as they all sat around the table eating lunch, a loud ringing noise interrupted them. "What is that?" asked Lindsey.

"Oh, the telephone! I wonder who could possibly be calling us?" Lena replied, getting up and heading for the wall phone. "Hello." After a pause, she said, "Oh my! Yes, yes she is staying with us. Yes. One minute!" She put her hand over the mouthpiece, "Ashley! It's your grandfather! He wants to talk to you!"

Ashley nearly choked on her soup. She got up and headed to the phone. Lena helped her cradle it against her shoulder. "Hello. This is Ashley Stokes. Grandfather?"

Everyone allowed her to have a private conversation and avoided listening in, until Ashley called for Lloyd. "Can you explain to him how to find us?" Lloyd took the phone; Ashley's face was wet with tears.

She went back to the table, nearly sobbing. "They, they want to come here and see me. I never knew I had any grandparents. What are they going to think of me?"

"They are going to go nuts over you, that's what," Lena said, putting her arms around Ashley, providing much needed moral support.

A bit later, Lloyd rejoined them. "They will be coming for supper tonight. Both of them use magic, though they are in their late sixties. Sampson will be teleporting them here at five. I gave him good directions. Lindsey, let's get the chores done early."

"What will they think of me? I mean like this?" she shrugged her shoulders. This was the first time that Lindsey had seen Ashley think less of herself because she had no arms.

"I told them what had happened to you. I think they understand," Lloyd said softly. "They will probably want to smother you with hugs and kisses. I know I sure would if I suddenly discovered I had a long lost granddaughter." Ashley managed a smile.

With guests coming in a little over four hours, everyone pitched in to get things ready. Lena had the table set with her best china. Polly whipped up a fancy dinner, roast pork with all the trimmings, including freshly baked bread. The girls cleaned up the house and tried to keep Ashley calmed down. Finally, they all showered and dressed and Ashley put on her newest sky blue, silky top and the new matching skirt that Lena had made for her. Lindsey fussed with her hair, brushing it and styling it as much as she could with the short hair.

With all in readiness, they all went outside to await the arrival of her grandparents. A popping sound echoed, and they saw the elderly couple materializing just beyond their porch, a perfect spell casting. Samson was sixty-six, with short white hair, a protruding belly, sporting a white moustache. He wore a very nice western style rancher's suit. Bertha was a year younger, with short white hair, heavily wrinkled face, but kindly. She wore a cowgirl outfit; both were true westerners.

"Lloyd Compton," he said, as he stepped forward. "Allow me to present your granddaughter, Ashley Stokes." Ashley stepped forward, extremely timidly, uncertain how she would be accepted. She could not help but see a strong resemblance of her father in Samson.

Both rushed forward, Bertha began bawling like a baby. Both threw their arms around Ashley, holding her so tightly that she thought she might get crushed. "Let me look at you, dear," Bertha manage to finally blurt out. "You have Josh's eyes and nose, doesn't she, Sam?"

"I think she looks an awful lot like her mother, at least that picture we have of her, Bert," he replied. "Honey, they told us you were dead too. We never knew that you were alive. Can you ever forgive us?"

"I never knew you existed either, not until Pam found you the other day."

"Well, come on inside. It's rather hot out here," Lloyd suggested, and they followed everyone inside. Ashley sat between her grandparents, and Lloyd introduced everyone else, though the Stokes could scarcely take their eyes off Ashley.

Eventually, Samson explained that the police of Chicago had called them to notify them of their son's tragic death. They were indeed told that the whole family had perished, probably because Ashley was in critical condition at the hospital and not given much chance of survival. "Then, yesterday morning we got the news. When you entered your DNA at the bank in Chicago, it triggered notification of next of kin. We got a notice that you were alive and where you were staying," he explained.

Over dinner and as they most definitely stared at how Ashley managed to eat, they heard her long story. Bertha cried so much that she barely touched her meal, until Ashley finished her tale. "We owe everything to Pam here; she was the one who uncovered everything," Ashley praised Pam. "Now I'm going to the best magic school in the country with some really terrific friends and I actually am rich! Mom left me her old bank account, ten thousand dollars! Only one time did I ever have so much as five dollars in my pocket before."

Over coffee and desert—the kids had tea—Samson explained that they were now living in a retirement community. Having no other children, they had sold their house and moved into the center several years ago. Bertha had arthritis and could no longer keep house, even with magic spells. "Ashley, if you want to come and live with us, we can try to buy a new house, hire a maid to help Bertha," Samson suggested. "We don't know how we can make up for fourteen lost years."

Lloyd was diplomatic. "She is going to Bradbury's this fall. As you know, she will be there nine months of the year. It would not be practical for you folks to buy a house just for three months of the year. Surely, she can come and visit you often at your retirement center. There are enough of us around that we can teleport her to visit you frequently. Next year, she will be learning to teleport herself and can come as often as you both desire. While she is here with us, she has many of her classmates with which to play and learn."

"Are you sure that it's all right for her to stay with you? I mean she isn't going to be a burden on you?" asked Samson.

"No, she does her chores around here to help. She is one fiercely independent young woman, anything but a burden, sir. Besides, until she learns to teleport, it is easier on you two to come and visit here. We have a large house, plenty of space. Even got spare bedrooms, if you two wish to stay for a few days at a time, especially around Christmas?" That brought big smiles to both their faces.

"You are right, Lloyd," Bertha sighed. "We are too old to be trying to raise a teenager properly. Some mornings, my hands won't even hold my coffee. Dear, we would love to visit with you as much as we can. Perhaps you can come and visit us for a day or two, but I'm afraid there is nothing to interest you at all at the retirement center, just a bunch of us old folks. However, we will make sure that you want for nothing, Ashley. We don't have a fortune, but what we do have is going to be yours. We had planned to leave everything to charity, but

Samson has already changed our will, leaving what we have to you. It is the best we can do for you now at our age, besides smothering you with all the love we possibly can."

She went on, "But there is one thing that I want to give to you right now, Ashley. Samson, will you do it? My hands don't work so well any more. This was my mother's locket, a family heirloom. I put a picture of Josh and Lisa inside, just for you, Ashley." Samson took the golden locket and carefully placed it around her neck for her. He fumbled with the opening mechanism. Even his hands were not working all that well, Ashley noticed. There was a tiny picture of her parents. Ashley cried, and Bertha put her arms around her and held her tight for some time.

Around nine, both grandparents tired, and Lloyd volunteered to teleport them to their home in Denver. He promised to bring Ashley to them for lunch tomorrow. After long hugs, Lloyd took them home. When Ashley crawled into bed that night, pulling the covers up with her teeth, Lindsey noticed that she slept with her locket. She smiled; it was something to treasure, as she treasured her father's last letter to her.

When Ashley and Lloyd returned from the lunch with her grandparents, Lindsey's request for a new computer laptop for Ashley had been granted, and it had arrived. Already, Pam had set to work adding a few new features, including voice recognition software. She fixed up Ashley's email address book with everyone's addresses. She even started a personal database, putting in her grandparent's birthdays and their wedding anniversary. When Lindsey and Pam presented her the new laptop, Ashley cried and hugged both girls.

"Now we need to transfer anything you want to keep over from your old machine," Pam explained. Since Ashley had no idea how this was done, Pam volunteered to do it. However, as Ashley scrolled through the files, only a handful of emails needed to be moved over to her new machine. Once done, Pam removed all traces of Ashley's data on the old, slow laptop. Since Lena didn't have a computer, Ashley decided to give it to Lena. Hence, Pam quickly reset the email system for Lena, adding all their email addresses to the new address book.

"For me? Really? A computer? Oh, Ashley, you shouldn't have. Maybe you will need it," Lena exclaimed, very much surprised. "I don't even know how to use it."

"I've got a new one from Bradbury's which is much better than this one, Lena. Pam has my new one all fixed up for me, and she has fixed this one up for you. I can show you how to run it, but I am, well, rather slow at it. Pam is blazingly fast. She ought to show you how to use it," Ashley explained. She felt a feeling deep inside her that she had seldom felt before. She was giving something of value to someone who needed it.

Lena looked at Pam and flushed. "Really, I know nothing about them. I think it would be less intimidating if you would show me. Please go very slowly," Lena admitted. Pam chuckled and left them. Indeed, typing with her toes, Ashley did get the job done, just very slowly, compared to Pam. Lena definitely appreciated the slow pace.

An hour later, Lena had sent a "hello" email to all the girls, who sent her back a reply. "Gee, this is rather a fine way to stay in communication with Lindsey. I always hated to call her, for fear I would be interrupting her studies or classes or something. Thank you, Ashley." Lena gave her another hug. Ashley beamed.

"Now, I've got something for you to try on. The prom dress is finished, unless we need to make a few alterations. It is sky blue silk and the latest fashion, at least that's what the storekeeper told me. I don't pay much attention to fashions, mind you. I do hope it meets with your approval. Now, first, you need to slip into this long slip, dear." Lena allowed Ashley to wiggle into the slippery white full-length slip on her own. After all, she needed to continue her independence, Lena concluded, though it was hard to resist the temptation just to help her into it.

"This feels so nice! I've never worn a slip before," Ashley commented. Next, she did her wiggling once more, sliding into the prom dress.

"I made it a bit wide at the waist so you could slip into and out of it. Usually, they have zippers or buttons of snaps up the back. Instead, there is this waist band that can be tied. I don't know if you can tie it yourself or not. If not, perhaps one of the girls can tie it for you."

Ashley began experimenting and though it took some doing, she actually produced a decent bow. "I added a long walking slit for you, since you need a wide range of motion with your legs. While you stand, it looks fabulously long, but you can still get your legs up to your head. Now let's see how you look." She had Ashley stand before the full-length mirror while she checked over the fit of the dress.

"There, now you have a totally unique prom dress. No one else has one exactly like yours. I do love the look at your shoulders, dear. It definitely displays your unique, beautiful form. You are going to knock the boys head over heels with your looks." Ashley blushed. That had never yet happened, ever. She had knocked the boys solidly in their privates, but that was an entirely different thing.

"How do I look?" Ashley asked the girls. Lena had suggested that she show her dress to the others.

"Wow! You look, well, ravishing!" Pam replied, very much impressed with her unique look.

"That's the latest style too," Audrey added. "It's similar to mine, only mine had arms."

"Beautiful. You look incredibly pretty, Ashley," Lindsey added. "Just perfect!"

"Really, I do?" Ashley asked, still not very certain. The three continued to praise her new look, and she decided that it must be true—that she looked good in the dress.

On Saturday afternoon, the four girls were put in charge of fancying up the home for the party. After all, this was the first party in their new home, and Lena felt like going all out. By suppertime, they had gold and silver streamers hanging from the ceiling. The furniture was moved out of the way, leaving a large dance floor in both the living room and the family room. All four girls wore their fancy dresses, spending much of the time giggling over their looks.

Just as they sat down for supper, Fred arrived, looking frazzled, tough week at work. However, he brought Monique with him, which delighted Pam as well as Monique.

Monique said, "Hi everyone, 'lo Pam." She stopped in

her tracks, staring at the new addition.

"Monique, this is our new third year student, Ashley Stokes. Ashley, this is my girlfriend, Monique Blackburn, from Red Hall. She lives in Greeley," Pam quickly did the introductions.

Monique, wearing her fancy man-looking outfit, with her hair tied back, said, "Wow! Pleased to meet you, Ashley. Incredible look, incredible style! Love your look." Ashley flushed at the unexpected comments; she never had them before now, especially from strangers.

"Hi, thanks. It's brand new. Lena made it for me. It's the nicest dress I have ever worn. You look, well, sort of different," Ashley replied, uncertain of how to respond.

Monique and Pam exchanged loving hugs, and she sat down beside Pam. "I think Pam looks better in her prom dress, so I dress like the man," Monique explained.

The adults began chatting about the various troubles that Fred had spent the week handling. More and more criminal acts were being committed, primarily against the norms. Ashley, sitting across from Monique and Pam, watched them as much as she could without seeming to stare openly. Yet, when they began to dine, Monique definitely watched how Ashley managed, which Ashley was quite used to, though she hated it.

Once the supper was finished, the Whitewater clan appeared in the front room. Fern and Amanda wore their fancy dresses as well, while Jim and Tom wore their suits. Sandy also wore her fanciest dress. Even R. B. and Luci looked well dressed. After the many hello's, R. B. took Ashley aside.

"Dear, I need a few minutes with you, alone. I have a little something for you." Ashley, a bit flustered, led him down to her bedroom.

"Okay, you sit and let me replace your leg wand holder." She did and watched him remove her well-worn leather contraption. He then strapped a very fine looking leather holder onto her leg and then waved his wand over it. "Bonding magic," he explained. "The new holder is now bonding itself to you, personally. "Can you feel the magical energies around your leg, kind of tingles?"

"Yes, it sort of tickles."

"Good. There, now it has accepted you, much as a Staff of Power accepts its new master. There are four command words for your new holder. Holder: On. Holder: Off. Wand to Me. Wand to Holder. You try them, starting with Holder: Off." She repeated the words and the entire holder magically removed itself from her leg.

"Wow! How can it do that?" she asked.

"Magic, my dear child, magic. Now try getting it back on."

"Holder: On," she said and the new device affixed itself to her leg. R. B. inserted her wand into the holder. Next, she said, "Wand to Me." Shocked, the wand was instantly between her toes! She was so startled that she dropped the wand on the floor. Hastily, she picked it back up with her toes. "Wand to Holder." Instantly, the wand appeared securely inside the holder.

"Ah, perfect. Perfect. When the wand is inside the holder, it will not fall out, even if you are upside down. That's an added safety feature. I suggest that you practice with it a little so you don't drop your wand every time you go to retrieve it. I do believe you will find wand accessing far faster and more efficient this way."

"Thank you, R. B.!" she exclaimed, and gave him a big hug, using her leg to hold him tightly to her. He gave her a loving kiss on her forehead.

"Now we'd best get back to the dance. Luci might become very jealous of you, you see." She flushed, even though she knew it was a kindly tease. The two rejoined the others, but Ashley immediately had to show all the others what R. B. had created for her.

Then, the dance began. This time, everyone waltzed to the same music, only Jim and Tom tried to vote for rock and roll and were totally out-voted. Jim whispered to Lindsey, "Would you mind if I danced with Ashley tonight?" He was about to add in all sorts of reasons why he should.

"Please, I think it would do wonders for her morale, thanks. I'll dance with Audrey."

"May I have this dance, Miss Stokes?" Jim gallantly

asked Ashley, who was very surprised that he asked her.

"Ah, well, if Lindsey doesn't mind. Sure, but I only have practiced dancing in class. No one has ever danced with me before, so I'm probably no good at this. I'm warning you, if you make fun of me, I will kick you where it hurts." She laid in her usual self-defense attitude.

Jim put his arms around her, and they began to waltz. He sensed just how unsure she was and was as gentle as he could be. Audrey and Lindsey danced near them as well, along with Monique and Pam. Fern and Amanda paired off as well. Lindsey kept an eye on her charge, just in case any trouble arose. Besides, she was a tiny bit jealous of Ashley just now.

As they danced, Jim found it unusual not to be holding her hands in his, and he found himself sliding his arms up and down her silky sides. Ashley found her body sending her all manner of new sensations that she had never felt before. She loved every minute of it, even whispering to Jim to keep on sliding his hands over her shoulders, sides, and back.

A couple hours later, Amanda switched partners, dancing with Lindsey. She whispered, "I have to tell you this, Lindsey. I hope you don't get too upset by it, but I think that Jim has fallen head over heels for Ashley. He used to have that huge picture of you on his wall, but yesterday, he added one of Ashley beside it. Men! Does he think he can have two girl friends? Honestly, I'm sorry, Lindsey."

"I like Jim, but I'm not in love with him, at least I don't think so anyway. Besides, we've never even been on a real date. I think he is just a good friend. You really think he has fallen for Ashley? He's only just met her."

"She's as feisty as he is, like two peas in a pod," Amanda replied. "Me, I think we are too young to be falling in love and all that—after all we are only barely fourteen. Mom says that you will know it when you meet the right person. She says that something about your stomach going all crazy like. Well, nothing like that has happened to me yet, so I must not be in love with anyone yet."

"Me either. I like Jim a whole lot, but my stomach is normal. It would be really good for Ashley to have someone who cares for her when we go back to school, don't you think?"

Lindsey asked.

"Absolutely. I mean she has a rough time with everything and deserves a break, but honestly, Jim ought to sit down and talk to you about everything, that's what I think anyway."

Still, for the girls, the evening passed too quickly once more. As the Whitewater's were about to leave, Tom said, "Tomorrow after lunch, come on over, we need to start our long distance running practices."

"Great. I'll be there," Lindsey replied.

Jim added, "Bring Ashley with you; we'll make a runner out of her."

"What? Run? In the heat?" she answered. Jim grinned, and they vanished before she could say anything else. The girls collapsed onto the sofas.

Monique said, "Mom is planning a lawn party next Saturday night. She's asked me to ask if all of you want to come."

"Great. Mom, can I go?" Pam asked her mother, who was still waltzing with her father, even though the music had long ended.

"Sure, I don't see why not. Do you agree, Fred?"

"If the four of you wish to go, that seems reasonable to me. Safety in numbers. There has not been too much trouble in Greeley. What time should we have them arrive, Monique?"

"About six. We have croquet, Jarts, and a whole bunch of lawn games to play. See if Amanda and Fern can come too, please. It's a girl's-only garden party thing, but Jim and Tom can come too." With that settled, Fred finally pulled himself away from Polly and took Monique home. The nice thing about using teleport spells was that he was only gone two minutes, which didn't spoil the mood the two were in, Pam noted.

After rearranging the rooms and grabbing a snack, the girls retired for the night. Alone with Lindsey, Ashley asked timidly, "Lindsey, could you please help me take off my clothes? I don't want to risk tearing them." Lindsey smiled; this was the first time that Ashley had asked for some assistance. Quickly, she helped slide the gorgeous gown over her head and then the slip. For the first time, Lindsey could

337

see the scars on each of her shoulders, though she tried not to stare at them. Without asking, she also helped her slip into her new nightgown.

"Thanks. Say, I didn't mean to steal Jim away from you the whole night. I'm sorry; time rather vanished. I don't know why."

"Don't fret over that. Jim and I are just very good friends. It's not as if we are in love or dating or anything like that. Although, Amanda has said that Jim used to have a crush on me, but he's three years older than I am, so I hardly think that counts. Can you keep a secret?" Ashley nodded, "Amanda also told me that now Jim may have a crush on you too!"

"Well, I've never felt like this before. I wish I had a mother to talk about things with, but I don't. I've just been on my own."

"Well, I don't know much either, but you can talk to me." The two talked for over an hour before they finally went to sleep. Lindsey realized that Ashley was feeling emotions that she had not had before. In many ways, she and Lindsey were very similar.

Chapter 18—The Summer

Chores. That was the theme in the morning. "Now that things have settled down around here, well, as much as they are going to, it looks like it's time that we get the chores spelled out. Essentially, there are four areas of chores. One, the house needs vacuuming and dusting once a week, and the laundry done. Two, the many vegetable gardens need weeding, and the ripe produce picked. Three, the animals need to be cared for, cows milked, eggs gathered. Fourth, the fields will need some weeding and cultivating," Lena explained for the benefit of all the girls, though she knew that Lindsey already knew these things.

"Now I don't mean to offend you, Ashley, but some chores around here are going to be terribly difficult for you. I want to work with you to find those things you can do easily. Let's start by having Ashley in charge of the vacuuming and dusting. Fridays will be laundry day. Ashley is in charge of doing all our laundry. Also, Ashley can help Audrey, who is in charge of the many vegetable patches, since she is the undisputed plant expert here." The girls chuckled; Audrey had proved that to them last fall, helping them survive plant biology.

"That leaves the animals for Pam and Lindsey. As far as the large fields go, we will all work together on that large project, and I will be in charge of that one, since I make most of my income from those crops and the breeding of the horses. I suspect that once you get going on these, you will probably only need a few hours a day on the chores. Polly."

Polly smiled; it was her turn. "Lena and I have decided that you girls are definitely growing up on us, becoming young ladies. It's time that each of you learns how to cook, plan meals, and prepare them. After all, I would expect within a few more years, you will also be getting married." The girls groaned over that suggestion.

"Lena and I are going to begin teaching you housewife activities. I'll tell you right now, that it is very rare to find a husband who will cook, clean, and do laundry for you. Fred can barely make coffee." Pam giggled; that was true. She remembered when he once tried to make breakfast in bed for her mother; the kitchen ended up being a total mess.

A little later, an exasperated Pam said, "You mean I really have to put my hands on them?"

"How else are you going to milk the cow?" Lindsey tried a bit of persuasion. Pam was definitely a city girl, she concluded.

As much as Pam struggled to get the hang of dealing with the many animals, Audrey was just the opposite; she relished working in the gardens. Her exotic wild flower patch had already sprouted, and she continued talking to her new plants and caring for them.

Inside, Ashley found new challenges that she'd never faced, cleaning. At least Lena was very patient, showing her what needed to be done and not trying to tell her how to accomplish it. At first, she tried dusting using the Pledge and the dust rag. While it was challenging, she managed it, slowly. Yet, she could not raise her legs high enough to reach many places and soon resorted to using magic. After all, Lena did not say that she could not do it that way.

Running the vacuum cleaner was even more difficult for her until she realized that she could use one foot to guide it by holding the upright machine near its base. Still, hopping around on one foot made it work. Although she tried using her Clean spell, the spell only cleaned a relatively small area. She put her algebra to work and sighed as she worked out that hundreds of Clean spells would be needed to clean the floors of the entire house. Hence, she began to find ways of working with the machine. Secretly, she was very thankful that Lena was so patient with her and did not stand around keeping an eye on her, as many of her foster mothers had.

When she finally finished the huge living room, Lena appeared and praised her work. "Very clean. Nicely done, Ashley. I think that if you do about this much each day, every day, you will be able to keep the house clean. Perhaps you can make a schedule of which rooms get cleaned on which days. The living room here is positively the largest room."

"Thanks, that was a workout for me. I, I've realized that I have a lot to learn—I mean about the simple things of keeping house. I've never had to do cleaning before. It is a whole lot harder for me to do than I ever imagined."

"Good girl. Just remember, Ashley, it doesn't matter how long it takes you to get a room clean, only that it is clean when you are done. I think that holds true for nearly everyone, whether they have arms or not. Come here and sit beside me a moment. Seeing you working out how to handle the vacuum reminded me of Lindsey, when she was six years old. She had no hands in those days, and she so wanted to help with the chores. One day, she decided that she would milk the cows for me. I showed her how I did it and then sat back and let her work out how she could manage it. My heart nearly broke watching her trying to make her arms do what my fingers could easily do. It took her an hour longer than it would have taken me to just go ahead and do it. Yet I let her take her time. I never will forget the look on her face when she proudly carried the heavy bucket of milk into the house."

"I know this world is all setup for people with arms and hands. You just have to be cleverer than the rest of us, brighter, and patient. Never give up. Stick to it and get the job done, whatever it may be. Then, you can hold your head up proudly."

Ashley laid her head on Lena's shoulder and cried. "I always kept telling myself that I was just perfect—that it was everyone else that was messed up. But it's not true, is it? I'm the one that is nearly worthless without arms." She cried for some time. Lena suspected that she had never cried like this before or admitted this to anyone, and she just held Ashley closely and tightly for a time.

When she stopped crying, Lena said softly, "Ashley, you are not worthless, not even remotely worthless. True, many, many people that you meet will immediately jump to that conclusion, just because of your lack of arms. That is their mistake. You are just fine only, unlike the rest of us, you must find new and different ways to accomplish the same tasks. I could never write a check with my foot, let alone feed myself using my foot. You can do so many things that the rest of us can't possibly do that it isn't even funny. Just be patient and find ways that you can achieve the same result. Who cares how long it takes? Just get it done and done right. If you do that, you will never, ever lose your own self-respect. That's how I have lived my life: get the job done and done right; ignore how long it takes. You won't find many women who can run an entire ranch by themselves. At least now I have some help from Lloyd, though just between you and me, he is a city slicker and knows very little about running a ranch."

"You know, that's really what I have been doing all these years, finding ways to do things; and you are right, just get it done. I always feel great when I get something done. This is so strange, Lena, I can talk with you so easily, almost as if you were my mom. Are you officially now my foster mother? I never did figure that out."

"No, not officially. I just agreed to provide you with a safe place to live for the summers and vacations from school. However, Ashley, if you want, I could apply to the State of Colorado to become your foster mother, or even better, if you wish and the rest of my family agrees, we could adopt you, and then I would be your mother. That's something to think about. After all, you might not like it here. I mean we are out on the desolate High Plains. Not much out here to interest young girls."

"I've never had a mom or really anyone to talk to about things—I mean women's things. Like last night, I felt so strangely wonderful dancing with Jim, his arms sliding up and down my sides and back. What does that mean? Is that supposed to be love? What does it mean when Lindsey says that Amanda says that Jim might have a crush on me? I thought Jim was Lindsey's friend."

"Oh yes, Jim and Lindsey have been good friends for two years now, but you, like Lindsey, are growing up, Ashley. These are perfectly normal feelings you are having. I too love to have the strong arms and hands of Lloyd holding onto me." They chatted for some time until Polly called out from the kitchen.

All four girls reported in to Polly for their first lessons in cooking. "First, you plan the meal, based upon what you had in the previous days, what you have in stock, and on how much variety you wish to have. Yesterday, we had stew for lunch. That means we shouldn't have stew today." The girls giggled. "I suggest soup and sandwiches. Next, having made the decision on what to make, you need an accurate assessment of just how much to make. How many will be eating lunch with us?"

"Seven," Pam replied quickly. Polly explained how to estimate the number of cans of soup they would need to heat and how many sandwiches to make. Today, she had Lindsey make the soup, while Pam got to prepare the sandwiches. Audrey and Ashley had to set the table.

Once more, Ashley came face to face with challenges she had not had before. Carrying the dishes into the table proved a tough challenge; she and Audrey worked out a division of labor. Ashley could get the dishes and silverware out of the cupboards and drawers, so Audrey then carried them to the table and set up the table. Lindsey watching this decided to teach Ashley the Move Object spell; then she would have a way to set the table herself.

With lunch finished and the dishes cleaned up, the girls headed over to the Whitewater's ranch. However, Audrey decided to stay behind today; she wanted to get more carvings done for her Web store. Pam also backed out. Since they were likely running, she wanted no part of that. It was just Ashley and Lindsey who stepped into the Whitewater's front room.

"Hi Ashley, Lindsey," Tom said, slipping on his track shoes. Sandy already had hers on and was waiting for the others.

Jim came in all set to run. "Hi Ashley. Glad you could come. Are you a runner?"

"Er, no. I've never done much except when I was forced to in PE class. Why?"

"Well, we all are on our track and soccer team. Got second place in the Nationals a month ago," Jim explained. "However, two of our team has graduated. They were sixth years. Now we are short two runners. We just have to find two others to join our team or we don't get to race or have a team. We have to have nine members or it is a no-go."

Tom added, "And we seem to have run out of Whitewater's." Everyone laughed; all four of them were on the team. "You don't have to run the five mile relay race, because we've got the four of us for that. We are short our hundred meter sprinter and a quarter miler for the mile relay race."

"Oh yes, I watched some at school. One guy runs a while and then hands the baton off to the next one, right?" Ashley replied.

"Yes, perfect. Nothing to it, really, just got to run fast," Tom tried to make it sound easy.

"But I haven't any arms to hold the baton, let alone pass it or take it from someone else," Ashley had already worked out just how she could gracefully get out of running races.

"Not a problem. We already dealt with that with Lindsey here. You see, she made the team her first year, that's when she had no hands. You can't use any magic in the race, but that didn't stop us. We put the baton in a pouch around her waist, and she started the race. Jim then came along and took it from her pouch. It's all perfectly legal and in the rules. Nothing in the rules says that you have to have arms or hands to race, just no magic. So are you game to give it a try, Ashley?"

"What? You mean run?"

"Sure, you can do it," Jim added.

Amanda came to her defense, "Guys, it is probably lots harder to run without any arms to help you."

"I haven't got any running shoes," Ashley spoke up, trying to think of other ways out of it.

"You can wear a pair of mine," Fern volunteered. "Our feet are about the same size. I'll loan you a pair of sweat socks, otherwise you will get blisters, which would be just awful for you."

"But I might not be any good or be too slow," she replied honestly.

"You won't know unless you try, now will you," Jim egged her on. "Look, if you don't try, you are going to force me to tickle you relentlessly!"

"You wouldn't dare," Ashley glared at him.

"Oh wouldn't I?" he teased back. Ashley decided not to call his bluff.

"But I am nearly helpless like this," she protested a few minutes later, after Fern had put her heavy socks on Ashley and tied her spare track shoes on her feet. "I can't use my feet as hands."

"You don't need hands while running," Jim countered. "Come on; let's give it a try. We can run around our ranch today and see how it goes."

Off they went. Jim was careful to hold the door open for Ashley and to make sure that nothing came her way that needed hands, like the gates around the place. Already the temperature was in the high eighties. Soon the sweat began pouring off the runners. Tom and Jim purposely kept the pace rather slow and kept a constant eye on how Ashley was doing.

At last, Fern had enough. "Gang, I'm your short distance runner. Why don't Ashley and I fall behind, cool down, and let you long distance runners have at it for a while? After all, you four are the key to winning the races. There are more points for your race than ours."

Tom agreed, and the four increased their speed, leaving Fern and Ashley behind. "Just because I'm an Apache doesn't mean that I like to run forever like they do," Fern commented. "I think you did just fine for your first run. Just between you and me, running in the mile relay race is easy 'cause you only have to run about thirteen hundred feet. Not like those four; they have to run five miles each! Ugh." Ashley grinned.

"Come on; let's try something." Fern took Ashley to their barn and found the old waistband carrier that Lindsey had used when she first began running. She put their old baton in it and tied it to Ashley's waist. They jogged beside each other and Fern practiced retrieving the baton. After doing this ten times, Fern had the movement down. Ashley felt better about the whole thing as well. Both girls were soaking wet and finished with the running. Still the others had not reappeared.

Fern took Ashley inside, and they showered and dressed, chatting all the time. Finally, the others came inside, dripping sweat everywhere. "Hit the showers before you have to re-clean the whole house," chided Luci, who passed by carrying a sack of garbage out to the dumpster. A while later,

Fern told them about how they had practiced passing the baton, and Jim complimented them both.

Amanda said, "We ought to work out like this every other day to get in shape if we go to the Nationals again. How about tomorrow we go for a long horse ride? We can show Ashley and the others all of our ranch and maybe even the arroyo." Everyone agreed, although Ashley said nothing. She had no idea how she could possibly ride a horse!

That night as Lindsey and Ashley looked over their emails before bed, Ashley finally said what had been eating away at her since Amanda's announcement of going riding. "I don't know how to ride a horse, Lindsey. I have been thinking about it, and I don't see how I can do it. Perhaps I have finally run into something that I really can't do." She was fighting back big tears as she actually admitted this to Lindsey.

"Oh, you can do it. You don't need hands to ride, actually. When cowboys go calf roping at the rodeos, they use both hands on the lassoing. In reality, you control your horse with your legs and balance. Only idiots control their horses by pulling hard on the reins. You lean in the direction you want the horse to turn and gently lay the reins over its neck to that side. Betsy takes gentle commands like that very well. You can ride her. I suppose that you could hold the reins in your teeth, but after a while, if that is too hard, we can always lead your horse. You will love riding. I know it. Trust me." Ashley managed a smile, but had nightmares about falling off a horse, unable to keep from falling.

Around one the next afternoon, the Whitewater's and Sandy came galloping up to the Compton's barn. Already, Lindsey had their horses saddled and ready, giving lessons to the three girls, none of whom had ridden before. "These three have never been riding before, so we have to watch out for them," Lindsey explained.

Jim held Betsy for Ashley and steadied her as she mounted with a great effort on her part. He then gave her some lessons, while Tom and Lindsey did the same with Pam and Audrey. Lindsey rode Dandy today, primarily because he needed some work. She sat high above the others on this tall draft horse.

Slowly, they walked the horses to one end of the Compton's ranch, allowing the three to get comfortable with the horses. Then, they began riding the perimeter, Lindsey pointing out all the sights. At last, they arrived at the gate that led into the arroyo.

Audrey suddenly said, "Hey, I need to ride down there." She pointed to a spot beyond the turn off or side gully that led up to the Whitewater ranch. Once more, they took it slow, because they were going downhill, a new experience for the three novice riders.

"Here's where we turn to go up to our ranch," Jim explained to Ashley, riding beside him.

"But I need to go down there," Audrey insisted. Amanda led them on down the arroyo.

Shortly, Ashley shouted between her teeth, "Hurry up, someone is in bad trouble down there." Amanda turned to look at Ashley and then quickened their pace. Ashley wished she had kept quiet, struggling to stay in the saddle and not slip off.

At the far end of the arroyo where the gully turned to the left, they halted. Debris littered the ground, but there was an unconscious man lying on the ground. "It's Grey Eagle," Amanda called out, as she reached the man first. Jim helped Ashley dismount, while Tom assisted Audrey, Lindsey, and Pam. Everyone crowded around the man.

Sandy suggested, "Looks as if he has been beaten up and dumped here."

"I've Messaged dad, and he'll be here in a minute," Fern told the others. "He said don't mess up the area or touch him. He might have internal injuries."

A minute later, R. B. appeared wand at the ready. "Glad you found him. He's on our side. He's alive. Tom, you and Jim look for signs. I'm taking him to the doc at once. Back as soon as I can." He waved his wand once more, touched the prone man, and the two vanished.

"You all stay back, Jim and I will look for tracks," Tom ordered. Amanda decided to look for magical energy traces. She saw those left by her father's coming and going—those were bright and fresh. After a bit of concentration, she announced, "Someone used a Levitation spell to bring him here and dumped him. I can see the residual energy of that spell here."

Ashley's eyes opened wide. She had been told that Amanda was a budding Tracker, but now she was seeing it in action. She strained her senses, but didn't see anything. Tom added, "Got two sets of boot prints coming and going."

Jim added, "Two horses here; looks like they brought him here by horseback and dumped him. Two of them. Probably last night."

R. B. appeared and reviewed his son's findings and those of Amanda's. "Well done, all of you. Doc thinks he will be all right. Nasty beating though. Lucky you came upon him; this is a remote location out here."

"Ashley's doing, Audrey's too," Amanda replied.

"I would like to collect some of those logs for my carvings," Audrey confessed. "That's what drew me here, the magnificent wood. Ashley sensed the man in trouble."

"Very good, Ashley. You probably saved Grey Eagle's life," R. B. complimented her. "I'm going back to tell the Tribal Rangers what we found here and check on Grey Eagle. As soon as he regains consciousness, maybe he can tell us who did this to him. Catch you later." Poof. Once more, he was gone.

The group helped Audrey collect a dozen chunks of the dried wood, as she chose each one specifically for the image that was contained deep within the wood. None of the others really understood what she was saying about that, however.

They mounted and continued their ride around the perimeter of the Whitewater ranch, before heading back to the Compton's barn. When they had dismounted, Jim said, "Next time, Ashley we will ride faster, if you are ready for it."

"My legs feel spongy," she said, "but it was fun. There is nothing like this in the city at all!"

Later, Lindsey and Pam had the opportunity to assist in preparing the dinner meal, while Ashley and Audrey did the table setting. During their meal, Tom dropped by to relay the latest news about Grey Eagle.

"He regained consciousness, and it looks like he will be all right in time. Good thing we found him though or it might well be a different story. He told dad that three of the hot heads, who are openly supporting Dominus, attacked him and beat him up. He had no idea how he got out there in the arroyo. Dad's helping the Tribal Rangers find and arrest them right now."

Everyone asked Tom questions, but Ashley interrupted them, "R. B.'s going into a trap; he's going to be injured, and one of them is going to take him to a place called line shack at Eagle Rock, wherever that may be."

"What? Dad's in danger?" Tom exclaimed. "I gotta go!"

"Wait, I'll come to," Lloyd volunteered.

"I will bring my staff, Tom, I can suck up their spells, while you clobber them," Lindsey added, commanding her staff to her. There was no time to argue, as Tom raced for the front teleportation area, Lloyd at his heals. Lindsey joined them, but as Lloyd started to protest, the device activated, and the three arrived at the Whitewater ranch.

"Dad's in trouble! Come on; we are going to his rescue," Tom called out. Both Jim and Amanda raced to join Tom, who was beginning his Teleport spell.

"Hold on a second," Lloyd ordered. "We don't know where your dad is right now."

"Yes, they were heading to Doe's ranch. Come on; I'll take us there," Tom replied. A second later, they arrived about a hundred feet from the ranch house. The Doe home was more of a shack, badly in need of repair. Great slabs of paint were peeling off the outside walls. Three official trucks with flashing red lights were parked nearby.

As they got their bearings, Tom spied Ben dragging an unconscious man out of the building. "Hey Tom, bad news. Doe blasted your dad and took him away. We got the other two, however. We'll launch a complete search for your dad as soon as we get these locked up." Tom and Jim badgered him about how could they have let anything happen to R. B.

While they were talking, Amanda began looking for magical energy traces. The rundown home was full of spell residue. These she ignored, she was looking for the long, thin line that accompanied a Teleport spell, one that would lead her to her father. "There it is! I see it. Teleport, goes that way."

"Hey, that is towards Eagle Rock!" Tom exclaimed.

"Ashley, I could kiss you!" Fortunately, she was not here. "Ben, we think he has taken dad to Eagle Rock and the abandoned shanty there. That's where we'll be. Come on gang."

"Hold on a minute," Lindsey interrupted him. "Let me cast my protection spells on you first." Three minutes later, she finished. Each had the Skin of Stone and the Lesser Invulnerability protections on them.

"I'm not familiar with this place," Lloyd said to Tom. "Take us there, but some distance away.

"Don't we need a plan or something?" asked Amanda. "We can't go charging in there. What if he kills dad?"

"Okay, Lindsey and I will draw his attention on to us. You three go invisible and see if you can sneak inside and cast a Hold spell on him," Lloyd suggested. "Since I'm with the Department of Defense, I should be able to hold his attention. Lindsey, you absorb all the incoming spells that you can. Your mother will kill me if I let any harm come to you."

"What if he has protection spells on him?" asked Amanda. "Why don't I try to stay well away from you two and keep on casting lots of Dispel Magic spells on him. Sooner or later, I should be able to knock them down."

"Hey, she is right. If he had the same protection spells on himself as we do, my Hold isn't going to work," Tom replied.

"Okay, I'll also stay off to one side and cast my Dispels as well," Jim concluded. "That way we stand a better chance of knocking them off so you can get him without harming dad. No Balls of Fire please!" Lindsey thought that was more than plainly obvious.

Again, the group held hands. Amanda, Tom, and Jim cast their Invisibility spells and Tom took them safely to Eagle Rock some distance from the run down shanty. Giant boulders dotted the landscape all around them. Ahead sat a weathered, half rotting, one room cabin, which had been a temporary shelter for field hands working the range in this area many years ago. Several sages grew near the door.

"We need to give them time to get into position, Lindsey. Stay alert." Lloyd looked around at the boulders. "Darn good place for an ambush as well."

Just then, a message fluttered in front of Lindsey's eyes.

Energy trail leads into cabin. A.

She relayed this to Lloyd. "Good, then we have the right place. Good bet he is inside and not out here." The two waited for another couple minutes before taking action.

"Doe, this is the Department of Defense. We have your cabin surrounded. Give yourself up, and you will not be harmed. We know that you have R. B. in side. If you harm him further, I will personally see that you are executed instead of taken back for trial," Lloyd spoke very loudly.

The two heard a noise, like a chair sliding across the floor, coming from the inside. Then, Lindsey saw the start of a Ball of Fire coming their way. "Suck It," she commanded, and the magical energy arced into her staff. Lloyd shot a volley of Magical Missiles back towards the hidden attacker; his idea was just to keep their opponent's attention. They really needed to be able to see this man.

"Keep an eye open from where the spells are coming. He has to be able to see us too," Lloyd whispered to Lindsey. "Ah the door," he said and launched another volley of missiles at the head of the wizard, who shot another spell back at the two of them. Again, Lindsey took no chances and had her staff absorb that one too.

"Ah, see, my missiles did nothing to him, so he's got protections on as well," Lloyd pointed out to his daughter, as if this was more of a training mission than a real live, life and death combat. "Next time he opens the door, I will take out the door. See if you can also shoot a Dispel Magic on him right after my spell goes off."

"But what about his spell back at us?" Lindsey asked.

"Good point. Maybe the others will take the opportunity. You'd better. . ." He didn't get to finish. The door opened again as Doe shot another spell at the two. This time a cloud of poisonous gas began to appear around them. Lindsey began coughing, but managed to get most of the spell absorbed at the very last instant. The wooden door disintegrated from Lloyd's powerful spell, revealing the Indian inside.

He stood there for a moment, his mind registering what

had just happened. That was all it took for Jim and Amanda. Each was now on either side of the door, some twenty feet away. Both fired their Dispel Magic spell on him. Amanda saw a nullification of energy effect, and she knew that something had been cancelled. However, now both of them were plainly visible to the man inside.

Doe was agile, whipping off two quick spells. A pile of thick webs landed on Jim, entrapping him. Two dozen Western Diamondback rattlesnakes began slithering toward Amanda, intending to strike her. She tried to run, but the snakes were closing in from all sides.

Lloyd acted, swishing his wand, he dispelled the summoning of the snakes, which now acted very confused and began heading back to the rocks from which they had come in answer to Doe's summons. This cost him valuable time however, and Doe shot a lightning bolt at him, while Lindsey was also trying to dispel the snakes. Because of their protections, the bolt had no impact upon him, thanks to Lindsey's insistence on the casting of her staff's protection spells beforehand.

Doe, outnumbered, suddenly disappeared. Neither Lloyd nor Lindsey could see him. "Watch out, stay alert," Lloyd yelled, knowing that Doe could now be anywhere, attacking them with total and complete surprise.

"No you don't!" yelled Amanda, she waved her wand and shot her Sparkling Dust spell over the man, who was now five feet from the door, racing toward the rocks, from where he intended to blast them all with a surprise attack.

Simultaneously, Doe was hit with two spells. Lloyd, who had been saving his power spell until the right moment, cast his Stun spell. Tom, who had snuck in through a hole in the back wall, shot his Hold spell, hitting Doe squarely in his back, taking him by compete surprise. Doe stood there motionless, stunned, and held.

"Got him!" yelled Tom, "Come on; dad's in here." They all raced to the cabin, though Lindsey stopped beside Jim and cast her Dispel Magic spell three times before the webs vanished and Jim could finally get up off the ground.

"He's alive," Amanda called out.

"Thanks, Lindsey. We'd better keep an eye on Doe here. I'm going to confiscate his wand. Cover me," Jim asked.

Lindsey didn't quite know what that meant, so she positioned herself in front to Doe and prepared to smash him with her staff if he moved. Jim gingerly snatched his wand, half expecting to get shocked or something worse. Nothing happened. The two then stood guard over him.

Inside, Tom, Amanda, and Lloyd found R. B. unconscious on the floor. A nasty head wound had bled a little onto the incredibly dusty floor. "His pulse is strong," Lloyd commented. "Let's get him medical attention at once."

"I'll take him to doc's. Can you take care of Doe?" Tom asked. Lloyd nodded. Amanda helped lift up her dad, and Tom teleported all three to the reservation's resident doctor. Lloyd went back outside.

"Tom and Amanda took R. B. to the doctor. He's alive and vital signs are strong. Now we need to get this guy safely into custody." Lloyd summoned a bit of rope and securely tied the man's hands.

"Now where should we take him, Jim? This is a tribal arrest, not a Department of Defense affair."

"We've got a jail. I can teleport us there, aiming high. I don't want to risk being a little off. Tom's better with this spell than I am, sir."

"That's fine, high is good. We can all Gentle Fall if needed," Lloyd agreed. They held onto Jim, who cast his spell. A minute later, all four Gentle Fell to the ground, just outside the reservation's jail. Several of the trucks had already arrived, bringing the other two whom they had captured.

Jim went inside and shortly returned with Ben. "So you got him, did you? How's R. B.?" Ben asked, motioning for one of his deputies to take Doe inside and lock him up.

Lloyd replied, "Nasty knock on his head. Tom and Amanda have taken him to your doctor's."

"Thanks for the good work. Hop in my truck, I'll take you all there right now," Ben replied. Lindsey and Jim climbed into the truck bed, while Lloyd joined Ben inside. The dust flew, and she concentrated on holding on to the sides. At the local doctor's office, they found R. B. conscious and being bandaged up.

"I hear you got Doe," R. B. said, while the doctor finished taping the bandage on his forehead. "Oh, I'm all right," he protested, "well, just a little woozy."

"Make him rest for a few days," the doctor told Tom. The group chatted a bit, filling in R. B. and Ben on the capture of Doe. At last, Lloyd teleported them all to the Whitewater ranch. Ben promised to come over tomorrow to get a full statement from R. B.

Once back home, Luci fretted over R. B., insisting he get to bed immediately. After thanking them all, he allowed her to lead him off to bed. "We'd better get back. Lena will be more than anxious about us," Lloyd said, and the two used the floor device to arrive in their front room.

"We are back, safe and sound. Captured Doe and rescued R. B. He's got a nasty bump on his forehead, but he is otherwise fine," Lloyd gave the quick version to satisfy everyone's curiosity. "Ashley, very, very well done. Your observations were precisely correct. You have everyone's heartfelt thanks!" he complimented her, and she smiled broadly. Of course, everyone wanted to hear all the details, which Lloyd allowed Lindsey to relate, adding a few comments here and there.

The next day, it was Ashley and Audrey's turn to cook lunch and supper, while Lindsey and Pam dealt with the table setting. Ashley suddenly came face to face with a very daunting task indeed. She had never cooked any meals herself, making it a double whammy that she faced.

Polly said quietly, "Dear, my advice is to work out how to do it without using magic if you possibly can. We should use magic only as a way to speed something up, not as the only way possible. There is no rush; take your time, and let's see if you can work out how to make the soup. We need six cans in that large pot. Just bring it to a boil, and it's done, though you will have to stir if periodically so that it doesn't stick to the bottom."

At lunch, Ashley swore that soup had never tasted so good to her before. She had managed the entire operation herself without using any magic. However, the pot itself was too heavy for her to lift, so Audrey lent a hand getting it off the stove and onto the table. Slowly, Ashley was gaining more pride in herself and her abilities to get the job done.

Saturday came quickly. They ate dinner a little earlier than normal so that the girls could have more time to get ready for Monique's party. Ashley was very intimidated by the prospect of going somewhere and being with many other people whom she did not know. She was now comfortable around everyone one here, but Monique and a lawn party were something else. Lindsey insisted that she wear her form fitting blue top with her new shorts. Indeed, all four girls wore tops with shorts. It was middle June and the nights were now quite warm. It took both Fred and Lloyd to teleport all them to the Blackburn residence on the outskirts of Greeley. The two men brought the group right to their front door.

The Blackburn home was a very nice, red brick, single story dwelling, with a two-car garage. Two tall pine trees grew in front along with very green grass, not a trace of weeds could be seen, suburbia.

Fred rang the doorbell, and Monique opened it a moment later. She, too, wore a blue top with shorts, though her lips were as red as always. "Hi, glad you could make it. Everyone's out back. Hi Pam. Guess I should take you to meet everyone first, but I want to show you our house and my room sometime."

The house was fairly new and very well kept, spotless, Lena observed. Out back, numerous lawn chairs lined one side of the tall, fenced-in back yard, some hundred feet deep and thirty wide. Three people rose to meet them. "This is my father, Doctor Henry Blackburn. He works at the Greeley Medical Center, Magical Healing Department." He was a tall, thin man, thirty-five years old, with a small black moustache. "This is my mother, Lottie." She was a year younger, also with black hair and eyes. She, too, wore crimson lipstick. Her dress was a flowered print and looked every bit the suburban housewife, though she too was a witch.

"This is my little sister, Ellie. She will be a first year at Bradbury's this fall, Red Hall too." She looked very much like Monique, but she was not allowed to wear makeup as yet. Ellie exuded enthusiasm.

One by one, Monique introduced the others. Fred, Polly, and Pam were first, of course, for she really wanted her parents to meet Pam. Next, she introduced Lloyd, Lena, Lindsey, Audrey, and Ashley. Ellie stared quite a lot at Ashley, although trying to make it not noticeable.

No sooner had they all been introduced when the doorbell rang again. Monique raced to get it and soon brought the six Whitewaters out to meet her family. R. B. still wore a bandage on his forehead, though.

For a time, Henry and Lottie chatted with the girls. Henry, who had read Doctor's Caterwall's paper on the re-growing of Lindsey's hands, twice, insisted on examining her hands. Monique had told them many stories of their adventures, and both parents wanted to hear them first hand. Ellie also was keenly interested and could not take her eyes off Pam, Lindsey, Amanda, and, of course, Ashley. Finally, R. B. and Tom were asked to relate the latest attack on R. B., and Doctor Blackburn insisted on examining R. B.'s head, much to R. B.'s annoyance.

An hour later, the adults and the boys began a game of lawn Jarts, so Monique took the opportunity to show the girls around their house and her room, in particular. Ellie followed them everywhere, much to the annoyance of Monique. Pam flushed when she saw a large photo of herself on Monique's dresser. Lindsey just smiled. Her room was definitely red. The bedspread was red satin; the drapes were red silk. Her rug, a deep crimson. Even her dresser was a reddish mahogany. Lindsey noted that Monique's room was spotless; everything was in its proper place, and she figured that she had probably spent the day cleaning it up to get it to look this good.

What got their attention was the bookshelf covering one wall. Computer books filled its shelves. "A little light reading," Monique sloughed off Audrey's bookshelf staring. Lindsey realized that Monique must be a computer genius like Pam was, so perhaps that was why they liked each other so well.

A while later, they all went back outside, having stopped by the large cooler for some sodas. Lindsey carried Ashley's over to the lawn chair, setting it conveniently where she could reach it with her feet. Ashley shot Lindsey a glance as if to say thanks.

"How about a game of croquet?" Monique asked.

"Er, sorry, I have never played," Lindsey lamented. Monique quickly explained the rules and added, "I get the red ball."

Ellie protested, "But you always get the red ball, Moni. Why can't I have the red ball once in a while?"

"Cause I am older," Monique replied.

"Dibs on the yellow ball," Lindsey called out.

As the girls got their mallets and balls and looked at the end stake to find the order of play, Ashley made her decision. She had never played croquet either, but could she manage, that was her concern. It was more than a little daunting. She was very self-conscious as she watched the others begin. Fortunately, her turn was last.

"You can play?" asked Ellie, when Ashley, holding the mallet between her neck and shoulders, walked up to the starting stake.

"I've never played. I hope I don't hold you up. I have to figure out a way to do this with my feet." Everyone stared, as she sat down on the grass and began to fiddle with the mallet. She hated this, but she was determined not to show it and somehow to play too! This was a challenge, she soon discovered, but though her shot did not send the ball far, because of the two close-set starting hoops, she managed to get going. Next, because she was last, many other balls were lying spaced out in front of hers, with Monique's red ball far in the lead after only the first turn.

"If your ball hits someone else's ball, you can either railroad them or take a free shot," Monique explained. Several free shots later, Ashley had gotten her orange ball through the next hoop and on her way towards the center hoop.

Jim, who had just lost miserably at Jarts, wandered over. He said, "Hey, can I play too? I'll be black and go last." Two minutes later and Jim had caught up to Ashley. Then, he hit her ball. "Got you. Say bye bye to your ball, Ashley. Railroading time."

"Don't you dare! I'll kick you," Ashley exclaimed

vehemently. Holding his ball securely with his foot, he sent Ashley's ball flying over to the fence. It bounced back several feet.

Ashley chased after him and indeed kicked him in his rear. All the girls laughed wildly. "Oh, now you've gone and done it, Miss Ashley! Tickle time for you!" Jim started chasing Ashley around the yard, tickling her sides whenever he got close. Finally, she stopped, laughing madly and watching the others take their turns.

Monique's red ball ended up close to the next far right hoop. By the time Ashley's turn came again, there was a massive pile of balls near the center hoop. Awkwardly, she carried her mallet over to her ball, sat down, and worked out her stroke with her feet. Again, she could not get much force on the hit, just enough to lightly touch another ball. Soon, by tapping many of the other balls, gaining her free shots, she got hers through the center hoop and headed towards Monique's ball.

Jim's next shot, aiming for Lindsey's yellow ball, actually missed. He had overshot and was now beyond the center hoop. He was forced to back up on his next turn, by which time everyone else had gotten through the center hoop. "See what happens when you pick on me?" Ashley teased him. He groaned.

While Monique eventually won, Ashley's orange ball was one turn behind her. Pam was right behind Ashley. Jim came in last. "I demand a rematch!" he declared, and everyone roared with laughter.

Since the adults were all sitting down, sipping coffee, and chatting, Monique suggested, "Why don't we play Jarts?" The objective was to toss your three Jarts some twenty-five feet and have them land and stick in the ground inside the foot in diameter hoop. "One point for each Jart that is inside the hoop," Monique explained.

Again, Ashley decided to go last, observing first how the others tossed the missiles and trying to figure out how she could toss them. Finally, she had an idea. She sat down with her legs facing the distant hoop. She picked up the dart between her toes and used her legs to lob it towards the hoop.

On her third try, she managed to get one inside the hoop, to everyone's amazement. However, she now had the hang of it, as long as the distance remained constant, she felt she could lob them consistently.

After the first round, Monique was in the lead with two points. Lindsey had zero along with Jim. "First one to get to ten wins," Ellie explained. She added, "Someone, please beat Moni. She always wins." Monique flashed her white teeth between her red lips in a big smile.

Sometime later, Ashley, continuing to lob them in a consistent manner, got her ten points. Monique only had eight. Audrey was next with seven; Pam had six. Jim and Lindsey each had three. "Yes! Ashley beat Moni!" Ellie began teasing and singing away. "Moni got beat by Ashley. Moni got beat by an armless girl, ha, ha, Moni."

"Ellie, that will be enough of that!" Lottie scolded Ellie, who was forced to stop teasing her older sister.

"Impressive display, Ashley," Henry said. "You have played Jarts before, have you?"

"Er, no sir, never," Ashley replied.

"Even more impressive. Well done. I think that we are all glad you came. Someone has finally beaten Monique at Jarts!" he praised her.

"Anyone for pizza?" Lottie asked. A chorus of affirmative replies came in return. Soon, ten Domino pizza boxes were spread out, and everyone began choosing which kind they desired. By now it was starting to get dark, Lottie waved her wand and a large number of outdoor lanterns turned on, illuminating the yard.

Lindsey overheard Henry commenting to Lloyd and R. B. "We are seeing far more magical related injuries this year here in Greeley. This Dominus business is stirring up all the low life. Crimes against the normal folk are way up. I've already done ten surgeries this week alone. He is ruining all of our lives with his silly manifesto."

Pam then began to outline all the crime statistics. She was well versed in this, and she definitely impressed Henry with her knowledge and intelligence.

A little later, Henry took Ashley aside for a private chat.

He asked if he could see her shoulders. She thought this a bit weird, but then he was a doctor. "Ever think about having arms re-grown, Ashley?" he asked, professionally.

Ashley immediately was defensive. "No, not at all. Why would I want to be like everyone else? I don't need arms, when I have two good feet. You all don't make hardly any use of your feet."

"I like your attitude, Ashley. You see, to magically re-grow missing body parts, one must have a little bit of that part still present. In your case, they have removed even the arm balls from the sockets, leaving nothing left on which to rebuild the rest of your arms. It would be exceedingly difficult to make such an attempt in your case. That's why I said I like your attitude. I have had a number of patients who have lost all of a limb, mostly through automobile accidents. They whine, plead, even beg me to attempt to regrow their missing limb, but with nothing left, it is nearly impossible to do so. I professionally think that you have adjusted absolutely terrifically. My compliments, Miss Ashley Stokes. Keep up the good work."

She smiled, finally deciding that he was complimenting her. However, deep inside, his words were terrifying—nearly impossible for her ever to have her arms back. Admittedly, she never believed that she could have them regrown. Until now, she had no money to pay for such an operation. However, he had just slammed the door on any future dream or wish that she might be able to have it done. Her stomach threatened to throw up her pizza, and she hastily went for a walk around the yard, pretending to admire the flowers and shrubs near the back fence.

Monique came up to her and whispered, "Ashley, you are old enough to wear some makeup. When you want to experiment and see what it can do for your looks, let me know. I'd love to show you and teach you proper techniques. I've already volunteered to do the same for Pam and the others. It is the very least I can do for you all. Really, a little can go a long way towards making you look very appealing, as in the fashion magazines. If you are interested, we can find some time to dabble when we get back to school."

"Sure, thanks," Ashley said without really realizing what she was agreeing to do. She rather wanted to be alone just now. Monique gave her a big hug, which surprised Ashley.

Just then, a loud explosion rattled the windows of the house, even the ground shook. Flames appeared on the horizon. "What was that?" echoed around the backyard.

"It's coming from the gas storage depot," Monique answered. "An explosion." That much was obvious. Shortly, many sirens began wailing not too far from their home.

"I think that now would be a good time for us all to head home," Lloyd suggested. As they were thanking their hosts, Henry's pager went off.

"I've got to go. Emergency at the hospital. Many injured. Sorry, duty calls. It has been wonderful meeting all of you. We should do this again soon." He kissed Lottie goodbye and teleported away.

Monique hugged each girl in turn, as they said their goodbyes. A few minutes later, everyone returned to their homes. When Pam finished her bath, she had an email from Monique waiting for her telling her what had happened. Dominus supporters had blown up the gas depot. No one knew why, though. Six norms were injured.

Around midnight, Lena heard a noise in the kitchen and got up to investigate. Ashley was sitting at the table, her head resting on its top. Lena realized that she had been crying and quietly took a seat next to the young girl. She put her hand on Ashley's shoulders. She had overheard part of Doctor Henry's comments to her, and she had seen her react, running to the back of the yard. She knew that Ashley was not interested in the flowers and bushes there.

"It hurts, honey, doesn't it," she whispered, putting gentle pressure on her back to nudge her onto her lap.

Ashley moved to lean on Lena, throwing her head on Lena's shoulder, tears still coming. "He said they couldn't make me new arms."

Patting her lovingly, Lena said softly, "I know. I know. I heard him too."

"It's not like I was planning to try, but. . ." she cried and couldn't finish her sentence.

"I know. You had no means even to try to get them fixed. You've had to convince yourself that you didn't need them anyway. Still, hearing that you couldn't get arms even if you wanted them and had the means, that really hurts. Rather knocks the hope out of you, am I right?"

"Yes, yes. I've spent all these years trying to convince myself I don't need them, but just hearing that I can't—well, it hurts so bad."

"I know. I know." She continued to hold Ashley tightly, rubbing her shoulders and back, like she was her own child. After a time she whispered, "But you are alive and doing well. You are healthy. You are managing to do nearly everything anyone else is doing. Now that *is* something to be quite proud of, Ashley. You are not a quitter. You are a fighter. I couldn't be more proud of you, even if you were my own daughter." She kissed her head lovingly.

"Really?" Ashley pulled back to look on Lena's face. Was she just playing with her emotions?

"Really." Ashley stared at Lena's face and was convinced she was telling her the truth.

After a bit of silence, Ashley asked, "Monique said that I would look more attractive if I wore some makeup. Is that really true? I really have no one that I can ask about it. Lindsey doesn't know much about it either."

Lena chuckled, "Dear, I'm one of the few old fashioned women around who believes that what you see is what you get. Never worn any in my life. Besides, I never had any money for such frivolities nor did I have the desire to look like the women in the fancy magazines. As for attracting husbands, I've had two of the finest men I've ever known, Sam Rabnor, Lindsey's father, and now Lloyd. I think it is you and your personality that matters, not how you look, unless you want to be a fashion model or things like that. Not much use in wearing makeup while running a ranch."

Ashley was silent for a bit. Then, she volunteered, "But who would want me? I mean who would want to marry me when I'm like this?" She shrugged her shoulders. Lena realized that Ashley had just opened up her deepest fears to her.

"Only the greatest man in the world—at least in your

eyes! It was like that with Sam and me. I never knew that he was a wizard—not in the entire time we were married. I never knew that he was one of the most famous wizards in our world. I only knew that he was the most honest, kind, hardworking, loving, gentlest, greatest man in the world. He thought I was the best woman he'd ever met. So that's who's going to want you: the greatest guy in the world. To him, whether you wear makeup or not, whether you have arms or not will make no slightest difference to him. He will love you exactly as you are. No need to pretend to be any different than you are. Those that do pretend usually lose badly later on."

"Is, is that what love is about?" Ashley asked timidly.

"You bet it is."

After another pause, Ashley whispered, "I wish you were my mother. I can talk to you so easily. If I could choose, I'd choose you to be my mom. Not a foster mother—they were all awful—I mean a real mom."

"Well, actually, Ashley, you could get that wish, you know. We could adopt you, and then you would be stuck with me as your mother ever after." Lena teased her slightly, because she had stopped crying and was feeling much better.

"You could? Me? Like I am?"

"Well, I would need to ask Lloyd and Lindsey, since they are part of my family that you would be joining. Are you sure that you would really want me as your mother, you know, giving you lots of orders and impossible chores to do around here?" she teased her a bit more, bringing a smile to Ashley's face.

"Yes, yes," she pressed herself as tightly to Lena as she could. Lena's arm responded by holding her tightly to her.

"I'll speak to them in the morning. It's late. We should be getting ourselves into bed. I'll tuck you in."

"No one's tucked me in before," Ashley replied softly. A minute later, Lena pulled back the covers as the young girl climbed into bed. She pulled the covers up, leaned over, and kissed Ashley on the forehead, before stealing quietly out of the room. Lindsey was sound asleep across the room.

"I guess Ashley got really tired out last night," Lindsey said wiping the sleep from her eyes as she sat down at the early morning breakfast table with her mom and dad.

"She and I were up late having a long talk. What would you two think about our officially adopting Ashley as our daughter?" Lena sprung her question on both of them. "She really desperately needs a mother and family of her own. She told me that she really would love to have me as her mother last night. I want to do it, but I told her I would have to ask you both, since you are part of my family as well."

"Fine by me. I'd have two daughters to dote over. Besides, you are right. She really needs some stability in her life just now," Lloyd replied.

"I'd have a sister? Cool! We've only known her for a few weeks, but I really like her a whole lot. Can we do that mom? Adopt her? It's fine by me, but what about Audrey?" Lindsey answered.

"What about me?" Audrey said, as she walked into the kitchen, stretching and yawning. She'd only heard the mention of her name.

"Ashley wants us to adopt her so she can have the mother and father that she desperately needs," Lena explained.

"Hey, now that is a good change on her part. Honestly, I saw that she needed that since the first day she came here. Is that even possible? You would do that for her? I mean that is taking on quite a lot of responsibilities—her with no arms and all," Audrey replied.

"Yes, it is possible, Audrey, but what about you? If we adopt Ashley, we can't ignore you. That wouldn't be fair to you." Lena explained.

"Oh I don't need to be adopted. I'm so grateful for you letting me have a place to live and grow my plants. I've turned down a family who wanted to adopt me six years ago. Really, I'm doing just fine, only I just need friends, like everyone here. To me, having so many great friends, especially adults, is what is important. After all, I'm fourteen now, almost grown up, really. Now that I have my little web business with my carvings, I'm all set. I have always been very independent, you see. Do you need to adopt me so that I can continue to live here?" she suddenly wondered if that was going to be a problem.

"Oh dear me no! You are welcome to live here with us as long as you desire," Lloyd replied hastily.

"And do your chores around here to help out," Lena teased her a little.

Audrey breathed a sigh of relief. "Whew, for a second there. . ."

"That's okay, dear. We owed it to you to ask. After all if we are considering adopting Ashley, it would be awful of us not to check with you as well," Lena added.

"Oh, yes, I do see what you mean. In a way, you are right. Now that you mention it, I would have felt rather funny if you had not said anything to me about it," Audrey admitted. "I'm truly content with the way things are here, only I want to throw some money into the pile to help out, now that my web store is making money."

"Well, that is admirable of you, Audrey. Only please don't toss in more than you can realistically afford," Lena cautioned, adding, "Perhaps I should help you work out a budget and show you how to do solid financial planning. So many people haven't a clue how to handle finances."

"That would be great! Thanks. I've never had any real money coming in before," Audrey replied.

"You are most welcome. Besides, my vegetable gardens have never done so well in all the years I've had them. You have a magic touch, thanks," Lena added. Audrey smiled.

"I must say, Audrey, that you are one of the most mature young women that I have ever met," Lloyd complimented her, and she blushed, pleased with his honest words. She knew that she was in the right place at the right time—that this was her special skill in operation once more.

"You're going to be my sister!" exclaimed Lindsey very excitedly an hour later when Ashley finally woke up and wandered into the kitchen.

"What?"

"Yes, they all agreed to adopt you into our family. Lloyd is going to see what must be done today while he is at his office handling Department of Defense things," Lena explained to Ashley.

"Congratulations!" Audrey said encouragingly, giving Ashley a hug.

Ashley could only cry. She moved to Lena, who again held her tightly, allowing her to rest her head on her shoulder for a time.

"Now then, hurry up and eat your breakfast. Chores are waiting. Polly and I are going to sit down with you three and go over meal planning before lunch time," Lena told the girls.

At lunchtime, Lloyd returned smiling. "I do like quiet Sundays at the office," he told everyone. "Not a whole lot to handle. I did get the initial papers we need to fill out to start the adoption process. Looks like this is going to be a long, drawn out affair to get it done."

Lloyd also had a twinkle in his eye. "Girls, I have been thinking. What would you say to a short vacation in the Canyon Lands? I know that we can't leave the crops for very long, say a weekend trip? Invite the Whitewater kids and Monique, if she wishes to come too."

Three girls jumped him with hugs. This was turning out to be the best of summers for Lindsey.

The End.

A Favor to Other Readers

How about helping other readers? Many readers rely on reviews to make the decision whether to buy a book. You can help them make their decision by leaving your opinions and viewpoint in a short review of the positive things of this book. Writing the review and expressing your opinion only takes a few minutes, and other readers will appreciate your efforts.

Click this link: Volume 2 The Board of Governors scroll down to Customer Reviews; click on Write a Review, and enter your review. Thank you.

Author Information

Visit My Amazon.com Author Page
Vic Broquard Author Page

Follow My Blog
Vic Broquard's Blog

Follow Me on Social Media
Facebook
Google+
LinkedIn
YouTube

Other Books by Vic Broquard

Without Warning (fantasy)

The Trident Series: (fantasy)
      Volume 1 The Trident and the Book
      Volume 2 The Trident and the Scepter
      Volume 3 The Trident and the Resurrection

The Adventures of Elizabeth Stanton Series: (science fiction)
      Volume 1 The Evolution of the Path
      Volume 2 The Great Messiah
      Volume 3 Of Kings and Queens and Troubadours
      Volume 4 Chaos in the Aftermath
      Volume 5 Power Plays
      Volume 6 Age of Exploration
      Volume 7 Abducted
      Volume 8 The Emperor and Empress
      Volume 9 A Job Worth Doing
      Volume 10 Degradation
      Volume 11 The Second Crusade
      Volume 12 When Worlds Collide
      Volume 13 Dark Ages

The Lindsey Barron Series: (fantasy)
      Volume 1 The Rod of the Apocalypse
      Volume 2 The Board of Governors
      Volume 3 The Crown of Moses
      Volume 4 Dominus for President
      Volume 5 The National Health Care Program
      Volume 6 States Justice
      Volume 7 Cross and Double-cross

Zoran Chronicles Series: (fantasy)
      Volume 1 A Dragon in Our Town
      Volume 2 Dragons, Power, Courts, and War

Lindsey Barron Series Volume 2 The Board of Governors

Planet of the Orange-red Sun Series: (science fiction)

The Return of the Wizards: Twelve Companions – The Making of Wizards (fantasy)

www.ingramcontent.com/pod-product-compliance
Lightning Source LLC
Chambersburg PA
CBHW072113250626
47159CB00007B/2430